The Salamander
and
Other Gothic Tales

VLADIMIR ODOEVSKY

The Salamander
and
Other Gothic Tales

Translated with an Introduction by

Neil Cornwell

Northwestern University Press

Northwestern University Press
Evanston, Illinois 60201-2807

First published 1992 by Bristol Classical Press,
an imprint of Gerald Duckworth & Co. Ltd.
Copyright © 1992 by Neil Cornwell.
Northwestern University Press edition published 1992 by arrangement
with Gerald Duckworth & Co. Ltd.
Printed in Great Britain

ISBN: 0-8101-1062-8

Library of Congress Cataloging-in-Publication Data

Odoevskii, V.F. (Vladimir Fedorovich), kniâz'. 1803-1869.
  [Short stories. English. Selections]
  The salamander & other Gothic tales / Vladimir Odoevsky:
translated with an introduction by Neil Cornwell.
     p. cm.
  Translated from Russian.
  Includes bibliographical references.
  ISBN 0-8101-1062-8
     1. Odoevskii, V.F. (Vladimir Fedorovich), kniâz'. 1803-1869-
-Translations into English. I. Title. II. Title: Salamander and
other Gothic tales.
PG3337.03A23 1992
891.73'3—dc20   92-25756
                                                                 CIP

The paper used in this publication meets the minimum requirements of the
American National Standard for Information Sciences—Permanence of
Paper for Printed Library Materials, ANSI Z39.48-1984.

CONTENTS

INTRODUCTION

Prince Vladimir Fyodorovich Odoevsky (1804-69) was one of the most extraordinarily versatile figures of nineteenth-century Russia. Despite a full career as a public servant, which lasted from 1826 until his death, he enjoyed fame as a romantic writer, children's writer, thinker, musicologist, educationalist, philanthropist, amateur scientist and general 'Renaissance man'. A man of many pseudonyms, he even published gastronomic pieces under the name of 'Mister Puff'. 'The Russian Hoffmann' or 'the Russian Faust' he has frequently been dubbed: in some ways (though he did not write poetry and the comparison doubtless flatters) 'the Russian Goethe' would be nearer the mark. A reputation for eccentricity, 'encyclopaedism' and dilettantism led to his being taken less seriously for much of his lifetime than was his due. Following many years of neglect, his reputation enjoyed one minor revival in the early part of this century and another in the 1950s, when important collections of his literary, musical and educational writings were published. A few of his children's stories remain highly popular, but it is as a leading representative of high Russian romanticism that he now finds his niche: a recent Moscow paperback edition of his 'Tales and Stories' enjoyed a print-run of no less than two million, seven hundred thousand copies.

The last in the line of one of Russia's oldest families (which traced its lineage back to Rurik and was therefore equal in seniority to the Romanovs) and in later life officially Russia's 'premier nobleman', Odoevsky nevertheless always had to work for a living. The family fortune had been dissipated during the eighteenth century and Odoevsky's father had married beneath him – virtually into the peasantry. These factors, together with an upbringing largely by Moscow relatives (his father had died in 1808 and his mother re-married), made Odoevsky something of an aristocratic outsider who, despite years of loyal government service, regained little political trust following his tenuous links with the Decembrist revolt which at the end of 1825 inaugurated and determined the reactionary reign of Nicholas I.

1

Odoevsky's first flourish of literary success (echoed in the story 'New Year') occurred in the first half of the 1820s, when he presided over the Society of Wisdom Lovers, a philosophical circle influenced mainly by Schelling, which included among its adherents some of the principal originators of both Westernising and Slavophile thought. He also co-edited the almanac *Mnemosyne* (1824-5) which, over its four issues, was as culturally vital as it was financially hopeless.

Following the Decembrist upheaval, Odoevsky married, entered governmental service, moved to St Petersburg and immersed himself ever deeper in the esoteric and occult philosophy which lay at the roots of European romanticism, channelling his thought into creative activity which was to reach fruition only in the 1830s – a decade to which we shall shortly return.

He lived in St Petersburg until 1862, during which period his literary career again blossomed and then declined. He held a number of important administrative posts, became in the 1840s strenuously involved in educational and philanthropic projects and was always a leading personality in Russian musical life. In this field he actively promoted both the home product (particularly the music of Glinka) and the pick of the West: Bach, Mozart, Beethoven – and subsequently the 'moderns', Berlioz and Wagner. He played an important backstage part too in the continued development of Russian literary journalism, as co-founder of Pushkin's *The Contemporary* and principal backer of *Annals of the Fatherland* (in which thick journals many of his own tales made their first appearance).

Not least, Odoevsky hosted one of the main literary and musical salons of St Petersburg and later Moscow. His circle remained, for over forty years, a meeting place for artistic celebrities from home and abroad. The Russian literary scene was nothing if not incestuous and Odoevsky was involved with everyone who was anyone, from Griboedov and Pushkin to Turgenev and Tolstoy; he befriended and encouraged the brooding Lermontov, the prickly young Dostoevsky and later the aspiring Tchaikovsky. Back in the 1830s, in the heyday of his salon, it had been remarked that 'on Odoevsky's divan sits the whole of Russian literature'.

Ever to be counted among the more progressive elements of the nobility, though wary of radicalism and revolution, Odoevsky was, as his later diaries show, an enthusiastic supporter of the reforms of Alexander II. At the same time, he wearied of the social and financial strains of Petersburg life and in 1862 took up appointment to the Moscow Senate. At the time of his death, in 1869, he was up to his ears in more projects than ever: musical, historical, scientific and, once again, literary.

Introduction

If Odoevsky is to be credited with a particular forté in his literary production, it lies in his unusual creations of cycles of stories. The 'cycle', as opposed to the mere collection, requires at least oblique thematic and stylistic connections, or threads, between its member stories. Several of these attempts remain uncompleted – still others were never more than pie in the sky. However, two which did achieve completion are now to be counted among the fundamental works of Russian romantic prose: *Variegated Tales* (1833), the first real fruit of Odoevsky's 'mature' literary period, is a delicate collection of parodies on strands of Russian and European romantic themes; and the remarkable *Russian Nights* (completed in 1844), which includes some fine individual stories (ranging from the Gothic, to the musical and the anti-Utopian), is surrounded by a substantial philosophical frame-tale, addressing many of the preoccupations of Russian intellectual circles of the 1830s.

The decade-and-a-half, from about 1829 until the issuing of his three-volumed 'Collected Works' in 1844 and subsequent virtual retirement from literature, indeed saw the flowering of Odoevsky's literary achievement. The present selection is drawn from this period and includes just one story from *Variegated Tales* ('The Tale of a Dead Body, Belonging to No One Knows Whom'), but none from *Russian Nights*, which was translated in toto in 1965. Neither have we included two other sides of Odoevsky's versatile fictional output: the society tale (of which 'Princess Mimi' and 'Princess Zizi' are the best examples) and his science fiction (see the unfinished futuristic tale 'The Year 4338').

Instead the emphasis here falls largely on Odoevsky's Gothic fiction, which includes some of his most stimulating writing and yet has been particularly neglected. Of the eight tales here featured, my translation of 'The Live Corpse' has been published in an earlier anthology (and is revised for the present volume). 'The Sylph' has appeared in two earlier translations, but has been re-translated for this collection. The other six stories appear here in English for the first time and the selection is arranged in chronological order. Even in Russian, several works have only in recent years made their first reappearance in print this century; indeed 'Letter IV' receives its first airing here in any form since 1844.

'New Year' represents a backward glance at the literary circles of the early 1820s and is, in its own way, a mini society tale, expressing poignant nostalgia over the decline of good fellowship. 'The Tale of a Dead Body, Belonging to No One Knows Whom' and 'The Story of a Cock, a Cat and a Frog', both set in the fictitious provincial area of Rezhensk, are examples of Odoevsky's ready wit and a Gogolian tendency towards whimsical

3

black comedy: the former story is an early instance of Odoevsky's use of the fantastic, while the latter tale elaborates on the Gogolian Mirgorod model of grotesque provincial life.

'Letter IV' [to Countess Ye. P. R...] is one of a series of letters to Yevdokia ('Dodo') Petrovna Rostopchina, herself a writer and society hostess, 'on apparitions, superstitious fears, sensual deceptions, magic, cabbalism, alchemy and other mysterious sciences'. Odoevsky also dedicated 'The Live Corpse' and 'The Cosmorama' to the Countess, who shared his theosophical interests. 'Letter IV' comprises a viable short story in its own right ('an excellent subject for a tale of terror', as Odoevsky puts it) and is notable too for featuring Count Saint-Germain, a legendary but historical figure used by Pushkin in his Gothic masterpiece *The Queen of Spades* (1833), who has recently re-surfaced in Umberto Eco's occult extravaganza, *Foucault's Pendulum*.

'The Live Corpse' is a striking tale of out-of-body experience, based ultimately this time on dream, which influenced Dostoevsky's later fantastical stories, 'Bobok' and 'The Dream of a Ridiculous Man'. It is of interest for its exploitation of mixed narrative techniques – largely proto-stream of consciousness alternating with dramatic dialogue – and linguistic register (including thieves' argot), but is also notable for being the clearest statement of Odoevsky's philosophical preoccupation with cause and effect: the ultimate impact on a single life and on posterity of every action and even every thought. This theme, which is present also in 'The Cosmorama' and 'The Salamander', was later taken up by Tolstoy in 'The False Coupon' and 'The Death of Ivan Ilyich' and is implicit too in the philosophy of *War and Peace*.

The main Gothic meat of the collection, however, is to be found in three tales traditionally seen as the most significant and the most elaborate of what have been termed Odoevsky's 'works of mystical content': 'The Sylph', 'The Cosmorama' and 'The Salamander', all written in a particularly productive period at the end of the 1830s.

'The Sylph' is subtitled 'from the notes of a reasonable man' (Odoevsky was ever suspicious of reliance on reason *per se*) and begins with seven letters from one Mikhail Platonovich to his friend and eventual editor, the 'reasonable man', who has little grasp of the artistic spirit [ironically, the 'authorial' confession, with which the tale ends, displays great rationality, both by purporting to understand 'nothing in this story' and by mangling the protagonist's name as 'Platon Mikhailovich']). Bored with provincial life, he discovers the cabbalistic books and folios of his deceased uncle's secret library and immerses himself in the pursuit of sylphs. The reasonable man's account of the 'saving' of his friend for marriage and a

conventional provincial lifestyle frames the extracts from Mikhail Platonovich's journal, in which the poetic saga of his relationship with a sylph
(involving an alternative artistic vision – indeed an alternative reality – and
the separation of time and space, leading to 'the soul of the soul' where
'poetry is truth') gradually descends from the sublime to incoherent
jottings.

'The Cosmorama' represents Odoevsky's most overt fictional depiction
of his interest in the concept of dualism (or *dvoemirie*), drawn from his
study of such mystical thinkers as Jacob Böhme, John Pordage, Sweden-
borg and Saint-Martin. The construction of a 'cosmorama' occurs in one of
Odoevsky's children's stories, while it appears that he himself possessed
some such 'toy', as he recorded in his travel notes (Mainz, 1847) that: 'In
the steamship cabin an Englishman and a Belgian did not know how to
work my travelling *kosmorama*; each time they wanted to see by looking
into the magnifying lens, instead of the frosted glass'. With the mystical
powers bestowed upon it in this tale, the cosmorama takes on a capability
comparable to that of Borges' 'Aleph' (in his story of that name) – itself
said to be 'one of the points in space containing all points' and 'the micro-
cosm of alchemists and cabalists'. The cosmorama, however, is only the
starting point of the visions of the protagonist Vladimir, which in fact reach
their most extravagant Aleph-like quality after the destruction of the allegedly magical toy. The scope of Vladimir's perception, both of the
dissolution of space and time and the apprehension of an inner or parallel
world, may be seen to counterpoint the purely mechanistic powers of
Kipriano, the Improvisor from *Russian Nights*, while his visions, together
with those portrayed in 'The Sylph' and 'The Salamander', come disturb-
ingly close, as romantic writing occasionally could, to what has more
recently been labelled 'near death experience'.

'The Cosmorama' is Odoevsky's most fully blown romantic tale: perhaps this is why, from its original publication in 1840, it had to wait until
1988 for a reprinting (even Odoevsky himself unaccountably omitted it
from his 1844 'Collected Works'). It includes as full a gamut of occult and
Gothic paraphernalia as may be encountered in any work of Russian romanticism: the walking dead, crime and torture, amorous intrigue, second
sight, supernatural arson and spontaneous human combustion. This grotesque phantasmagoria is, however, skilfully interwoven between vision
and 'reality', accompanied with a slight edge of undercutting irony. Indeed,
unlike 'The Sylph' or 'The Live Corpse', it cannot be conclusively explained in terms of madness or dream (although insanity remains one
strongly plausible interpretation): riddles still remain, as we are warned in
the 'publisher's preface', not least the mysterious personalities of Doctor

Bin and the unfortunate Sophia (the evolution of whose name from 'Sonia' is undoubtedly to be seen in occult terms). The promised sequel to 'The Cosmorama' never materialised, although there is some evidence that one had been seriously intended.

'The Salamander' is, *Russian Nights* as a totality excepted, Odoevsky's longest work of prose fiction and the nearest he came, at least in finished form, to writing on the scale of a novel. Indeed, 'The Salamander' has a curious bi-partite structure, termed by Odoevsky a 'dilogy' (as compared to the more common 'trilogy' form), which, while comprising a genuine continuation in narrative terms, signals a radical break in the work as regards narrational mode, chronological leap and generic emphasis. The first part (first published separately as 'The Southern Shore of Finland at the Beginning of the Eighteenth Century') has many of the characteristics of the historical novel and could almost have been entitled 'The Finn of Peter the Great' (as opposed to Pushkin's 'The Negro' of same). Another striking attribute is its pervasion by Finnish folklore, derived from the researches of Odoevsky's friend Yakov Grot and his translations from *The Kalevala* (which had made its first appearance in Helsinki in 1835).

In its second part 'Elsa', 'The Salamander' (the overall title being imposed in 1844 on first integral publication) shifts dramatically into the genre of Gothic tale. The main characters continue, but the magical folk-loric elements are transferred to an alchemical search for the philosopher's stone. And yet, as in all things occult, there remains a mysterious connection. The first part uses omniscient third-person narration. 'Elsa', however, switches abruptly to a seemingly authorial narrative, and is mainly a flash-back from the nineteenth century; the sub-narrator (the apparent author's uncle) is the real Odoevskian figure: a characteristic self-parody in the guise of elderly eccentric and slightly impatient adept in all matters arcane. This type, indeed, anticipates many a psychic doctor to come in subsequent European Gothic fiction. The central character, Yakko the Finn (Peter the Great's former favourite, now fallen on hard times), is transposed from hero to villain and, with his affirmation that 'all is permitted to a rich man', he takes his place in a firm line of Russian moral delinquents stretching from Pushkin's Hermann (in *The Queen of Spades*) to Dostoevsky's Raskolnikov and various Karamazovs. Again, a goodly range of Gothic appurtenances are on display and the tale reaches a rousing finale.

Odoevsky's propensity, revealed in a number of tales here, for open, multiple or alternative endings shows his natural instinct for the pure fantastic: not just in the use of Gothic detail and thematic content, but in classic terms of ambiguity and hesitation, the representation of opposites and the inadequacies of language to express a deeper reality. Notable too is the exploitation of other devices from romantic poetics: distancing by means of varied and multiple forms of narration and use of the fragment or manuscript, as well as other forms of fragmentary composition.

Odoevsky lacks, it has to be said, the masterly concision of Pushkin, the stylistic elegance of Lermontov and the sheer linguistic verve of Gogol (although at the height of his fame, in the 1830s, his reputation was not far short of theirs), but his relative verbosity brings him closer, arguably, to the English style of writing of the first half of the nineteenth century. His themes too are close to the romanticism of both European and the English-based literatures: comparisons can be made with, not only Hoffmann, but Charles Brockden Brown and of course, Poe; Mary Shelley, Maturin and Odoevsky's near contemporary, Sheridan Le Fanu. Particularly intriguing is the proximity between Odoevsky's 'The Sylph' (1837) and 'The Diamond Lens', a story written some twenty years later by the Irish-American author Fitz-James O'Brien (explicable, until recently, only in terms of common alchemical sources; now an element of plagarism, via French translation, can be established).

It is only in recent years, with the revival of interest in romanticism in the former Soviet Union, that some of Odoevsky's works have again seen the light of day. It is hoped that an English translation of these tales will help mark a wider stage in the resurrection of the Russian Gothic.

Acknowledgments

Permission is gratefully acknowledged from Ardis Publishers to reprint (in revised form) the translation of 'The Live Corpse', first published in *Russian Romantic Prose: An Anthology* (1979); and from Oxford University Press for quotations from Keith Bosley's translation of *The Kalevala* (The World's Classics, 1989). For assistance with Finnish references in 'The Salamander' I am grateful to Ian Press and, indirectly, Michael Branch.

Further Reading

Fetzer, Leland (ed. and trans.), *Pre-Revolutionary Russian Science Fiction: An Anthology*, (Ardis, Ann Arbor, 1982)
Korovin, Valentin (ed.), *Russian 19th Century Gothic Tales* (Raduga, Moscow, 1984)
Odoevsky, V.F., *Russian Nights*, trans. by Olga Koshansky-Olienikov and Ralph E. Matlaw, (Dutton, New York, 1965; reprinted Northwestern University Press, Evanston, 1992)
Proffer, Carl R., *Russian Romantic Prose: An Anthology* (Translation Press, Ann Arbor, 1979)
Rydel, Christine (ed.), *The Ardis Anthology of Russian Romanticism*, (Ardis, Ann Arbor, 1984)

See also

Brown, William Edward, *A History of Russian Literature of the Romantic Period*, 4 vols (Ardis, Ann Arbor, 1986)
Campbell, J.S., *V.F. Odoyevsky and the Formation of Russian Musical Taste in the Nineteenth Century*, (Garland, New York, 1989)
Cornwell, Neil, *V.F. Odoyevsky: His Life, Times and Milieu* (Athlone Press, London/Athens; Ohio University Press, Ohio, 1986)
Mersereau, John Jr, *Russian Romantic Fiction*, (Ardis, Ann Arbor, 1983)
Reid, Robert (ed.), *Problems of Russian Romanticism* (Gower, Aldershot, 1986)

NEW YEAR

(from the Notes of a Lazy Man)

'If you noted down every day of your life, then whose life wouldn't be curious?' – said someone.

To this, I could very boldly retort: 'Mine'. What can be curious in the life of a man who has done absolutely nothing in this world! I have felt, I have suffered, I have thought on behalf of others, about others and for others. I write my notes, read them over, and I find in them only one thing: myself. Such self-effacement on my part must dispose the readers in my favour; let's see whether I am mistaken in my calculation. Here are a few days *not from my* life; if they don't bore you too much, I'll tell you about a few more.

Act I

– Wine! Wine! Hurry up and pour it; it's five to twelve already.

– That's not true, there's still a whole half hour left before New Year...
– replied Vyacheslav, pointing proudly at his wooden clock, with the roses on its dial and its cast-iron weights.

– That's by your clock: it's always a good hour slow!...

– But then it sometimes races two hours ahead; it comes to the same thing, – remarked one inveterate wit.

– That's not true, it is very accurate, – objected Vyacheslav with some annoyance, – I check it every day by the town clock....

– Look how proud he is of his clock! – continued the wit. – He bought it from some carrier for a rouble and hung it on his wall, look, it's just like a drawing room....

– That's not true: it was bought from a clockmaker and it cost twenty-five roubles....

– I declare to you, gentlemen, that because of this wonderful purchase

9

we shall today be worse off by two bottles....

Thus we shouted, clamoured, argued and gabbled all sorts of nonsense on New Year's Eve in Vyacheslav's small second-floor room. There were about twelve of us; we had all just left the university. Vyacheslav was slightly better off than the rest of us, but also rather more dandified and at the same time a past master both at entertaining and in domesticity. For example, Vyacheslav always had some cheese on top of his tobacco and so-called wine from the Rhenish cellar. In his room, instead of the classic student's iron bed-stead with a flannelette cover, stood a divan fitted with striped gingham; on that divan lay leather cushions, from which the pillow-slips were removed in the daytime. Beside the divan stretched a carpet of woven selvedge, which gave the divan the air of a luxurious ottoman. Books lay not on the floor, as was the usual fashion, but on a shelf nailed to the wall under a calico curtain; not only was there a writing table, but another table as well, separate, although without a drawer. Over the only window there hung a piece of linen. There was even a Voltaire armchair. Finally, the famous clock proudly swung its pendulum, giving the final touch to the furnishing of the room.

Such well-appointed surroundings aroused universal envy and universal surprise and, at the same time, gave sufficient reason for Vyacheslav's apartment always to be our place of meeting. And so it was that day. A month before, Vyacheslav had momentously invited us to see in the New Year with him, even promising to make hot punch. Naturally, no one refused. We knew that he had been busying himself over the preparations, that the pie had been ordered and that, over and above his usual so-called wine, there would be at least three bottles of champagne!

After all the laughter and noise, by twelve o'clock all was as it should have been.

How we all sat down in six square metres, I really don't remember any more, but there was room for everyone: on the divan, on the window-ledge, on the table, on the shelf; on the armchair there sat, I think, three! On the table everything was ready and set out: the huge pie, a huge cheese, the bottles and, of course, a skull – so that our feasting should the more resemble that of Lucullus. Twelve pipes were smoked in solemn silence: but no sooner had the wooden clock tinkled twelve than we clinked glasses and cried 'hurrah!' for the New Year. It's true, the champagne was a little warm, and the hot pie was a bit on the cool side, but no one noticed. The conversation was merry. We had only just escaped from scholarly confinement: we were only just entering society. A wide road was opening before us – such scope for the youthful imagination! So many plans, so many dreams; such self-confidence and such nobility! Oh, happy times! Where are you?...

Moreover, we were people of some prominence: we had already experienced the delight of seeing ourselves in print – a delight which, for the first time, is indescribable! We already belonged to a literary grouping; we had defended one conscientious journalist against his rivals and had got extremely steamed up in the process. It's true, we had landed in hot water because of that. At first the repressors of literary glory had been on the point of taking us, we new authors, under their fatherly patronage; but we, in a fit of impartiality, in reply to their flattery, had nettled all these gentlemen mercilessly. Such ingratitude on our part angered them exceedingly. At that shameful stage in the development of our criticism, literary abuse would overstep all limits of decorum; literature itself was a totally extraneous matter in critical articles: they were pure invective, a vulgar battle of vulgar jokes, double entendres, the most malicious calumnies and offensive constructions. It goes without saying, that in this inglorious battle the only winners were those who had nothing to lose as far as their good name was concerned. My friends and I were totally deluded. We imagined ourselves engaged in the subtle philosophical disputes of the portico or the academy, or at least the drawing room; in actual fact we were slumming it. All around it smelt of lard and tar; talk was of the price of sturgeon; they were cursing away, stroking their filthy beards and rolling up their sleeves – while we were thinking up polite taunts, witty allusions or dialectical subtleties, and hunting through our Homer or our Virgil for the most severe epigram to pit against our foes, fearing all the while to disturb their sensitivities.... It was easy to guess the result of such an uneven fight. No one took the trouble to consult their Homer, so as to grasp the full sarcasm of our epigrams; the scoffing of our opponents had a thousand times more effect on the reading public – both because it was ruder and because it had less to do with literature.

Fortunately, that painful time passed. If the residue of the victorious heroes of that epoch were now to feel like renewing the combat which then went so to their advantage, such an enterprise would hardly be crowned with success; widespread scorn has little by little weighed down on those who deserved scorn, and they will not rise again! But then – then was another matter. Many of us were affected by these gentlemen with the manners of lackeys; the laughs were on us and, shameful though it is to admit, the stupid jokes of our critics resounded in our ears. We could feel the sheer justice of our case – and so much the more infuriating for us was the injustice of general opinion. In his mature years, a man gets used to human injustice and takes it in his stride, the bitter with the sweet; but in one's youth, when one so wants to believe in everything lofty and fine, the injustice of people hits home and impresses an inexpressible despondency on the soul. To this state of mind may be ascribed that Byronism with which the young are all too often reproached, when frequently all that is to blame is their kindheartedness and nobility of spirit. The soulless have no need of melancholia.

Be that as it may, the attacks of our infamous foes and their triumph with public opinion drew the comrades of our little circle closer together. We relaxed together; each one knew the other's troubles; each in his own way valued the efforts of his friend. Common injustice even had its uses: with good cheer, we spurred each other on towards new labours and with each new day were stricter with ourselves.

Our conversation on the threshold of the New Year was filled with this ardent, vigorous, youthful life. So many fine hopes! So many plans, confused with Attic epigrams against our persecutors!... Vyacheslav was the life and soul of the company: he momentously persuaded us that the New Year must without fail be begun with something effective and himself, in his capacity as poet, seized a sheet of paper and began to improvise some verses, while proposing that we should each choose for ourselves some effective, important work, to which we would be required to devote ourselves during the course of the year. His proposal was accepted with alacrity – and on that day we threatened to inflict on the reading public a number of systems of philosophy, courses of mathematics, novels and dictionaries. From such immediate tasks we turned our attention to the long-term; all fields and careers were taken up: someone promised to elevate the bellicose name of his ancestors by means of scholarship; another to bring to our industrial world all the expertise of Europe; another to sacrifice his life in the Tsar's service on the field of battle, or in arduous civilian labours. We believed in ourselves, and in each other, for our thoughts were pure, our hearts knew no intrigue. Meanwhile, Vyacheslav finished his verses, in which he alluded to the tasks we had allotted ourselves. There is no need to say that we proclaimed him a true poet and convincingly proved to him that his destiny in this life was *to develop the idea of poetry*. For a long time afterwards, whenever we met we would greet each other with, in lieu of the usual 'hello', our poet's verses: they put a radiant, optimistic complexion on all our thoughts and feelings.

We parted with the light of day, promising each other all to gather on this day every year at Vyacheslav's, any hindrance notwithstanding, to give full account of the fulfilment of our vows.

For several years we were inseparable. The fortunes of many of us underwent great change; the selvaged carpet was replaced by the intricate weaves of English manufacture; the small room turned into a splendidly luxurious mansion; the champagne chilled in silver buckets filled with a chemical freezer; but, in honour of our old student life, we met without ceremony, in plain frock-coats, and as before shared the most candid thoughts and feelings. Meanwhile, some of our tasks had been commenced, the greater part of them uncompleted, while the rest had given way to other projects. Little by little, fortune dispersed us around the corners of the globe; those remaining met as before, on the first day of the year; those absent would write back, saying that they would be mentally transported to their friends on that day: whether from the metropolis of the Hagia Sophia, from the banks of the Orinoco, from the foot of Mount Elbrus, or from the hills of ancient Rome.

Act II

A few more years went by. Fortune took me to various countries. I arrived in Moscow one New Year's Eve. I looked for Vyacheslav, but he was not there: he had moved outside Moscow, about ten kilometres away. In the same carriage, I travelled on, out of Moscow, and arrived towards midnight. The horses quickly carried me across the yard, which remained uncleared of snow; a light could still be glimpsed in the stately house. After walking through several dimly lit rooms, I reached the study. Vyacheslav was on his knees in front of the cradle of a sleeping infant; smiling at him was a woman in the full bloom of beauty. He spotted me and made a sign that I should speak more quietly:

– He's only just got to sleep, – whispered Vyacheslav; his wife repeated the same words. For several minutes I found the sight of this family scene quite moving. It was obvious from everything that this house was lived in, and was no mere bivouac. Everything had been thought out with an English intuition for family life, the everyday: the table was covered with books and papers, the furniture was comfortable, as is essential to a busy man; everywhere there was an untidiness which constituted a mean between the tidiness of an indolent man and the negligence of sloth; reading-stands on the armchairs, a piano, a partly painted canvas, some journals lying open and, finally, a memento of our former life – the wooden clock from his student days. I didn't have time to look around further before the baby dropped off into the deep sleep of innocence. Vyacheslav got up from the cradle and hugged me.

– This is my old friend – he said, introducing me to his wife, – today is New Year's Eve. We must see it in, just like in the old days.

The three of us sat down at a small table; at twelve o'clock we clinked glasses and began to reminisce, to recall our friends.... Many were missing: having died a glorious death on the field of battle, or a no less glorious death exhausted by office work and nights without sleep; killed by a hopeless passion, an irrevocable loss or human injustice. Already half of us no longer existed on this earth!

There were no shouts, no youthful raptures at this peaceful celebration, no precipitate promises or frivolous hopes. We spoke in whispers, so as not to wake the child. Frequently we paused in mid-sentence to look in on the sleeping infant. We spoke not of the future, but only of the past and the present. Our conversation was that quiet family babble, where what is of interest is not the words spoken, but the person uttering them: where half the thoughts are guessed and people speak, seemingly, only to provide a pretext for looking at each other.

– My time has past – said Vyacheslav finally. – My verses have gone on to the fire; my endeavours have not come off. There is no calling back one's youthful vigour. A great poet I cannot be, and a mediocre one I have no wish to be. But what I have not managed to do myself, I shall try to accomplish through him – added Vyacheslav, pointing to the cradle. –Here is my true vocation now, here is my youthful vigour, here my hopes for the future. I shall dedicate my life to him. He will have no other mentor than me; he won't have a minute not shared with me, for in upbringing every minute is important: one moment can destroy whole years of effort. A father who does not take proper care of his son is, to my way of thinking, the greatest of criminals. Who knows? Nature produces a weak, seemingly unnecessary leaf on a plant, which grows only so as to preserve a tender shoot and then – it withers inconspicuously. Doesn't the same thing happen with people? Perhaps I am this weak, coarse leaf, and my son the shoot of something great; perhaps in this cradle lies a poet, a musician, a painter, to whom Providence has entrusted the whole future of humanity. I shall wither inconspicuously, but everything that is in my son I shall expose to the world; in this, I believe, lies the sole meaning of this secondary life of mine!

At this point, Vyacheslav began telling me of the plans which he was making for the education of his son. His library was filled with all the books he could get on education: he showed me a pile of lengthy extracts. He was studying in earnest, but in the way we used to in the old days, like a student preparing for a tough examination.

I left Vyacheslav quite early; we had scarcely drunk a quarter of the bottle. He, as a family man, didn't care to turn night into day. I didn't want to force him to alter his strictly established routine. The hours I had spent with him long remained with me as a sentimental but inexpressible memory.

Act III

A few more years passed. Then once, on New Year's Eve, fortune brought me to P. I knew that Vyacheslav had taken up residence in the city over two years before. I left my carriage and trunks at the inn and, as in the old days, without changing, got into the first cab I found – just as I was, still in my travelling clothes – and rushed off as fast as possible to my old friend. The swift movement of the gleaming carriages charging along the street brought me, from want of habit, to a state of numbness; I was scarcely able to pronounce my name to the porter who met me on Vyacheslav's porch. I think he took me for a madman because, for a time, he looked me in the eye and didn't utter a word in reply.

– The master is just leaving, the mistress has left already, – he said finally.

– What nonsense! That cannot be.

– The carriage has already been brought up, the master is finishing dressing....

– That cannot be.

– Will you permit me to announce you?

– I don't need to be announced.

– All the same, though....

I pushed the faithful retainer aside and hurried at a run through a series of brightly lit rooms. All was a-bustle; in the far room I found Vyacheslav, in full ceremonial get-up, in front of the mirror. He was terribly cross because one of his shoes had detached itself from his foot; a hairdresser was adjusting a hair-piece for him.

Vyacheslav was both pleased and embarrassed to see me.

– Oh, my dear fellow! – he said disappointedly, turning first to the footman, then to the hairdresser. – Tighten this lace.... Why ever didn't you let me know that you were here?

– I'm straight off the long distance coach.

– I would have got out of it somehow. You don't know what life here means... fix this tuft... not a minute to yourself, no time to live, and you don't even feel as though you are living....

– You're going out. I won't detain you....

– Oh, how annoying! I would much rather stay here with you... the hair-piece is slipping here... but it's impossible, believe me, it's impossible....

– I believe you, I believe you; you have some kind of important business....

15

– Important business! I promised Prince B. a hand of whist... my gloves... he's a man on whom much depends – I couldn't turn him down. Oh, how good it would be to see in the New Year in our old style, to reminisce... my hat....

– Please don't stand on ceremony....

At this point his son came in, with his tutor.

– Adieu, father.

– Ah, are you back already? Did you enjoy your masked ball? Now, goodbye, go to bed... tighten this lace a bit more.... God bless. Oh, my God! It's half past eleven already.... Goodbye then, my dear, dear fellow! You remember the old days? Carriage, my carriage!...

Vyacheslav rushed out at full pelt. I walked quietly after him, looking at the fine rooms – they were brilliant, but cold; the study was impeccably tidy, everything in place: the letters, the ink-well, above the fireplace a *rococo* clock, on the table an open city directory....

That New Year I greeted alone, a jug of mineral water in front of me, in a wayfarers' hotel.

1831

16

THE TALE OF A DEAD BODY, BELONGING TO NO ONE KNOWS WHOM

> It's true that the district clerk, coming out of
> the tavern on all fours, saw the moon
> dancing on the sky for no apparent reason,
> and swore about it all over the village; but
> the villagers shook their heads and even
> made a laughing stock of him.
>
> Gogol, *Evenings on a Farm*

The following declaration by the district court was posted around the market villages of the Rezhensk area:

> It is hereby declared by the Rezhensk local court that, within its jurisdiction, on the Morkovkino-Natashino village commonland, on the 21st November last, was found a body belonging to no one knows whom, of the male sex, clad in a threadbare grey cloth greatcoat, in a cotton sash, in a red cloth waistcoat partly green, in a coarse red shirt; on the head a peaked cap of old coarse rag with a leather peak. The deceased is about 43 years of age, 6 feet $1^{1}/_{2}$ inches tall, with light-brown hair, pallid face, smooth skinned, grey eyes, clean shaven, chin streaked with grey, nose large and somewhat to one side, of slight build. It is hereby declared: should there be former relatives of, or the owner of, the above-mentioned body, such persons are asked kindly to let themselves be known to the village of Morkovkino-Natashino, where investigations into the above-mentioned body belonging to no one knows whom are being conducted. And if none such can be found, kindly let this be known to the above-mentioned village of Morkovkino.

Three weeks went by in which owners of the dead body were awaited. No one appeared and finally the assessor and the district physician went off to visit a landowner of the village of Morkovkino. The clerk Sevastyanich, who was also posted to the investigation, was quartered in the escheat shed. In the same shed, in the storeroom, was the dead body, which the court intended to unseal and bury the next day, according to the usual procedure. The generous landowner, for Sevastyanich's consolation in his solitary state, sent him down from the manorial yard a dressed goose and a good litre of home-distilled liquor for his stomach.

It was already dark. Sevastyanich, being a conscientious fellow, instead of clambering up on the sleeping ledge beside the recently stoked stove, as would be the wont of his colleagues, decided, for the good of his soul, to get down to the preparation of all the papers for the next morning's session. All the more estimable was the fact that, although only the bones of the goose remained, only a quarter of his jug of liquor had been drained. As a preparatory measure, he adjusted the wick of the iron night-light, deliberately preserved for such occasions by the elder of Morkovkino village, and then pulled out an old greasy notebook from his leather bag.

Sevastyanich could not look at this without emotion: in it were all the copies of the various decrees concerning local authority affairs which had come down to him from his father, a local scrivener of blessed memory by virtue of the attribute of having been discharged from his duties in the town of Rezhensk for slander, bribery and indecent conduct. Such, moreover, was the case elucidated against him, that henceforth he would be appointable nowhere and no petitions from him would be accepted – for which status he enjoyed the respect of the entire district. Sevastyanich involuntarily recalled that this notebook was the unique codex by which the Rezhensk district court conducted its business; that he, Sevastyanich, alone was capable of interpreting the mysterious symbols of the Sibylline Book; that by means of its magic power he held in obedience both the Chief-of-Police and the assessors and compelled all the inhabitants of the precinct to come running to him for advice and instruction. For this reason he looked after it like the apple of his eye, showed it to no one and brought it out only in case of extreme need. With a smile he lingered over those pages on which, partly in the hand of his late father and partly in his own, were, here blotted out and there written anew, various insignificant particles, such as: *not*, *but* and so on, and in this perfectly natural way it occurred to Sevastyanich how stupid other people were, and how clever were he and his father.

Meanwhile he had knocked back a second quarter of his jug of spirit and begun work. But while his practised hand curved loops on the paper, his self-esteem, awakened by the sight of the notebook, was at work. He remembered how many times he had transported dead bodies to the borders of the neighbouring district and thus spared his Chief-of-Police unnecessary trouble. Yes and, generally speaking, whether it is making decisions, or reporting to the authorities on the impossibility of fulfilling their injunctions: everywhere and in everything, there is Sevastyanich. With a smile he recalled one ploy which he had contrived: deflecting a general search in any direction. He remembered how, quite recently by this innocent means, he had saved one of his associates: this associate had done something for which he could well have had to undertake a certain not altogether pleasant journey. The questioning had taken place and the general search had been ordered; but on this occasion Sevastyanich suggested they hold responsible, before anyone else, a certain literate fellow and suitable confederate; a document was compiled in accordance with the words of the literate fellow, which the literate fellow duly signed, crossing himself; and Sevastyanich himself approached first one resident, then another and then a third, with the question: 'And you as well, and you as well?' – and began to sort them out so quickly that, while the residents were still scratching their ears and bowing, preparing to reply, he managed to question every one of them; and the literate fellow, in view of the illiteracy of his comrades, again signed, crossing himself, their *unanimous* testimony. With no less pleasure, Sevastyanich recalled how he, when the Chief-of-Police was faced with a demand for the restitution of a considerable accounting deficit, managed to involve up to fifteen people in the mess, to spread the deficit over the whole lot of them, and then place all of them under open amnesty. In short, Sevastyanich saw that in all the remarkable cases of the Rezhensk district court he had been the one and only culprit, instigator and executor; that without him the assessor would have been finished, as would the Chief-of-Police, the District Judge and the Marshal of Nobility; that by himself alone was the ancient glory of the Rezhensk district maintained, and unwittingly there crossed Sevastyanich's mind a sweet sense of his own merit. It was true that from afar, as if from the clouds, his eyes caught a glimpse of the angry eyes of the Governor and the questioning face of the secretary of the criminal chamber. But he looked at the windows covered with snow; he thought of the three hundred kilometres which separated him from this horrific spectre. To enliven his spirits he sank the third quarter of his jug of spirit – and his thoughts became much more cheery: he imagined his cheerful little Rezhensk house, acquired on his wits; big jars of fruit liqueur on the window-ledge between two balsam pots; the kitchen cupboard full of crockery, between which in the middle, in the place of honour, was the crystal pepper-pot on its porcelain saucer: and there was his plump, pale-faced Lukeria Petrovna. She was holding a rich, fine-ground loaf. A heifer, fattened up for Christmastide, was looking at Sevastyanich. A large tea-pot and samovar bowed to him and moved towards him. There was the warm stove-ledge, and beside the stove-ledge the feather bed with the damask blanket and, under the feather bed, a rolled-up piece of fabric, and in the fabric some white gingham and in the gingham a leather book-holder, and in the book...some grey papers.

At this point, Sevastyanich's imagination took him back to the years of his youth; he pictured his poor everyday life in his father's house: how he often went hungry through his mother's meanness; how he was sent to the sacristan to learn to read and write. He laughed his head off recalling how once with his friends he climbed into his teacher's garden behind the apple trees and frightened the sacristan, who took him for a real thief; how he was flogged for this and in revenge fed his teacher a meat dish on Good Friday, of all days. Then it came back to him: how finally he surpassed all his friends of his age and got as far as reading the Apostles in the parish church, starting in the thickest bass voice and finishing in the thinnest of voices, to the surprise of the whole town; how the Chief-of-Police, spotting the boy's potential, attached him to the district court; how he began to sharpen his wits. He married his dearest Lukeria Petrovna and received the rank of provincial registrar, in which capacity to this day he continues to feather his nest. He was overcome by emotion and in his joy he drained the last quarter of the bewitching beverage as well. At this point it occurred to Sevastyanich that not only was he a fine official, but a great fellow al-together: the way they all listen when, at a ripe hour of an evening's session, he will start on the tale of Bova Korolevich, the adventures of Vanka Kain or the journey of the merchant Korobeynikov to Jerusalem – incessant harp playing, indeed! And Sevastyanich began to muse: how great it would be if he had the strength of Bova Korolevich and could grab someone by the hand – and the hand would be off! – or someone by the head – and the head would be off! Then he would have liked to have a look and see what sort of an island Cyprus was – according to Korobeynikov, abundant with lamp-oil and Greek soap, and where people ride on donkeys and camels – and he began to laugh at the inhabitants of that place, who hadn't the wit to harness these to sledges. At this point, the following argument began to form in his mind: he considered that either the books were lying, or that the Greeks must really be a very stupid race, because he himself had questioned Greeks – those coming to Rezhensk fair with soap and spice cake, who, he would have thought, must have known what actually goes on in their country – as to why they had sacked the city of Troy, as Korobeynikov actually wrote, yet left the Imperial City to the

Turks! And no sense could be got out of these people: what Troy was exactly the Greeks couldn't tell him, saying that probably this city had been built and captured during their absence. While he was preoccupied with this important question, there passed before his eyes Arabian brigands, the Dead Sea, the procession of the interment of the cat, the Pharaoh's palace with its gilt interior, and the ostrich: as high as a man, with a duck's head and a stone in its hoof....

His reflections were interrupted by the following words, uttered by someone beside him:

– Ivan Sevastyanich, old chap! I come to you with the most humble petition.

These words brought Sevastyanich back to his role as a clerk and, from habit, he began writing much faster, lowered his head as much as he could and, not lifting his eyes from the paper, replied in a drawling voice:

– What can I do-oo for you?

– You represent the court which has appealed to the owners of the dead body picked up at Morkovkino.

– Ye-es.

– Well, you see, it's my body.

– Ye-es.

– So, could you possibly be so good as to hand it over to me as soon as possible?

– Ye-es.

– You can, of course, rely on my gratitude....

– Ye-es. So who was the deceased, a serf of your's, was he?...

– No, Ivan Sevastyanich, what do you mean a serf? The body is mine, my own....

– Ye-es.

– You can imagine what it's like for me without a body... could you please help me out with this favour, as soon as possible?

– All in good time, sir, but it's a bit tricky to do this sort of thing, just like that – it's not a pancake, you know, you can't just wrap it round your finger. Inquiries have to be made.... If you were to make a small contribution....

– Oh, please have no doubt about that. Just hand over my body and, by all means, fifty roubles....

At these words, Sevastyanich raised his eyes, but saw no one and said:

– But come in here, don't stand out there in the freezing cold.

– But I'm here, Ivan Sevastyanich, I'm standing beside you.

Sevastyanich adjusted the lampshade, rubbed his eyes, but, still seeing nothing, he muttered:

– Devil take it! – have I been struck blind or something? I don't see you, my dear sir.

– There's nothing odd in that! How can you expect to see me? I haven't got my body!

– To tell you the truth, I don't quite follow you. Let me at least have a look at you.

– As you wish, I can show myself to you for a minute… except that it's a very difficult business….

And at these words, in a dark corner, there began to appear some sort of a formless face; first appearing, then lost, like a young man arriving at a ball for the first time: he feels like approaching the ladies but is afraid to, thrusts his head out from the crowd and then hides again… .

– Excuse me, sir – said the voice while this was taking place – be good enough to excuse me, but you cannot imagine how difficult it is to show yourself without a body! Please be good enough to hand it over as soon as possible. As I keep saying, I wouldn't begrudge fifty roubles.

– Glad to be at your service, sir, but to tell you the truth I don't quite follow you… do you have a petition?…

– For goodness sake, what petition? How could I have written it without a body? If you would please be good enough and take the trouble….

– It's all very well saying take the trouble, sir, but I keep telling you, I don't understand what the hell's going on….

Sevastyanich pulled out a sheet of stamped paper.

– Now tell me, if you'd be so good: do you at least have a rank, name and patronymic?

– Of course…. I am called Zveuillet, Jean-Louis.

– Your rank, sir?

– Foreigner.

And Sevastyanich wrote on the stamped paper in large letters: 'To the Rezhensk local court from the foreign adolescent of the nobility Savelii Zhaluev an explanation.'

– What next?

– Kindly just write. I'll tell you what to put; write: I possess….

– A fixed possession, is it? – asked Sevastyanich.

– No, sir: I possess an unfortunate weakness….

– For strong drink, is it? Oh, that's highly shameful….

– No, sir: I possess an unfortunate weakness for leaving my body….

– What the devil! – shouted Sevastyanich, throwing down his pen – what do you take me for, sir!

– I assure you that I am speaking the absolute truth. Just write and never mind anything else. There's fifty roubles for you for a single petition and another fifty when you've sorted the business out....

And Sevastyanich again took up his pen.

'On the 20th of October last I was driving my covered wagon on personal business on the Rezhensk highway, sitting in the open part, and as it was cold outside and the roads of the Rezhensk district are especially bad...'.

– Now, just wait a minute here – objected Sevastyanich. – We certainly can't write that; that's personal and putting personal remarks in with official business is not allowed....

– That's all right by me; well then, simply put: outside it was so cold that I was afraid of my soul freezing, and in general I so wanted to get to the night's lodging as soon as I could... that I lost patience... and, in my usual way, jumped out of my body....

– Pardon me! – exclaimed Sevastyanich.

– Never mind, never mind, carry on; what can I do if that's my usual way... there's nothing illegal about it, after all, isn't that so?

– We-ell, yes – replied Sevastyanich – and what next?

– Please write: I jumped out of my body, covered it over completely in the back of the wagon...'so that it wouldn't fall out; I tied its hands with the reins and set off for the post-station, in the hope that the horse itself would gallop off to its familiar yard.

– It must be said – remarked Sevastyanich – that in this matter you acted very imprudently.

– Having arrived at the post-station, I climbed on to the stove, to warm up my soul, and when, according to my calculation, the horse should have been returning to the coaching inn... I went out to check but, however, the whole night through neither horse nor body returned. The next morning I hurried off to the place where I had left the wagon...but it was no longer there.... I suppose my lifeless body fell out of the wagon because of the pot-holes and was picked up by the passing Chief-of-Police, and the horse joined up with a string of carts.... After three weeks of fruitless searching, and now informed of the Rezhensk district court appealing to the owners of a body which has been found, I most humbly request that my body be returned to me, as its lawful owner...to which I would add the most humble request, in order that the above-mentioned court should be so kind as to give the instruction to place, in the meanwhile, that body of mine in cold water, in order that it should recover; if there should be, from the occurrence of falling, in that oft-mentioned body any damage at all, or should it have been adversely affected in some part by frost, then order it to be put right by the district physician at my expense and attend to all of the above as the law commands, to which effect I now sign.

– Well, be good enough to sign it, then – said Sevastyanich, as he finished writing the document.

– Sign it! That's easily said! You've been told that I don't have my hands with me – they stayed with my body; you sign it for me, to the effect that, for lack of hands....

– No! Excuse me – objected Sevastyanich – that's not the form, and requests not written according to form are forbidden acceptance as decrees; if you like, it can be: for lack of literacy....

– Whatever you think best! it's all the same to me.

And Sevastyanich signed it: 'To this explanation, for lack of literacy, by personal request of the petitioner, provincial registrar Ivan Sevastyanich, son of Blagoserdov, has added his signature'.

– I'm most deeply obliged to you, my dear Ivan Sevastyanich! Now, please do all you can, so that this case is resolved with the utmost haste; you cannot conceive of how awkward it is to be without one's body!... Well, I'm disappearing for the time being, to see my wife; you may be sure, I won't begrudge you over this.

– Wait a minute, wait a minute, your honour! – shouted Sevastyanich – there's a contradiction in this request. How did you manage to cover yourself, or pack your body into the wagon, without any hands? Oh, to hell with it! I can't make any sense of it.

But there was no reply. Sevastyanich read the request through once more and started to think it over, to think and think....

When he awoke, the night-light was out and the morning light was forcing its way through the window, which had been covered over with a bag. With some annoyance, he looked at the empty liquor flask standing in front of him; this annoyance had knocked the nocturnal happening clean out of his head; he gathered up his papers without looking at them and went off to the main house, in the hope of there obtaining a hair of the dog.

The assessor, having knocked back a glass of vodka, settled down to look through Sevastyanich's papers and came across the request of the foreign adolescent of the nobility.

– Well, Sevastyanich, old mate – he shouted, upon reading it – you must have been well and truly away with it last night; what a lot of rubbish you've written! Listen to this, Andrey Ignatevich – he added, turning to the district physician – this is the sort of petitioner Sevastyanich is putting forward to us. And he read the curious request through to the district physician, word for word, splitting his sides.

– Well, let's go, gentlemen, – he said finally, – and unseal this garrulous body, yes, and if it doesn't respond, then we'll bury it while the going is good; it's time we got back to town.

These words brought the nocturnal happening back to Sevastyanich and, no matter how strangely it struck him, he remembered the fifty roubles promised him by the petitioner if he sorted out the matter of his body, and seriously began to demand of the assessor and the physician that the body should not be unsealed because this might spoil it, so that it would be no use for anything, and that the request should be noted in the entry-book according to the usual procedure.

Needless to say, this demand of Sevastyanich was answered with a recommendation that he should sober up; the body was unsealed, nothing was found on it and it was buried.

After these events, the corpse's request began to do the rounds; all over the place it was copied, supplemented, embellished and read, and for a long time the old women of Rezhensk would cross themselves with horror whenever they heard of it.

Legend has not preserved the outcome of this unusual happening: in one neighbouring district they said that, at the same time as the physician touched the body with his lancet, its owner jumped into it, the body got up and ran off, and that Sevastyanich chased after it for ages round the village, shouting for all he was worth, 'Catch him, catch that deceased!'.

In another district they claim that the owner, to this day, every morning and evening, comes to Sevastyanich, saying: – Ivan Sevastyanich, old chap, what about my body? When are you going to hand it over to me? – and that Sevastyanich, without turning a hair, replies: 'Ah, well, inquiries are still being made'. All of twenty years have passed since then.

1833

THE STORY OF A COCK, A CAT
AND A FROG

A Provincial Tale

For Dmitrii V. Putyata

Critic: What is the object of your tale?
Author: *(bowing humbly)* Telling it to you.

During her days in the town of Rezhensk, my late grandmother was the witness of a certain strange occurrence: being sure that it is necessary for the public to know everything concerning me, or my relatives and friends, I will relate this occurrence in every detail, as it was related to me, and in my usual fashion, without adding a single word of my own.

Many years ago we had in our town, in the calling of town mayor, a retired ensign named Ivan Trofimovich Zernushkin. Long had he already been carrying out this office – and no wonder, everyone was so pleased with him: he never interfered with anything; he allowed everyone to do as they liked; and, there again, he didn't allow anyone to intervene in his own affairs. Certain jokers, who had visited St Petersburg, often pestered him about various – in our parts, improbable and harmful – innovations; for example, they claimed that it wouldn't be a bad idea to inspect, at least now and then, shops with stores of comestibles, because the Rezhensk traders were in the habit, I don't know why, of selling mutton from Christmas to Shrovetide and fish in Lent, but the sort of fish – God forgive us! – that would make you run a mile from the market; others added that it wouldn't be a bad idea to sprinkle a bit of sand on the streets and forbid the throwing down of all kinds of rubbish from the houses, because of which apparently you couldn't get down the streets in autumn and from which the air was allegedly infected; there were even those who maintained that it was essential to bring in at least one fire hose, with ladders, boat-hooks, axes and other fancy tools.

Ivan Trofimovich, to all these unreasonable demands, replied highly sensibly, wittily and firmly. He proved that traders do not foist their goods on anyone and that everyone should themselves watch what they are buying; that only idlers and dishonourable people could demand supervision by the town mayor over such a matter, which the worst cook must know all about. Regarding the pavement, he said that God sends the rain and the good weather and, obviously, that was the way it was supposed to be, that in the autumn the streets were knee-deep in mud: moreover, good people stay at home and don't roam around the streets, and when a Russian does find it necessary to, then he'll get through anything. And if, he added, nothing was thrown out on to the streets, the pigs of the poorer classes would have nothing to eat in the autumn and wintertime. As for the air, air is not a human being·and cannot infect. Concerning the fire hose, Ivan Trofimovich proved that there had been no such thing before in Rezhensk, and now, when three parts of it had already burnt down, there was no point in going to such lengths for the fourth; that finally he, Ivan, Trofim's son, Zernushkin, retired ensign of a carbine regiment, had not exactly been born yesterday, and he knew himself how to perform his office, how to run the town and answer to the authorities. Such prudent arguments, repeated more than once, soon closed the lips of these jokers, especially when once, in a moment of anger, Ivan Trofimovich added that his, the town mayor's, duties, lay not in concerning himself with mud on the pavements and rotten fish, but with those who start spreading vicious rumours in the metropolis and stirring up resentment against the town services.

Everyone in the town praised Ivan Trofimovich for his firm disposition and ways and, thanks be to God, in our town of Rezhensk everything to this day has remained as it was: the streets are knee-deep in mud and you can't get through the markets. The only difference is, that instead of a fire hose, we recently acquired a fine green barrel with two equally green boat-hooks, but, by the terms of Ivan Trofimovich's will, they are never taken out to a fire, for if they were, they might easily get spoiled; they are preserved under lock and key in a purpose-built shed. Time proved the prudent instruction of Ivan Trofimovich to be correct: soon afterwards a passing official considered it his duty to report to the governor on the excellent arrangements for the fire-fighting equipment in the town of Rezhensk.

However that may be, Ivan Trofimovich, having divested himself of the tiresome requests of these Rezhensk jokers, addressed himself to his favourite occupations, of which he had two: namely, his tea and his cat. Yes my dear sirs! Ivan Trofimovich was very fond of tea and was even a great expert on the subject.

For this reason, he often went round the shops to collect tea samples from the merchants, so as to make no mistake. In this manner, Ivan Trofimovich would pick up a quarter here and a half pound there. Not that he would mix all the samples together, no! As a genuine expert, he would drink each one separately, and whoever's tea he praised, that merchant would bring him a present. It is said, however, to Ivan Trofimovich's honour – such a kind-hearted person was he! – that in these instances he was guided not so much by the quality of the tea, as by either whose turn it was among the merchants, or by various pertaining circumstances: thus, for example, any one of them who had something on his mind would probably know that Ivan Trofimovich would come to him for a sample. Not that this could be called a bribe! No! Our Rezhensk shopkeepers loved Ivan Trofimovich so much that they took him everything out of respect! In any case, there was no reason to give bribes: things were not as they are nowadays. Of course, in those days the town was not without its quarrels, its envy, its malice – it's just that then things were done differently; the litigants would go to Ivan Trofimovich and both of them would talk and talk – one would outshout the other; and Ivan Trofimovich would listen and listen, administer a shove to one of them and another to the other – he would offend nobody, our late mayor – and the litigants would then push and shove between themselves, as like as not come to blows, unburden their souls, and thereupon make it up in the tavern and, what's more, drink the health of Ivan Trofimovich. Happy old days were those!

Ivan Trofimovich certainly liked his tea drinking, but no less did he love his cat. It was not just that he loved his cat, no! But he loved his cat to walk round his neck, fawning and rubbing itself against him and whispering in his ear. And in truth, what a cat he had! Nowadays there are no such cats any more! Big, glossy, black, with its face, chest and paws white as snow, just like gloves. It goes without saying, there were no mice to be found at Ivan Trofimovich's place. And what endearing ways it had! I'm telling you, there are no such cats any more. Ivan Trofimovich would wake up and the cat would be straight up to him on the bed, first stretching and then arching its back, purring and then miaowing – and its green eyes would roll like emeralds. Then Ivan Trofimovich would get up, light the fire, put the kettle on the stove, put on his fleecy greatcoat, pick up his bag and set off to the market, with the cat behind him. Here the dogs are barking, the carts are rumbling and the people are shouting, but it doesn't worry the cat: it just jumps across the puddles and shakes its paws. Into whichever shop Ivan Trofimovich would go, there with him would go his cat – to the surprise of the entire town! And there's the cat where the fish is, where the newly chopped scraps are: it eats and purrs away! Ivan Trofimovich would return home, take his kettle, sit at the table by the window, and never mind that the cat is already fed. Don't imagine that it, like the cats of nowadays, would curl up into a ball and go off to sleep – no! – it would steal on to the table, between the cups and the sugar basin, and, not brushing against anything, would either sit on the window-ledge in the sun, or snuggle up to Ivan Trofimovich on his shoulder, purring and purring away, and rubbing and rubbing round his neck and whispering into Ivan Trofimovich's ear; Ivan Trofimovich would stroke it, and then take a sip of his tea.... Thus the long days would pass.

One of our latest writers has described the mute minutes of family happiness, when not a single thought enters the head and in one's heart is born a certain silent, inexpressible feeling; but who will describe the happiness of Ivan Trofimovich in this solitude! His warm residence, warm sheepskin, multicoloured wallpaper, mice burying the cat all over the wall, three-cornered hat, sword; the sun shines, there's a pillar of steam from the tea, everyone bows passing the window, around his neck Vaska's warm fur and no one else: neither children, nor wife, nor cook, and three hundred kilometres from the provincial capital! And this silent, inexpressible happiness was repeated every day; not once a day, but twice, in the morning and after dinner, and sometimes even in between times! There were two aims in Ivan Trofimovich's life: to drink as much tea as he could and to hold Vaska round his neck in silence. This thought never left him even for a minute; he fell asleep with it, dreamed of it and awoke with it. To this thought were tied his every action, his every desire and every slightest movement of his soul – which had no other thoughts in it. If someone came to him on some matter, if something important happened in the town, he would put everything off, so as not to miss his appointed hour for tea. If they spoke of the government inspector – well, he feared him only because he would feel awkward appearing together with Vaska.

But there is no eternal happiness in this life! Ivan Trofimovich had a namesake, and even some sort of a relation – among the gentry – the widow Marfa Osipovna Zernushkina. Some business might befall her in the town of Rezhensk, such as when someone had bewitched her mill, or put mercury in her weir. Marfa Osipovna was a lively, clever, miserly woman and, although she wasn't literate, she knew more about legal matters than many a legal clerk: therefore she would decide to plead her own cases herself, in her own person, and she needed Ivan Trofimovich to lend a hand on her behalf, for kinship's sake. She travelled in to see him, straight to his house. There could be no question of any temptation here, because the two of them were, between them, something over a hundred years old. Kind Ivan Trofimovich led her most cordially into his small parlour. And so, of course, in such a meeting, the distant cousins took great pleasure. There was talk about this and about that, about the old days, about the new ways, about the harvest. Vaska was right there, fawning, rubbing against them, purring, miaowing and looking at them with screwed up eyes....

– Oh! What a friend you've got there! – said Marfa Osipovna – have you had him long, old chap?

– Oh yes, a long time now, old girl! Eight years; since the last time we saw each other....

– And how should we see each other, old chap! Eighteen kilometres are no joke! You have your duties and I'm not so young any more. Three days, old chap, I dragged over to you on Shanks' pony! I nearly drowned in the mud, and I kept to the main road all the way. You know, we've had a new road built! Pussy-cat! Pussy-cat! How marvellous he is! Now, I see, you're set up in your own little house! Don't you want to get married, then? I saw a fully grown cock in your yard, and here there's an outlandish cat: now, we would say, according to our old wives' tales, a cock and a cat means a wife, old chap!

– Oh really, Marfa Osipovna, old girl, as far as that cock's concerned, I'd as soon be without him. What a squawker, drat him! He doesn't let your eyes close. Perhaps I'll give him to you, and for nothing....

– Thank you, Ivan Trofimovich, old chap. But whatever for?

– Oh, it's nothing, old girl! Blood is thicker than water. But that Vaska of mine! I can really say, Marfa Osipovna, that my Vaska is dearer than some wife. If you knew what an entertainer he is, what a joker. It's not only that he goes hunting, but he sings songs and keeps my neck warm; no, old girl, he doesn't get a crumb from me, but he goes around the town with me and takes quickrent from the shopkeepers!...

– Really, you don't say!

It would be impossible to list all the stories of Ivan Trofimovich and all the questions of Marfa Osipovna; so I, like the authors of sentimental novels, when matters reach some dreadful point of climax, leave it to the reader's imagination to add to everything that has been told, not fully told or re-told during this encounter.

Several days went by. One day after dinner, sitting at the tea table, Marfa Osipovna said to Ivan Trofimovich:

– I'm keeping my eye on you, old chap!... – Yes! – replied Ivan Trofimovich, – on what?

– On something bad!

– What do you mean, bad?

– Just that! bad....

– What's bad then, old girl?

– Just that: why do you allow the cat to whisper in your ear?

– Whisper in my ear?

– Yes, there, you see? You chased him away, old chap, but he's climbed up to your ear again.

– I really must admit, Marfa Osipovna, that I don't see what's wrong with it. It's warm and nice.

– I'll tell you what's wrong with it, Ivan Trofimovich. He'll whisper up a toad in your head for you.

– What do you mean, whisper up a toad?

– That's right, so that one way or another you'll get a toad in your head.

– What are you talking about, old girl? Get a toad in my head!... How could it get there?

– As you please, Ivan Trofimovich! Believe it or not, these are not my words I'm giving you, but what I heard from my parents. You remember my late father: he was not given to dropping idle words; and he frequently – may he rest in peace! – used to say that if a cat whispers in someone's ear, then that person will definitely get a toad in his head.

'What's this silly woman on about?' – thought Ivan Trofimovich to himself, lying down in bed and stroking Vaska. 'The very idea; a cat can whisper up a toad! The things these women think up!'

However, first one thing and then another came into Ivan Trofimovich's head. Now it would seem to Ivan Trofimovich that something was knocking in his head and as if he had a headache. And he would wonder, 'is it aching, or not? It's aching, it's really aching!... No it's not aching, it's really not aching!..'.

When he got up in the morning, Ivan Trofimovich, like a sensible man, decided that in the circumstances, the best thing was to ask a knowledgable person. He had a close friend, Bogdan Ivanovich, the district physician. He had not seen him for a long time now. 'Yes, let's go and see Bogdasha', – said Ivan Trofimovich – 'and ask him: he's an expert and will probably be able to tell me the whole truth'. This was no sooner said than done.

Ivan Trofimovich did not wish to admit that he had believed the old wives' tittle-tattle, but, being a subtle man, he commenced the conversation obliquely. After the usual greetings, Ivan Trofimovich said to the physician:

– What's going on, Bogdan Ivanovich, old chap? In our town everyone's complaining of headaches. What would this be from?

– Oh, it's not surprising, Ivan Trofimovich! – replied the physician. It's autumn time now and at this time of the year haemorrhoids are on the increase.

– And really, can you only get a headache from haemorrhoids?

– No, you can get a headache from various causes: from a cold, from intoxication, from indigestion.

– And from what other causes can you get a headache?

– From what others?

– Well, for example, is it true, old chap, that a person can sometimes get a toad in the head?

– There's no shortage of wonders in the human body! There are examples even of that.

– What! There are?

– Yes, but fortunately it's very rare.

– What wonders there are in this world! So how can you help in such an unfortunate case?

– Well, then you have to undergo an operation.

– An operation!

– Yes! And a very difficult one. The head is opened up.

– The head opened up? How can you do that?

– Well, like this, you see: there's this instrument; it's like the lid of a teapot, except it's got sharp teeth all round, like a fret-saw.

– Well?

– The hair is shaved off the head, the skin is cut all round and then you start twisting this instrument round and round the skull: it cuts a circle out of it.

– Well?

– Well, they take the circular area off: if there's a frog or something else in that area, then....

– What do you mean, if it's in that area!... if it's in another area?

– Well, then they twist it round the head again.

Ivan Trofimovich's legs went numb; however, he pulled himself together and said: – How can they do that, old chap? Cut the whole head up, like a pumpkin!... What happens to the person during this time?

– What should happen? He lies there unconscious.

– And are they still alive after such a torment?

– I have to admit, Ivan Trofimovich, they nearly always die.

Plunged into meditation, Ivan Trofimovich left the physician. 'The woman wasn't lying!' – he said on the road home – 'she wasn't lying! What a terrible business!' And, arriving home, he found Marfa Osipovna already preparing to leave.

– Where are you rushing off to, old girl?

– I can't waste time, Ivan Trofimovich! Thanks to you, all my business is sorted out; any odds and ends outstanding, you will settle without me. Thank you for your hospitality....

– Not at all, old girl, not at all!

When Marfa Osipovna was quite ready to get into the carriage, Ivan Trofimovich reluctantly said to her:

– Listen, old girl: I've given you the cock...take...the cat as well!

That was just what Marfa Osipovna had been waiting for.

– Oh! Whatever for? – she replied, – Vaska's your only consolation....

– No, old girl! I'm, you see, a single man, there's no one to tidy up the house, and in any case the cat's a bit of a devil; he jumps all over the place, gets everywhere and breaks things...you have plenty of space in the country.

– That's quite right, Ivan Trofimovich! Give him to me, then, give him to me. And in return, I'll bring you honey for your tea and dried mushrooms for Lent... You do fast, I'm sure?...

Tears almost welled up in Ivan Trofimovich when it came to parting with Vaska; but there was nothing for it. The cock was put in a bast basket, Vaska in a bag and Marfa Osipovna in the carriage; the whole lot shook and rolled on its way.

From that day, life became unbearable for Ivan Trofimovich. He was always sad, he was always cold round the neck; even his tea tasted bitter, no matter how much sugar he took. Going into the living room, he would seem to hear Vaska purring; when he walked round the town, he couldn't help turning round to admire him: then he would snatch at his cold neck – and there was no Vaska!...

One day, when Ivan Trofimovich was sitting at his tea table, a cup of tea cooling in front of him, a friend called in to see him.

– Hello there, Ivan Trofimovich, old chap! How are you getting on then, these days – is everything fine?

– No, my dear fellow!... I don't feel too well: even my tea doesn't slip down the way it should.

– What's wrong with you, Ivan Trofimovich?

– God knows! My head aches now and then, and I feel so down and sad; I don't even feel like looking at anything.

– Oh, Ivan Trofimovich, old chap! Would you like me to put you on to a good medicine?

– Do me a good turn, my dear fellow!

– Add a drop of grape vodka to your tea – and just you see!

– What do you mean, my dear fellow! I've never taken anything intoxicating in my life and I don't even know the taste of it.

33

– Just try. It's not going to turn you into a drunkard!... Grape vodka in tea, I'm telling you, is the best medicine for all illnesses. Physicians usually try to dissuade you from it because it does them out of their profits, but I've experienced its efficacy myself. I remember when a bridge of mine near the mound collapsed under my carriage: the coachman managed to hold on somehow, but I got thrown into the slop pit – up to my ears in water, old chap! Soaked to the skin, I was! I got home – it was a freezing day – and I had such a shaking fever through and through that I was seeing stars: a knocking in my head, teeth rattling, arms and legs buckling. What did I do? – Hey, missus! give me some tea, give me some vodka! I just downed a couple of glasses and the next day it had gone. Well, that's first-hand experience!... What other medicine would have done the trick? You listen to me, Ivan Trofimovich, try it: really, you'll thank me! You do have some grape vodka, don't you?...

– I keep it for visitors.

– Well, then, try it! Once, anyway – it won't cost you anything!

Ivan Trofimovich listened to his friend and tried it; he was just on the point of pulling a face, when he said: 'It's a funny thing!... The vodka gives the tea a better taste! We'll see what good it does.'

After two cups, indeed, Ivan Trofimovich felt much brighter. He repeated this enjoyable experience a second day, then a third, then a fourth, and so on.

One day Ivan Trofimovich was woken up by a severe headache: he jumped out of bed as though possessed. Straight for the grape vodka! He drank some and it helped. After a while he had a second attack, even worse than the first; again the vodka – and again it helped. Then a third one – and the grape vodka did not help this time. In vain, Ivan Trofimovich increased his medicinal intake: he just felt worse and worse. Ivan Trofimovich got cold feet; he felt as if something was moving and scratching inside his head: it was awful!

And from that time, Ivan Trofimovich had terrible dreams. First he would think that his skull was a whole nest of frogs and all kinds of reptiles. Or then he would think that he himself had turned into a huge, fat toad: and he was wretched and ashamed!... He wanted to put on his frock-coat to cover himself up, but his frock-coat wouldn't stretch far enough! Just sleeves dangling in the air!... Or then finally, he would think that he had the whole town of Rezhensk in his head – shouting, noise, the creaking of carts... and down the streets walked not people, but frogs on their hind legs, lolloping from leg to leg!...

Ivan Trofimovich was scared stiff! Throwing his shame to the winds, he dashed off to the doctor.

The Story of a Cock, a Cat and a Frog

– Bogdan Ivanovich, old chap! Help me, save me!

– What's happened to you, Ivan Trofimovich? Let me feel your pulse....

– Never mind that, old chap!... What's my pulse got to do with it? Do you remember the recent chat we had about a particular strange illness?...

– Well, yes, I do. What about it?

– Well, old chap, this same illness has just struck me, sinner that I am....

– I don't understand, Ivan Trofimovich....

– What don't you understand, old chap? I've got a toad in the head. Yes!.. a toad, do you understand? A toad in the head....

– Goodness me, Ivan Trofimovich! Where did you get that from?

– How did I get it? I'm not going to keep anything from you, old chap, any more than from my spiritual father; I'll tell you everything. I got attached to my cat.... Remember, I had a cat, such a marvellous, warm one – deuce it! – a black, glossy one.... It took to whispering in my ear, the cursed thing: whispering and whispering and it whispered a toad into it....

The doctor burst out laughing, for all he was worth.

– Oh dear me, Ivan Trofimovich! With your intelligence, you believe that sort of rubbish?...

– You may laugh, old chap, laugh as much as you like! – exclaimed Ivan Trofimovich through his tears. – You don't know what's going on in my head, but I do. I can feel some cursed thing scratching in there – my head's splitting; it's aching and aching – I'm almost out of my wits! What an awful thing it is! I'm in my sixth decade on this earth, in my fortieth year of service; I've always served faithfully and truthfully, I faced the Turk and was in the firing line, I got to the position of town mayor, and I never had such a thing happen to me before, and now, in my old age, to have such a disgrace visited upon me!... Help me, old chap, help me in any way you can; if not, I'll lay hands on myself!...

The doctor, seeing that all his exhortations would be in vain at this juncture, decided not to contradict the old man any more and said:

– Now listen to me, Ivan Trofimovich! If you really have got this illness, you'll have to have a little patience: I've already told you, I think that I have only heard some notion of some such strange illness, but I may vouchsafe to you that I've never seen it with my own eyes, nor have I read of it in books. Give me a little time to think about it a bit and consult my books. I shall lose no time in giving you the answer, but for now take this powder to get your temperature down and put some cabbage leaves round your head, and then, God willing, we'll see what has to be done.

As Ivan Trofimovich went out, the doctor set himself to think. The blood of his student days began involuntarily to throb in his veins; he recalled the delight with which he and his fellow students would learn of the admission to the clinic of some unusual patient or unusual corpse. 'What a misfortune!' – they cried to one another, – 'they've brought in six whole, fine bodies!' And if there should chance to be among the bodies some freak with six fingers, with the heart on the right, with a double stomach: this was happiness, this was delight!... New knowledge! The hope of a discovery! The elucidation of one's observations! New professional talk! New methods!

This type of enjoyment for our district physician had already faded long since; it was fifteen years since he had left the capital; word of scarcely any of the observations made in the course of that period had reached him, over a period of fifteen years of this medical century! He had no Academy nearby, nor journals, nor libraries, only an almost mechanical type of work and the need to earn his subsistence amid uneducated people: there was no one with whom to verify even the simplest observation; not a minute to set up one's own experiments! The whole twenty-four hours a day were taken up with rounds, inquests and the most trivial tasks of life. With despair, the doctor looked at his meagre range of books: Lorenz Heister's 'Anatomy', published in 1775; some 'Complete Doctor' or other, from the same era; the college dissertation by his friend: 'On the fluid of the nervous system'; his own dissertation for his medical degree, which in its day had caused quite a stir: 'On the appropriate designation of glands', with its epigraph from Heister: 'Which gland is which it is hard for doctors to say, for they are all very ignorant on this'; a few issues of *The Moscow Gazette*, his student notebooks and that was all!

How could he get anywhere with this? Where could he find, not only the means of treatment, but even the description of his patient's illness?...

In annoyance, and in the certainty of finding nothing, he took down his mentor, Heister, and, finding the chapter 'On the head', read: 'Constituent parts (*contentae partes*) are: the brain (*cerebrum*).... Beside the cranial brain is the *dura mater*, or the hard membrane over the brain, consisting of sinewy fibre...'.

He threw the book down: he had read all this and re-read it, learned and re-learned it!...

Then there occurred to him another book which he had once been given at the university as a prize for diligence, and which he had painstakingly coverd with paper and carefully kept apart from the other books, by dint of its expensive binding: this was a translation of the book *On presentiments and visions*, which had only just appeared.

On unwrapping this book, he came across the place describing the well-known episode of the famous Boerhaave in a Harlem orphanage. One of the girls in the house had collapsed with convulsions: so, upon looking at her, did a second, a third, a fourth and similarly every one of them, to the last. Boerhaave, seeing that this was an action induced only by imagination, ordered a brazier to be brought into the room, with coals and tongs, and announced that the first one to collapse with convulsions would be burned on the hand with red-hot tongs. This treatment so alarmed the patients that they all recovered instantly.

Having read this account, Bogdan Ivanovich started thinking. Carrying on reading, he found a description of a patient who imagined that his legs were made of crystal and whom a maidservant cured by dropping a bundle of firewood on his legs. Then he found the description of a patient who imagined that a fly was sitting on his nose and constantly waved his hand about, trying in vain to get rid of it. 'The quick-witted doctor' – so it said in the book – 'having assured the patient that he had the remedy for it, struck him on the nose with his lancet, thereupon showing the patient a fly which he had ready beforehand'. The words 'quick-witted doctor' and 'the famous Boerhaave' stopped Bogdan Ivanovich in his tracks.

– Supposing, he said to himself, I could manage to put into practice some such cure! I would describe in detail the temperament of my patient, his monomaniacal attacks, the remedy for his cure thought up by me, and my complete success, my fame, would spread over the whole world, I would send my report to the Academy...even the foreign newspapers would proclaim to the world how rare and remarkable in the annals of science are such incidents, what difficulties Ivan Trofimovich presented regarding treatment, how the 'quick-witted' doctor skilfully exploited the condition of the nervous juices in his patient, and so on, and so on; and perhaps this would get me called to Petersburg, accepted into the Academy?... Oh rapture! oh joy!... That's it!

And Bogdan Ivanovich hurriedly collected all the instruments he had – bent and straight scissors, bent and straight knives; he added to these everything he could lay his hands on in his meagre household: skewers, pie filling, the remnants of innocent tongs – everything, just in case. After this, in a nearby bog, he caught a huge frog, bent back its legs, put it into the pocket of his camisole and, with this store of equipment and his brows knitted as severely as possible, he appeared at Ivan Trofimovich's. Without saying a word, he laid out on the table, beside the very window-sill on which Vaska had usually sat, all his gadgets of war. Ivan Trofimovich paled.

– What's that? – cried the town mayor with horror.

– I've been pondering it for a long time and hunting through books for information about your illness, Ivan Trofimovich, – said the physician momentously – and I find that the only remedy for your salvation is an operation; it's true, it's an awful one.

– Operation! – cried Ivan Trofimovich – you mean boring through my head!... No, not for anything on earth! It would be better just to die of it, rather than dying under your knife.

– But it's the only remedy.

– No! Not for anything on earth!

– But you are feeling unbearable pain in your head, which will get worse and worse....

– No! It wasn't anything!.. it's all gone now....

– But two hours before this?...

– It's gone, I'm telling you! Completely gone!

All the efforts of the physician were in vain: he saw that his aim of frightening the patient had been too successful and decided that he needed to moderate it a little.

– But, listen! – he said. – This operation is really not as dangerous as you think, you know....

– Oh no, my dear fellow! You won't get the better of me: I am quite a cunning chap myself. I remember all the awful things you told me. I've only got to think about it, and my head almost comes off my shoulders.

– But I assure you, the way I do it is so skilful, so careful, that you won't even feel it....

– What's the good of your skill, when you're trying to drill through my skull!... Do you take me for a fool, or something?

The physician was in despair. He approached Ivan Trofimovich with his skewer, and with his lancet and with his tongs: Ivan Trofimovich would have none of it. In the end, the town mayor got really angry and 'the physician likewise; the decisive moment had been reached: on this depended Bogdan Ivanovich's future fame, his wealth, the Academy and articles in the press and a destiny to be envied among his learned profession. Armed with the lancet, he threw himself in despair upon his patient, trying at least to touch his head and demonstrate the achievement such an operation would be. But Ivan Trofimovich suddenly summoned up his former youthful strength...they struggled away: the table was upside down; cups and teapot were in smithereens; for both of them it was life or death!... And at that very minute, taking advantage of one of the physician's lunges, the cold witness and innocent participant in the incident plopped out on to the floor.

– What's that? – cried Ivan Trofimovich in surprise. – You damned scoundrel! You not only wanted to destroy me, but to plant some reptile in my head as well!... Get out of here, damn you!...out, I tell you!...

And with these words, Ivan Trofimovich, putting everything he had into it, threw Bogdan Ivanovich out of the window....

To this day, in the archives of the Rezhensk district court, is preserved 'the complaint of retired ensign of a carbine infantry regiment, the town mayor of Rezhensk, Ivan, Trofim's son, Zernushkin, against physician of the same district, Bogdan, Ivan's son, Goremykin, over the smashing of faience cups and a teapot, and over his clear intention to bring destruction upon him, Zernushkin, and implant in his head a certain reptile'.

The old men say, however, that from that day Ivan Trofimovich was freed for good from his attacks.

1834

THE SYLPH

(From the Notes of a Reasonable Man)

Dedicated to Anastasia Sergeyevna Pashkova

We shall crown the poet with flowers and
lead him away from the city.

Plato

A kingdom has three pillars: the poet, the
sword and the law.

Legends of the northern bards

Poets will be used only on appointed days
for the composition of anthems to public
edicts.

*One of the industrial companies
of the 18th century*

! ? ! ?

the 19th century.

Letter 1

At last I am in my late uncle's village. I am writing to you sitting in my
grandfather's huge armchair by the window. True, the view before my eyes
is not especially magnificent: the kitchen garden, two or three apple trees, a
rectangular pond, a bare field and that's it. Uncle was obviously no great
shakes with the estate. I would like to know what he used to do, living here

for fifteen years without a break. Did he really, like one of my neighbours, get up early in the morning at about five, sit swilling tea and laying out patience right up until dinner, have dinner, lie down for a rest and then keep at the patience again right up until night, and go on like that three hundred and sixty-five days a year? I don't understand it. I've asked people what my uncle did to pass the time and they told me 'well, that's more or less it'. I really like this reply. There's something poetic about a life like that and I hope soon to be following my uncle's example: it's true, the late lamented knew what was what!

In fact I do feel more composed here than in town and the doctors did just the right thing in sending me here. They probably really did it to get me off their hands, but I shall get the better of them, I think. My spleen, believe it or not, has almost gone. They are wrong if they think that a dissipated life can cure patients of my ilk. It's not true: the high society whirl drives you mad and so do books, while here, you can imagine my delight, I hardly see anyone and I haven't brought a single book with me! You can't describe happiness like this – you have to experience it. When there's a book lying on the table, then you can't help but reach for it, you open it and you read it. The beginning is enticing, promises you the earth, but you get a bit further and all you see is soap bubbles and you get the horrible feeling that all scholars have experienced, from the year dot to this year, inclusive: seek and ye shall not find! This feeling has tormented me for as long as I have been conscious and it is to this that I attribute those moments of spleen which the doctors like to put down to bile.

However, do not think that I have been living like a complete recluse. In the time-honoured way I, as the new landowner, have paid visits to all my neighbours, of whom there are mercifully few. I have talked about hunting with them, which I can't stand, about farming, which I don't understand, and about their families, of whom I have never heard in my life. But all these gentlemen are so cordial, so hospitable and so open-hearted that I have been quite taken by them. You cannot imagine how attracted I am by their total indifference and ignorance about everything that goes on outside their back yard; the delight with which I listen to their outlandish judgements on the only issue of *Moscow News* received in the whole district. They read everything in this number, which they keep wrapped in wallpaper just in case, from the delivery of horses to the capital to the science reports, inclusive. The former, of course, they read with great interest and the latter for a laugh, with which I join in with all sincerity, although for a different reason – for which I earn universal respect. Previously they were rather afraid of me and thought that, as an arrival from the capital, I would lecture them on chemistry or crop rotation. But, when I told them that, in my opinon, it was better to know nothing than to know as much as our scientists know, that nothing was more detrimental to human happiness than being knowledgable, and that ignorance never hindered digestion, then they clearly saw that I was a good chap and a most splendid person and they started telling me various jokes of theirs about the bright sparks who, flying in the face of reason, introduce potato growing, threshing, coarse flour and other fancy novelties into their villages: talk about laugh! And it serves these bright sparks right – why do they bother? The slightly smarter of my new friends discuss politics, too. By force of habit, they are still most perturbed by the Sultan of Turkey and they are quite concerned by the altercation between Tigil-Buzi and Gafis-Buzi; also they can't make out why Charles X is being called Don Carlos.... Ah, happy folk! We preserve ourselves from the disgust with which politics fills the soul by artificial means, that is by refusing to read the papers; they do it by the most natural means, by reading but not understanding....

Indeed, looking at them I am more and more convinced that true happiness can lie only in knowing everything or in knowing nothing, and as the former is not yet possible, then a person must choose the latter. I propagate this thought in various ways to my neighbours and they are quite taken with it, and I am most amused by the emotion with which they listen to me. There is one thing about me that they don't understand: and that is why I, being an absolutely splendid chap, do not drink punch and do not keep hunting dogs. But I am hopeful that they'll get used to this and I shall succeed, if only in our district, in getting rid of this worthless enlightenment which only serves to exhaust a man's patience and to set itself against his natural, inner inclination: which is to sit around doing nothing.... But to hell with philosophy! It can mess around with the thoughts of the most bestial of men.... Speaking of the bestial, some of my neighbours have the most attractive daughters who, however, are not so much to be compared with flowers as with garden vegetables – plump, buxom and robust – and there's not a word to be got out of them. One of my nearest neighbours, a very rich man, has a daughter whom I think is called Katenka and whom one might consider an exception to the general rule if she didn't share the habit of biting her tongue and blushing at every word you say to her. I tussled with her for close to half an hour and I still can't decide whether she has a mind under that lovely skin, and that skin really is lovely. There is something so sweet, so childish, about her sleepy little eyes and her little turned up nose that you can't help wanting to cover her with kisses. I find it highly desirable, as they say here, to make this little doll talk and I am priming myself at our next meeting to open our conversation with the words of the one and only Ivan Fyodorovich Shponka: 'In the summer we

get a lot of flies',* and then I shall discover whether anything more protracted comes out of it than the chat Ivan Fyodorovich had with his
betrothed.

Goodbye. Write to me more often, but don't expect letters from me very
often. I really enjoy reading your letters, but I enjoy not answering them
almost as much.

Letter II

(Two months after the first)

Talk about the constancy of the human spirit! How long ago was it that I
was rejoicing that I didn't have a single book with me? Not a month had
passed before I began to crave books. It began at the point when my
neighbours were boring me to death. You were quite right when you wrote
that I ought not to regale them with my ironic comments on the learned and
that my words, by raising their stupid self-esteem, would only bewilder
them all the more. Yes, my friend! I am now persuaded that there is no
salvation in ignorance. I soon discovered all the very same passions here
that used to frighten me among so-called educated people: the same ambi-
tion, the same vanity, the same envy, the same selfishness, the same spite,
the same flattery and the same meanness; the only difference being that all
these passions are stronger here, more open and more vicious, while at the
same time their subjects are more petty. I will go further: an educated man
is entertained by his very education, and his spirit at least is not in a state of
complete humiliation every minute of his existence: music, a painting, a
luxury gadget – all this reduces the time available for depravity.... But
getting to know my friends better was an awful experience. Egoism perco-
lates, so to speak, their whole make-up. Cheating somebody over a
purchase, winning an unjust lawsuit, taking bribes: all these are considered
to be the acts – not to be done on the quiet, but directly and overtly – of an
intelligent man. Currying favour with someone from whom some benefit
may be gained is the duty of a well-bred man. Longstanding grudges and
vendettas are treated as a matter of course. Drunkenness, gambling and
debauchery – of a kind which would never enter the head of an educated
person – are regarded as harmless, permissible forms of relaxation. And
still these people are unhappy, they complain and curse their lives. And
what do you expect? All this immorality and all this complete oblivious-

* Gogol (*Author's note*)

ness to human dignity are passed down from grandfather to father and father to son in the form of paternal exhortation and example and they infect whole generations.

I realised, from my close observations of these gentlemen, how closely immorality is bound up with ignorance, and ignorance with unhappiness. Not for nothing does Christianity call upon man to forget his present life. The more attention a man pays to his material needs, the greater significance he attaches to his domestic affairs, to his domestic woes, to what people say, to their attitude towards him, to trivial enjoyment, in a word to all the trivia of life – the more unhappy he will be. All this trivia will become the goal of his existence. He worries about it all, gets angry, uses up every minute of the day, sacrifices his most sacred inner being; and as all this trivia is endless, his soul is subjected to myriad irritations and his character is ruined. All the higher, abstract, reassuring concepts are forgotten; tolerance, that highest of virtues, disappears and a man involuntarily becomes malicious, quick-tempered, rancorous, intolerant; his soul descends into sheer hell. We see examples of this every day. The man who is always worried that due and proper respect may not have been paid to him; the mistress of the house who is completely absorbed in the running of her household; the moneylender who is incessantly occupied in the calculation of interest rates; the government clerk who loses amid bureaucratic pedantry all real ideal of service; the man who forgets his dignity in the lowest forms of accountancy. Take a look at these people in their domestic circle, in their relations with subordinates – they are awful. Their life is one of unrelieved worry, never achieving its goal, for they are so preoccupied by the means for living that they never find the time to live!

As a result of such sad observations on my friends in the country, I locked myself in and ordered that none of them be admitted to me. Left alone, I wandered about my room, looked at my rectangular pond a few times, and nearly had a good go at drawing it, but you know that I was never much good with the pencil. Work away as I would, it would turn out a ghastly mess. I would have taken up poetry, but I only got as far, as usual, as the tedious argument between thoughts, feet and rhymes. I was even on the point of starting singing, although I never could get *di tanti palpiti* right. Finally, alas!, I summoned my uncle's old steward and, despite myself, I asked him: 'Did my uncle really have no library at all?' The grey-haired old man bowed low and replied: 'No, master, we never had such a thing.' 'But what is there, then', I asked, 'in those sealed cupboards that I saw in the mezzanine?' 'There are books in them, master. After your uncle died, your aunt went and sealed the cupboards and said no one was to touch them any more.'

'Open them up, then.'

The Sylph

We went up to the mezzanine. The steward pulled off the wax seals, which were barely holding anyway, the cupboard was opened and what did I see? Something I had never suspected – Uncle had been a great mystic. The cupboards were filled with the works of Paracelsus, *The Count of Gabalis*, Arnold of Villanova, Raimondo Lulli and other alchemists and cabbalists. I even noticed remnants of some chemical apparatus in the cupboard. The old boy must have been searching for the philosopher's stone.... The old rogue! And the way he kept it secret!

There was nothing else for it; I got down to those books which had now been found; so imagine me, a nineteenth-century man, poring over huge folios and assiduously reading their content: on prime matter, on elemental electricity, on the soul of the sun, on northern dampness, on stellar spirits and all sorts of things like that. It is amusing, and tedious, and interesting. With all this business I almost forgot about my pretty neighbour, although her father (the one decent, though still boring, man in the whole district) often visits and is trying very hard to keep in with me. Everything that I hear of her suggests that she is what they used to call in the old days a good match, that is to say she has a large dowry. Incidentally, I have heard by heresay that she does a lot of good; for example, she marries off poor girls, giving them money for the wedding, and often pacifies the wrath of her father, a very quick-tempered man. All the local people call her an angel – a highly unusual thing around here. By the way, these girls always seem to have a strong inclination to marry off others, if not themselves. Why would this be?...

Letter III

(Two months later)

You are thinking, I suppose, that I have not only fallen in love, but even got married. You are mistaken. I am busy with something quite different. I am drinking – and do you know what? What idleness won't think up! I am drinking – water.... Don't laugh: you have to know what kind of water. Rummaging around in my uncle's library, I found a book in manuscript containing various formulae for conjuring up elemental spirits. Many of these were funny to the extreme. Here the liver of a white crow was required, there the salt of glass, elsewhere adamantine wood. For the most part, all these compounds were such that you could not have procured them from any apothecary. Among other formulae, I found the following one:

Elemental spirits are very fond of people and the slightest effort on the part of a human is sufficient to enter upon relations with them. Thus, for example, in order to see the spirits which waft on the air it is enough to collect sunbeams in a glass vessel with water in it and to drink it daily. By this mysterious means the sun's spirit will enter the human little by little and his eyes will open on to a new world. Whomsoever should decide to engage with them by means of a noble metal, he will comprehend the very language of the elemental spirits and their way of life and his existence will unite with the existence of his chosen spirit, who will grant him knowledge of such secrets of · nature that...but more we dare not say.... *Sapienti sat*.... Much, much has already been said for the enlightenment of your mind, gentle reader....

and so on, and so on. This method seemed so simple that I determined to try it out, if only so as to earn the right to boast that I had tried out a cabbalistic mystery on myself. I started to remember the Undine who so consoled me in childhood but, not wanting anything to do with her uncle, I took it into my head to see a sylph. With this in mind – what will idleness come up with next? – I threw a turquoise signet-ring into a vase of water, I placed this water in the sun and towards evening, before going to bed, I drink from it. So far I have found that it's very health-giving at least; I haven't seen any elemental force as yet, but I'm certainly sleeping better.

Do you know that I am still reading my cabbalists and alchemists and, do you know, what's more, I find these books really entertaining. How cordial and open their authors seem to be. 'Our business', they say, 'is very simple: a woman could accomplish it, without leaving her spindle – you just have to be able to understand us.' 'I saw it done', says one, 'I was present when Paracelsus turned eleven pounds of lead into gold'. 'I myself', says another, 'I myself know how to extract prime matter from nature, by means of which I myself can easily turn any metal into another one at will.' 'Last year', says a third, 'I made very good sapphire out of clay', and so on. They all, after this sort of open declaration, follow on with a brief but vigorous prayer. I find this performance particularly touching. The man speaks with scorn of what they call laymen's learning – that means us! – and with proud self-assurance attains, or thinks he will attain, the ultimate limits of human power, and then at this lofty point humbles himself, uttering a grateful, simple-hearted prayer to the almighty. You cannot help believing in the knowledge of such a man. Only an ignoramus can be an atheist, just as only an atheist can be an ignoramus.

We proud industrialists of the nineteenth century, we are wrong to ignore these books and not even to want to know of them. Among the various silly notions demonstrating the infancy of physics, I have found many profound thoughts. Many of these thoughts may have seemed fallacious in the eighteenth century, but now most of them are finding confirmation in the new discoveries. The same thing has happened to them as to the dragon, which thirty years ago was considered a fabulous creature and which has now actually been discovered amid the antedeluvian beasts. Tell me, must we doubt the possibility of turning lead into gold now, since we have found the means of creating water, which for so long had been considered a primary element? What chemist would refuse to undertake an experiment to break up a diamond and then restore it to its original state? And why is the idea of making gold any more ridiculous than the idea of making diamonds? In short, laugh at me as you wish, but I can only repeat that these forgotten men are worthy of our attention. If one can't believe everything they say, neither can one doubt that their works allude to a kind of knowledge that has now been lost and which it would be no bad thing to discover again. You will be convinced of this when I send you an extract from my uncle's library.

Letter IV

In my last letter I forgot to tell you the very thing which had prompted me to begin it. The thing is, my friend, that I find myself in a strange position and I am asking your advice. I have already written to you several times of Katenka, my neighbour's daughter. I finally succeeded in getting her to talk and I have discovered that, not only does she have an innate intelligence and a pure heart, but another completely unexpected quality: to wit, she is head over heels in love with me. Yesterday her father paid me a call and told me something that I had heard of only in passing when handing all my affairs over to the steward. We have an ongoing lawsuit over several thousand acres of woodland which are the main source of income for my peasants; this lawsuit has already been going on for over thirty years and if I lose it in the end my peasants will be completely ruined. You can see that this is a very important matter. My neighbour told me all about this in the greatest detail and ended by suggesting a reconciliation. And in order that this peace should be durable, he dropped a very subtle hint that he would very much like to have me as his son-in-law. This scene was pure vaudeville but it made me start thinking. Well, what about it? My youth is already past, a great man I am not to be, and I am bored with everything. Katia is a very sweet, obedient and reticent girl. By marrying her I would put an end to this stupid lawsuit and do at least one good deed in my life: I should assure the welfare of the people who are dependent on me. In short, I would really like to marry Katia, start living like a sedate landowner, hand over the running of everything to my wife, and myself keep quiet for days on end, smoking my pipe. That would be paradise, wouldn't it?...

All this preamble is just to tell you that I have decided to get married, but I haven't yet told Katia's father, and I won't tell him until I get a reply from you to the following questions: what do you think, am I fit to be a married man? Will I be saved from the spleen by a wife who, don't forget, is in the habit of not saying a word for whole days and who, consequently, has no way of annoying me? In short, should I go on waiting until I do something new, unexpected and original, or have I simply, as they say, passed my peak and have nothing left to worry about except the quantity of spermaceti that can be produced from my person? I am waiting impatiently for your reply.

Letter V

Thank you, my friend, for your decisiveness, your advice and your blessing. No sooner did I receive your letter than I galloped over to my Katia's father and made a formal proposal. If you could have seen how delighted Katia was and how she blushed! She even came out with the following words to me, in which her entire pure and innocent soul overflowed: 'I don't know', she said to me, 'whether I shall manage it, but I shall try to make you as happy as I myself will be.' These words are very simple, but if you had only heard the expression with which they were spoken! You know that there is often more feeling concealed in a single word than in a long speech. I could see a whole world of thoughts in Katia's words: they must have cost her dearly and I was able to appreciate the strength her love must have given her to overcome her maiden's timidity. The actions of someone are important in comparison with their strength and I had always thought that the overcoming of timidity was beyond Katia.... After this, as you can imagine, we embraced and kissed and the old man burst into tears. After Lent we shall hold a merry feast for our wedding. You absolutely must come and stay: drop everything, I want you to be the witness of what is called my happiness. Do come, if only out of curiosity, to have a look at the bride and groom, the like of whom you really won't have seen before: they sit opposite one another, they simply stare at one another, both keep silent and both are very content.

Letter VI

(Several weeks later)

I don't know how to begin this letter. You will think I am mad. You will laugh at me and berate me.... I don't mind. I don't mind even if you don't believe me, but I cannot doubt what I have seen and what I see every day with my own eyes. No! Not everything in my uncle's formulae is nonsense. Indeed, this is a remnant of the ancient mysteries which exist in nature to this day, and there is much that we still don't know, much that we have forgotten and much truth that we take to be ravings. This is what has happened to me: read on and be amazed! My conversations with Katia, as you may easily imagine, did not make me forget my vase of solar water. As you know, inquisitiveness – or, to put it simply, curiosity – is my basic element: it interferes in all my affairs, messes everything up and makes a mess of my life. I shall never be rid of it. There is always something luring me, something waiting in the distance: my soul will be bursting and suffering and where does it get me? But, to get back to business.... Last night I went up to the vase and noticed some sort of movement in my signet-ring. At first I thought it was an optical illusion and, to make sure, I picked the vase up. But hardly had I caused the slightest perturbation when my ring disintegrated into small blue and gold sparks that spread out through the water in thin threads and soon disappeared altogether, except that the water all turned gold, shot with blue. I replaced the vase and my ring coagulated again on the bottom. I must admit to an involuntary shudder. I called my servant and asked him whether he noticed anything in my vase; he replied that he did not. Then I realised that this strange phenomenon was visible only to me. In order not to give my servant a pretext to laugh at me, I dismissed him with a remark that the water seemed dirty to me. Remaining alone, I repeated my experiment for a long time, pondering over this strange phenomenon. I poured the water from one vase to another several times. Each time the same phenomenon recurred with a surprising exactness – and at the same time it remained inexplicable by any of the laws of physics. Can this really be the case? Had I really been fated to be the witness of this strange mystery? It seems to me so important, that I really do intend to get to the bottom of it. I have been getting down to my books as never before and, now that this experiment has taken place before my very eyes, I am getting a better and better grasp of that intercourse between man and this other inaccessible world. What is going to happen next?

Letter VII

No, my friend, you were mistaken and so was I. I am predestined to be the witness of a great mystery of nature and to make it known to people, to remind them of that wondrous force that lies within their power and which they have forgotten; to remind them that we are surrounded by other worlds hitherto unknown to them. And how simple are all the acts of nature! What simple means she employs in the production of those deeds which amaze and horrify man! Listen to me and marvel.

Yesterday, engrossed as I was in scrutinising my wondrous ring, I again noticed some sort of movement in it: I peered closer and blue waves were streaming over the water, in which irridescent opalescent rays were reflected. The turquoise had become opal, from which there rose into the water a sort of sun-like radiance. All the water was in a state of agitation. Golden jets spurted upwards and dissipated into blue sparks. There was an amalgam here of all possible colours, which now would merge in countless tints and then visibly separate. Finally the irridescent radiance disappeared and a pale greenish colour took its place. Pink threads permeated the greenish waves, intermingling with each other for some time, and then merged at the bottom of the vessel into a beautiful, magnificent rose – and then everything died down. The water turned clear and only the petals of the gorgeous bloom swayed lightly. Several days have gone by thus; every day since then I get up early, go over to my mysterious rose and expect a new miracle: but in vain. The rose is blooming peacefully and merely filling my whole room with an inexpressible fragrance. I instinctively recalled reading in one cabbalistic book that elemental spirits pass through all the realms of nature before they attain their real form. It's marvellous! Marvellous!

(A few days later)

Today I went up to my rose and noticed something new in the middle of it.... To take a proper look at it, I picked up the vase and decided again to transfer the water into another one. But hardly was the water in motion, when once again green and pink threads extended from the rose and flowed together with the water in a variegated stream and my beautiful flower appeared once more at the bottom of the vase. Everything calmed down but something had flashed across the middle of it. The leaves opened little by little and – I couldn't believe my eyes – between the orange stamens there reposed – I wonder whether you'll believe me? – there reposed an amazing, indescribable, unbelievable creature: in short, a woman, barely visible to the eye! How am I to describe to you the joy, tinged with horror, which I felt at that moment! This woman was no child. Imagine the miniature portrait of a beautiful woman in full bloom and you will get a dim notion of the miracle which lay before my eyes. She reposed casually on her soft couch and her russet brown curls, wavering from the rippling of the water, now revealed and now concealed from my eyes her immaculate charms. She appeared to be immersed in a deep sleep and I, my eyes fixed avidly on her, held my breath, so as not to disturb her sweet composure.

Oh, now I believe the cabbalists. I am surprised even that I should have looked upon them before with derision and mistrust. No, if any truth does exist in this world, then it exists only in their lucubrations! Only now have I grasped that they are not like our usual run of scientists. They do not argue among themselves, do not contradict one another; they all talk about one and the same mystery. Only their expressions differ, but they are quite intelligible to someone who has divined their arcane purport.... Farewell! Having really resolved to get to the bottom of all of nature's mysteries, I am breaking off my relations with people. A different, new and mysterious world is opening for me. Only for posterity do I preserve a record of my discoveries. So, my friend, I am destined for great things in this life!...

Gavril Sofronovich Rezhensky's Letter to the Publisher

My dear Sir,

Forgive me that, although I do not have the honour of being personally acquainted with you, but in accordance with information concerning your close friendship with Mikhail Platonovich, I venture to trouble you with my letter. You are, of course, not unaware that I was engaged in a lawsuit over a considerable quantity of lumber and kindling forest with his late uncle, to whom he now finds himself the legal heir. Having felt an attraction towards my elder daughter Katerina Gavrilovna, your friend proposed himself as my son-in-law, to which proposal I, as you are aware, gave my consent. Consequent upon this, in expectation of mutual advantage, I stopped the case in its tracks. But now I find myself in a state of extreme perplexity. Shortly after the betrothal, when the announcement had been sent out to all our aquaintances and my daughter's dowry had been got together at last, and all the necessary papers had been cleared, Mikhail Platonovich suddenly ceased his visitations to me. Ascribing this to reasons of ill health, I sent a servant over to him and, eventually, despite my own infirmity, went to see him myself. It seemed to me improper and even offensive to remind him that he had forgotten his fiancée; and if he had at least apologised! All he did was to tell me about some important business he had undertaken, which he had to complete before the wedding and which for some considerable duration would demand his unremitting attention and supervision. I supposed that he wanted to set up a potash factory, of which he had previously spoken; I thought that he wanted to surprise me by providing a wedding gift, showing that, if put to the test, he could manage something practical, on account of my having often reproved him for his empty lifestyle. However, I noticed no preparations for such a factory and still see none. I proposed waiting to see what would happen, when yesterday, to my great surprise, I learned that he has locked himself in and admits no one: even his food is served to him through the casement. At this point, my dear sir, the strangest thought came into my head. His late uncle lived in that same house and had a name in the district for dabbling in the black books. I myself, sir, once studied at the university; a bit behind the times I may be, but I don't believe in black magic. However, man is all too easily impaired, especially such a philosopher as your friend! What most of all convinces me that something unfortunate has befallen Mikhail Platonovich is the rumour which has reached me indirectly, that he sits for days on end looking at a carafe of water. In these circumstances, my dear sir, I address the most humble request to you: immediately hasten your arrival here to bring Mikhail Platonovich to his senses, out of concern for him and so as I may know how to proceed – whether to recommence the lawsuit or to stick to our settlement. As for me, after the insult inflicted by your friend, I shall not darken his doors, although Katia implores me with bitter tears so to do.

In expectation of our imminent meeting, I have the honour, etc. etc.

My Account

On receipt of this letter, I considered it my duty first of all to approach a doctor I know, a very experienced and learned man. I showed him my friend's letters, told him all about his situation and asked him whether he could make any sense of any of this. 'It is all quite clear', the doctor told me, 'and nothing new to a medical man.... Your friend has simply gone out of his mind...'.

'But read his letters again', I protested, 'is there in them even the least sign of madness? Leave aside their strange subject-matter, and they seem a cool and collected description of a physical phenomenon...'.

'That is all quite clear', repeated the doctor. 'You know that we can distinguish various kinds of madness – *vesaniae*. The first kind covers all forms of frenzy and this does not pertain to your friend. The second kind consists of: firstly, a disposition towards apparitions – *hallucinationes*; secondly, a certainty of communication with spirits – *demonomania*. It is perfectly clear that your friend, a born hypochondriac, in the country and alone, without any amusements, engrossed himself in reading all kinds of rubbish. This reading has affected his cerebral nerves; the nerves...'.

For a long time yet the doctor carried on explaining to me in what way a person can be in complete possession of his faculties and yet be a madman, seeing what he does not see and hearing what he does not hear. To my profound regret, I cannot report these explanations to the reader, because I understood nothing of them; but, convinced by the doctor's arguments, I decided to invite him to travel with me to my friend's village.

Mikhail Platonovich lay in bed, pale and wan. For a period of several days he had taken no food. As we approached, he did not recognise us, although his eyes were open: some sort of a wild light was blazing in them. To all our questions he replied not a word.... On the table lay sheets of paper covered with writing. I was able to make out only a few lines of it. Here they are:

Fragments

(From the journal of Mikhail Platonovich)

'Who are you?'

'I do not have a name. I have no need of one...'.

'Where are you from?'

'I am yours – that's all I know. I belong to you and to no one else... but why are you here? Here it's stuffy and cold! Where we live the sun shimmers, the flowers emit sound, the sounds perfume.... Follow me...follow me! How heavy your clothing is – throw it off, throw it off...and still it's a long way, a long way to our world...but I shall not leave you! How dead everything is in your dwelling place...all that's alive is covered by a cold membrane: tear it, tear through it!'

...So your knowledge is here?... Your art is here?... You split time from time and space from space, desire from hope, thought from its fulfilment, and you do not die of boredom? Follow me, follow me! Quickly, quickly....

...Is this you, proud Rome, capital of centuries and of nations? How the

53

convolvulus has distended over your ruins.... But the ruins are stirring, bare columns rise from the green sward and stand erect in orderly formation, an arch has bowed valiantly across them, shaking off its eternal dust, the rostrum drifts in like a frivolous mosaic; on the rostrum throng living people, the potent sounds of an ancient tongue mingle with the murmur of the waves – an orator in a white robe and laurel wreath is raising his hands.... And it has all vanished: the splendid buildings bend to the ground; pillars stoop low, arches plunge into the earth – the convolvulus again weaves over the ruins, and all is silent. A bell calls to prayer, the basilica is opened, audible are the sounds of a mellisonant instrument – thousands of harmonious modulations vibrate beneath my fingers, thought strives after thought, flying away the one after another like dreams...if one could have seized and stopped them? And the submissive instrument again repeats, like a faithful echo, all the transient and irrevocable movements of the soul.... The basilica has emptied, the lunar brightness falls on statues without number; they step down from their places and walk past me, full of life. Their speech is ancient and new, their smiles are portentous and their glances grand. But once more their pedestals support them and once more the lunar brightness falls on statues.... But it is late...a happy, quiet refuge awaits us. The Tiber shimmers in the windows. Beyond it the Capitol of the eternal city.... An enchanting picture! It has fused into the tight frame of our fireplace...yes! There we have another Rome, another Tiber, another Capitol. How merrily the fire is crackling.... Embrace me, charming maid.... A sparkling beverage foams in a pearl goblet...drink...drink it.... Out there snowflakes are falling and blocking the road – here your embraces are warming me....

Speed on, speed on, my swift steeds, over the brittle snow, raise the icy dust by the column. The sun is shining in every speck: roses have burst forth on her charming face, she clings to me with fragrant lips.... Where did you learn the art of kissing? Everything in you is burning and the seething liquid courses through every nerve in my body.... Speed on, speed on, my swift steeds, over the brittle snow. What? is that not the cry of battle? Some new enmity between heaven and earth?... No, either brother has betrayed brother or an innocent damsel is in the clutches of crime.... Yet the sun is shining and the air is cool? No, the earth has shaken, the sun has dimmed, a storm has precipitated from the heavens, saving the victim and flushing away the felon, and again the sun is shining and the air is quiet and cool, brother is kissing brother and strength bows before innocence.... Follow me, follow me.... There is another world, a new world.... Look, the crystal has opened up, there is a new sun inside it.... The great mystery of the crystals is being enacted there: let us lift the curtain...crowds of inhabitants of the transparent world are celebrating their life with all the flowers of the rainbow. Here the air, the sun and life are eternal light: they scoop up the fragrant resins from the plant world, perfect them into brilliant rainbows and seal them with the fiery element.... Follow me, follow me! We are still on the first step.... Streams flow over vaults without number: they spurt swiftly upwards and swiftly cascade to the ground. Above them a vigorous prism refracts the sun's rays. The sun's rays meander through veins and the fountain transmits into the air their irridescent sparks. These now rain down on floral petals, now meander in a long ribbon through a patterned mesh. Vital spirits, chained to eternally seething stills, transform the living liquid into an aromatic vapour which drifts over the vaults and falls as heavy rain into the mysterious vessel of botanic life.... Here, in the inner sanctum, the embryo of life struggles with the embryo of death, living juices petrify, congealing in metallic veins, while dead elements are transformed by the spiritual essence.... Follow me, follow me!... On an elevated throne human thought is seated, linked to the whole world by golden chains. Spirits of nature prostrate themselves in the dust before it. The light of life rises in the east; in the west, dreams swarm in the rays of sunset and, at the mercy of thought's whim, now merge into a single harmonious form, now dissipate in volatile clouds.... At the foot of this altar she gripped me in her embrace...we had left the earth behind!

Look, there in the boundless deep floats your speck of dust: there are the curses of man, there the mother's sobs, there the murmur of worldly need, there the mockery of the evil-doers, there the sufferings of the poet. Here everything merges into delightful harmony; here your speck of dust is no suffering world, but a mellifluous instrument, whose harmonious sounds gently pulsate the etherial waves.

Bid farewell to the poetic *earthly* world! Yes, you do have poetry on Earth too! Ah, the tattered laurels of your bliss! Poor folk! Strange people! In your rancid depths you have found that even suffering is happiness! You give suffering a poetic sheen! You are proud of your suffering: you want the denizens of the other world to envy your life! In our world there is no suffering: that is the lot only of the imperfect world – the creation of an imperfect being! Humanity is free either to prostrate itself before it, or to throw it off, like the threadbare clothing from a traveller's back as he catches sight of his native land....

Do you really think that I did not know you? From my very infancy I have accompanied you in the puffing of the breeze, in the rays of the spring sun, in the drops of fragrant dew, in the unearthly dreamings of the poet! When man's pride in his strength is reborn, when deep scorn descends from his eyes upon the impoverished images of the sublunar world, when his soul, shaking off the dust of mortal torments, mockingly defiles nature as it quivers before him – then we hover above you, then we await the moment to deliver you from the gross bonds of matter: it is then that you are worthy of our image!... See whether there is suffering in my kiss: there is no time in it, it will last into eternity, and every moment for us is a new ecstasy!... Oh, do not betray me! Do not betray yourself! Beware the temptations of your crude and contemned nature!

Look, there in the distance, on your Earth the poet prostrates himself before a heap of stones, overgrown with the insensitive organism of botanic strength. 'Nature!', he cries in rapture, 'sublime nature, what is higher than you in this world? What is human thought before you?' And blind, inanimate nature laughs at him and at the moment of the supreme rejoicing of human thought dispatches an icy avalanche, thus destroying both human being and human thought! Only in the soul of the soul are the summits high! Only in the soul of the soul are the chasms deep! Dead nature dares not venture into their depths; an independent and strong human world is in their depths. Look, *here* the poet's life is sacred! *Here* poetry is truth! Here everything left unsaid by the poet is said; here his earthly sufferings are transformed into an immeasurable series of ecstasies....

Oh, love me! I shall never fade: eternally fair, my virginal breast will throb against your breast! Eternal ecstasy will be new and complete for you – and in my embraces, an impossible desire will become an eternally possible realisation!...

This infant – this is our child! He does not expect a father's care, he does not arouse false doubts, he has fulfilled your hopes in advance; he is youthful, yet grown up: he smiles and does not sob – for him no sufferings are possible, if only you do not recall your crude, contemned vale.... No, you will not kill us with a single desire!

But come on, come on – there is yet another, a higher world: there thought itself merges with desire. Follow me, follow me!...

From this point it was almost impossible to make anything out; there were only disconnected, mixed-up words: 'love...plant...electricity...human being...spirit...'. Finally, the last lines were written in some strange kind of letters that were unknown to me and broke off on every page....

Having cleared all these ravings out of the way, we got down to business and started off by putting our dreamer into a bouillon bath. Our patient began to shake all over: 'a good sign!', exclaimed the doctor. There was a highly strange expression in the patient's eyes – something of repentance, of entreaty and of the anguish of parting: he gave way to profuse tears... I drew the doctor's attention to this facial expression...the doctor replied: *'facies hippocratica!'*

An hour later – another bouillon bath and a spoonful of medicine. We had trouble enough in accomplishing this: the patient suffered torments and held out, but finally swallowed it. 'We've won!', cried the doctor.

The doctor insisted that we should do all we could to try and pull our patient out of his torpor and activate his sensuousness. And so we did: first a bath, then a spoonful of tasty medicine, then a spoonful of bouillon and, thanks to our reasonable attentions, the patient began visibly to recover. Eventually his appetite returned and he even began to eat without our ministrations....

I endeavoured not to remind my friend about anything that had happened and to direct his attention to more basic and useful matters: to wit, the circumstances of his estate, the advantages of establishing thereupon a potash factory, and of switching his peasants from the quitrent to the corvée system.... But my friend listened to me as though in a dream, contradicted nothing I said, obeyed me implicitly and drank and ate whatever was served to him, while at the same time taking no active interest in anything.

What could not be accomplished by all the doctor's medicines was achieved by my chats about our rakish youth and, in particular, a few excellent bottles of Lafitte, which I had had the forsight to bring with me. This remedy, together with servings of marvellous rare roast beef, put my friend completely back on his feet, so much so that I even ventured to broach the subject of his fiancée. He heard me out attentively and agreed with me in everything. Being a thorough sort of chap, I lost no time in taking advantage of his favourable disposition, galloped off to his future father-in-law, sorted everything out, settled the dispute between them, drew up the dowry, dressed my crackpot in his old uniform, got him to the church and, having wished him every happiness, set off on my journey home, where a case was awaiting me in the Civic Chambers, and, I must confess, I hit the road feeling exceedingly pleased with myself and with my success. In Moscow all his relatives, needless to say, showered me with favours and gratitude.

Having set my affairs in order, a few months later I deemed it proper, however, to pay a visit to the young couple, the more so as I had received no news from the young blade.

It was morning when I caught him in. He was sitting in his dressing gown with a pipe clenched in his teeth. His wife was pouring tea. The sun was shining through the window and a huge tree laden with ripe pears peeped in. He seemed pleased enough to see me, but remained generally uncommunicative....

I chose a moment when his wife was out of the room and said, with a shake of the head:
– Well, then, aren't you happy?
Well, what do you think? He started talking? What didn't he say!
– Happy! – he repeated with an ironic smile, – do you know what you meant to say with that word? You inwardly congratulated yourself and thought: 'What a reasonable fellow I am! I cured this madman, married him off and now, thanks to me, he is happy…happy!' You call to mind all the praise of my aunts and uncles, of all those so-called reasonable people, and your self-esteem perks up and rockets…isn't that it?
– If that were the case… – I said.
– Then be satisfied with their praise and gratitude, but don't expect mine. No! Katia loves me, our estate is settled, the revenues are collected on time – in a word, you gave me a happiness, but not mine: you got the wrong size. You, such reasonable gentlefolk, are like the carpenter who was ordered to make a case for some expensive physics instruments: he didn't measure it properly and the instruments wouldn't go in – so what did he do? The case was ready and beautifully polished. The tradesman re-ground the instruments – a curve more here, a curve less there, and they went into the box and fitted nicely. They were a pleasure to look at, but there was one problem: the instruments were wrecked. Gentlemen! instruments are not for cases, but cases are for instruments! Make the box according to the instruments and not the instruments according to the box.
– What do you mean by that?
– You are very pleased that you have, what you call, cured me: that is to say, blunted my perceptions, covered them with some impenetrable shell, made them dead to any world except your box…. Wonderful! The instrument fits, but it is wrecked: it had been made for a different purpose…. Now, when in the midst of the daily round I can feel my abdominal cavity expanding by the hour and my head subsiding into animalistic sleep, I recall with despair that time when, in your opinion, I was in a state of madness, when a charming creature flew down to me from the invisible world, when it opened to me sacraments which now I cannot even express, but which were comprehensible to me… where is that happiness? Give it back to me!
– You, my friend, are a poet and that's all there is to it, – I said with annoyance, – write poetry….
– Write poetry! – objected the patient, – write poetry! Your poetry is also a box. You have merely pigeon-holed poetry: this is your prose, this is your poetry, this is your music, this your painting, and this your what have you. But perhaps I am the practitioner of a kind of art that does not yet

exist, which is neither poetry, nor music, nor painting – an art which I would have had to discover and which, perhaps, will now die for a hundred millenia: find it for me! Perhaps it will console me for the loss of my former world!

He bowed his head, his eyes took on a strange expression and he said to himself: 'It's gone – it won't come back – she has died - she couldn't bear it – perish! perish!' – and so on and so forth.

However, this was his last attack. Thereafter, to my knowledge, my friend became a thoroughly respectable man: he took up hunting, started a potash factory, introduced crop rotation, won several lawsuits over land in masterly fashion (he goes in for the open field system). His health is robust: he has acquired rosy cheeks and a very respectable paunch. (N.B. He takes bouillon baths to this day – they really help him a lot.) There is only one thing: they say that he hits the bottle a bit with his cronies – and sometimes even without his cronies. They also say that no chambermaid can get past him with impunity – but who doesn't have some vices in this world? At least, he is now a man, like the others.

Such was the story related to me by one of my acquaintances – a highly reasonable man – who favoured me with Platon Mikhailovich's letters. I must confess that I have understood nothing in this narrative: will its readers be a little luckier?

1837

LETTER IV
[TO COUNTESS YE.P. ROSTOPCHINA]

I should now like to give you an account, Countess, of those optical illusions known under the name of *hallucinations*: those which have given most occasion to stories about ghosts. But perhaps you will ask me: by what means can I persuade you that a ghost is really only an optical illusion?... A rather difficult question. Often, a person subject to hallucination tells of his vision so vividly, so plausibly; sometimes a clear-cut illusion can be established, for example, in the case of Pascal, who continually thought that he had an abyss beside him; but there are cases where verification with our own eyes cannot take place, for example, when the occurrence being related, and affirmed by large numbers of witnesses, happened at a time or place distant from us; sometimes, alas, we must remain mute simply from our lack of information. Of course, much which now seems to us marvellous, incomprehensible, susceptible to doubt or to complete rejection, will be a comprehensible and quite usual thing for our descendants, just as what was miraculous and improbable for the ancients now belongs for us among the most usual of things. One of the remarkable people of our time,* defending his poetic theory of industry, which exceeded the bounds of the possible, and which has now joined the treasures of history, said:

> Suppose that in the age of Augustus someone had invented gunpowder and the compass and, having concealed his invention, had worked on its refinement for a period of twenty years and finally had got as far as what we now call artillery and mines: imagine that the inventor had then appeared before the famous people of the age of Augustus, holding in one hand a powder cartridge and in the other a compass, and made the following speech: 'Gentlemen! With this,

* Fourier (*Author's note*)

black powder it is possible to change the entire military strategy of Alexander the Great and Julius Caesar; with this black powder I can blow the Capitol into the air (by means of a mine), demolish the city walls a mile away (with bombs and such things), in a single minute turn all of Rome to ruins (by the explosion of a large quantity of powder), at a distance of 500 paces annihilate all the Roman legions (artillery), bring the strength of the weakest warrior up to that of the strongest (with a gun), and finally, with the help of this black powder I can carry thunder and lightning in my pocket (a pocket pistol). With the help of this other instrument (the compass), I can direct the motion of a ship, by night as well as by day, in a storm as well as in calm; I can lose sight of the shore without navigating by the stars.

There is no doubt that the brilliant Maecenas and Agrippa, hearing such a speech, would have considered the orator a madman but, incidentally, there is not a single word in that speech which does not relate to what are now the most simple and common objects. And we are in the same position in relation to our descendants. How many such phenomena are there, which now appear incredible to us, but which have perhaps really happened, but are repudiated by our proud ignorance alone! Probably, before the discovery of electricity, reasonable people considered it nonsense: tales of a flame appearing sometimes at the top of a mast, which the ancients called Castor and Pollux; tales of sparks appearing on an iron spire on I don't remember which mountain and serving the surrounding inhabitants as portents of a storm; before the invention of the thermometer and hydrometer, how many times had perhaps a country landowner's wife, who would be concerned about her yarning, cursed her spinners for the yarn sometimes being smooth and another time rough, and added (probably to this day she is still adding) to the fairy tales of assurance given to her servant girl that, in dry weather, yarn goes rough. All this is now understood and should not arouse any surprise.

There is no doubt that many such phenomena, which we now ascribe to superstition and prejudice, will some day enter the ranks of the perfectly common. You have probably heard of the famous Count Saint-Germain; there is a lot of idle chatter about him, but there is no doubt that this famous charlatan possessed great knowledge for his day; if we consider ninety-nine per cent of everything told about him to be false, there would still remain that one per cent which could have happened and which, for that matter, has not been explained. Remember that Robertson, whose phantasmagoria and galvanic experiments are now so well known, was seriously considered a sorcerer for thirty years, despite the fact that he usually began his presentations with the announcement that he was not a sorcerer, but merely a natural scientist. Supposing he had posed as a sorcerer? Count Saint-Germain, by contrast, liked to surround himself with mystery, but there is scarcely any doubt at all that he knew much that we don't know now. Phenomena of so-called animal magnetism are to us these days, if not clear, then manifest. Altogether, this man's life deserves far more attention than is usually supposed. Here is one of the little known anecdotes about him which is of almost historical authenticity:

At the beginning of the eighteenth century, there lived in Paris a very rich man by the name of Dumas; in the source from which I gleaned this information, his rank, the street and the house in which he lived are signified in detail; I consider it unnecessary to go into these details here. Dumas' family comprised a son and a daughter; beyond that, there was a maid in residence, who was in charge of the running of the house.

Because of his wealth, Dumas was accused, as was usual in those days, of magic and of having dealings with spirits; this rumour was particularly strengthened by the fact that, on the top floor of his house, Dumas had a room; from this room the master of the house used to observe the stars and calculate, according to astrological rules, the influence of the stars on the fate of those born under this or that constellation. Many people used to come to him for information of this type.

Every Friday after dinner, at exactly three o'clock, Dumas would go off to the mysterious room and lock himself in; after that, there would be heard, every Friday, the heavy hoofbeats on the street of a huge mule, which would stop at the gates of the bewitched house. This mule might have been considered the finest animal in the world – if it hadn't had on its left side a gaping bloody wound of revolting appearance. On this mule sat a man, its equal in height and burliness, proud and important in appearance – but on his forehead were three open weals, so red that they could be taken for burning coals; at least, this is what everyone thought, for, at the sight of this terrible rider, passers-by would turn round and close their eyes.

For a thirty-year period (Dumas was ninety years old) both the mounted man and his mule appeared constantly on a Friday, and no one knew where they came from, nor where they went; this was because, if anyone followed them, which happened fairly often, they always lost sight of them in the vicinity of the Cimetière des Innocents. The mounted man, arriving at Dumas' house, would leave the mule untethered in the yard; he himself, without being announced, would go up to the top room; without knocking, he would unlock the door, which was bound inside and out with iron, and lock himself in with his host for an hour; then he would descend alone, get on his mule, and ride away at full speed. It would be much later, already evening, by the time Dumas emerged.

Such conduct gave rise to various rumours in the neighbourhood. Dumas' son was no longer young, being about fifty years old. Every year it was intended that he should get married, but nevertheless he still remained a bachelor, just as his sister stayed spinster, and she was already forty-five and, according to local gossip, a great hypocrite, spiteful and a reveller in scandal.

Dumas himself enjoyed extraordinarily good health. Neither feebleness nor wrinkles bore witness to his age; he was seasoned and strong. It was even said that he constantly enjoyed the favours of the fair sex and a multitude of anecdotes about him circulated in the precinct on this score; even in this respect, he was considered a very dangerous man.

One morning, the thirty-first of December 1700, on a Wednesday (note, not a Friday!), at about ten o'clock, the hurried pounding of the great mule was heard. Dumas happened to be in his room. The unknown figure dismounted from his mule and as usual, without being announced, appeared in front of Dumas, who probably was not expecting him at all, since, upon seeing the figure, the old man cried out in horror. An argument broke out between them; both spoke heatedly; the argument lasted for some time. Finally, the mysterious rider came out of the room and the mule tore off with him at such a speed that neighbours claimed not to have been able to follow them, even with their eyes.

When, in his turn, old man Dumas descended, his children could hardly recognise him. He was no longer the previous hale and hearty old man: death was stamped on his pale, cold face, now furrowed with wrinkles; his eyes had faded terribly. He declared to his son and daughter that he would not dine with them and soon indicated a wish to return to his secret room; he could no longer climb up there on his own, and his son and daughter had to take him by the arm and drag him up the stairs which, as it seemed, he would not be able to descend unaided. They told him this and he instructed them to come for him at four o'clock. The son, on Dumas' instructions, locked the door from the outside and took the key with him.

What happened in that room is not known. At four o'clock some petitioner turned up in the son's room, saying he had business with his father; the son asked him to help bring the old man down. They opened the door and went in – and the room was empty: Dumas had vanished.

All searching was in vain. They called architects, stone-masons, joiners, carpenters, stove-setters; they examined and ransacked the corners and the walls of the little room, but found no trace of a secret exit, and the most active inquiries of the police could uncover nothing concerning this unusual abduction.

Then suspicion fell on the Dumas children. They dispensed large sums to prove their innocence, and first one and then the other died, without having received any information on the death of their father. From that day on, the rider, who over a period of thirty years had visited the old man each week, appeared no more; gradually the whole business was forgotten. However, the recollection of it was not entirely effaced and this is what happened fifty years later:

Marshal Villeroi, who was highly inclined to superstition, frequently regaled his royal pupil Louis XV with all sorts of tales about spirits and ghosts. A child's first impressions are never effaced. When he became king, Louis XV still listened eagerly to such stories and was not averse even to dealings with the spirit world.

Among the horrific stories which had most appealed to the king in his young days, the story of the disappearance of Dumas had made the biggest impression on him. He liked recounting this occurrence and observing what affect it produced on his listeners. Once the king related it in the presence of the Count Saint-Germain. The Count volunteered to ascertain the outcome of the story of Dumas and to explain the details which remained unknown. The Marquise de Pompadour, who heard this conversation, joined the Count in his suggestion and begged the king to allow him to get to the bottom of the mysterious event. The remaining parties to the conversation supported her, and the Count was duly detailed to go through with his suggestion.

'Now, Your Majesty,' he said, bowing: 'I ask for just ten minutes'. Then, with great composure, he began to draw lines and to write down various algebraic and astrological symbols, which he then painstakingly scrutinized; less than ten minutes had passed before he again turned to the king:

'Your Majesty!' he said: 'the experts and the workmen who sought to trace Dumas were either bought off by persons who wanted to cover the business up, or they knew their trade very badly. This was the situation, in a corner of the room beside the entrance: one panel there was movable and covered a staircase which goes around all the rooms; at the bottom of the staircase there is a sort of cellar; this is where Dumas went, having taken a beverage which restored his strength; but here, after drinking a strong dose of opiate, he fell asleep and didn't wake again.'

– And so it was the evil spirit who visited him? – asked the king. 'Your Majesty,' replied the Count: 'I cannot lift the final veil covering this secret without risking, should things go contrary, the greatest dangers.'

The king was silent and did not question the Count further; but Madame de Pompadour, who was more inquisitive, informed the Chief-of-Police of the Count's discoveries, asking him to institute fresh inquiries immediately at the place in question. The Chief-of-Police carried out her wish; this much is clear from the dossier found in the police archives. They found the movable panel, the staircase, the underground room and, therein, amid a great number of astrological and chemical instruments, the corpse of Dumas, still covered by his clothing. He lay on the ground; beside him were found pieces from a broken agate vessel and a crystal phial; on one of the pieces, the merest trace of opium still remained.

Rumours spread through France that the dénouement of this story had been invented by the Marquise de Pompadour and the Chief-of-Police, for the amusement of the king. This supposition is even stranger than the original occurrence; such a complicated dénouement would entail so many physical difficulties that the hoax could easily have been revealed, a rumour could have reached the king and such deception would not have redounded to the benefit either of the police chief, or the Marquise herself. However, were the supposition to be true, the whereabouts of old man Dumas would still remain a total mystery. You may believe or not believe this story, Countess, but either way you must admit that this occurrence would make an excellent subject for a tale of terror.

1839

THE LIVE CORPSE

Dedicated to Countess Ye.P. Rostopchina

'Tell me, if you'd be so kind, how would you translate into Russian the word *solidarnost'* (solidaritas)?

'That's easy – *collective guarantee*,' replied the walking dictionary.

'Near, but not quite! I wanted to give expression (in letters) to that psychological law by which not one word pronounced by a man, not one action, is forgotten, is lost in the world, but without fail produces some kind of action; so that responsibility is connected with each word, with each apparently insignificant action, with each impulse of a man's soul.'

'About that it would be necessary to write a whole book.'

From a novel lost in the Lethe.

What's this? – it seems I've died?...really! That's got it off my chest, anyhow...what can I say? Like a bad joke.... My legs and hands are cold, it's getting me in the throat, choking me, a cracking in my head, my heart's stopping, as if body and soul are splitting up.... So? It seems that's it, then? It's strange, very strange – the soul's splitting from the body! Where is my soul, anyway?... Where's my body? Here! Where are my arms, then, and legs?... Good gracious me! Here it is, lying on the bed as if nothing had happened...only the mouth's a bit twisted. Confound it! That's me lying there – no, it's not me! – No! It really is me; just like looking in the mirror; I am something entirely different: I – look, arms, legs, head – they're all there, here there's nothing, absolutely nothing, yet I can still hear and see.... Here's my bedroom; the sun's shining in the window; here's my table; my watch is on the table, it says half past nine; my niece has fainted, my sons are in tears – everything's as it should be; that's enough,

66

now...what are you crying for? What? They can't hear! I can't even hear my own voice, yet I seem to be speaking very distinctly. Let's try a bit louder – nothing! Just as if a light breeze were blowing – it's uncanny, it really is uncanny! I must be dreaming, mustn't I? I remember: yesterday I was perfectly hale and hearty and played whist, and had a bit of luck, too; I can see where I put the money – and I ate a good supper, and chatted with my cronies about this and that, and read for a bit at bedtime, and fell fast asleep – when, suddenly for no reason, I feel a pain, a pain.... I want to cry out – I can't; I want to move – I can't.... Then I don't remember a thing – until I suddenly woke up...how can I say woke up? I mean I found myself here...where's here? Words can't describe it! It must be a dream. Don't you believe me? Wait a minute, I'll conduct an experiment: I'll pinch my finger – but I haven't got a finger, I really haven't.... Wait a minute, what can we think of next? Let's have a look in the mirror – the mirror never lies; here's my mirror – oh, confound it! I'm not there, either, but I can see everything else in it: the whole room, the children, the bed, lying on the bed, there's... who? Me? – nothing's happened! I'm in front of the mirror – yet I'm not there in the mirror.... It can't be, it's uncanny! I should send for our great philosophers and scholars: come on then, gentlemen, explain this one: I'm here, and yet I'm not here; I'm alive, and yet not alive; I'm moving, and yet not moving.... What's that? The clock's striking: one, two, three...ten; oh well, it's time to go to the office – I've got something interesting to do there. I've got to put one over on that no-good Perepalkin, who's always telling tales about me.... 'Hey! Filka! I want to get dressed!..'. Who, me? How can I get dressed? It's impossible! There used to be a time when I had nothing to put on, and now it's even worse – there's nothing to put anything on.... Still, it wouldn't be a bad idea to look in at the office...but how do I get there? I can't order a carriage; there's nothing for it but to go on foot, although it's unbecoming. It should be easy enough for me to move from one place to another...let's have a try; since the doors are open.... Here's my study, the drawing room, the hall; here I am on the street... how easy it is; I don't hear the ground under me, I just float along – as fast as I like, and as quiet.... Yes, really, it's not bad – I don't even have to take steps.... Ah, here are some people I know! 'Good day, your honour! Your honour is nice and early today?'... He's gone past and didn't take the slightest notice.... Here's another one: 'Good day, Ivan Petrovich!' Not a dickie-bird out of him, either – that's strange! My goodness! – here's a carriage coming at full pelt! Slow down a bit, slow down! You're going to flatten me with that shaft – are you blind or something!... I'm done for! The carriage galloped right through me, and I don't seem to have felt a thing – cleaved in two and it's as though nothing happened, it's just uncanny. Still, though, if that's what's happened then, really, it can't be too bad a state to be in: it's nice and easy, with no worries; no need to shave or wash or wear a stitch, I can go where I like – as free as a bird; I can go all over the country without a travel warrant, with no dangers threatening – what happened just now? A carriage ran through me and it didn't matter a damn! So that's death, then, so that's what it's like.... And reward, punishment? Though it's true to say, I wasn't really expecting any reward – I've done nothing to deserve any; and there's nothing really to punish me for, either; there were a few little sins...who doesn't have any? I can truthfully say: I never did any good, nor any evil, without due cause to anyone – really...you know: I'm just a straightforward man. Now, naturally, when you are expecting trouble, then from time to time you might, as you might say, trip your neighbour and send him flying...well, what else can you do? If a man comes after you with a knife, are you really going to offer him your neck? I lived sensibly enough, I grew up on copper coins, and then inherited the silver, and left my children a pretty penny; I didn't even send them to any institution, so as to watch more closely over their moral development, but I educated them myself and taught them the most important thing – *how to live in society*, and if they follow my lessons, then they'll go far. To tell the truth, I hardly ever, so to speak, troubled my conscience – naturally, sometimes, according to circumstances, I stretched it a bit.... Yes! Of course, I did stretch it a bit – but only when it was all right to stretch it...who is an enemy to himself? However, leaving all that aside: esteemed by everyone, respected by everyone, I came from nothing, got on in the world and did it all myself.... I wish to God that everyone would conduct their affairs in this way.... Ah, here's the office! Let's see what's going on here. There's the watchman dozing as always – you can't do anything with him. 'Sidorenko! Sidorenko!' – he doesn't hear, and the doors are shut.... How can I stand here? You could wait for an age in this hall – it would be all the same if it were something important.... Ah! Here's someone coming...my clerk – now, the door's ajar.... 'Bless my soul! I say, excuse me! You've slammed it', – but no, I've gone through the wood.... So, that's not so bad then, is it?... How come I didn't think of that before? So, it seems, for me there are no doors and no locks; does that mean there are no secrets from me either? Well, then, that's really not bad at all – that could be highly convenient in the right circumstances.... Ah, the lazy devils! Instead of attending to their business, there they are, some of them on the table, some of them on the window-seat, lounging about, idly chatting. They might have stood up, the louts, they might have bowed: have to instill a bit of order.... Ah! Here's the chief clerk; we'll soon see, he'll put the wind up them a bit....

Chief Clerk: Gentlemen! Could we not return to our desks? We can chatter just as well sitting at our papers; isn't it just as good? There, is that any hindrance? It stands to reason – why not chat there? I remember how we used to, back in the old days, we used to play cards in the office, with due caution of course, and all right it was too, really! We used to have small tables then: we'd lay our papers out, and out with the cards for Boston; if the boss came – cards away under the papers; the boss comes in and everything's just as it should be; but what about you lot, nowadays? Lounging about on the tables, on the window seats; if Vasilii Kuzmich comes in, how can you suddenly jump to it? Running about, disorder – you won't half catch it, especially now, when he's expecting a decoration – you know how angry he gets at times like that....

One of the Clerks: It's a bit early for Vasilii Kuzmich. He was playing cards 'til three o'clock last night.

(They all know, damn them!...)

Second: That's not true – he was at Karolina Karlovna's....

(They know about that, too, the villains!...)

Third: Not at all – he was at Natalia Kazimirovna's....

(And that, too...who would have thought it?...)

Fourth: Has he really got two affairs going at the same time? An old man like him?...

Third: Old man? You see if he doesn't outlive us all! Eating, drinking, he doesn't give a damn! Well might he play the stuffshirt...he outdoes us all....

Pah! What good for nothings! I didn't know you before.... And I don't want to hear any more.... Mischief-makers, chatterboxes!... Just you wait!... I've forgotten my state again; I can't stop them!... How infuriating: I'd like to get them dismissed from the service.... What can I do here? Oh, the devil take them!... They have to amuse themselves with something. I know, I'll go and see what the prince has to say when he hears of my decease, how sorry he'll be.... Let's get a move on. There's Kirila Petrovich on his own in the waiting room, and in tears – probably about me: exactly, one friend on his own is never unfaithful! A good thing you didn't know about one little matter.... I dropped a little word about you which will harrow you for life – well, there was nothing else for it: why were you appointed to the very position that I wanted?... Who is an enemy to himself? But apart from that, I always helped you in everything, and well might you weep for me. Ah! The doors to the prince are opening.... Let's go in....

Kirila Petrovich: I have come to bring Your Excellency unexpected and sorrowful news: Vasilii Kuzmich has departed this life....

Prince: What's that you're saying? Why, only yesterday....

Kirila Petrovich: Early today he had a stroke; they sent for me at eight o'clock – he was even then barely breathing; all medical assistance...at nine o'clock he gave his soul up to God.... It's a great loss, Your Excellency.

Prince: Yes, I must admit, such people are scarce; the man was truly esteemed.

Kirila Petrovich: A diligent official....

Prince: A veracious man.

Kirila Petrovich: A straightforward, upright soul! Whatever he said, you could take as Gospel....

Prince: And just fancy! As if by design, only today a statement came about him....

Kirila Petrovich (*crying*): Ah, the poor man! And he was so waiting for it....

Prince: What can we do! Obviously, he was fated to die without promotion.... What a pity!...

Kirila Petrovich (*breaking down*): Yes! Indeed, nothing's any good to him now....

Vasilii Kuzmich: How do you mean, no good?... If you please, Your Excellency! Why this insult? Oh yes! I forgot...now not even a promotion is any good.... Ah, it's painful! Obviously, now, I really have died.... But why should I have, though? What call had I to die! I hadn't sent in my resignation; as if promotion grew on trees.... Who would have been any the worse for that? Even for a dead man it's nice to.... Ah, I never guessed that would happen! I should have allowed for it.... It's infuriating, sickening....

Kirila Petrovich: Yes, now nothing's any good to him! But he has left a family...if Your Excellency....

Prince: Of course! Most willingly. Draw me up a memorandum.... But, I must just say to you, your sincere concern for Vasilii Kuzmich does you great credit.

Kirila Petrovich: How could I feel otherwise, Your Excellency. He was a true and devoted friend to me....

Prince (*smiling*): Well, not altogether....

Kirila Petrovich (*wiping away tears*): Not altogether? What do you mean by that, Your Excellency?...

Prince: Oh, well, it's all in the past now, so I'll tell you: when you didn't receive that position – who stopped you, do you know? None other than Vasilii Kuzmich.... It's painful to have to tell you, but that's the way it is....

70

The Live Corpse

Vasilii Kuzmich: Oh, dear!

Kirila Petrovich: You overwhelm me, Your Excellency! Whatever could he have said about me?

Prince: Well, nothing much; he just remarked in general that you are an unreliable person....

Kirila Petrovich: Pardon me, Your Excellency, that word by itself means nothing – you would have to have proof....

Prince: I know, I spoke up for you; but Vasilii Kuzmich just kept saying: 'Believe me, I've known him a long time; he's unreliable, unreliable altogether...' That matter, as you know, didn't depend on me; Vasilii Kuzmich carried weight – and everyone stuck with him.

Kirila Petrovich: Ah, the hypocrite, the hypocrite! If that's the way the land lies, let me report to you, Your Excellency: he assured me that it was you who were against me, that he, however much he argued with you, however much he spoke up for me....

Prince: He was simply lying.

Kirila Petrovich: Take it from me, Your Excellency, there was never anyone on earth more treacherous than that man; he would play the simpleton, and was always saying: 'I am a simple man, I am a simple man', and looking everyone straight in the eye – and then he does his utmost to do you down; he took in everybody, Your Excellency, did everybody down.... If there was the slightest advantage in it for him...he would sell his father, pawn his son, slander his own mother...he really would!

Prince: At least, you can't detract from one thing: he was an efficient man.

Kirila Petrovich: What do you mean efficient? Your Excellency, he was a thorough-going idler: he was just a past master at sending out memos. You just look into his work – he didn't do a thing. When could he have done? From morning 'til evening he was either carrying on intrigues or playing whist. Nothing was sacred to him: the more important the business, the more difficult, the sooner he'd pile it on to someone else. Oh, he wasn't half clever when it came to that.... He would always find some pretext that would never enter your head.... And then, when others had done all the work, he would twist the whole thing round, as though he'd done it himself.... Oh, such a cunning devil!...

Prince: But all the same, he was not a mercenary sort of man....

Kirila Petrovich (getting excited): Wasn't he? Such a mercenary sort the world has never seen. He didn't bother with the little things so much, because he was cautious, like a hare; but just you remember his commissions in other parts: where did he get all his wealth from?...

Prince: What? Really? Is that really true?

Kirila Petrovich (continuing to get excited): Yes, for goodness sake.

Wasn't I with him? I know all about it – he took everyone in, sold them out.... but there's no proof – he covered up his tracks....

Vasilii Kuzmich: Dear, oh dear!

Prince: I'm very grateful that you've revealed all this to me. I can only regret that it didn't occur to you to do so somewhat earlier....

Kirila Petrovich: Ah, Your Excellency! What could I do? It's a long-standing tie, friendship – a powerful restraint.

Prince: And a protection to which you were beholden, isn't that so? Well, good day to you, sir.... (*Goes out*)

Vasilii Kuzmich: So, you caught it then, old man. That's what comes of telling tales....

Kirila Petrovich (*coming to his senses*): Oh! I've blundered, I got too excited.... The damned hypocrite, the murdering swine! Even in death he's doing the dirty on me....

Vasilii Kuzmich: Indeed, it's not such a bad thing that I've died; not such a bad joke they've played on me. Well, why listen to him! I'll flit along to my other friends: may be someone will remember something good about me. Ah, it really is nice, flying about from place to place.

(*Friends of Vasilii Kuzmich at dinner*)

First friend: So, there we are, my dear fellow! In two days time we'll be at Vasilii Kuzmich's funeral! Who would have thought it? Only today he was to have come to me for dinner; I was going to give him Strasbourg pie: he was so fond of that, was the late lamented.

Second friend: And the pie is splendid – I can't say otherwise....

Vasilii Kuzmich: Yes! I can see it's splendid! It's a strange thing: I'm not hungry, but I wouldn't say no to a bit.... Look at those truffles! What a pity there's no way of....

Third friend: A marvellous pie! Let's have another portion for Vasilii Kuzmich.... (*They all laugh*)

Vasilii Kuzmich: Oh! The villains!

First friend: Hm! Vasilii Kuzmich would have taken a different portion from that – he didn't half enjoy his food, the deceased, may God forgive him....

Second friend: He was a terrible old glutton! If you ask me, that's what caused his stroke....

Third friend: Yes, that's what the doctors say.... They say that yesterday he ate so much for supper, you could hardly bear to watch.... And so, hasn't anyone heard, who's going to get his job?...

First friend: Not yet. But have some pity for the deceased, please, for humanity's sake.

The Live Corpse

Third friend: He was a master at whist....

All: Oh! A past master!...

First friend: He had, you know, such a grasp of it....

Second friend: What's on at the theatre at the moment?

(Gossip about town news, about the weather.... Vasilii Kuzmich listens: not a word about him; he glances at every dish. The dinner finishes; they all sit down to cards; Vasilii Kuzmich watches the game.)

Vasilii Kuzmich: What's his game? Ah, I see – a grand slam! Trump him, trump him, Marka Ivanovich – no! He's followed suit! Oh, really, how could you? With that hand – you've gone over their queen.... Ah! If I could have played that hand – what a pity there's no way I can...again the wrong one! Marka Ivanich! You, my dear sir, are not remembering your cards...allow me to tell you, I am a simple and straightforward man, what I feel in my heart is on my tongue.... Oh, what am I chattering to them for – they can't hear!... How infuriating! They've played one rubber.... and another.... Oh, dear me, my hands are itching, how infuriating! Now they're serving tea – I don't feel thirsty, but I wouldn't mind drinking a cup – it's the same tea that Marka Ivanich has sent, direct from Kiakhta: how fragrant it is – wonderful! Even just a drop.... Oh! it's infuriating.

Now the game has finished; they're going for their hats, saying goodbye: 'Goodbye, goodbye, Marka Ivanich?' – he pays no heed.... Well, where shall I go now? I'm not at all sleepy. Unless I go for a stroll round town; the carriages have started to thin out a bit already – everything's gone quiet; the lights are going out in the houses; everyone's in bed – everything forgotten; sleeping away to their heart's content; and as for me, poor chap – I haven't even anywhere to lay my head. But, hang on, now? Why don't I go and see Karolina Ivanovna.... Maybe she's crying over me, the poor creature? Huh! her light is still on – obviously, she can't sleep a wink; she's grieving for me, the poor thing! Let's see. She's sitting in her study.... Dear me! She's not alone! It's that handsome devil that I met once on the stairs at her place, the one I got jealous over – and she kept assuring me that she didn't know him from Adam, that no doubt he was visiting other tenants! Ah, the baggage! Let's listen to what they're saying. What are those papers she has in her hands; ah! my I.O.U.s. What does she want with them?

Karolina Ivanovna: So, listen Vaniusha: you pay attention, now. I don't know how this sort of thing is done: you have to produce these I.O.U.s, or something: how, where, when – find out all that, my dear. I don't want to lose them, whatever I do; if you only knew what they cost me!

Oh, the world never saw such an old skinflint as that Aristidov; and talk about jealousy – he wasn't half jealous, and do you think I got any pleasure out of him? – not on your life! I had to extort these from him by force; and as if that wasn't enough – oh no, he was always saying: 'Come on Karolinushka, show me my promissory notes – I've forgotten what date was on them'; he almost tore them out of my hand once. And if it wasn't that, he was coming to ask for a loan – from me! Just for a little while, he'd say. He was a disgrace! It's a good thing he pegged out; now you and I can really live it up, my dear Vaniusha....

Vasilii Kuzmich: Ah, the baggage! She's embracing him, kissing! – Ooh, it's infuriating to watch! It's enough to make me burst a blood vessel – and there's nothing I can do about it! To hell with her, the worthless traitress – and what if she did give herself to me?... A fine one she is, the damned.... O-ooh! You shameless.... I could spit on you. Oh, you're not a patch on Natalia Kazimirovna.... Let's have a look, and see if that one's up to anything – if she hasn't found herself a consoler, too. Here's her little apartment! And no light. Let's have a look – she isn't sick, is she? – No! Fast asleep and snoring as if nothing had happened. Not from grief, surely? How could it be from grief! There's a masquerade gown thrown down by the bed: she was at a masked ball! So that's her way of mourning.... And how peacefully she reclines! Sprawled out in such abandon...she looks so good! What a treasure...akh! What a pity.... Well, there's no use complaining – nothing I can do about it.... Where should I go now? Just home...is that what I should do, in fact?... How silent it is on the streets – the slightest movement is audible.... And what sort of gentlemen are these, sitting by the corner...they're looking at something, as if they were waiting for someone; probably up to no good.... Let's see. Hey! It's that rogue Filka, my valet, who absconded.... Ah, the good for nothing...he's talking about something....

Filka's mate: 'Ere. Where did you learn to knock things off, then? From a family of sharpers, are you?

Filka: What d'ye mean? I had no chance to be what I am now. My father was a strict and honest man, made no allowances and taught us to be good; knocking things off never crossed my mind.... 'Til I landed in the service of Vasilii Kuzmich, the one who'll be having the posh funeral....

Filka's mate: You mean, was he really on the fiddle?

Filka: He was a big villain, was the late lamented.... You know, palm wide open. Petitioners were always after him, you know, with backhanders....

Filka's mate: Hold it, looks like the watchman.

Filka: No! It's some drunken prick or other.... Where's our look-out got to?...

Filka's mate: He can't suddenly have....

Filka: Oh! Goddamn it! I'm chilled to the marrow....

Filka's mate: Never mind, soon as it's light we'll go to the caf.... Yeh, so the petitioners used to come....

Filka: Oh yes! they came...and Vasilii Kuzmich thought I was a simpleton.... Look, he'd say, a friend of mine's come; whatever he gives you, you bring it to me, and there'll be a little something for you; well, I got the point, all right; I could see that Vasilii Kuzmich, you see, didn't have the nerve to take money straight into his hand, and he wanted, you know, if anything happened, to put all the blame on me. So, I thought to myself, why should I do all that for nothing? So, I got my cut from Vasilii Kuzmich, and a bonus from the petitioner....

Filka's mate: Cor, mate! A fine old time you 'ad.

Filka: So it was! But the trouble was, as soon as them backhanders had passed through my fingers, I'd be eating my heart out – I wanted more! And with Vasilii Kuzmich I didn't know if I was coming or going; come on, Filka, here you are, do this and do that – you take it from me, strike me down if I tell a lie – and various such devil-may-care tricks he taught me – so that at first I felt ashamed, especially whenever I remembered my father's words, but then it occurred to me: what's wrong with working for your own profit? Vasilii Kuzmich – I'm no match for him, and he knows what to do all right, and he's looked up to and respected by everyone... why look a gift-horse in the mouth? If it's fiddling, well, it's fiddling. So, once I'd thought it all out – I went for a really big sum one time, and had to make myself scarce – and so, from then it's gone on, the further I go, the deeper I am in; and now, instead of an honest life – I 'ave to watch it, or it'll be the slammer for me.

Filka's mate: Look, look, the look-out's signalling....

Filka: Ah! At last! (*Gets up*)

Filka's mate: Got yer crow-bar?

Filka: And me knife, too....

Vasilii Kuzmich: Ah, you no-good! Just look, and to think I taught him! I certainly didn't teach him that.... Now he'll go and rob, maybe even commit murder.... How can he be stopped?... Stop him! How can I stop him? Who could hear me? Oh, it's terrible! Where can I go, so as not to see and not to hear...home, quickly...perhaps I won't hear...here I am, home. They haven't taken my body away yet – no, it's still early. Ah, my niece can't sleep, she's crying, the poor soul!.... She's a good girl, you can't say otherwise; just like her late father! Not an evil thought would enter his head, you could deceive him ten times over, and he wouldn't notice a thing! A good soul...yes, so all he had left was his good soul when he set off for the next world: he's somewhere around now; if I could only meet him, we wouldn't half have a thing or two to talk over. Now, don't cry Liza, my dear! Grief won't help, it will pass – you'll get over it. You'll see, you'll get married, you'll forget all your grief.... Well, and what are my sons doing? They're not sleeping, either – but they're not crying, though.... It sounds like a lively conversation, let's listen.

Piotr: I don't care what you say, Grisha. If we don't clinch this, if we let this opportunity pass, who knows what creek we'll be up....

Grisha: That's just it. But I'd feel ashamed, somehow; I mean we know very well that she's the daughter of our late uncle....

Piotr: We know, but the court doesn't know, and will rule according to the evidence on paper....

Grisha: Yes, but I do feel sorry for Liza. She's so good and kind! So helpless.... We did used to play with her when we were young...you know what I mean, that feeling of....

Piotr: Have you finished philosophising? No wonder our deceased papa used to berate you! He use to say that, with your philosophising, you'd be trash all your life: and that's the way it's turning out....

Grisha: I remember what father used to say...but all the same, what do you think Liza will do? Where will she get a roof over her head?

Piotr: Oh, who cares? Listen, brother Grisha, I'll tell you straight: our father was really a very clever man, and he proved he was clever: he started with a sou and ended up with a million; you remember his favourite saying: 'cover your own roof; you won't get soaked through someone else's'. And that's it. And here we are, two hundred thousand each, Grisha; you won't find that lying around the streets....

Grisha: That's right.... But what arrangements did Vasilii Kuzmich make?

Piotr: He made arrangements all right – and I know what. You were too young, you don't remember, but I remember. When Uncle was dying, he said: 'I didn't have time – my illness has got me – and there's an important matter: Liza's papers are not in order. If you die, God forbid, other inheritors will flock round and take her inheritance from her. Be so good, and petition for all the documents to prove her parentage – if not, she'll be in trouble. In any case, I had all the bank-bonds transferred into an unspecified name, so that, if anything happens, Liza won't be without a crust of bread. I want them to remain with you and, when she grows up, give them to her – and meanwhile get all her papers for her...don't forget – and you, Petrusha, you remind your father...'. A year went by after Uncle's death – I was still young then and foolish, I didn't understand what was what in this world – I remembered Uncle's instruction and mentioned it to father. And Vasilii Kuzmich looked at me, frowned and said: 'Are you trying to teach your father something, then?' – 'I just thought, father, that with all your other affairs...'. – 'That I might forget, is that it?' – asked father. 'No, Petrusha, whatever business I might have, I never forget the most important business, remember that'. At the time, I didn't quite understand those words, but then, when I began to reach the age of wisdom, I got the point; so, one day, I began talking to father, not without a reason, about Liza's papers. The old fellow looked at me even more attentively than before, and seemed to guess what was on my mind. 'You're learning a lot, you'll soon be growing up', he said, you know, putting on that benevolent smile of his, and then he clapped me on the shoulder and said: 'Listen to me, Petrusha, I can see you're going to be no fool...do you know what money means? You don't? Well, I'll tell you: money is – what we breathe by; everything on this earth is trifling, it's all nonsense, balderdash...there's only one thing on this earth: *money*! Remember that, Petrusha – and you'll go far...'.

Vasilii Kuzmich: Now, when did I say that to him?... Ah, quite! I did say it...what a rogue! – he's remembered – that's what he's driving at....

Grisha: Well, so what do you think?...

Piotr: I think that, as of now, the matter stands as follows: that is, the bonds for four hundred thousand in an unspecified name are lying in father's chest of drawers – while Liza gets nothing, not having been her father's daughter....

Grisha: How's that?

Piotr: Simple! We just keep quiet, and the four hundred thousand are our's....

Grisha: Ah, but brother, I'd be ashamed to....

Piotr: Oh, philosophy again! Ashamed of what? Of keeping quiet? A fine thing, speaking out would be.... Listen to me, four hundred thousand – four hundred.... Can you count, or not?...

Grisha: But what about father, what instructions did he leave?

Piotr: What indeed? It was the truth that the late lamented spoke: 'What ever happens, don't lose your head, don't forget the most important thing.' Let's go and have a look in his papers... lucky I took the keys....

Grisha: Oh, this is horrible. It's...you know...it's forgery....

Piotr: Oh, those books have knocked all the sense out of you! Rubbish you always were and rubbish you'll always be.... There's no time to lose: it'll soon be morning. I'll go alone if you're afraid...you sit here and compose verses at your leisure....

Vasilii Kuzmich: Now, I see. This fellow doesn't miss a trick – he's a sharp lad, all right! It's a pity about Liza, though; but still, she's not my daughter.... There he is; he's started rummaging; he's got the scent all right: he's found Liza's bonds, straight off. He's looking pensive...rummaging in the papers... pensive again.... Now what? Into his pocket? Dear me! That's naughty of you, Petrusha.... How can you? He's filched them! Dear, oh dear! What's going to come of this?...

Piotr (*returning to his brother's room, in some alarm*): There are no instructions at all.... I rummaged through everything....

Grisha: Well, then...that's good....

Piotr: Yes, very good! What have you been doing here?

Grisha: Two fine lines for an elegy just came to me: 'Oh gold! Despicable metal, you! What level will you reduce us to?' Only the rhyme's not all that good....

Piotr: Listen, Grisha, I've brought you some rhymes, and some very rich ones, too.... Look, brother mine! I'm an honest man, as you can see, I could enjoy the lot, but I don't want to. You're still my brother, rubbish or no. Here's half of it, hide it away, quickly...and make sure you don't blab about it.

Grisha: How could you? How could you? How could you take it without the relatives being here, before the inspection?...

Piotr: What? Wait for the inspection? Oh, you – philosopher! You've given me an idea....

Grisha: I have?

Piotr: Who else? You said yourself that perhaps Vasilii Kuzmich made some kind of written provision, maybe he left some kind of instructions: I took you at your word and went to look, found no instructions, and so, I thought: supposing it was found somewhere? Well, you have to know which side your bread is buttered! And if we hide the money, no one will be the wiser; let them search all they like and then put the seals on: 'We know nothing and say nothing; as the bonds were, so the bonds will stay!' So all the bonds will stay in father's name, which means it'll all come to us.... Not bad, eh?

Grisha: So...but all the same...I don't know....

Piotr: Are you going to take the money, or not? If you're not going to take it, then maybe I'll take it all myself....

Grisha: Well, all right. Hand it over, then....

Vasilii Kuzmich: No! There's something sad budding here, but I'm not sure what...strange, somehow! It's both perfectly reasonable and bad, and yet, it's perfectly reasonable.... There's something I can't quite grasp...but it's getting stuffy here, I'll go up for some air, seeing that it's morning already...the shops are opening...people are going out...they're happy...but I'm just bored somehow.... I'll just pop into this sweetshop. Ah! they're delivering newspapers...might as well have a read of one.... Oh! my obituary! Let's have a look (*reads:*)

'Deceased on this day such and such, Vasilii Kuzmich Aristidov, deeply mourned by family, friends, colleagues and subordinates alike, indeed by all who knew and loved him. And who did not love this estimable man? Who is not aware of his penetrating mind, his tireless activities, his steadfast straightforwardness? Who did not value his frank and open character? Who did not respect his family virtue and moral purity? Dedicating his whole life to indefatigable labours, he, not wishing to entrust his children to a state institution, found the time personally to direct their education, and managed to bring them up to be citizens as worthy as himself. Let us not forget that, despite his important and arduous duties, our esteemed Vasilii Kuzmich also devoted time to literature; versed in several European languages, he was endowed with refined taste and a subtle fastidiousness. At this point, by the by, we should remind our enemies – those who envy us, our detractors, our strict connoisseurs and judges – that our esteemed Vasilii Kuzmich always gave us our just due: over the course of many years, he was a stalwart subscriber and a reader of our newspaper...'. Hm, they're a bit off the mark there. I've never subscribed to them; they sent it to me free...yes...as a good-will gesture.... Well, what else do they say?

'...He well knew and believed that we are ready to sacrifice life itself for the truth, that our diligence, loyalty...moral purity...in the public interest...'.

Well, whatever next! What's this postscript?

'...We consider it our duty to inform our readers that there remain a number of copies of this year's editions of our newspapers, and that...subscriptions may be taken out with the following bookseller, who is well known for his honesty and efficiency...'.

Oh, that's just their own business; they were glad of something to stick it on the end of, I suppose...but still, I'm grateful to the scoundrels for their kind words....

What's all this noise on the street! Aha, they're coming back from the funeral. Mine is it? Let's listen in to what they're saying about me.

– A really smart operator, he was...there was just one thing wrong....
Let's move on.

– A really tasty business....

– Whatever you'd do with him, he would always get out of it!...

– A very thorough man....

– Without shame and without conscience....

– Gvozdin went up in the world through him....

– He completely ruined me and the children....

– He took bribes and he still destroyed people – it's true, the more you gave him....

– He never took....

– He did, but cleverly, through his valet....

– You don't say?

– Who should know better than I do?

– From the living and from the dead....

Huh, confound it! It's not nice to listen to.... How could you live after that? You're always on your guard, you weigh up every step, you manage your affairs nicely, then you die – and it all comes out! No! You can't say otherwise, it's sad and infuriating – you can't even stop anyone's mouth! Now where shall I get to?... Where? Just wander around the town, seeing that it's day....

But it's getting dark already! I don't know why, but I find night frightening somehow.... I mean, what is there for me to fear now?.. Yet, something's pricking me under the heart.... Where shall I go? Ah! is that the theatre lit up? I haven't been there for a long time, especially as I don't need to pay to get in. Let's see, now, what are they doing there? *The Magic Flute* – I've never seen it. Oh, yes, opera! I never did like music – never my cup of tea, somehow.... Oh, well, never mind, just to kill an evening....

What kind of an allegory is this supposed to be? A man going through fire and water...being subjected to various ordeals...let's have a closer look (*on the stage*). Huh! the water's cardboard, the fire is, too...and a young fellow laughing with an actress... it's the same here as everywhere: from the outside it looks like God knows what, and on the inside it's nothing, fancy paper and strings, which work everything. (*Addresses the audience:*) Ah! Not a bad view of the public from here! Listen, gentlemen, what you are seeing here is complete nonsense; young lads in tall hats – magicians or something – talking stuff and nonsense about virtue and rewards, such as they may be among you – it's all untrue. They talk like that because they get money for it; whoever thought up all that was also in it for the money; that's the whole trick! Believe me: I have really passed through water and fire, and nothing came of it; I lived, had money – it was good, but now what am I? Nothing! Can you hear me, then? Nobody can hear, they're all watching the stage...it must be something good, let's move back a bit. (*In the stalls:*) So! I thought as much! To reward virtue, great deeds – the fulfilment of all desires: light, rest and love – yes! Just wait.... All the same, what would you think if you really got to some cosy little warm place, seeing nothing, hearing nothing and forgetting about everything!... The curtain's come down – that's all! Everyone's going home: a family, friends are waiting for every one of them...and me? No one's waiting for me! This stupid play has just depressed me. Where shall I go? Shall I just stay here in the empty dark theatre.... Akh! If I could only go to sleep! Before, if something nasty happened, you could lie in your bed, close your eyes, and forget about everything, and now there's no sleep, even! It's so sad.... (*Flying around the city.*) Ugh! Just passing these houses, it's getting quite awful; all you can hear is: abuse going on here, cursing there, people laughing about me somewhere else...and there's nothing to stop your ears with, and you can't close your eyes – you see everything and hear everything.... Where's this I'm being drawn to?... Out of town, is it?... Ah! the cemetery! Yes! Here's my grave...here's my little warm place! This is where he's lying! Ooh, dear me! There's a worm crawling over his face! All the same, he's happier than I am; at least, he doesn't feel anything.... And even for me it's better here than back there; at least I can't hear people talking.... Oh, it's sad! so sad!...

I seem to have started losing track of the days.... I don't know, now, how much time has passed.... And why should I know? My only comfort is that at my grave...it's quiet! You've only got to make a move somewhere and the abuse and cursing starts all over again!... But still, I'd like to have a look and see what's happening in my house.... Let's make a move...now, on the road! What's drawing me now?... Some poor little apartment.... Hey! Liza, my niece, in here...the boys must have kicked her out of the house. Oh, that's very bad! Who's that with her? Ah! Young Valkirin, the one who used to flirt with her.... Dear oh dear! I hope no trouble comes of it.... What are they talking about?...

Valkirin: Tell me, Lizaveta Dmitrievna, did your late father really not leave you any papers at all?

Liza: Any, such as there were, were given over to Vasilii Kuzmich by father.... But what's the matter with you, Vyacheslav? You're as pale as death!...

Valkirin: Don't ask me, Lizaveta Dmitrievna! It's terrible... terrible!... That you had four hundred thousand, that's certain, and that it was stolen – that's even more certain.... I started a case, I was taking steps, and do you know what refutation your brothers had prepared? They maintained that Dmitrii Kuzmich never had a daughter!...

Liza: He didn't? Then what about me?

Valkirin: They know: you, I and they know, but there's no written proof among the papers....

Liza: What! I'm not my father's daughter? What am I, then?

Valkirin: Until proof is found, you are nothing, you are an impostor.

Liza: Oh my God! How terrible!... But how is this possible? Ask anyone! Everyone knows that I'm my father's daughter....

Valkirin: I'll tell you again: everyone knows; but it's not in the documents, and that's what's important....

Liza: What do we do now?

Valkirin: There's no time to lose; I've managed to get myself some time off, and this very night I'm setting off for your father's former estate; I'll probably be able to find some trace or other there....

Vasilii Kuzmich: Yes, just you wait! A fat lot you'll find!

Liza: Vyacheslav, I don't know how to thank you...everyone's abandoned me, thrown me out – only you....

Valkirin: You know what reward I want! Just one thing, your hand....

Liza: Oh! It has long been yours, but not now, not this minute...you are poor yourself. I don't want you to marry a pauper, and your father will never agree to that.... I don't want to be the cause of strife in your family, especially now, when I'm...I can't bring myself to say it...not even my father's daughter! (*Sobs*)

Valkirin: Just say one word...and I won't let anything stop me...tomorrow you will be my wife.

Liza: No, you're a wonderful person, but I don't want to take advantage of your selflessness, just as you don't want to humiliate me: your proposal now is almost an act of charity, for which I shall reproach myself.... Be content with the fact that my hand and my love belong to you.... God will take care of everything; and then nothing will prevent our happiness.

Vasilii Kuzmich: They throw themselves into each other's arms, both of them are crying, the poor things! I even feel sorry for them; but how can I help? Ah, if I'd known, I would have left her something to live on.... And those rogues have grabbed the lot for themselves.... But the truth is, what can I do now? Isn't it all the same if they or some others got it?... Huh!... it's a shame! It tugs at the heartstrings, I can't look at them any more!... No, it's horrible here.... I'm better off away, out of town, where I don't have to see or hear anything!...

It seems to be a bit easier to breathe here; it isn't half boring roaming the big highways alone, but still it's better than.... Huh! I seem to know this area.... Yes! Of course! This is the town where I really lived it up in my day. Do they remember me here, or am I forgotten?... There's the house I lived in; let's see what's going on inside.... Ah! Here's my former subordinate! How nice to see a familiar face! There's some newcomer with him and he's very excited; let's listen to what they're saying.

Newcomer: Do you really mean to tell me that nothing has been preserved of that precious collection?

Provincial official: I've told you, Vasilii Kuzmich ordered everything to be destroyed.

Newcomer: But to what purpose?

Provincial official: Simply for the sake of tidiness and order. As I remember it now, he was seated at whist, he called me over to him and said: 'Look here, old man, you've got a lot of old lumber, haven't you? Wherever do you stick it all? It's just taking up space, and here I am with nowhere to put my people'. I started stammering something about it being very old, and he just about jumped down my throat: I'll thank you not to try to be clever, old man! I'll thank you to collect up all that old junk, get it weighed and sold, and hand the money over to me. Then clean out the rooms, so that my people will be able to move in there the day after tomorrow'.

Newcomer: So, what did you do?

Provincial official: I had to carry out his orders. All the scrolls I sold to the candle shops, and the other stuff to the scrap dealer.

Newcomer: What stuff? Was there other stuff?

Provincial official: Yes, just old things: clothes, pole-axes and all kinds of things that you couldn't even put a name to.... For example, there was a clock – they say it was about four hundred years old, but so old that you wouldn't look twice at it, it wasn't even decent looking. We sold it to the locksmith for eleven and a half roubles; all the old clothes, I'm telling you....

Newcomer: My God, what a loss!

Provincial official: I was sorry to see it go myself, but what could I do? But why are you so interested in it?

Newcomer: How can I best explain it to you? Among those papers was preserved the only copy of a certain document of extreme historical importance; I used up all my not inconsiderable property in order to trace it; I traveled round dozens of towns, and finally was fully convinced that this document was nowhere to be found, when in your.... Now whole decades of my labours have been lost, a vital gap in our history will remain for ever, and I must return empty-handed, without hope and...without money.... Tell me, didn't you have an old mural on the walls as well?

Provincial official: Mural? Oh yes, of course, sir. It was rubbed off on Vasilii Kuzmich's orders.

Newcomer: But what kind of a barbarian was this Vasilii Kuzmich of yours?

Provincial official: He wasn't so much a barbarian; he didn't really do anything too villainous; more a twister, I'd say.... You see, let me tell you....

Vasilii Kuzmich: Let's skip the oration to me...we'll move on! (*Flies through the town*) What's this? I can hear sobbing.... My name is being mentioned again.

Voice in hovel: May that Vasilii Kuzmich rot in hell! The life I could have been leading now!... He got round me then, blast him: don't worry, my dear, he said, I'll fix everything; if you stir things up you'll be even worse off. I'll be responsible for everything, you leave it all to me; I'll fix everything...and this is how he fixed it, damn him! And, like a fool, I believed him and let time slip by, and here I am now, dying of hunger, with five orphans and now it turns out he was rich and important! How can the world put up with such people?

Vasilii Kuzmich: Another oration! Let's go past! There's no rest! The only thing's to fly off to the back of beyond!... Ah, here's another town; what's this? Seems to be jolly here, there's a fair on.... Oh, no! They're talking about me again: they're saying that everyone's been ruined because the store-house was not built where it should have been; there are no roads to it, and the goods get spoilt.... Ah, yes, it's true! But what else could be done? I was chasing a nice little widow, and she wanted the fair to be opposite her house; what a carry-on I had to fix that! What didn't I have to do in the way of intrigue and deceit to prove that right here was the very best and most convenient place...and what did it all lead to? Let's go past! But, what do you think? What kind of a set-up is this, anyway? Surely, if you've died, you've died – and that should be that. But no – whatever you got up to, it all hits you right in the eye, it all cries out, it's all cast up at you...it really is a strange set-up....

I've no more strength left! I've been roaming all over the place! I've flown all round the earth's globe! And wherever I pop down to earth, I'm being remembered, everywhere.... It's strange! After all, is that what I was like on earth? Judged from any reasonable point of view, I was no upstart, never tried to appear too clever, didn't exactly work my fingers to the bone, and achieved precisely nothing – and look at the traces I left behind me! And how oddly all these things are strung together, one after another! You see a man in prison, whom you've never clapped eyes on before; you go and find out what's what – and I find that it's all through my good offices! Another one's taken off to the ends of the earth – and again it's through my good offices. Widows and orphans, debtors and creditors, old men, young men – they all remember me, and what for? All for trivia, yes, really for trivia: I assure you, I'm a straightforward and open man, be it a stroke of the pen, or just a word, said or left unsaid.... No, truly, I've no strength left! It's getting too horrible! And besides, I so want to go home, I've such an urge to get back. And, here I am, back! Again I've stopped over Liza's apartment.... What poverty! Has she got used to such a life? She's so emaciated, the poor thing, you wouldn't know her; where has her beauty gone? She's slaving over the washing and tears are falling; I expect she's thinking of me, too.... And who's this going to see her? Some gentleman or other, the way he's dressed: obviously a rich man; what's he doing calling on her? And look how pleased she is to see him, the way she jumped up!

Liza: Filipp Andreyevich, I thought you had completely forgotten me.

Gentleman: Why, no young lady, how could I! I've been rather busy, you know, ministry affairs.... Well, and how are you keeping?

Liza: Ah, not so well, Filipp Andreyevich, not so well at all! My lawyer says that there's no hope of finding my papers.

Gentleman: Never mind, never mind, young lady. We'll arrange all that....

Liza: Ah, you truly are my benefactor! Without you, I would have perished altogether; I am still living on the money you lent me when I sold your silver – and still I have, I'm afraid, no means of repaying it.

Gentleman: Never mind, never mind, young lady! We'll settle all that later; I am very much in your debt...you understand, for me, a man of my position, it's somehow indelicate to be selling things – but at the same time I need the money...you understand.

Vasilii Kuzmich: Now that I've had a good look at him, I know that face! Yes, it's that rogue Filka, my valet, dressed up! Well, there'll be trouble here!...

Liza: I quite understand, and I'm ready to be of service in any way I can; I said that that silver was my mother's, and in any case the monogram on the silver happened to be the same as mine.

Filka: That's fine...by the way, I can't stay long with you; I called in just for a minute; I was at the pawnbroker's, to redeem some things there, and now I have to go and see the minister. I'm afraid to carry them about – they might get lost. Would you allow me to leave the things with you?

Liza: With pleasure. Ah, what wonderful diamonds, necklaces, diadems...and so many of them!

Filka: Yes! Wonderful, wonderful, and very expensive. Please hide them somewhere safe.

Vasilii Kuzmich: Liza, Liza! What are you doing? Those things are stolen, this man's a thief, he's Filka.... She doesn't hear a thing.... It's hopeless!

Filka: Oh no! If you please, not in the chest of drawers: they might get stolen; thieves usually search the chest of drawers before anywhere – I know all about it....

Liza: Do you – how?

Filka: I'll tell you what, behind the stove. It's much safer there!

Liza: Oh, what fun!

Filka: Well, now, goodbye. I'll be seeing you again.... (*Filka goes out and in the doorway meets a policeman, steps back a pace; turns pale*)

Vasilii Kuzmich: Ah, poor Liza! She is not the guilty one! Do you hear, she's not the guilty one! No, they can't hear! How can I explain to them.... She's in hysterics; she can't utter a word.... Now here's someone else.... Ah, it's Valkirin; perhaps he will rescue her...he's beside himself with shock...he's having it out with the policeman, who's telling him all about Liza's conduct, about her long-standing relations with this thief, about the silver she sold. Liza recognises Valkirin, rushes to him, he pushes her away.... No, I can't look at any more of it. I'd rather be in the grave, my one and only refuge!...

So, life's one thing and death's another! What a horrible difference! In life, whatever you may have done, you can still put it right; but once you cross that threshold – your whole past is irretrievable! Did such a simple thought never enter my head in the whole course of my life? It's true, I did hear it in passing, I came across it in books; it did creep in, between other phrases. Everyone's the same there: people talk, talk, and keep on talking, so that you think it's all just idle gossip! But what deep thoughts can lie hidden beneath the most simple words: 'there's no return from the grave!' Ah, if I'd only realised that before!... Poor Liza! Whenever I think of her, my soul dies another death! And the whole blame is mine, mine alone! I inspired that miserable idea in my sons – and how! By a careless word, an everyday ordinary joke! But am I guilty? I thought that I would have time to secure Liza! It's true, I looked after my own offspring best, but I would never have brought my brother's daughter to the predicament that she's in now! Is there really not a spark of feeling in my sons?... But from where would they have got such a spark? Certainly not from me; no sooner did I notice any suspicion of what you might call poetic ravings than I tried to kill it by ridicule or reasoning; I wanted to make my sons into *men of reason*; I wanted to preserve them from weakness, from philanthropy, from every-thing that I call trifling! And look at the men they became! My exhortations they profited by; my morality they were able to surmise!... Oh! I can't bear to stay here any longer – there's no rest for me here, either! I can't hear any other voices, but I can hear my own...oh! it's my conscience, my conscience! What an awful word! How strange it sounds aloud! It has quite a different ring to it, from the ring it had *there*. It's like some kind of monster, which crushes, suffocates and gnaws at my heart. Before, I thought that conscience was something more or less like decency; I thought that if a man is careful about his behaviour, observes all social stipulations, does not fall foul of public opinion and says what everyone else says, then that was all there was to conscience and morality.... It doesn't bear thinking about! Ah, my sons, my sons! Is the same thing in store for you, too? If you were different, if something else had inspired you, perhaps you would have understood my sufferings; you would have tried to obliterate the traces of the evil which I committed; you would have understood that only in this way can my torments be eased.... But it's all to no avail! A long, an eternal, life lies ahead of me and my deeds, like the seeds of a poisonous plant, will all grow and multiply!... What will come of it in the end? It's horrible, horrible!...

Here's the prison. I see poor Liza there...but what's the matter with her? She's not crying any more, her eyes are gazing around....

Good lord! She's near to madness.... My sons, do you know that?... Where are they? The younger one's asleep, the elder one's sitting at his papers.... My God, what's that written on them? He's accusing Liza of debauchery, he's supporting the suspicion of theft, subtly hinting at vicious tendencies allegedly noticed while she was still in my house.... And how skilfully, how cunningly lies are woven in with truth! My lessons were not lost on him, he has understood the art of living.... as I understood it! But what's wrong with him now? The way he glanced at his sleeping brother: what a horrible expression on his face! Oh, I wish I could penetrate his inner thoughts... there...I can hear his heart speaking. Oh no, it's horrible! He's saying to himself: 'This piece of trash will always be a hindrance to me in everything; where did he get his pity from, his sense of repentance and protectiveness? And supposing he were stupid enough to blurt everything out? That would really do it! Indeed – if only he could conveniently die now!... Hmmm, that's not a bad idea! Why not give him a hand? All it takes is a few drops in this glass.... I'll what you might call regale him with coffee.... Why not? The very thing! A drug at hand, and a glass of water beside him on the table; he'll take a drink of it half asleep – and that will be that.'

Petrusha! My son! What are you doing? Stop! He's your brother!... Can't you see me? I'm at your feet...no! He can't see or hear anything, he's going over to the table, a phial in his hand.... The deed is done!

My God! Is there really no *judgement* or *punishment* for me? But what's happening now around me? Where have all these horrible faces come from? I know them! It's my brother reproaching me! Widows and orphans abused by me! The whole world of my evil deeds! The air is shuddering, the sky is collapsing...they're calling, calling for me....

That morning Vasilii Kuzmich awoke very late! For a long time he couldn't wake up properly; he kept rubbing his eyes and gazed round in confusion.

'What a stupid dream!' he said finally. – What a fever I've broken out in. What horrors I dreamed and how vivid they were; exactly like reality.... Whatever brought that on? Oh yes, yesterday I dined somewhat extravagantly, then the devil prompted me to have a bed-time read of some fantastic fairy-tale.... Oh, these story-tellers! They can't write anything useful, pleasant, soothing! They have to dig up all the dirt under the sun! They ought to be forbidden to write! Well, I mean to say! You read it and let it sink in – and then all kinds of balderdash enter your head; really, they should be forbidden to write, simply forbidden altogether.... Well, I mean to say! They don't even allow a decent man to get to sleep peacefully! Ugh! It's still making my flesh creep now.... Oh, it's mid-day already; huh! I didn't half stay up late last night; now I'll have no time to do anything! Still, you have to have some relaxation. Who shall I go and see? Karolina Karlovna or Natalia Kazimirovna?

1838 (published 1844)

THE COSMORAMA

(Dedicated to Countess Ye.P. Rostopchina)

Quidquid est in externo est etiam in interno.

The Neoplatonists

A Warning From The Publisher

A passion for rooting among old books often brings me to curious discoveries. In the fullness of time I hope to communicate the greater part of
these to the educated public. However, to many of them I consider it
imperative to attach a preamble, an introduction, a commentary and other
scholarly appurtenances. All this, I need hardly say, demands a lot of time
and therefore I have decided to present certain of my findings to the reader
simply in the state in which they were obtained.

In the first instance, I intend to share with the public a strange manuscript, which I bought at an auction, together with piles of old bills and
house-keeping papers. Who wrote this manuscript, and when, is not
known, but the important thing is that the first part of it, which amounts to
a self-contained composition, is written on notepaper in a handwriting
sufficiently modern and even attractive for me to have been able to dispatch it for printing without copying it. Consequently, there are here no
additions of mine; but it may be that some of my readers may carp as to
why I have left many passages in it without explanation. I hasten to reassure them with the news that I am preparing annotations to it, amounting to
four hundred, of which two hundred are already finished. In these annotations, all the events described in the manuscript will be explained as clearly
as two times two make four, so that readers will be left without the slightest
misunderstanding: these notes will fill a respectable quarto volume and will
be published as a separate book. Meanwhile I am working incessantly on

an elucidation of the continuation of this manuscript, which unfortunately is written extremely unclearly, and I shall lose no time in imparting it to an eager public. For the moment I shall limit myself to the cautionary remark that the sequel has a certain connection with the pages now being published, but embraces the other half of it's author's life.

Manuscript

If I had had any reason to presuppose that my existence would be a chain of incomprehensible, marvellous adventures, I would have preserved for posterity every tiniest detail. But my life at its outset was so simple, so like any other person's life, that it never occurred to me either to note down my each and every day, or even to recollect it. The wondrous circumstances, in which I had roles as witness, active participant and victim, flowed so imperceptively into my existence, encroached so naturally upon the circumstances of my everyday life, that I could not fully appreciate the total strangeness of my position.

I have to admit that, struck by everything which I have seen, being certainly in no condition to distinguish reality from simple play of the imagination, I to this day cannot really account for my sensations. All the rest is almost blotted out from my memory. Despite every effort, I recall only those circumstances which have to do with appearances of the other or, to put it more aptly, *extraneous* life – I do not know what else to call that wondrous state in which I find myself, the mysterious links to which began in my childhood, from an age before I can even remember, and are reiterated to this very day with a horribly logical consistency which is unexpected and almost against my will. Obliged to shun people, in the hourly fear that the slightest movement in my soul will be transformed into a crime, I avoid any such thing and in desperation entrust my life to paper and seek in vain by rational effort a means of escaping the mysterious nets which have entrapped me. But I notice that everything which I have said so far may be comprehensible only to me, or to someone who has undergone my experiences, and so I hasten to get on with the story of the actual events. There is in this story nothing invented, nothing embroidered for adornment. Sometimes I have written in detail, sometimes in brief, depending on how my memory has served me – thus have I endeavoured to protect myself against the smallest element of fiction. I shall not undertake explanations for the events which have befallen me, for what is incomprehensible to the reader remains incomprehensible to me too. Perhaps someone who may know something of the real key to the hieroglyphs of

human life will be able to make more than I can from my own story. That is
my only purpose!

I was not more than five years old when, passing through my aunt's room
once, I noticed on her table a sort of a box, covered with coloured paper on
which flowers, faces and various figures were sketched in gold. All this
glitter stopped me in my tracks and rivetted my childish attention. My aunt
came into the room. 'What is that?', I asked impatiently.

– It's a toy, which our Doctor Bin sent you, but it will only be given to
you when you are clever enough. – With these words my aunt pushed the
box nearer to the wall, so that from a distance I could only see the top of it,
into which there had been stuck a magnificent flag, the brightest scarlet in
colour.

(I should warn my readers that I had neither father nor mother and that I
was brought up in my uncle's house.)

My childish curiosity was aroused both by the appearance of the box
and by my aunt's words. A toy and, what is more, a toy which was
intended for me! In vain did I pace around the room, looking first from one
and then from another angle, so as to look at the tempting box: my aunt
was immovable on the subject. Soon it struck nine o'clock and I was put to
bed. However, I couldn't sleep; hardly would I close my eyes but the box
would be before me with all its gold flowers and flags. I fancied that it
would melt away, that beautiful children in gold dresses would emerge
from it and beckon me over – then I would awake. Finally, I was absolutely
unable to sleep, despite all the exhortations of my nanny; when she threatened me with my aunt, however, I changed my tack. My childish mind had
soon worked out that, if I went to sleep, nanny would perhaps leave my
room and my aunt would now be in the lounge: I pretended to be asleep. It
worked. Nanny left the room. I jumped smartly out of bed and made my
way to my aunt's study. It was only a momentary matter to move a chair
over to the table, to clamber on to the chair and to get my hands on the
enchanting and cherished box. Only now, in the dull light of the nocturnal
lamp, did I notice that there was a round piece of glass in the box, through
which light could be seen. I looked round to make sure that my aunt was
not coming and then put my eyes to this glass window and caught sight of a
series of beautiful, richly turned-out rooms, around which there walked
richly dressed people who were unknown to me. Everywhere lamps and
mirrors were shining, as though it were some sort of a celebration. But
imagine my surprise when I recognised my aunt in one of the further
rooms. Beside her stood a man and he was passionately kissing her hand,
while my aunt was embracing Uncle. However, this man was not Uncle:

Uncle was fairly stout, with black hair and wore a frock coat, but this man was a handsome, slim, fair-haired officer with a moustache and spurs. I couldn't get enough of looking at them. My fascination was interrupted by the tweaking of an ear: I turned round and before me stood my aunt.

– Oh, Auntie! How can you be here? I just now saw you in there....

– What rubbish!...

– What do you mean, Auntie! A fair-haired, gallant-looking officer was kissing your hand....

My aunt shuddered, lost her temper, started shouting and led me by the ear to my bedroom.

The next morning, when I came to greet my aunt, she was sitting at her table. The mysterious box was in front of her, but its lid had been removed and my aunt was pulling various cut-out pictures from it. I stood still, afraid to budge, thinking that I would catch it for my prank of the night before, but, to my surprise, my aunt did not scold me, but, showing me the cut-out pictures, asked: 'Well, where did you see me in these? Show me.' I looked through the pictures for a long time: there were shepherds, cows, Tyroleans and Turks; there were also richly dressed ladies and officers, but I could not find either my aunt or the fair-haired officer among them. Nevertheless, this inspection satisfied my curiosity: the box lost all its enchantment for me and soon a bay horse on wheels induced me to forget all about it.

Soon after this, in the nursery, I heard the nannies telling each other that we had a new arrival in the house, a hussar chap, and so on. When I went in to see my uncle, he had with him my aunt on one side in the armchair and, on the other, my fair-haired officer. He barely had time to utter a few kind words to me before I exclaimed:

– Yes, I know you, sir!

– What do you mean, you know him? – my uncle asked in surprise.

– I have seen you before....

– Where have you seen him? What are you talking about, Volodia? – said my aunt in an angry voice.

– In the box, – I replied, quite guilelessly.

My aunt burst out laughing:

– Oh, he's seen a hussar in the cosmorama, – she said.

My uncle also laughed. During that time Doctor Bin had walked in. They explained to him the reason for the general mirth, and he said to me, with a smile: 'Yes exactly, Volodia, you did see him there'.

I very much liked Paul (as my aunt's distant cousin was called) and especially his hussar's uniform. I was always running off to see Paul, since he was living in the house – in a room behind the conservatory. Moreover, he seemed to be very interested in toys, because, when he was sitting in my aunt's room, he would constantly send me off to the nursery for some toy or other.

On one occasion, which really surprised me, I brought Paul a wonderful clown which I had just been given and which did remarkable things with its arms and legs. I held the strings, while Paul held my aunt's hand behind the chair; my aunt was crying. I thought that my aunt must have felt moved by the clown, so I put it aside and out of boredom started to do something else. I got two pieces of wax and a piece of thread; the one end I stuck to one half of the door and the other end to the other half. My aunt and Paul looked at me in astonishment.

– What are you doing, Volodia? – my aunt asked me, – who taught you to do that?

– Uncle was doing it this morning.

Both my aunt and Paul shuddered.

– Where was he doing it? – asked my aunt.

– Around the conservatory door, – I replied.

At this point, my aunt and Paul exchanged glances in a very strange fashion.

– Where's that bay of yours? – Paul asked me, – bring it here to me, I'd like to have a go on him.

I ran off helter-skelter for the nursery; but some involuntary urge forced me stop at the other side of the door, and I could see that my aunt and Paul made off hurriedly towards the conservatory door which, do not forget, led to my aunt's study, examining it closely, and that Paul had stepped over the thread which my uncle had fixed there that morning. After that Paul and my aunt laughed for some time.

That day they were more than usually affectionate to me.

These were the two most remarkable events of my childhood which have remained in my memory. None of the rest deserves the attention of my gentle reader. I was taken to a distant female relative, who sent me to boarding-school. While at boarding-school I used to receive letters from my uncle, from Simbirsk, and from my aunt, from Switzerland, sometimes with postscripts from Paul. With time the letters became less and less frequent. After boarding-school I immediately entered government service, where I received the news that my uncle had died, leaving me as his sole inheritor. Many years have passed since then; I have had time to have my fill of the service, experience hunger, cold and my fair share of spleen and of hopes foiled. Finally I got myself some leave to visit my native Moscow. I was in the most Byronic state of mind, firmly intending to do a little philandering.

93

Despite the time which had elapsed since the day of my departure from Moscow, I felt an inexplicable sensation on entering my uncle's house, which had now become my own. You would have to go through a long, long life, restless and full of passions and dreams, bitter experience and protracted thought, in order to comprehend the feeling produced by the sight of one's old home, in which every room, table and mirror is redolent with events from childhood. This phenomenon is difficult to explain, but it does exist and everyone has some experience of it. Perhaps we think and feel more in childhood than is generally supposed, but we are not capable of ascribing meaning to these thoughts and feelings in words, and for that reason we forget them. It may be that the events of our inner life remain rooted to the material objects which surrounded us in childhood and which serve us in the same capacity – as thought signs – as do words in normal life. And then, long years later, when we meet these objects again, that old forgotten world of our virginal soul arises before us and these silent witnesses tell us the secrets of our inner being that otherwise would have been completely lost to us. Thus does the naturalist, returning from his lengthy perambulations, recall with joy the rare plants, shells and minerals which he has collected and partly forgotten, and each one of them reminds him of a train of thought aroused within him amid the dangers of his life of wanderings.

At least, this was the feeling with which I ran through the series of rooms which reminded me of my life in infancy. I quickly got to my aunt's study. Everything there was in its place: the carpet which I used to play on; bits of toys in the corner; the fire-place under the mirror, in which, it seemed, the coals had gone out only yesterday; on the table, in the same spot, stood the cosmorama, which time had turned black.

I ordered the fire-place to be stoked up and settled down in the armchair upon which, in previous days, I had barely been able to clamber. Taking in all my surroundings, I couldn't help but start recalling all the events of my childhood days. Day after day flashed past in front of me, like a shadow pantomime. Eventually I got up to the incidents described above, involving my aunt and Paul. Her portrait hung above the divan; she was a fine dark-haired woman, whose swarthy colouring and expressive eyes revealed the fiery story of the inner fluctuations of her heart. Opposite there hung the portrait of my uncle, a portly – even fat – man, in whose, to all appearance, simple glance could be seen nevertheless a subtle Russian sharpness. Between the facial expression of both portraits was an absolute chasm. Comparing them now, I understood everything which had seemed incomprehensible to me in childhood.

My eyes involuntarily lit upon the cosmorama, which played such a key role in my recollections. I tried to comprehend how I could have seen in its images what happened in reality, and before it had happened. Absorbed thus in meditation, I went up to it, moved it over towards me and to my utter surprise noticed in its dusty glass a light which even more vividly reminded me of what I had seen in my childhood. I must admit that it was not without an unwitting shudder and not without giving some thought to my action that I put my eyes to the enchanted glass. A cold sweat ran down my face when, in the long gallery of the cosmorama, I again saw that series of rooms which had been presented to me in childhood: the same decoration, the same columns, the same pictures, the same celebration. But the faces were different: I recognised many of my present acquaintances and finally, in a distant room, myself. I was standing beside a beautiful woman and saying to her the most tender things, which in a toneless whisper reverberated in my ear....

I leaped away in horror, ran out of the room to the other half of the house, called a servant over and questioned him on various points of nonsense, solely so as to have a living being in my presence. After a lengthy conversation, I noticed that my interlocutor was beginning to nod off. I took pity on him and dismissed him. Meanwhile day was already starting to break; the sight of it calmed my agitated blood. I threw myself on to the divan and fell into a troubled sleep. What I had seen in the cosmorama appeared to me incessantly in my dreams; the cosmorama itself seemed to take on the shape of a huge building, in which everything – the columns, the walls, the pictures, the people – everything spoke in a language that was incomprehensible to me, but which produced in me a horror that made my flesh creep.

In the morning a servant woke me with the news that an old acquaintance of my uncle, Doctor Bin, was here to see me. I ordered him to be admitted. When he walked into the room, it struck me that he had not changed at all since that time when I had last seen him, about twenty years before. He wore the same blue frock-coat with the bronze figured buttons; he had the same tuft of grey hair which hung down over his dull tranquil eyes, the same ever-smiling appearance as when he had forced me to swallow a spoonful of rhubarb, the same walking-stick with the gold knob, on which, at one time, I used to take rides. After a lengthy chat and plenty of reminiscing, I unwittingly brought the conversation round to the cosmorama, which he had given me when I was a boy.

– Do you mean it's still in one piece? – asked the doctor, with a smile. – In those days it was the first cosmorama in Moscow; now they're in all the toyshops. That's the dissemination of enlightenment! – he added, with an expression of mock-ingenuousness.

Meanwhile, I was taking the doctor off to show him his antique gift. I must admit that it was not without an involuntary shudder that I crossed over the threshold of my aunt's study; but the doctor's presence, and especially his calm and banal expression, reassured me.

– Here's your miraculous cosmorama, – I said to him, pointing to it.... But I didn't finish what I was saying: a brilliance which flashed across the convex glass took away all my attention.

In the depths of the cosmorama I distinctly made out myself and, beside me, Doctor Bin: but he was not at all the same, although he had kept the same clothing. In his eyes, which had seemed to me so ingenuous, I could see an expression of deep sorrow. Everything that in the room was ridiculous took on an appearance of grandeur in the enchanted glass. There he was holding me by the arm, saying something inaudible, and I was listening respectfully to him.

– You see, you see! – I said to the doctor, pointing to the glass, – do you see yourself there, and me? – With these words, I went to put the lid on the box, when at that moment the words being pronounced in that strange scene became audible to me; when the doctor took hold of my hand and started feeling my pulse, saying 'what's wrong with you?', his double suddenly smiled.

'Don't believe him, – he said, – or, to put it in a better way, don't believe me in your world. There I don't know myself what I do, but here I understand my actions which, in your world, are presented in the form of *unconscious motivation*. There I gave you a toy, without myself knowing why, but here I had the intention of forewarning your uncle – and my benefactor – of the unhappiness which was threatening all your family. I underestimated in my calculations of human wisdom: you in your childhood chanced on the charmed signs which were inscribed by a powerful hand on the magic glass. From that moment I had unwittingly passed you a miraculous, fortunate and at the same time calamitous capability. From that moment there opened in your soul a door, which will always be opening for you unexpectedly, against your will, according to laws which even to me here are unfathomable. Oh, you ill-starred fortunate! You – you can see everything – everything, without the covering, without the astral shroud which *there* is impenetrable, even for me. I have to pass my own thoughts to myself by means of a series of routine trivia, by means of symbols, of secret incentives, of dark hints which I frequently take the wrong way, or which I don't take at all. But you needn't rejoice: if you only knew how I grieve over my fatal gift, over human pride which has dazzled me; I did not suspect, fool that I am, that that miraculous door within you had opened equally for good and evil, for bliss and for perdition...and, I repeat, it will never more close. Take care of yourself, my son – take care of me.... For your every action, for your every thought, for every feeling, I am equally responsible. Initiate! Preserve yourself from that fatal law to which astral wisdom is subservient! Do not destroy your initiator!'... The apparition began to sob.

– Do you hear, do you hear? – I said, – what are you saying there? – I cried out in horror.

Doctor Bin was looking at me with troubled surprise.

– You are not well today, – he said. – You've had a long journey, you've seen your old house, remembered the past; all this has disturbed your nerves: let me prescribe a potion for you.

'Do you know what I am thinking there, in your world, – replied the doctor's double, – I simply think that you have gone mad. That's the way it's bound to be – in your world he who speaks the language of our world must seem mad. How strange I am, how pitiful in that image! And I haven't the powers to instruct, to knock any sense into myself. There my feelings are crude, my mind is swaddled, astral sounds are in my ear – I do not hear myself, I do not see myself! What torture! And beyond that, who knows, perhaps in another higher world still I seem even more strange and pitiful. Oh, misery!'

– Let's go out of here, my dear Vladimir Petrovich, – said the real Doctor Bin, – you need a diet and your bed and it's a bit cold here: it's making my flesh creep.

I removed my hand fom the glass. Everything in it disappeared. The doctor led me out of the room and, in a daze, I followed him like a child.

The potion worked. The next day I was much calmer and I put every-thing I had seen down to distraught nerves. Doctor Bin made so bold as to order the destruction of this strange cosmorama, which had so deeply shocked my active imagination, whether through my recollections or through some other cause unknown to me. I must confess, I was very content with this instruction of the doctor's, as though some big load had fallen from my chest. I made a quick recovery and eventually the doctor permitted me, ordered me even, to go out and try as far as possible to look for something else to think about and any kind of distraction. 'This is absolutely essential for your nervous disorder', the doctor said.

Opportunely, I remembered that I had not yet paid any visits to my friends and relations. Having called at heaps of houses and used up almost all my calling cards, I stopped my carriage at Petrovskii Boulevard and got out with the intention of going on foot as far as the Rozhestvenskii monastery. I involuntarily stopped almost at every step, recalling the past and admiring the streets of Moscow, which seem so picturesque after the monotonous walls of Petersburg, drawn out in ranks. A small side-street on the Truba extended to a hill, on which were scattered little houses which had been built to spite all the rules of architecture and were, perhaps, all the more attractive for that. Its mixed character had appealed to me during boyhood and its capricious negligence now struck me again. Trees protruded around the courtyards, which were barely fenced, and between the trees stretched various domestic properties. Above a three-storeyed house and one particular window, painted red, there towered a green lattice in the form of a dovecot which seemed to weigh down on the whole house. About twenty years before, this dovecot had been an object of astonishment for me: I knew this house very well. It had not changed at all since then, except that a new single-storey extension had been built on at the side and, as though deliberately, had been painted yellow. From the upland the interior of the yard was visible. Yardbirds strode majestically around it and a crowd of domestics were bustling merrily around a garrulous cake- maker.

Now I looked at that house through other eyes and clearly saw all the absurdity and vulgarity of its design but, that notwithstanding, its appearance awakened in my soul feelings which are never awakened by those fine Petersburg houses, which always seem ready to shuffle along the pavement together with the city's pedestrians and which, like its inhabitants, are so neat, so boring and so cold. Here, on the contrary, everything bore the stamp of a lively, untrammeled home life; here it was obvious that people lived for themselves and not for others and, most importantly, they were reckoning on living not just for the minute, but for a whole generation.

Absorbed thus in philosophical reflection, I inadvertently glanced at the gates and caught sight of the name of one of my aunts, for whom I had fruitlessly searched the Mokhovaia. I hurried through the gate which, by ancient Moscow custom was never locked. A few servants were asleep in the anteroom, it being mid-day. I went quietly past them into the dining room, the antechamber, the reception chamber and, finally, into the so-called boscage-room, where, under the shade of arborial etchings, sat my aunt, laying out her game of patience. She cried out on catching sight of me, but when I gave her my name her surprise was transformed into joy.

– So, you just about remembered me, young man! – she said. – You've been in Moscow exactly two weeks today, and haven't managed to look in on me.

– What, Aunt, you know all that already?

– How can I not know, young man! I saw it in the papers. Oh, you society people these days, we only get to know about you from the papers.

I see it there: Lieutenant *** has arrived. Bah!, I said, that's my nephew! I notice the day of his arrival, the tenth; and today is the twenty-fourth.

– I assure you, Aunt, that I couldn't find you.

– Young man! If you had wanted to find me, you would have found me. Yes, what are you talking about? You would only have had to write a line! And to think that I used to carry you in my arms when you were small, well, I can hardly say often, but if you had only come to greet me on a Sunday....

I must admit, I did not know what to reply to her, how to explain politely to her that I could barely have remembered her name since the age of five. Fortunately, she changed the subject.

– But what kind of a way was that to come in? You were not announced: it's true, there's no one in the vestibule. There you are, young man, sixty years I've been living on this earth and I can't run my house properly. Sonia, Sonia! Ring the bell.

At these words a girl of about seventeen, in a white dress, came into the room. She did not have time to ring the bell....

– Ah, young man, you need to be introduced: she's a relation of yours, of course, though a distant one.... Of course! the daughter of Prince Mislavsky, of your cousin once removed. Sonia, this is your cousin Vladimir Petrovich. You've often heard about him; you see what a fine fellow he is!

Sonia went a little red, lowered her pretty little eyes and muttered something sweet. I spoke a few words to her and we sat down.

– But still, young man, it's no wonder that you didn't find me, – went on my loquacious aunt. – You see, I sold my house and then bought this one. You see what character it has, but, to tell you the truth, that's not why I bought it, but because it's near the Rozhestvenskii monastery, where all my darling relatives lie. But the house, it goes without saying, is fine and warm, and the little features it has: you see what a marvellous boscage-room; when they light a candle in the corridor, in here it's like a moonlit night.

Indeed, glancing at the wall I noticed a crudely cut space in the wall like a half moon, into which a piece of greenish glass had been fitted.

– You see, young man, how marvellously it's thought out. In the day it shines into the corridor, and at night in to me. I expect you remember my old house?

– Of course, Auntie! – I replied, smiling unwittingly.

– And now, let me boast about my new house.

With these words my aunt stood up and Sonia followed her. She led us through a series of rooms which seemed to be joined to one another for no reason; however, on closer inspection, it could easily be seen that everything in them had been thought out for convenience and for a quiet life. Everywhere there were bright windows, wide stoves to lie on, little doors which seemed out of place, but which at the same time afforded more convenient communication between the inhabitants of the house. Finally, we got to Sonia's room, which distinguished itself from the other rooms by its special cleanliness and order: by the wall stood a small clavichord, on the table a bouquet of flowers, beside it an old Bible. On the large old-style chest of drawers with bronze bits I noticed several old books, the titles of which made me smile.

– And this is where Sonia has her room, – said my aunt. – You see how everything of hers is in its place. I can't but say what a clean girl she is. There's only one problem I have with her: she doesn't like work, she just likes to keep reading books. Now, perhaps you will tell her what sort of work reading is for a girl, and it's all in German – she had a German governess, you see.

I wanted to say a few words in defence of this attractive girl who just kept quiet, blushed and lowered her eyes to the ground, but my aunt interrupted me.

– That's enough of your fa-la-la, young man! We know you're a Petersburg man-about-town. It's no good listening to you, or the gal will think she's actually playing the part.

From that moment I looked upon Sonia quite differently. Nothing helps to get to know a person as much as the appearance of the room in which they spend most of their life, and it is not for nothing that the new novelists so assiduously describe the furnishings of their heroes. Nowadays, with even greater justice, one can modify the old proverb: 'Tell me where you live, and I'll tell you who you are'.

Obviously, my aunt was a desperate enthusiast for buying houses and building. She told me in great detail how she had found this house, how she had bought it, how she had renovated it, what the contractors, carpenters, beams, panels and nails had cost her. I replied to her in insignificant phrases and, with the attention of a connoisseur, examined Sonia, who kept ever quiet. And she was, there's nothing else to be said, attractive: with light-brown hair strewn over her shoulders à la Valière, which without any poetic deception could be called chestnut, black sparkling eyes, a sharp little nose, elegant little feet – but all this evaporated before the particularly harmonious expression of her face, which was impossible to capture in any phrase.... I took advantage of a moment when my aunt was catching her breath and said to Sonia: 'So you like reading, then?'

– Yes, I like reading sometimes....

– But you don't seem to have many books?

– Does a person need many?

Such a question, applied to books, seemed to me rather amusing.

– You know German. Have you read Goethe, Schiller and Shakespeare in Schlegel's translation?

– No.

– Allow me to bring you these books....

– I would be very grateful.

– Yes, young man, goodness knows what you will load her up with, – said my aunt.

– Oh, Aunt, rest assured....

– I must ask you, young man, only to bring those which are permitted.

– Oh, but absolutely!

– It's a funny thing! Here I am at the age of sixty and I can't understand what consolation people find in books. When I was young, I asked once, which was the best book in the world? I was told *Rossiada*, by Senator Kheraskov. So I set about reading it, but it was so boring, young man, that I didn't get through ten pages of it. At that point I thought to myself that if the best book in the world is so boring, what must the rest of them be like? And I still don't know whether I am stupid, or it's something else, but from then on I haven't read anything apart from the newspapers, and even then only about who's in town.

To this literary critique by my aunt, I could find nothing to reply, except to say that there are books and books, and tastes and tastes. My aunt returned to the reception room and Sophia and I followed slowly behind her; for the moment we remained almost alone.

– Don't laugh at Auntie, – Sophia said, as though guessing my thoughts, – she is right; it's very difficult to understand books. For example, my guardian loved the fable 'The Dragon-Fly and the Ant'; I could never see what was so good about it. My guardian always used to say: what a fine chap the ant is! But I always felt sorry for the poor dragon-fly and cross with the cruel ant. I used to say to everyone, couldn't we ask the author to change that fable, but they all laughed at me.

– That's not surprising, my dear cousin, because the author of that fable died even before the French Revolution.

– What was that?

I involuntarily smiled at such endearing ignorance and tried in a few short words to give my questioner some conception of that horrific event.

Sophia was visibly disturbed, tears coming to her eyes.

– I didn't expect that, – she said, after a short silence.

– What did you expect?

– What you call the French Revolution must definitely have come about

101

from the fable 'The Dragon-Fly and the Ant'.

I burst out laughing. My aunt then intervened in our conversation:

– What's going on there? There she is, cackling away with you like nobody's business – and with me she's as quiet as a mouse. What are you chirping on to her about?

– My cousin and I are discussing the French Revolution.

– I remember, I remember it, young man. That's when coffee and sugar went up....

– That's more or less it, Auntie....

– Then they started to give up powder. I was living in Petersburg then. Then the French came – they were so funny, they looked as if they had come straight from the bath-house. Now we've got a bit more used to it. What a time that was, young man!

For a long time my aunt chattered on about that time, confusing all times, and saying how impossible it was to find cloves or cinnamon; that, instead of olive oil, they made salads with cream, and so on.

Finally I managed to take leave of my aunt, naturally, after solemn promises to visit her as often as possible. This time, there was no pretence: Sonia had really caught my eye.

The next day, books arrived – and I myself followed. The following day and the day after that – the same thing.

– How did you like my books? – I asked Sophia one day.

– Excuse me, but I permitted myself to note down what I liked in them....

– Not at all, I'm very glad. There's nothing I'd like more than to see your comments!

Sophia brought me the books. In the Shakespeare, she had noted the sentence: 'There are more things in heaven and earth, Horatio, / Than are dreamt of in your philosophy'. In Goethe's *Faust* only that short scene where Faust and Mephistopheles are galloping over the deserted plain was marked.

– What appealed to you about that scene in particular?

– Don't you see, – Sophia replied simple-heartedly, – that Mephistopheles is in a hurry; he chases Faust, tells him that they are casting spells there, but is Mephistopheles really afraid of witchcraft?

– In fact, I have never understood that scene!

– How is that possible? It is the most comprehensible, the most lucid scene! Do you really not see that Mephistopheles is deceiving Faust? He is afraid – it's not witchcraft here; here it's something quite different.... Oh, if Faust had only stopped!...

– Where do you see all that? – I asked in amazement. – I... I assure you,
– she replied with peculiar expression.

I smiled; she was embarrassed.... – Perhaps I am mistaken, – she added,
her eyes lowered.

– And didn't you note anything else in my books?

– Yes, lots and lots of things, except that I would have liked to, so to
speak, sift....

– What do you mean, sift?

– Yes! So that what remained would be what weighs on the heart.

– Tell me, what sort of books do you like?

– I like the sort that, when you read them, you feel pity for people and
want to help them, and then you feel like dying.

– Dying? Do you know what I am going to say to you, cousin? The truth
won't make you angry?

– Oh no; I really love the truth....

– There is much that is strange in you. You have a peculiar sort of view
of things. Remember, the other day, when I was joking about something,
you said to me: 'Don't joke like that, you should be careful of words, for
not one of our words is ever lost; sometimes we don't know what we are
saying with our words!' Then, when I remarked that you dress not exactly
in the latest fashion, you replied: 'What does it matter? You've hardly time
to dress yourself three thousand times before it's all over: this dress will be
taken from us, the next one will be taken, and we shall be asked only what
good remains in us, not how well we were dressed'. You must agree that
such remarks are strange by any standards, let alone from the tongue of a
young girl. Where did you pick up such thoughts?

– I don't know, – replied Sophia, a little frighened, – sometimes there is
something inside me which speaks in me; I lend an ear to it and just speak,
without thinking – and often what I say I don't understand myself.

– That's not good. You should always think about what you are saying
and say only what you clearly understand....

– That's what Auntie tells me, as well; but I don't know how to explain
it; when it starts talking inside, I forget that I should think first – and I
speak or I keep quiet. That's why I keep quiet so often, so that Auntie
won't scold me; but with you I somehow feel more like speaking.... to me,
I don't know why, you are sort of pitiful....

– In what way do I seem pitiful to you?

– That's just it! I don't know myself – but when I look at you, I feel so
sorry for you, so sorry that it's impossible to tell you: I keep wanting to, so
to speak, console you, and I say to you, I say... well, I don't know what
myself.

103

Despite all the charm contained in that pure and innocent confession, I considered it necessary to continue in my moralistic role.

– Listen, cousin: I cannot be ungrateful to you for your kind feelings towards me; but, believe me, you have about you the kind of disposition which could be very dangerous.

– Dangerous? But why?

– You should try to amuse yourself a bit, not to listen to whatever, as you put it, speaks to you inside....

– I can't. I assure you, I can't. When the voice inside starts talking, I cannot come out with anything, except what it wants me to....

– Do you know that you have in you a leaning towards mysticism? No good will come of that.

– What is mysticism?

This question showed me what a delusion I was under. I smiled unwittingly.

– Tell me, who was your tutor?

– When I lived with my guardian, I had my German nanny, dear old Louisa; she's dead now....

– And no-one else?

– No-one else.

– And what did she teach you?

– Cooking, embroidering with satin-stitch, how to knit woollens, visiting the sick....

– Didn't you read anything with her?

– Of course! German vocabularies, grammar... and yes! I forgot: latterly we read a little book.

– Which one?

– I don't know, but, wait a minute, I'll show you a passage from this book. Louisa wrote it out in my album when she said goodbye. Perhaps you will recognise which book it is from.

In Sophia's album I read a fairy tale which, in some strange way, has always remained imprinted on my memory:

Two men were born in a deep cave, into which the sun's rays never penetrated. They could not get out of the cave other than by a very steep and narrow ladder and, from an insufficiency of daylight, they lit candles. One of these men was poor, suffered every privation, slept on the bare floor and barely had any sustenance. The other was rich, slept on a soft bed, had a servant and dined from a luxurious table. Neither of them had ever seen the sun, but both had their own conception of it. The poor man imagined that the sun was a great and distinguished personage who gives alms to everyone and he kept thinking about how he could have a word with this magnate. The poor man was quite sure that the sun would take pity on his situation and help him. He used to ask visitors to the cave how he could get to see the sun and breathe fresh air – another delight that he had not experienced. The visitors would reply that, for that, he would have to go up the narrow and steep ladder. The rich man, by contrast, questioned the visitors more closely and found out that the sun was a huge planet which warms and shines; that, upon leaving the cave, he would see a thousand things of which he had no conception. But, when the visitors told him that for this he had to go up the steep ladder, the rich man decided that this would be a useless exertion, that he might tire and stumble, perhaps falling and breaking his neck, that it would be much more sensible to get by without the sun, because in the cave he had a hearth which warmed him and a candle which gave light. Moreover, painstakingly collecting and writing down all the stories he had heard, he soon assured himself that much in them was exaggerated and that he himself had a much better conception of the sun than had those who had seen it. The one, in spite of the steepness of the ladder, did not shirk the exertion and managed to get out of the cave; when he gasped the fresh air, when he saw the beauty of the sky, when he felt the sun's warmth – then he forgot the false concept he had previously had, forgot the previous cold and privation, and, falling on his knees, gave thanks to God for this joy which had been incomprehensible to him previously. The other remained in the stinking cave, in front of his dim candle, and kept on laughing about his former comrade!

– That's one of Krummacher's apologues, I think, – I said to Sophia.
– I don't know, – she replied.
– He's not bad, a bit confusing, as the Germans usually are; but look, he says the same thing as I was just saying: that a person has to work at things, to make comparisons and to think....
– And believe, – answered Sophia, with lowered eyes.
– Yes, of course, and believe, – I replied, with all the condescension of a man belonging to the nineteenth century.
Sophia looked at me attentively. – I have other inscriptions as well in my album. Have a look, there are some beautiful thoughts there, some very, very profound ones.
I leafed over a few pages; in the album were isolated phrases, seemingly taken from some primer, such as:

A pure heart is the greatest of riches. Do as much good as you can, don't expect any reward, this is not for you. If we should take careful note of ourselves, we should see that, for every bad deed, sooner or later punishment follows. People seek happiness all around them, but it is in one's own heart.

And so on. My sweet cousin read these phrases out with the most serious expression and with particular emphasis lingered on every word. She was amazingly funny, and sweet....

Such were my chats with my cousin; however, they took place rarely, both because my aunt hindered our conversations and because my cousin herself was not always talkative. Her ignorance of all that went on outside her little circle, and her opinions which were improbably childish, reduced me to both laughter and pity. But, at the same time, I had never felt such tranquility in my soul: in her few words, in her actions and in her movements there was such peace, such gentleness, such balm, that it seemed as though the very air which she breathed had the property of taming all the rebellious passions, of scattering all the dark thoughts which sometimes clustered in my heart. Often, when the discordant opinions, the horrific questions, all the consequences of the mental conceit of our century cramped my soul, when in a trice it would go through all the ordeals of doubt and I would be horrified at the conclusions which could be reached by an inflexible, wordly logic – then just one open-hearted glance, a single unsophisticated question from that ingenuous girl would involuntarily restore pristine purity to my soul. I would forget all the overbearing thoughts which had stirred up my reason, and life would seem to me comprehensible, lucid, full of peace and harmony.

At first, my aunt was very pleased by my frequent visits, but eventually she gave me to sense that she understood why I was coming so often. Her straightforward remark, which she had meant to be very subtle, forced me to collect myself and to peer more deeply into the inner recesses of my mind. What were my feelings for Sophia? Was my feeling for her love? No, love had never begun to take root, and it was not likely to. Sophia, with her simple-heartedness, with her childish strangeness and her maxims drawn from literary clippings, could amuse me – but that was all. She was too much of a child, too infantile. Her mind was innocent and as fresh as could be; she was most concerned with her aunt, and then with the household and only then with me. No, she was not the creature who could capture the imagination of a young man at the height of his powers, but already experienced.... I had already got beyond that age when any pretty little face could turn my head: a woman for me had to be a friend with whom I could share not only feelings, but ideas as well. Sophia was not at a stage to understand either the one or the other; and to be the constant moralist, although flattering to the ego, would be rather tedious. I did not wish to arouse the sort of society gossip which could harm a blameless girl; of putting an end to it by the usual means, that is by marriage, I had no intention. For this reason I began to visit my aunt much less often – and in any case I had no time: I had started on a different pursuit.

One day at a ball I met with a woman who stopped me in my tracks. It seemed to me that I had seen her somewhere; her face was so familiar to me that I almost bowed to her. I asked what her name was; it was Countess Eliza B. This name was completely unknown to me. Soon I found out that she had lived in Odessa since childhood and, consequently, could not possibly have entered my circle of acquaintances.

I noticed that the Countess, too, was looking at me with no less surprise. When we got closer, she confessed to me that my face, as well, had seemed familiar to her from the first. This strange incident, of course, gave occasion for various conversations and suppositions. It involuntarily enticed us into that metaphysics of the heart which is liable to be so dangerous with a pretty woman.... This strange metaphysics, consisting of paradoxes, anecdotes, witticisms and philosophical musings, is partly characteristic of the normal scholastic metaphysics, that is to say it excommunicates you from society, it isolates you into a special world, though not alone, but together with a beautiful partner in conversation. You speak any nonsense and you are assured that you are understood; on both sides pride arises and is maintained, and pride is the chalice into which all human sins are poured: it glitters and jingles and its arabesque lures your gaze, while your lips involuntarily touch the seductive beverage.

The Countess and I shared this fatal vessel. I admired in her the playfulness of her mind, her beauty, her fervid imagination, the refinement of her heart. She admired in me my strength of character, the boldness of my thoughts, my erudition and my worldly success....

In short: we had already become essential to one another, and yet each of us barely knew the other's name, or position in society.

It is true that we were still innocent in every sense; no word of love had yet been pronounced between us. This was a funny word to a proud man of the nineteenth century; it had long been decomposed by it, dismantled into parts, each part valued, weighed and thrown out of the window, like a thing incompatible with our moral comfort. But I had long conversations with the Countess in the social world; I sat with her for long evenings; but her hand remained in mine on parting for a long time, too long; but when with a smile and a pale face she told me one day: 'My husband will be returning in a few days... you really must get to know him' – I, a man who has been through all the ordeals of life, could find no reply, could not recall even one trite phrase, and, like a lover in a novel, I pulled my hand away, ran off and hurled myself into my carriage....

It had entered neither of our heads, until that minute, to recall that the Countess had a husband!

Now things were different. I found myself in the situation of a man who had just jumped out from a magic circle in which various phantasmagoric visions had been presented before his eyes, forcing him to forget about life.... He blushes, getting vexed with himself as to why he had been in thrall.... Now the problem facing me was a dual one: it remained to me either to look upon this news with equanimity and, by taking advantage of my social rights, to continue my platonic affair with the Countess; or, calling on all my Don Quixotry for assistance and disdaining all conventions, all proprieties and all the conveniences of life, to assume the rights of a desperate lover. For the first time in my life I was in a state of indecision; I hardly slept the whole night – I couldn't sleep either from the passions stirred in my heart or from vexation at myself for this agitation; until this minute, I was so sure that I was no longer capable of such infantilism. In short, I felt within myself the presence of several independent beings who were struggling fiercely and could not overcome one another.

Early in the morning, I was brought a note from the Countess. It consisted of few words: 'In God's name come and see me today, today without fail. I have to see you.'

The words 'today' and 'have to' were underlined.

We had understood each other; at my rendezvous with the Countess, we quickly crossed that space which had separated us from direct expression of our secret, which we had been hiding from ourselves. The first act of our worldly comedy, usually so tedious and so alluring, was already played out: what remained was the catastrophe and the dénouement.

For a long time we could not utter a word, but silently looked at one another, each unfeelingy deferring to the other in the right to begin the conversation.

Finally, as the woman, as the creature of greater kindness, she addressed me in a quiet but firm voice:

– I called you here to say goodbye... our acquaintance must come to an end, it goes without saying, as far as we are concerned, – she added after a short pause, – but not as far as society is concerned; you understand me.... Our acquaintance! – she repeated in a lacerated voice and threw herself sobbing into an armchair.

I rushed over to her and seized her by the hand.... This gesture brought her to her senses.

– Stop now, – she said, – I am sure that you will not wish to take advantage of a moment of weakness.... I am sure that, even if I would forget myself, you would be the first to restore my memory.... But I myself will not forget that I am a wife and a mother.

Her face shone with an inexpressible nobility.

I stood still in front of her.... A kind of sorrow which my heart had never yet endured was tearing me asunder. I could feel my blood, like a hot spring, coursing through my veins: a fast pulse resounded in my temples, deafening me.... I called for assistance upon all the resources of reason, all the experience obtained in the cool computations of a life of some length.... But my intellect could dimly present me only with the dark sophisms of criminality, thoughts of anger and blood. These closed off from me in a crimson shroud all other feelings, thoughts and hopes.... At that moment the savage, inflamed by bestial incentive, was raging beneath the exterior of the educated, refined, prudent European.

I do not know what would have come out of this condition, when suddenly the door opened and a servant handed the Countess a letter. It was from the Count, by special delivery.

The Countess opened the envelope in some agitation and read a few lines: her hands shook and she turned pale.

The servant went out. The Countess handed me the letter. It was from an unknown person, informing the Countess that her husband was dangerously ill on the road towards Moscow, had been forced to stop at an inn, was unable to write himself and wanted to see the Countess.

I looked at her. In my mind there flashed a vague idea which was relected in my gaze.... She grasped this idea, covered her eyes with her hand, as though so as not to see it, and quickly rushed over to the bell.

– Post-horses! – she commanded the servant as he entered. – Ask Doctor Bin to come as soon as possible.

– You are going, then? – I asked.

– This minute.

– I shall follow.

– It's impossible!

– Everyone knows that I had long been intending to go to my village in Tver Province.

– At least leave it until the day after me.

– Agreed... but chance will force me to stop at the same post-station as you, and Doctor Bin has been a friend to me since childhood.

– We shall see, – said the Countess, – but goodbye for now.' – We parted.

I hurriedly returned home, put my affairs in order, calculated when to leave in order to stop at the post-station and ordered my servants to make it known that I had left for the country four days before. This was plausible, as I had been little seen in society for some while. Within thirty hours I was on the highway and soon my carriage had stopped at the gates of the inn, where my fate was to be decided.

I did not have time to go in, before I guessed from the general alarm that everything was already over.

– The Count is dead, – was the answer to my question and these words wildly and joyfully rang in my ears.

At such a moment it would be natural for any traveller, let alone an acquaintance, to appear before the Countess and offer her his services. I need not tell you that I hastened to take advantage of this obligation.

Almost at the door, I met Bin, who rushed to embrace me.

– What's going on here? – I asked.

– What indeed! – he replied, with his ingenuous smile, – a nervous fever.... He neglected it, thought he could get to Moscow – some hope! She is no fool, doesn't mess about: so I came – but it was already too late. What could I do here – there's no raising the dead.

I rushed to embrace the doctor; I don't know why, but probably for his last words. It was just as well that my good Ivan Ivanovich did not take it upon himself to seek out the reason for such uncommon tenderness.

– Pity her, the poor thing! – he continued.

– Who? – I asked, quivering all over.

– The Countess, of course.

– Is she really here? – I muttered, feigning ignorance, and hurriedly added, – what's wrong with her?

– Well, she hasn't slept or eaten for three days.

– May she receive visitors?

– No, she's just gone to sleep now, thank God. Let her calm down before the bearing-out.... You see the owners here are asking for him to be carried out to the church, as soon as possible, for the sake of the travellers.

There was nothing to be done. I concealed my agitation, ordered a room for myself, and then set about helping Ivan Ivanovich with all the necessary arrangements. The dear old chap could not praise me enough. 'You are a good fellow, – he said, – others would have just cleared off; it's good that you happened along, I would have been lost without you; it's true, we medics, I must confess, – he added with a smile – we often enough see people off to the next world, but I've never once contrived to bury anyone before'.

The bearing-out was that evening. The Countess seemed not to notice me and, I must confess, I was myself in no condition at that moment to speak to her. Strange feelings stirred in me at the sight of the deceased. He had been no longer young, but there was still a considerable freshness in his face: his short-termed illness had not yet had time to disfigure him. I looked at him with sincere regret, and then with an unwitting pride I gave a thought to the beautiful inheritance that he was leaving to me in his wake, and through these touching thoughts there flashed, more than once, through my mind the hellish words, preserved by history: 'The corpse of your enemy always smells sweet!' I could not forget these words, bestial as they are to the point of stupidity; they constantly resounded in my ear.

The service came to an end and we left the church. The Countess, as though guessing my intention, sent a servant to me to say that she thanked me for attending and that she herself would be prepared to receive me tomorrow. I obeyed.

The state of agitation in which I found myself throughout these days did not allow me to fall asleep before sunrise. Then a troubled sleep, full of hideous visions, closed my eyes for a few hours. When I awoke, I was told that the Countess had already returned from the church; I quickly dressed and went to her.

She received me. She wanted no pretence and did not display false despair, but a calm sadness was clearly expressed on her face. I shall not mention that the disorder of her attire, a black dress, rendered her still more charming.

For a long time we could say nothing to each other beyond trite phrases, but eventually our feelings got the better of us and we threw ourselves into each other's embraces. This was our first kiss, but a kiss of friendship, brotherly and sisterly.

We soon calmed down. She told me of her future plans: in two days' time, having discharged her last duty to the deceased, she would return to Moscow and from there would travel on, with her children, to her Ukrainian village. I replied that I also had a small estate in the Ukraine and we soon saw that we were fairly near neighbours. I could not believe my happiness; before my eyes a beautiful dream was being fulfilled and an ideal of my youth: seclusion, a warm climate, a beautiful intelligent woman and a long series of happy days, full of resuscitating love and composure.

And so two days went by. We saw each other almost every minute and our happiness was so complete, so unwittingly did words of hope and joy escape our hearts, that even Ivan Ivanovich began looking at us with a smile which he intended as derisive; in private he hinted to me that I should not let the little widow escape, all the more so since she had been very unhappy with the deceased, who had been a capricious, carnal and vindictive man. I now learned these details for the first time and they seemed to me the key to various thoughts and actions of the Countess. Despite the strangeness of our position, we could not help in these two days but become closer than in the previous months – what can you not talk over in twenty-four hours? Little by little, the Countess's character was revealed to me in its fullness, and her fiery soul in all its magnificence. We managed to entrust, one to the other, all our little secrets; I told her of my romantic despair; she confessed to me that, at our last rendezvous, she had been pretending for all she was worth and had even then been ready to throw herself into my embraces, whereupon the fatal letter had been delivered. Now and then we even allowed ourselves to laugh a little. Eliza had completely charmed me and, seemingly, found herself in similar thrall. Frequently her ardent gaze came to rest on me with its inexpressible love and with a tremble it sank to the ground; I made so bold only as to squeeze her hand. How furious I was with the social proprieties which would not allow me to compensate the Countess instantaneously with my love for all her previous sufferings! I must admit, I began to wait with impatience for what belonged to the earth to hurry up and be given to the earth, and was furious with the timescale ordained by law.

Eventually the third day dawned. Never yet had my sleep been calmer. Charming visions wafted before my bed-head: there were endless gardens, flooded with warm sunshine; everywhere – in the thicket of trees, in the coloured rainbows, I saw the beautiful face of my Eliza; everywhere she appeared to me, but in countless semi-transparent images, and all of them smiled, extended their arms to me, slinked across my face with their perfumed curls and in an ethereal line levitated into the air... But suddenly everything disappeared; a horrific crash rang out, the gardens turned into a bare rock and on that rock there appeared the dead man and the doctor, as I had seen him in the cosmorama; but his appearance was stern and sombre, while the dead man guffawed and threatened me with his shroud. I woke up. Cold sweat was pouring from me in streams. At that moment there was a knock at the door.

– The Countess asks you to come and see her this minute, – said the servant as he came in.

I jumped up. Terrifying claps of thunder were ringing out and the clouds made it almost dark in the room: it was illuminated only by a flash of lightning. Dust rose up in a column from the violent wind and spattered against the windowpanes. But I had no time to pay attention to the storm: I dressed hurriedly and raced off to Eliza. No. I shall never forget her facial expression at that minute: she was as pale as death, her hands were shaking, her eyes were motionless. Proprieties were by now out of place: the language and conventions of society were forgotten.

– What's wrong, Eliza?

– Nothing! It's nonsense! Stupidity! An idle dream!....

At these words I felt a cold convulsion.... 'Dream?' – I repeated with astonishment....

– Yes! But an awful dream! Listen! – she said, shuddering at every crash of thunder, – I went to sleep calmly.... I was thinking about our future plans, about you, about our happiness.... At first my dreams reiterated the joyous flights of my imagination.... Until suddenly my deceased husband appeared before me – no, this was not a dream – I saw him, he himself; I recognised those familiar, still pursed, almost smiling lips, that hellish twitch of the black eyebrows, which always signalled with him an outburst of vengeance, without fear or favour.... It's horrible, Vladimir! Horrible!... I recognised that implacable, leaden gaze which breaks into bloody sparks at the moment of anger. I caught the sound of that voice again, which turns into a savage whistle from rage and which I had thought I would never hear any more....

'I know everything, Eliza, – he said, – I see everything. Here everything is clear to me. You are very glad that I died; you are already ready to marry someone else.... My tender, true wife!... You fool! You thought you could find happiness – you don't know that your ruin and the ruin of our children is tied up with your criminal love.... But this will not be; no! Astral life is still strong in me – my soul is earthly and does not wish to part with the earth.... Everyone here has told me – only by returning to earth can I save my children, only on earth can I take vengeance on you; and so I shall return, I shall return to your embraces, my loyal spouse! I have purchased this return at an extortionate and terrible price – a price which you cannot even comprehend.... In return all hell will come down with me on your criminal head – get ready to receive me. But listen: on earth I shall forget all that I have learned here; conceal your feelings from me, conceal them: otherwise woe betide you, and woe betide me!..'. At this point he touched my face with cold hands which had turned blue, and I awoke. It's horrible! Horrible! I can still feel his touch on my face....

Poor Eliza could hardly finish speaking; her tongue went dumb and she was as if in a fever all over. She drew convulsively towards me, covering her eyes with her hands, as though seeking to shield herself from the threatening vision. Somewhat disturbed myself, I tried to console her with the usual phrases about agitated nerves, the physical effect on them of the storm and play of the imagination, and myself felt how futile were all these words, contrived during tranquil and untroubled moments of human sagacity, in the face of a horrifying reality. I kept on talking, and calling to mind all the similar cases I had read of in medical books, when suddenly a window blew open, a violent gust of wind howled into the room and a noise signifying something abnormal resounded round the house....

– It is he... he's coming! – screamed Eliza and, pointing quiveringly to the door, she gesticulated to me with her hand....

I ran out of the door. Confusion reigned in the house. At the end of a dark corridor I could see a crowd of people. This crowd was approaching.... In a state of shock, I hugged the wall, with no strength to challenge or collect my thoughts.... Yes! Eliza was not mistaken. It was he! he! I could see the crowd, part leading and part carrying him. I could see his pallid face. I could see his sunken eyes, from which deathly sleep had yet to depart.... I heard the surrounding cries of joy, of amazement and of horror.... I heard the incoherent tales of how the Count had come to life, how he had risen from his coffin, how he had encountered the sacristan in the doorway, how the doctor had helped him.... Thus it was not an apparition, but reality! The dead were returning to violate the happiness of the living.... I stood as though petrified. When the Count drew level with me, in the confined space, his hand, which was convulsively extended, slid across my face and I shuddered, as though an electric spark had raced through my body. Everything surrounding me became transparent: the walls, the land and the people now appeared to me in a light penumbra, through which I could clearly discern another world, other objects, other people.... Every nerve in my body received the gift of sight; my magic gaze embraced at the one instant the past and the present, plus both what actually was and what could have been. There is no possibility of describing this whole picture as human words are inadequate to relate it....

I saw Count B at different ages of his life.... I saw how, above his mother's bed-head, at the moment of his birth, hideous monsters were writhing about, greeting the newly-born with wild joy. Here was his upbringing: a vile monster came between him and his tutor – whispering to the one and to the other confiding thoughts of egoism, nonbelief, callousness and pride. Now the appearance of the young man in society: the same vile monstrosity directs his behaviour, instills in him a subtle sharpness, caution and treachery, arranging certain success for him. The Count in women's society: an irresistible attraction draws them to him, he caresses one after the other and laughs with his guardian monster. Here he is at the card table: the monster selects the suits and whispers in his ear which card to play; he beats his friend and ruins him, a family man, and riches consolidate his successes in society. Here he is duelling: the monster whispers in his ear all the sophistries of the duel, hardens his heart and raises his arm; he shoots – his opponent's blood spattered over him and cast its stain with its eternal drops. The monster covers the traces of his crime. In one of the seconds of the duel, I recognised my late uncle. Here is the Count in the office of some top brass: he artfully slanders an honest man, blackens his character, destroys his happiness and takes over his position. Here he is in court: under a mask of rectitude he hides an inexorably cruel heart; he sees an innocent man and realises his innocence, but condemns him in order to exploit his rights. Everything comes off for him: he gets rich, he enjoys the reputation of an honest, upright, firm citizen. Here he is offering his hand to Eliza: on this hand are drops of blood and tears; she does not see them and gives him her hand. Eliza is, for him, a means to various ends: he compels her to participate in his dark and secret deeds, threatens her with all manner of horrors which would stretch the imagination and when, subject to his hellish power, she complies, he laughs at her and plans further crimes....

All these occurrences in his life are miraculously, inexpressibly connected by living links. From them mysterious threads reach out to countless figures, who were either victims or participants in his crimes, often permeating through several generations and joining them to this horrific family tree. Among these people I recognised my uncle, my aunt, Paul: all of them were as though interwoven within this net, connecting me with Eliza and her husband. As if this were not enough: his every feeling, his every thought and every word had the shape of living, deformed beings, with which he, as it were, had populated the universe.... In the final analysis, this whole monstrous concatenation was interlinked back to him, the semi-corpse, and he had brought the whole of it with him into this world. Living links, in the form of his children, united him with Eliza; to them, by other routes, the threads of their father's various crimes were attached and these surfaced in the form of vicious propensities of unwitting motivation. Among the crowd, there floated innumerable strange images, whose horrible effect it would be impossible to express on paper; there was nothing funny in their deformity, as is sometimes the case in paintings. They all had a human likeness, but their forms, colours and especially their expressions were diverse in the extreme: the nearer they were to the dead man, the more horrific they seemed. Under the wretch's very head there drifted a being whose gaze I shall never forget: its face was a dull green colour; crimson hair, like blood, streamed over its shoulders; from earthen coloured eyes there dripped fiery tears which penetrated the entire composition of the dead man and revitalised one organ after another. Never shall I forget the expression of sadness and spite with which this unfathomable creature looked at me....

I shall not describe this scene further. How can anyone describe the interlacement of all the inner motivations that spring up in a human soul, of which each one here had its own separate, animate existence? How can one describe all those mysterious deeds accomplished in the world by these creatures, which are invisible to the ordinary eye? Each one of them magically engendered from itself new creatures which, in their turn, pierced the hearts of other people, remote in time and space. I could see what a horrific, logical reciprocity there was in the actions of these people; the accretion of the smallest acts, words and thoughts, over the course of centuries, into one huge crime, the basic cause of which is completely lost to contemporaries; and how this crime has put forth new roots and, in its turn, engendered new centres of criminality. Between these dark engines of human sin, there drifted also bright images, begotten of the souls of the pure and un-bloodstained. They also joined together in living links, also magically multiplied themselves and by their presence annhilated the actions of the children of darkness. But, I repeat, to describe everything which presented itself then to my gaze would require several volumes. In that minute, the whole history of our world from the beginning of time was accessible to me; the interior of human history was laid bare before me and the inexplicable, in terms of its outer series of events, now seemed to me very simple and clear. And so, for example, my gaze gradually passed along the magic ladder, where the moral feeling aroused in the good Spaniard at the sight of the fires of the Inquisition engendered in his descendent a feeling of exploitation and harshness towards the Mexicans, still maintaining an aspect of legality; and finally this same feeling in succeeding generations turned simply into brutality and total spiritual collapse. I saw how my own heart's momentary motivation had its origin in the affairs of people who existed several generations before me.... I understood how important is every human thought and word, how far their influence extends, what heavy responsibility for them lies on the soul and what evil for the whole of humanity can arise from the heart of one person exposed to the influence of unclean and hostile beings.... I understood that the phrase 'man is the world' is not an empty play on words, thought up for amusement.... Sometime, in calmer moments, I shall commit to paper this history of the moral beings which inhabit a person and are engendered by his will, and of which only traces are preserved in the worldly chronicles.

What I can now relate only gradually was, at the time of my vision, presented to me in one and the same instant. My being was, as it were, fragmented. On the one hand, I saw the developing picture of the whole of humanity; on the other, a picture of the people whose fate was tied to my fate. In this unusual state of the organism, my mind felt equally the sufferings of people distant from me in space and time and the sufferings of the woman for whom love was massaging my heart with a fiery stream! Oh, she suffered, suffered inexpressibly!... She would fall on her knees in front of her tormentor and implore him to leave her or to take her with him. At that moment it was as if a curtain had fallen from my eyes: I recognised in Eliza that same woman whom I had once seen in the cosmorama; I cannot comprehend how until now I had been unable to recall this, although her face had always seemed familiar to me. In this phantasmagorical scene, I was beside her; I was similarly bowing the knee before the Count's double; the doctor's double, sobbing, was trying to entice me from this family unit: he was saying something to me with great ardour, but I couldn't catch his speech, although I could see the movement of his lips. In my ear I could hear only the vague cries of monsters, hovering above us. The doctor raised his hand and was pointing somewhere; I strained all my attention and, through thousands of transient monstrous beings, thought I recognised the image of Sophia, but only for an instant, and this image seemed to me a distorted one....

During the whole of this strange spectacle I was in a state of paralysis: my mind did not know what my body was doing. When some semblance of susceptibility to external feelings had returned to me, I found myself in my room at the inn; beside me stood Doctor Bin with a phial in his hands....

– What? – I asked, coming to.

– All right! He's perfectly fit! A pulse like that, it's a miracle....

– Whose?

– The Count's! Wonderful deeds we've been doing! And to tell you the truth, I never imagined, and have never come across it in books, that there could be such a fierce swoon. Well, it was exactly as though he were dead. I thought I had had quite a bit of experience in my time; but there you are, as they say, you live and learn! And as for you, young man! And you were a military man, too; you took fright, thinking that a dead man was on the move.... I had a job rubbing some life back into you.... Where would you be without us, we medics! We're a valiant race.... I went out on to the street to see where the storm was coming from, and what did I see, but my dead patient staggering along and people fleeing from him in all directions. So I said to myself: 'Here's an intriguing case', went over to him, – I had to shout, and call people, and they weren't too keen on coming; I soon gave him a bit of this and that – now there's not a thing wrong with him and he'll live another twenty years. I shall certainly write this case up, explicate it and send it to Paris, to the academy, I shall thunder it around Europe – let them interpret it...it's impossible! a most intriguing case!...

The doctor went on talking for some time, but I didn't listen to him; but one thing I did understand: all this was not a dream and not delirium – a dead man really had returned to the living, reanimated with false life, and was taking my life's happiness away from me.... 'Horses!' – I cried.

I can hardly remember how and why I was brought back to Moscow: it seems I had not given any orders and it was my valet who sorted me out. For a long time I did not show myself in society and spent my days alone, in a state of unfeeling, which was interrupted by bouts of inexpressible suffering. I felt that all my abilities had been extinguished, my intellect had lost all judgement, and my heart remained without desires. My imagination reminded me only of that awful, incomprehensible spectacle, the very thought of which was enough to confuse all my thinking and to bring me to a state aproaching madness.

I inadvertently remembered my unsophisticated cousin. I remembered how she alone possessed the knack of calming my soul. How glad I was that at least some desire or other had stolen into my heart!

My aunt was ill, but she ordered that I be received. Pale and racked with illness, she was sitting in her armchair. Sophia was attending her, arranging the cushions and giving her sips to drink; she had scarcely looked at me, but she almost started crying.

– Oh! How sorry I feel for you! – she said through her tears.

– Who's that you're sorry for, young woman? – asked my aunt, in a breaking voice.

– Well, it's Vladimir Andreyevich! I don't know what the reason is, but I cannot look at him without tears....

– Well, you'd do better, young woman, to feel pity for me; there, you see, and he didn't think of visiting his sick aunt....

I do not know what reply I gave to this reproach of my aunt's, which was not her last. In the end she calmed down somewhat.

– You see, young man, I only speak like that because I love you. Why, Sophie and I have often talked about you....

– Oh, Auntie! Why are you telling fibs? We never even mentioned my cousin....

– So! So, after all! – yelled my aunt in a fury, – she has to put her spoke in! You'll have to make allowances, young man, for our simplicity. I was just wanting to pay you a compliment, you see, when my instructress, here, has to intervene. You'd do better, young woman, to worry about something else... – and she heaped reproaches on the poor girl.

I noticed that my aunt's personality had quite changed from her illness. She was bored with everybody and annoyed at everything; she particularly mercilessly scolded kind Sophia. Everything was wrong, no one was sufficiently concerned about her, no one understood her properly. She complained bitterly to me about Sophia, and then, from her, turned to her relatives and friends, sparing no one. With a surprising exactness, she recalled everything disagreeable in her life, blamed everyone, grumbled about everyone and once again brought all her reproaches down on Sophia.

I silently observed this unfortunate girl, who with angelic meekness heard the old woman out, while at the same time seeing what she could do for her. I was trying with my gaze to penetrate that invisible link which joined me to Sophia, to transmit my soul into her heart – but in vain: before me was just an ordinary girl, in a white dress, with a glass in her hands.

When my aunt had tired from speaking, I said to Sophia, almost in a whisper: 'So, you feel very sorry for me?'

– Yes! Very sorry and I don't know why.

– And I really pity *you*, – I said, indicating my aunt with my eyes.

– Never mind, – replied Sophia, – everything on earth is shortlived, both grief and joy; we shall die, something else will be....

– What frights are you talking about now! – cried my aunt, catching the last words. – What a consolation she is, young man, I must say. Something to amuse a sick person, to cheer them up? But oh no, she starts talking about death. Are you trying to drop hints, so I don't forget you in my will, or something? Do you want me in my grave as soon as can be? What a little self-seeker! Oh no, my young woman, I'll outlive you yet....

Sophia calmly looked the old woman in the eye and said: 'Auntie! you're not telling the truth...'.

My aunt lost her head: 'What do you mean, not telling the truth? So you are getting ready to bury me.... Just tell me, young man, can I endure this? Look what a serpent I've been cherishing here'.

Among the attendant maids I noted a rumbling disapproval; such words reached me as: 'She's wicked! That's nice! She'll be the death of her!'

In vain did I try to reassure my aunt that she had taken Sophia's words the wrong way: I only succeeded in annoying her still further. Finally, I decided to go; Sophia accompanied me.

– Why do you send Auntie into such frenzies? – I asked my cousin.

– It's nothing; she's angry with me for a little while, and then she will keep thinking about death; it's good for her....

– What an incomprehensible creature you are! – I exclaimed, – teach me about dying, too!

Sophia looked at me in astonishment.

– I don't know about it myself; though, the person who wants to learn is already half educated.

– What do you mean by that?...

– Nothing! That's what's written in my album....

At that moment the bell rang. 'Auntie is calling me, – murmured Sophia, - you see, I was right: her anger has passed now, now she will cry and crying is good, very good, especially when you don't know why you are crying'.

With these words she disappeared from view.

I returned home deep in thought, threw myself into an armchair and tried to take stock of my situation. First Sophia would appear to me to be some sort of a mysterious, good creature, who was guarding me, whose every word had a deep meaning, connected with my existence; then I would start to laugh at myself, and would recall that to my thoughts about Sophia my imagination had added what I had read in the old legends, that she was simply a good girl, but very ordinary, who, to the point or otherwise, liked to repeat the most childish maxims. These maxims probably only struck me in that, within the currents of the strong, positive thought of our century, they had been forgotten and seemed new, like the Gothic furniture in our drawing rooms. But at the same time, Sophia's words about death involuntarily sounded in my ears, involuntarily, so to speak, acted as a magnet to all my other thoughts and in the end conjoined into one centre all my spiritual powers. Little by little, all surrounding objects disappeared, as far as I was concerned; an inexplicable languor kindled my heart and my eyes unexpectedly filled with tears. This amazed me! 'Who is that crying in me?' – I exclaimed rather loudly, and it seemed to me as if someone was replying. I felt a wave of cold and I could not move my arm. I seemed to be rooted to the armchair and suddenly I began to feel within me that inexpressible sensation which usually preceded my visions and to which I had by now grown accustomed. And indeed, within a few moments my room had become transparent and in the distance, as though through a bright steam, I again saw the face of Sophia....

'No! – I said to myself: – let us gather our strength of mind and take a cold look at this phantasmagoria. It's good for a child to be frightened of it: but isn't there enough already which seems inexplicable?' And I fixed on this strange vision the sort of seering gaze with which the natural scientist examines a curious physical object.

The vision was covered as though with a greenish steam; Sophia's face became clearer, but seemed to me to take on a distorted look.

'Ah! – I said to myself: – the green colour is of some significance here; let's think about this properly: various gases also produce the sensation of the colour green to the eye; these gases have a stupefying quality - exactly so! The refraction of the green rays is connected with the narcotic effect on

120

our nerves, and conversely. Now, let's go a bit further: the apparition has become clearer? That's what it should do: that means that it's transparent. Exactly so! In microscopes they deliberately use greenish lenses for looking at transparent insects: their forms become clearer because of that...'.

In order to preserve my equanimity and not to submit to the power of the imagination, I noted down my observations on paper. But this soon became impossible: the vision came closer to me, everything became clearer, and at the same time all other objects paled. The paper on which I was writing, the table and my own body became as transparent as glass; whichever way I looked, the vision followed my gaze. I recognised Sophia in it: the same appearance, the same hair and the same smile, but the expression was different. She was looking at me with treacherous, voluptuous eyes and, in a brazen sort of fashion, proffering me her embraces.

– You don't know, – she was saying, – how I am longing to be married to you! You're rich, and I'll get something out of the old woman somehow, and we would be well off. Why don't you give in to me? However much I lead you on, however I flirt with you, I get nowhere. Do my severe words frighten you off, and does my virginal ignorance surprise you? Don't believe it! It's all a bait with which I'm trying to catch you, because you don't recognise happiness when you see it yourself. Just marry me – you'll see what I can really be like. You like amusement – so do I. You love squandering money – I can beat you at that. Our house will be a wonder; we'll give balls, and invite our relatives to them; then we'll ingratiate ourselves with them and we'll be showered with inheritances.... You'll see, I'm a past mistress in these things....

I was numbed, listening to this speech; such revulsion for Sophia was born in my heart that I can hardly express it. I remembered all her mysterious actions, all her double-meaninged words – everything was now clear to me! A cunning demon was hidden in her under a mask of innocence.... The vision disappeared – in the distance there remained only a brilliant point; this point gradually increased in size and approached – it was my Eliza! Oh, how can I narrate what then transpired with me? All my nerves trembled, my heart began to thump and my arms, of their own accord, reached out towards this vision of seduction. She seemed to be floating in the air – her curls, like a light vapour, twined and untwined; waves of transparent veil stretched over her splendid shoulders, grappled with her waist and flapped against her shapely pink legs. Her hands were clasped and she looked at me reproachfully.

– You are unfaithful and ungrateful! – she said, in a voice which, like melted lead, inflamed my heart, – you have already forgotten me! You child! You were frightened of a dead man! You've forgotten that I am

121

suffering, suffering beyond expression, beyond consolation. You've forgotten that between us there is an eternal vow which is indelible! Are you afraid of public opinion? Are you afraid of meeting the dead man? But I, I haven't changed. Your Eliza aches and weeps, she seeks you awake and in dreams – she is waiting for you. She doesn't care about anything; she's not afraid of anything; she will sacrifice everything for you....

– Eliza! I am yours, eternally yours! Nothing will separate us! – I cried, as though the vision could hear me.... Eliza sobbed, beckoned me, held out her hand to me – so close, that it seemed that I could grab it – until suddenly another hand came into view beside that of Eliza.... Between us appeared the mysterious doctor; he was dressed in tatters, his eyes were burning and his limbs were quivering. He appeared and then disappeared; he seemed to be struggling with some invisible force and trying to speak to me, but I could only pick up isolated words: 'Run... doom... mysterious revenge... is taking place... your uncle... moved him... to a mortal crime... his fate is decided... him... crushing... spirit of the earth... drive away... she is stained with innocent blood... he is doomed beyond all hope... he wants revenge for his ruin... horribly evil... for that reason he returned to earth... disaster... perdition...'.

But the doctor disappeared and Eliza remained alone. As before, she stretched out her hands to me and beckoned me, as she disappeared.... In despair, I watched her go....

A knock at the door interrupted my disappointment. One of my friends came in to see me.

– Where are you these days? You haven't been seen at all! What's wrong with you? You are not yourself....

– It's nothing; I was just... thinking.

– You will end up going mad, I promise you, and that without fail; and I hear you've had some little devils appearing to you....

– Yes! A nervous weakness.... But now it's gone....

– If only we could put you in the hands of a mesmerist, that would sort you out in no time....

– How is that?

– You have exactly that type of organism, the sort needed for.... You could have made a *clairvoyant*....

– A clairvoyant! – I yelled....

– Yes, but I don't advise you to experiment: I know that department very well; it's a disease that leads to madness. If a man wanders in a mesmeric dream, he'll then start to wander all the time....

– But you can be cured of this illness....

– Without a doubt: amusement, society, cold baths.... Really, think

about it. What's the use of sitting here? You'll only add to your troubles....
What are you going to do today, for example?

   – I was going to stay at home.

   – Rubbish, we'll go to the theatre, there's a new opera; I have a whole box at your disposal....

   I agreed.

Mesmerism!... It's amazing, I thought along the way, that this had not occurred to me before. I had heard something of it, but not much. Perhaps that is where I would find an explanation for my strange mental condition. I would have to flick through a few books on magnetism.

   Meanwhile we had arrived. There were few people yet in the theatre; the box beside our's remained unoccupied. On the poster in front of me, I read: 'The Vampire: an opera by Marschner'. I did not know the work and it was with curiosity that I listened to the first notes of the overture. Suddenly an involuntary movement made me look round; the door in the neighbouring box creaked; I looked – and in walked my Eliza. She looked at me, bowed amicably, and her pale face flushed. Her husband walked in behind her. I seemed to detect a whiff of the grave, but this was a flight of the imagination. I had not seen him in the two months or so since his revival. He had made a considerable recovery: his face had all but lost any signs of illness.... He whispered something in Eliza's ear and she replied just as quietly, but I realised that she had pronounced my name. My thoughts were becoming confused: what with my previous love for Eliza, my anger and jealousy, my visions and reality – all of this together was bringing me to a state of severe agitation, which I tried in vain to conceal under a mask of normal social composure. And this woman could have been mine, completely mine! Our love was not illicit; to me, she was a widow. She could dispose of her hand without a twinge of conscience: and there was this dead man – a dead man between us!

   I had lost all interest in the opera; profiting from my place in the box, I appeared to be looking at the stage, but I did not take my eyes off Eliza and her husband. She was more languid than previously, but more beautiful than ever. I mentally arrayed her in the dress in which she had appeared to me in that vision; my feelings became aroused and my mind could hardly contain itself within my body. From her, my gaze passed to my mystifying rival; at first glance his face had no particular expression, but, on closer inspection, one would be unwittingly convinced that the imprint of crime lay upon this face. In that part of the opera where the vampire asks a passer-by to turn him towards the shining of the moon, which will reanimate him, the Count shuddered convulsively. I fixed my eyes on him with great curiosity, but he coldly took up his lorgnette and guided it around the theatre: whether this had been a recollection of his adventure, a simple physical play of nerves, or an inner murmur of his mysterious destiny – one guess was as good as another.

The first act finished; etiquette required that I should speak to Eliza. I approached the balustrade of her box. She introduced me to her husband with great indifference. He spoke a few amicable phrases to me, with the familiarity natural to an experienced man of society. We conversed on the subjects of the opera and of society. The Count's conversation was witty and his remarks subtle: those of an obviously worldly man who, under a mask of indifference and mockery, conceals an intimate acquaintance with the multifarious branches of human knowledge. Being in such close proximity to him, I was able to examine those crimson sparks in his eyes, of which Eliza had spoken. However, this play of nature contained nothing unpleasant; on the contrary, it enlivened the Count's penetrating glance. Noticeable too was a kind of spite present in the convulsive movement of his thin lips, but this could be taken merely as the expression of normal worldly mockery.

The next day I received from the Count an invitation to a reception; not long afterwards to dinner *en petit comité* and so on. In short, almost every week I saw my Eliza at least once, joked with her husband, played with her children, who, although they were not very likeable, were extremely funny. They looked more like their father than their mother and were serious beyond their years, which I attributed to a strict upbringing. Their words frequently surprised me by their gravity and their mocking tone, but I, not without a certain displeasure, noticed on these childish faces clear enough signs already of that convulsive twitching of the lips which I found so unpleasant in the Count. As for conversation with the Countess, we, it goes without saying, were in need of no preparatory measures: we understood every hint, every gesture; however, no one from appearances would have been able to divine our long-standing relationship, for we conducted ourselves with caution and permitted ourselves even to look at each other only when the Count was sitting at cards, for which he had a passion beyond belief.

Thus several months went by. Not once had I yet managed to see Eliza alone, but she promised me an assignation and I lived with that hope.

Meanwhile, ruminating on all the strange incidents which had befallen me, I provided myself with all the available books on magnetism. Puységur, Deleuze, Wolfart and Kieser never left my table. Eventually, so I thought, I found the solution to my psychic state; I soon started to laugh at my previous fears, banished all gloomy, mystifying thoughts and finally persuaded myself that the whole mystery was contained in my physical organism, that what had been happening with me was something like the so-called 'second sight', which was very well known in Scotland. I discovered with joy that this type of nervous disease went away with the years and that there existed a means of eliminating it altogether. Following this information, I planned out for myself a style of life which should lead me to the desired goal. I battled strongly against the least tendency towards somnambulism, as I called my condition. Riding, incessant activity, the bath – all this together had an effect on the improvement of my physical health, and the idea of a meeting with Eliza drove all other thoughts from my head.

One day after dinner, when a group of social parasites gathered around Eliza, she insensitively started a conversation about superstitions and omens. 'There are some very intelligent people, – said Eliza coolly, – who believe in omens and, what is stranger still, have strong evidence for their belief; for example, my husband never misses a New Year's Eve reception, so as not to miss playing cards. He says that on that day he always feels an unusual sharpness, has an unusually keen memory; on that day such computations at cards enter his head, as he would not have imagined: on that day, he says, I study for the whole year'. This story produced a volley of comments, each one more vacuous than the last. I alone grasped the meaning of this anecdote: one glance from Eliza explained everything to me.

– It seems to be ten o'clock now, – she said after a little while....

– No, it's eleven already, – replied several simpletons.

– *Le temps m'a paru trop court dans votre société, messieurs...* – said Eliza in that special tone by which an intelligent woman lets it be felt that she does not at all think the same thing that she is saying; but for me it was enough.

So, New Year's Eve, and at ten o'clock.... No, never had I experienced greater joy! For the duration of days and days, to see the woman whom you had once held in your embraces, to see her and not to dare to take advantage of one's right, and finally to end up with that happy, rare moment.... You have to experience this feeling, which is incomprehensible in any other condition!

In the final days before New Year I could not sleep, lost my appetite and shuddered at every swing of the pendulum; I kept waking up all the time at night and looking at the clock, as though afraid of losing a minute.

Finally, New Year's Eve came. That night I had really not slept a single minute and I rose from my bed worn out, with a headache. In an indescribable agitation, I wandered from corner to corner and with my gaze followed the slow movement of the hands. Eight o'clock struck; I fell on the divan in complete exhaustion.... I was seriously afraid that I would be taken ill, and at such a time!... A light slumber began to come over me. I called my valet: 'Make some coffee and, if I go to sleep, wake me up at nine o'clock, but without fail – do you hear? If you leave me as much as a minute over time, I will drive you out of the house; if you wake me on time – there'll be a hundred roubles'.

With these words I sat in the armchair, bowed my head and fell into a deep sleep.... A horrific crash awoke me. I woke up and my hands and my face were wet and cold...at my feet lay a huge bronze clock, smashed to smithereens – my valet said that, sitting by it, I had probably caught it with my arm, although he had not noticed this. I seized the cup of coffee, when the sound of the other clock, from the next room, was heard. I started to count: it struck one, two, three... eight, nine, ten!.. eleven!.. twelve!... The cup flew at my valet. 'What have you done?' – I shouted, in a frenzy.

– It's not my fault, – replied the unfortunate valet, wiping himself; – I carried out your order exactly, I came over to wake you – you didn't wake up; I lifted you out of the armchair and you were pleased to reply, just: 'It's too early for me yet, early... for God's sake... don't destroy me', – and again you collapsed into the chair. In the end I decided to pour cold water over you, but nothing helped; you just repeated: 'Don't destroy me'. I was just on the point of sending for the doctor, but I didn't have time to get to the door before the clock, I don't know why, fell and you were pleased to wake up....

I paid no attention to my valet's words, dressed as hurriedly as I could, threw myself into my carriage and galloped off to the Countess.

To the question: 'Is the Count at home?' – the doorman replied: 'No, but the Countess is at home and receiving visitors'. I did not run up, but flew up the staircase! In the further room, Eliza was waiting for me. When she caught sight of me, she shrieked in despair: 'So late! The Count is due to return soon; we have lost irrecoverable time!'

I did not know what to reply, but moments were precious, it was no time for reproaches, and we rushed into each other's embraces. We had much, much to talk about: the past to tell about, the present and the future to make arrangements about. Fate had so capriciously played with us: one moment it had united us so closely, another it had for so long separated us by an entire abyss. Our life had been connected by fragments, like the momentary inspirations of a careless artist. So much in it remained unexplained, not understood, unfinished. I only then found out that Eliza's life was a

126

hell, filled with all kinds of tortures; that her husband's temper had become worse than ever; that he tormented her daily, simply for pleasure; that the children were a new source of suffering for her; that her husband had been pursuing and trying to kill every pure thought in them, every noble feeling; that he by words and example had been introducing them to concepts and passions that were horrible, even in a mature person; and when poor Eliza tried to save these blameless souls from infection, he trained the unfortunate babes to laugh at their mother.... The whole picture was ghastly. We talked for some time about the possibility of having recourse to the protection of the law, calculating all the probable successes and failures, all the advantages and disadvantages of such action.... But then our conversation began to dry up and continually broke off – the words dying on our burning lips; we had waited for this moment for so long. Eliza was so seductively attractive. Indignation aroused our feelings still further; her hand dug into my hand, her head was drawn to me, as though seeking protection.... We did not recall where we were or what was happening to us, and when Eliza in a state of amnesia languished on my breast...the door was not opened, but her husband appeared beside us.

I shall never forget that face. He was as pale as death, his hair was bristling on his head as though electrified; he shook as though in a fever, but remained silent, breathless and smiling. Eliza and I stood as though turned to stone; he grabbed us both by the hand...his face grimaced...his cheeks turned crimson...his eyes lit up...he silently fixed them on us.... It seemed to me that a fiery, bloody ray was being emitted from them.... A magic power had fettered my movements, I couldn't budge and I dared not remove my eyes from this terrible gaze.... The expression on his face became more ferocious with every instant, while his eyes shone ever brighter and his face became more purple.... Was it not a real fire reddening beneath his nerves?... His hand was burning my hand...another instant and he would be irridescent as hot iron.... Eliza screamed... the furniture started smoking...a blue flame ran over all the dead man's limbs...amid the sanguinary brilliance were revealed the white features of his bones.... Eliza's dress started to burn; in vain did I want to extract her hand from that revengeful clasp...the dead man's eyes followed her every movement and burned through her...his face turned an ashen colour, his hair went white and curled; only his lips cut across his face in a crimson stripe and smiled a treacherous smile.... The flame developed with an unimaginable swiftness: the curtains blazed up, as did the flowers and the pictures; the floor flared up, and the ceiling, and a thick smoke filled the whole room.... 'The children! the children!' – cried Eliza in a desperate voice. 'They're coming with us too!' – replied the dead man with a raucous guffaw....

From that moment I do not remember what happened to me.... A pungent, hot stench was choking me and forcing me to close my eyes. I could hear, as though in a dream, the howls of people and the crash of the house, which was collapsing around me.... I do not know how my hand was extricated from that of the dead man: I could feel myself free and an animal instinct made me throw myself in various directions, in order to avoid falling rafters.... At that moment only, I noticed in front of me a sort of white cloud.... I looked closely at it...the face of Sophia gleamed within this cloud...she was smiling sadly and beckoning to me.... I involuntarily followed her.... Where the apparition flew, there the flames bent back and fresh, fragrant air revived my breathing...I went on, and on....

Finally, I saw that I was back in my room.

For a long time I did not come to; I didn't know whether I was sleeping or not. I looked myself over: my clothes had not smouldered; only on my hand did there remain a black stain... the sight of this was a shock to my nerves and I again lost consciousness....

When I returned to my senses, I was lying in bed, without the strength to utter a word.

– Thank God! The crisis has ended! There is hope – said someone beside me. I recognised the voice of Doctor Bin. I made an effort to say a few words, but my tongue did not obey me.

After long days of complete silence, my first words were 'What about Eliza?'

– Quite all right! Quite all right! Thank God, she's fine and sends you her regards....

My strength was exhausted by the pronunciation of that question, but the Doctor's reply calmed me.

I began to recover. My friends started to visit. One day, when I was looking at my hand and trying to remember what the black stain on it meant, I was struck by hearing the Count's name, uttered by one of those present, but I could not make sense of the conversation.

– What about the Count? – I asked, raising myself up on the pillows.

– Yes, of course, you used to be a regular visitor there, – replied my acquaintance, – really, don't you know what happened to him? What a fate! On New Year's Eve he was playing cards at ***; luck was unusually favourable to him; he carried home an immense sum. But just imagine – that night a fire broke out in his house; everything was burned: he himself, his wife, the children, the house – as though they had never been. The police worked wonders, but all in vain: not a thread was saved. The firemen said that they had never seen a fire like it: they reckoned that even the stones were burning. In fact the house has entirely crumbled, there's not even a chimney sticking up....

I didn't finish listening to this story: that horrific night was vividly restored to my memory and terrible shudders shook my whole body.

– What have you done, gentlemen! – shouted Doctor Bin – but it was already too late: I was again approaching death's door. However, whether it was due to my youth, or to the Doctor's care, or my mysterious destiny – I don't know, but I remained among the living.

From then on, Doctor Bin became more cautious. He stopped allowing acquaintances in to see me and himself almost never left me....

One day – I was already sitting up in my armchair – there was no anxiety in me any more, but a heavy sadness, as heavy as lead, pressed on my heart. The doctor looked at me with an inexpressible sympathy.

– Listen, – I said, – I am now feeling reasonably strong already; don't conceal anything from me: not knowing torments me even more....

– Ask what you like, – replied the doctor dolefully, – I am ready to answer you....

– What about my aunt?

– She has died.

– And Sophia?

– Soon after her, – said the kind old man, almost in tears.

– When? How?

– She was completely healthy, but suddenly, on New Year's Eve, she had these incomprehensible attacks. I have never seen such an illness: it was as though all her body had suffered burns....

– Burns?...

– Yes! at least, that's what it looked like; that's the way I would put it to you, because you are not a medical expert; but it was, it stands to reason, a sort of acute water....

– And did she suffer for long?

– Oh no, thank God! If you had seen with what patience she bore her torments, how she asked about everyone, took an interest in everything.... Really, she was a true angel, although she was a little on the simple side. Yes and, by the way, she did not forget you: she tore out a sheet from her note book and asked me to give it to you, in her memory. This is it.

With a tremble I seized the precious sheet of paper. On it were written only the following words from some moralizing text: 'The highest form of love is to suffer for another...'. I pressed this sheet of paper to my lips with an inexpressible feeling. When I went to read it again, I noticed that under these words there were others. 'Everything has come true! – said the magical letter, – the sacrifice has been made! There's no need to feel sorry for me – I am happy! Your path is still a long one and its ending depends upon you. Remember my words: a pure heart is the highest blessing; search for it'.

Tears poured from my eyes, but these were not tears of despair.

I shall not describe the details of my recovery, but I shall attempt, albeit lightly, to chart the new sufferings which I had to undergo, for my path is long, as Sophia said.

On one occasion, sadly running through all the events of my life, I was trying to fathom the mysterious links which joined me to beings whom I loved and to people almost alien to me. There arose in me a strong desire to find out what was happening to Eliza.... I hardly had time to desire any such thing, before my mysterious door opened. I saw Eliza in front of me; she was exactly the same as on that last day, just as young and just as beautiful. She was sitting in deep silence and crying; an inexpressible sadness could be seen in all her features. Beside her were her children; they looked sorrowfully at Eliza, as though expecting something from her. Memories welled up in my breast and all my previous love for Eliza was resurrected. 'Eliza! Eliza!' -- I cried, stretching out my arms to her.

She looked at me with bitter reproach...and her dreaded husband appeared in front of her. He was still the same as in that last minute: his face the colour of ash, across which were slit, like a thin filament, his crimson lips; his hair white, curled up into a tangle. With a fierce and mocking air he looked at Eliza – and what then? She and the children turned pale – their faces, like their father's, turned ashen; their lips, extended in a crimson streak, reached towards their father in convulsive torment and twined themselves around his limbs.... I cried out in horror and covered my face with my hands.... The vision disappeared, but not for long. I just had to look at my hand and it would remind me of Eliza; I just had to recall her, my previous passion would awaken in my heart and she would appear before me again, would again look reproachfully at me, would again turn ashen and again convulsively reach towards her tormentor....

I decided not to repeat my horrific experience any more, and for the sake of Eliza's happiness I tried to forget about her. In order to amuse myself, I started to go out and to see my friends. But soon, as I recovered, I began to notice something strange in them: in the first instance they would recognise me and be glad to see me, but then, little by little, a certain coldness, almost revulsion even, would arise in them. They would make efforts to become friendly with me, and something would involuntarily antagonise them. Whoever started a conversation with me would, within a minute, try to break it off; in the clubs people would be turned away from me by some inscrutable force and they stopped visiting me. Servants, despite generous salaries and the unusual calmness of my disposition, did not stay with me more than a month. Even the street where I lived became less populated. No animal would attach itself to me. In the end, as I noted with horror, birds would never even land on the roof of my house. Only Doctor Bin remained faithful to me; but he too failed to understand me and, in my stories about the strange wasteland in which I found myself, he saw only a play of the imagination.

But that is not the half of it. It seemed as though all possible misfortunes were befalling me. Nothing whatever that I undertook had any success. In my villages, misfortunes followed one after the other. Lawsuits were started against me from all sides, while even old, long forgotten cases were renewed. In vain did I wish with all possible vigour to combat this attack by the fates. Nowhere amongst my associates did I find any advice, assistance or good will. The greatest injustices were perpetrated against me and were accepted by everyone as righteous deeds. I reached a state of complete despair....

One day, having heard of the loss of half my estate in a most unjust hearing, I flew into such a rage as I had never before experienced. I automatically turned over in my mind all the contrivances which had been used against me, all the misdirections of my judges, all the coldness of my acquaintances and my heart throbbed with annoyance... and once again the mysterious door opened before me and I could see all those faces because of whom I was inflamed with anger – a horrific spectacle! In the other world my moral anger assumed a physical force: it afflicted my enemies with all possible calamities, sending them violent convulsions, torments of conscience and all manner of malicious horrors.... They stretched out their hands towards me in lament and prayed for mercy, assuring me that in our world they were acting in accordance with some clandestine and insuperable motivation....

From that moment on, this calamitous door of my soul has never closed for as much as an instant. Day and night there crowd around me apparitions – of people known to me and unknown. I cannot as much as think of anyone, either with love or with anger; everyone who loved me or hated me, everyone who had the slightest dealings with me, who had ever had any connection with me: all were suffering and imploring me to avert my eyes....

In a state of inexpressible horror, tormented every minute, I fear to think, fear to feel, fear to love and hate! But is this a possible state for anyone? How can you train yourself not to think, not to feel? Thoughts appear unwittingly in my mind – and instantly before my eyes are transformed into a torment to humanity. I have given up all my connections, my wealth. I have buried myself alive in a small, remote village, in the depths of an impenetrable forest, not known to anyone. I am afraid to meet anyone, for everyone I look at falls ill. I am afraid to admire a flower, for that flower will instantly wither before my eyes.... It's awful! Awful!... And meanwhile that incomprehensible world, summoned by a magic force, seethes in front of me: all enticements appear before me there, all of life's seductions; the women are there, my family is there, all the enchantments of life are there; in vain do I close my eyes, in vain!

Whether this experience of mine will pass sooner or later – who can tell? Sometimes, when tears of pure, feverish repentance pour from my eyes, when, having cast aside pride, I with humility recognise all the deformity of my heart, the vision disappears and I calm down – but not for long! The fatal door has been opened: I, a denizen of this world, belong to the other one; I am an actor there against my will; there I – dreadful to relate – there I am an *instrument of torture!*

1839

THE SALAMANDER

Author's Foreword

In this tale readers will find an experimental story based for the most part on Finnish popular beliefs. To Grot, the translator of Tegnér's *Frithiofs saga*, who so usefully devoted his labours to Finland, we are obliged for the unexpected and highly curious disclosure of precious details on the character and the legends of the Finns, which are so strikingly distinct from the legends of all other peoples (see *The Contemporary*, 1839-40). We cannot judge the Finns without having penetrated their lands and acquainted ourselves with their family routine. Their innate passion for the miraculous is united with a strong poetic element and a half wild attachment to their land. In general, the Finns are kind, patient, obedient to the authorities, attached to their obligations, but distrustful and so cunning that, when they see a stranger, they can opportunely pretend not to understand him. Once annoyed, their vengeance knows no bounds. They live not in villages, but in isolated huts scattered among the granite rocks. They have little to do not only with other people but even with each other. That is why news of everything happening in the world reaches them in the form of distorted rumour. In every hut such a rumour is supplemented by some wonderful story (for the Finns are great storytellers) and thus, little by little, an event which happened yesterday is turned by them into a fabulous legend: a curious phenomenon, explicable to a certain extent by the way in which ancient myths are depicted. In general, the Finns could be called a people of antiquity who have been brought forward to our epoch. Lönnrot, the excellent Finnish poet, wandering over all parts of his country, has collected folk songs which had never been written down before; looking over them, he noticed a certain link between them. After further research, Lönnrot discovered that these folk songs are a part of a whole harmonious poem and thus he furnished new proof for adherents of Wolf's views on the origins of *The Iliad*. Legends of the events of the times of Peter and Charles XII are still alive in the memory of the Finns, but have been transformed into fabulous legend. A life close to nature has taught them to know the properties of grasses and roots; they are familiar too with the secrets of animal magnetism. All this has a magic role for them: witness the tales of the Russian peasants who settled in Finland. From the letter of a Russian peasant to the Emperor Alexander (Grot in *The Contemporary*) one can see how eagerly the Finns love to argue about everything they can find out about, and what viewpoint they have on things. In general the life, legends and beliefs of this people deserve attention in the highest degree and are an unvalued store of treasure for literary works.

I

The Southern shore of Finland at the beginning of the eighteenth century

Dedicated to Countess Emilia K-e Musina-Pushkina

'Gina, throw a bit more wood into the stove. It's no use being summer if it's still not warm, or else I can't feel the warm in my old age'. Gina stood up and threw a few pine logs into the hearth. The resinous bark flamed up strongly and covered the whole hut with a lively, cheerful light. The old woman heaved a sigh.

– You see, – she said, – when we had Pavali with us, I didn't carry the wood. Now the wood's coming to an end, who's going to bring us any to the hut?

And the old woman sat with her head in her hands.

– Never mind, he'll come yet; he'll drag back the wood and chop the kindling for Christmas, – said the old man in a shaky voice, which sounded as though he did not trust his own words.

And she fell silent. Meanwhile a boy of about twelve came out from behind the pile of brushwood, the adopted child of the poor Finn, and merrily pulled little Elsa, the grand-daughter of the old people, along behind him. But Elsa didn't want to go over to the stove and broke away from his clutches. Yakko teased her and laughed loudly, but catching sight of the sorrowful look of the old man, he fell silent and quietly sat down on the floor, opposite the fire.

The hut in which this minor scene was enacted was built right on the bank of the Vuoksi. Now the banks of the Vuoksi have been flattened out and cleared, and an even path with railings stretches over the rocks. Pavilions in the tasteless English fashion, well whitened, await idle travellers; but even now, as previously, horror overcomes the person who dares to glance into the terrifying gurgling abyss. The River Vuoksi is silent and calm in its flow; but unceasingly the rocks either lie across her, or squeeze her by narrowing her banks, and the river boils, seethes and bursts down towards its kindred sea, crawls on to the cliffs, throws its white foam into the air in waves and rips up huge pines. The pines fall into the deep and, in no time and within a kilometer of the rapids, the Vuoksi throws the debris of a huge tree on to the shore – and then again flows on silently and calmly. The river is like a good person, whom fate annoys at every step on life's path: strongly and angrily he struggles with fate, but after the struggle everything calms down in his soul and once again a clear sun shines on it.

For a hundred and thirty years there were neither roads nor pavilions on Imatra. Idle newcomers from Petersburg did not turn for amusement to the menacing strength of the natural surroundings. These retained all their virginal grandeur. But even then, as now, between the rapids there would slither the occasional fisherman's skiff. Full of courage, he would trust to his native river and calmly cast his nets between the gurgling chasms. On the bank was a Finnish hut, leaning against two cliffs. Between the stones, encrusted with yellow moss, the roots of the trees threaded their way and their branches interwove above the roof, which was packed down with green turf. The hut was dark; a four-cornered stove with ever-burning wood, a few stumps of pine, a pile of brushwood which served as a bed, and on the wall a kantele, the Finnish folk instrument like a horizontal harp with hair strings: that was all that adorned the poor dwelling of the fisherman.

The wind whistled through the porthole ventilating window, which was not shut fast, and sometimes ran over the strings of the kantele: the strings would sound sorrowfully and dissonantly. When the wind quietened down, the howl of the rapids could be heard. The walls of the old hut would tremble and the door would creak, swinging on its hinges. Sparks poured out from the stove, smoke issued in clouds from its opening. At times a strong squally rain poured through the roof and sprayed the inhabitants; but they, it seemed, were used to all this and paid no attention to any of it.

And so quite a long time passed in complete silence. Only occasionally Yakko turned his eyes towards the old man, as though wanting to ask him something but being afraid to, or he threw fresh pine twigs on to the fire in a carefree manner and watched with childish curiosity as little by little the green resinous needles burned up into golden sparks. Eventually Gina got up, reached down from a pole some bark mugs, whitened with flour, took a wooden bowl of sour milk from the stove and the whole family set about its frugal supper. Elsa alone, having received her portion, went off behind the brushwood again.

At that moment Yakko, who had been looking intently at the old man, said: 'I've wanted to ask you for a long time, Grandad, where did our Pavali go?'

– Where, – replied the old man, – surely you saw the soldiers taking him away?'

– But where did they take him?

– Where? to war with the Russians.

– And what's war, Grandad?

– Well, you see, Yakko, on one side you have the *Ruotsi*, the Swedes, and on the other the *Veineleisi*, the Russians, and they quarrel about who's going to get our land.

– But what's all that business got to do with us? – remarked Gina. – I wish they'd just fight amongst themselves and wouldn't keep troubling us. Why did they take away our Pavali? What's he to them?

– Ah, well they need guides, to show them the way.

– Show them the way? – said Gina. – And what about us? How are we supposed to live without Pavali? There's no one to bring in the wood, no one to grind the bark.

– Oh, he'll come, – repeated the old man in an unsure voice.

Yakko again turned his quick, inquisitive eyes on the old man.

– Do you remember Christmas, Grandad, you played the kantele and sang to us about our land, and about how the tribes fought over it. Are they the ones who are fighting now? I didn't understand any of it then; tell me all about it again, Grandad.

– No! That was in olden times, and this is now, – replied the old man, sighing.

– But why should they have our land? – said Gina. – Haven't they got their own?

The old man did not answer. He sorrowfully bowed his head, his grey locks hung down over his pale wrinkles, he folded his arms and, rocking his head, began to speak, as if just to himself:

A Finnish Legend

There is no land on earth more beautiful than our Suomi. We have the wide sea and the deep lakes and the evergreen pines. In other lands they also have the sun, but it will show itself, will shine for a bit and hide itself, like it does here in the winter. Our sun rests for half the year, and then shines for half the year; and in our fields, hardly has the evening dew settled, than the morning dew lifts. But in the olden days it was even better: we had the wondrous Sampo treasure, which was variegated, from multicoloured stones, and with such a lid that now no smiths could forge. In those days there was earthly paradise in Suomi. People did nothing, the Sampo did everything: it carried the wood and built the houses and ground the bark into bread and drew off the milk and strung the strings on the kantele and sang the songs, while people just lay in front of the fire, turning over from one side to the other. Everything was plentiful. But when Väinämöinen* got angry with us, the Sampo went off into the ground and immersed itself in stone, and on the ground only the kantele remained. In those days the people were not like they are now, but strapping and strong. They wanted to smash the stone, and they laboured long, but they didn't get to the Sampo and only heaped up loads of stones on our land. Since then other people got to know that there was this treasure in our land; first the *Ruotsi* and then the *Veineleisi*: and they are still fighting since then about who will get the Sampo. The Swedish people have a king and the Russians have a Tsar. They are both great mages. They know how to get the treasure out of the ground but neither of them wants to yield it to the other. They have long been preparing to take possession of it. But what is there that our mage Kukari doesn't know? He sees everything which has taken place, where the iron comes from and the fallen timber and all the earthly powers, but before the Tsar and the king even his miracle-working mind dims. The Tsar is obviously stronger than the king, for he knows how he was born. Hardly had the king come out of his maternal womb than he stamped his foot on the ground and said: what Iumala has given, Pergola will not take from me. And he went around the earth with an iron sword; wherever he came to, he would wave his sword and all the people round him would die. And

* A kind of Finnish Apollo (*Author's note*)

such was his wisdom that no one saw that he ate or drank, and he sleeps with just one eye, looking all the time with the other one at the sky and at the ground and seeing everything: what and how and from what things happen. There's one thing only that he didn't see: how the Tsar of the Russians came about. They say he came straight out of the sea. There was a severe storm, the waves washed over the earth, ships sank, rocks tumbled from the shores into the sea. The king sat on the shore, waved his iron sword and ordered the rocks to get up from the sea, but the rocks didn't obey. The king got angry, the sea raged even more, when suddenly it parted and from out of the water came the Tsar of the Russians. With one hand he raised the rocks and with the other he pointed all round and said: everything I see is mine. The king got even more angry and threw iron at the Tsar; the Tsar replied with the same. Then the king threw sulphur at him and saltpetre. The Tsar didn't have any sulphur or saltpetre. The battle became unequal. The Tsar collected all his Russians and started to march about the world with them; he even went beyond the far-away sea, where the sky leans against the earth. He comes to one place, strikes the earth with iron, and says: dig, and from the earth will come forth iron. He strikes somewhere else, and from the earth comes forth sulphur and saltpetre. In a third place – various treasures. But still he didn't get down to the Sampo, because the Sampo is only in our Suomi. Everything which the Tsar got, he took back to his land. But he spent so long marching about the wide world that all the people in his land grew old, and they all grew long beards. The Tsar got very angry. 'I want you all, – he told the Russians – to grow younger, because I need young, strong people'. And such was his wisdom that, from a single word, all the Russians got younger: they became healthy and strong, and their beards dropped off. Then the Tsar told the Russians to forge weapons against his enemy, the king of the Swedes. For three days slaves helped the Tsar zealously, with dust a fathom deep on their shoulders, a yard of soot on their heads and a thick layer of grime over their whole bodies. But the Tsar's sister found out about this. She comes along, has a look and says: 'Many are the smiths, brother, you've brought from over the far-away sea; I've been told to cast a Tsar's necklace, so that everyone would respect me as the Tsarina; and I've been told to cast a silver moon and a gold sun, so they would go round me shining, day and night. You won't cast them, brother, I'll send wicked words to stop you'. The Tsar got angry, hearing such things. 'There is no Tsar – he said – apart from me; I've got a Tsar's necklace, but not for you; there is a moon and sun, but they don't shine for you'. The Tsar's sister became sad and from annoyance started to comb her black hair: her hairs fell on the ground and from each hair there grew a poisonous potion. Then she broke her comb into pieces and from each tooth there came a giant with a bow and arrows. And the king of the Swedes found out about this, as did the Turk, the eternal enemy of all Christians. And they went forth together and fell upon the wise smith. Having seen this, the smith struck his hammer on the anvil and from a single blow the giants crumbled to dust. He struck again – and from the anvil there flew off pieces of iron and they showered down on the Turk. He struck a third time – and from the anvil sparks spattered, which set fire to the sulphur and saltpetre and scorched the king of the Swedes. The king threw himself into the sea, so as to put out the fire; the Tsar goes after him, comes to the sea, but the king is already over the sea. The Tsar wants to give chase. He looks round: there is no boat, but around him only sand from the sea-shore, bare stones, swamp and marsh. The Tsar collected his Russians and told them: 'Build me a city where I can live, while I am building a ship'. And they started to build a city, but as they laid the stone, so the marsh would suck it in. Many were the stones heaped there, rock upon rock, beam upon beam, but the swamp accepted them all and on the surface only marsh is to be seen. Meanwhile the Tsar had built his ship and, looking round, he saw that his city was not there yet. 'You can't do anything', he said to his people and with these words he began to lift stone after stone and forge in the air. Thus did he build the whole city and then he lowered it on to the ground. Meanwhile, the king, on the opposite shore, went up and down, thinking: what is the Tsar up to? The moon met him. The king bowed to the moon, saying: 'Ah, my dear moon, have you seen what the Tsar of the Russians is doing?' But the moon does not answer. The sun meets the king. He bows to the sun: 'Ah, my dear sun, have you seen what the Tsar of the Russians is doing?' But the sun doesn't answer. The king meets the sea, and he bows to the sea: 'Ah, my dear sea, have you seen what the Tsar of the Russians is doing?' The sea finally answered: 'I know what he's doing, he's drying the land and driving the waves into my heart; I'm getting cramped within my shores, like you, king, in your kingdom'. – Let's attack him, – said the king, – and perhaps we'll have a bit more room in this wide world. – And so they agreed, and went to war on the Tsar. The king got the sulphur ready and the red-hot coals, and the sea got into a rage and poured itself over its shores and crawled up to the roofs of the new city. The Tsar, who was resting after his day's work, woke up and what does he see? The sea wants to flood him! He struck strongly at the sea with his staff; the sea was confused, quickly flowed to its shores and only in fear did it wash over the Tsar's legs. 'Take my ships!' – shouted the Tsar in a menacing voice and the sea accepted them on to its wet shoulders. 'Freeze over', – said the Tsar and the sea was covered with a silvery ice. 'Blow, storm, into my sails', – said the Tsar and the ships started gliding over the slippery ice. The king, meanwhile, seeing that the sea had frozen, looked at it in joy. 'The sea has won, – he said, – and pulled the Russians under its ice-floe'. He looked again and something was looming over the white snow, getting nearer... nearer... oh, woe!.. the Russian ships were flying towards him. In vain did the king curse them; in vain did he bestrew them with red coal; from the ships there blew a stormy wind, which condensed the burning sulphur into a cloud and burned the king and the whole Swedish land. The king took fright and ran off to the Turk to ask for help. But such was his wisdom that he was both with the Turk over the seas and here on our shore at the same time. How will this bloody battle finish? Who will get our land? Who will get our treasure, the Sampo?

The old man fell silent; the old woman was long since dozing. Elsa occasionally looked out from behind the brushwood and then hid again. Only Yakko, it seemed, his shining eyes fixed on the old man, was afraid to miss a word.

The old man paid no attention to his audience; his speech dominated him completely. The words followed each other automatically. He himself listened to his own story with curiosity and was afraid to interrupt it.

Kukari told me – he continued after a short silence – that from a certain time he seemed to have strange dreams. He saw huge rocks raising themselves up from the shores of Suomi, swimming across under the legs of the Russian Tsar, so that he went up higher and higher; the Suomi people ran up the heap of rocks and the Tsar of the Russians was sheltering them with his huge hand. Then he seemed to see on the sea shore the rocks burst apart with a crash and from them comes a huge and shining city; there mages gather from all corners of the world and in loud voices conduct wise speeches with all the Suomi people. And above the city again is the Russian Tsar in a gold wreath; he is carried on heavenly clouds and from his wreath there fall on to Suomi golden sparks, which shine like a thousand suns. It's wonderful! Wonderful!

The old man became lost in thought. All went quiet in the poor hut and only the wind whistled into the porthole window and sorrowfully ran over the strings of the kantele. The rapids roared, the rain burst through the roof and long shadows from the hearth came and went around the beams of the hut, blackened as they were with smoke.

Suddenly Gina shuddered: 'What's that? Thunder?' – she cried.

In fact, in with the howl of the rapids, could be heard thunderous rolls; again and again – eventually one peal followed another.

– No, Gina, – said the old man, listening hard, – that's not thunder, it's cannons. Gina, the war has now reached us.

– Where's our Pavali now? What if he's standing under a cannon? It would kill him.

The old man was silent and could not conceal his unease.

– There it is again, and again... do you hear it, man... oh, tell me, where is our Pavali?

The old man was silent; his grey hair hung down over his pallid wrinkles, his eyes were motionless; something gloomy was reflected in them.

Gina started sobbing.

– Listen, Rusi, – she said, – I know you are a mage yourself, that you can see everything yourself that you want to, with your magic eye....

The old man looked angrily at Gina.

– Don't be angry with me, I'm your true, obedient wife; I have known your secret for forty years and I've never even spoken to you about it.... But now, what does it cost you? Find out, find out where our Pavali is... it will satisfy you as well....

The old man got up and started to walk around the hut, shaking his head with a look of indecision. Meanwhile the cannon shots were becoming more frequent and seemed to be getting nearer. Gina uttered a shriek at every boom and her whole body was shaking.

After a bit, the old man threw back his grey locks and said: 'So be it! That's enough crying; perhaps we'll find out where our Pavali is. Now, enough of that crying, you've been told!'

The old woman quitened down in a minute and just looked at the seer with imploring eyes.

The old man continued: 'Just look here then, Gina, go up on the stove and don't you dare turn round, or else it'll be the worse for you and for me. Yakko, clear off to the brushwood, close your eyes tight and lie still, until I call you'.

Everything was immediately carried out as the old man said. Then he lapsed into deep thought, moved his hand over his face and said in a sombre voice: 'Elsa, come here'.

Elsa stiffened up and didn't want to come out from the brushwood. The old man repeated his command and then Elsa crawled out from behind the brushwood and approached the old man, but pressed herself against the wall, quivering.

Almost by force, the old man led her over to the fire and sat on a stump. Hardly had the poor child's face begun to redden from the heat, than she shook even more and her whole body went into a convulsive movement. The old man took her by the head and held her tightly, so that the poor girl's face could not turn away from the hearth.

After a certain time, he said to her in a quiet but angry voice: 'Look for your father'. The child's convulsive movement became more agitated; poor Elsa struggled to break free of the old man's hands, but in vain: his iron hands rivetted her to the stump.

– Look, go on: where's your father? – the old man repeated in an even more angry voice.

Elsa quivered all the more, but fixed her eyes concentratedly on the hearth.

– I can see, – she said finally in a halting voice, – I can see my father... he's sitting on a stone... beside him there's a tree... no, not a tree... beside him there's a man... a soldier... and he's saying something to father... but I can't hear it....

– Listen, – said the old man menacingly.

– The soldier's telling father that he should give him his coat... father won't give it... they are arguing fiercely... oh, he's fighting with father... father has hit the soldier... oh, the soldier is shooting... father falls down... ah, father's died....

The old man jumped up from her at these words. Gina shrieked from the stove.... Elsa started sobbing and the old man hung his head in horror and murmured in a whisper: 'This is my punishment...'. Yakko shuddered under the brushwood....

In a short time, the clatter of horses' hoofs was heard... the inhabitants of the hut winced... a certain numbness came over them... now it was as if something was striking against the earth; soon the door opened from the knocking and a man burst in in a Finnish coat holding a musket, drenched with rain and splattered in blood and filth.

– A boat! Your boat! – he shouted in Swedish, – hurry up, your boat!

The old man looked at him and very coolly said: *än mujsta.**

---

* I don't understand – the usual phrase of a cunning Finn (*Author's note*)

– Do you hear what I'm saying? – shouted the Swede angrily, – My blasted horse has fallen... your boat!... Take me to the other bank straight away.

The old man turned his head with complete composure and wanted to repeat his previous '*än mujsta*', but Gina suddenly threw herself upon the new arrival: 'That's Pavali's coat, did you take it from Pavali? Did you kill Pavali? Where is he, where is he?'

The Swede did not understand Gina's words and pulled away angrily from her: 'What's all this talk! You've been told: your boat, I can't waste time; I have important dispatches.... Vyborg has been taken by the Russians... do you hear? Do you understand? Your boat... your boat, or I'll kill you'.

The old man looked at the Swede with a sombre expression and, without moving, again said: *än mujsta*.

Then the Swede lost patience. 'If you don't understand, – he yelled, – I'll show you in another way what I want...'.

With these words he grabbed the old man by his long hair and started pulling him out of the hut. Gina fixed on the Swede. 'You killed my son, and you want to kill my husband too!' – she cried, shielding the door and making an effort to help her husband. The exasperated Swede pushed Gina so hard that she banged her head against the doorpost.... The old man wanted to get to her, but the Swede didn't give him a chance and heaved him roughly out on to the river bank....

Outside it was clearing. The wind was breaking up the clouds and they were floating like smoke across the white sky. The trees were bending to the ground, while the foam of the rapids, whipped up by the storm, crashed with a terrific roar against the granite rocks. The first twilight rays were reflected in the grey waves as bloody stains....

– Where's the crossing point? – shouted the Swede, shaking the old man for all he was worth....

It seemed that this time the old man understood; he made no reply, but went straight off to the boat, which was tied up between the pines that grew along the upper reaches above the main rapids.

– So, you've understood at last, – said the Swede joyfully, – take me over, quickly.

The old Finn untied the boat and was on the point of seating the Swede in it, when the Swede grasped his intention.

– No! – he said, – you certainly are a cunning race, – you'll let me in and then clear off yourself; you get in up front!

With these words he shoved the old man into the boat, and the old man obeyed. With his experienced hands he took to the oars: it was obvious that this was not the first time that he had taken his boat through the dangerous rapids.... Occasionally he shot a glance at the Swede, but the Finn's face showed no trace of feeling.... Mid-stream the Swede shuddered: 'To the right! Over to the right, – he shouted – we're heading for the rapids'.

– *Än mujsta*, – replied the Finn, smiling maliciously....

– To the right, I tell you... otherwise... – At this point the Swede went for his musket, but it was too late. The boat was drawn down into the white foam; the robust guffaw of the old man and the cry of the Swede barely resounded above the waves.... Something black flickered momentarily among the whirls of foam – and everything disappeared for ever: the Finn, the Swede and the boat.

There was no witness to this scene, except for Yakko who, in fright, had run after the old man and at this horrific spectacle had stood petrified on the bank.

At that moment several horsemen in green uniforms galloped along the bank.... Suddenly the leading horse reared up.

– Look! – shouted the horseman in Russian – this is where the Swedish horse fell: he must be near here!

With these words the commander of the Russian detachment briskly dismounted, the others followed him and they all rushed together into the hut. Gina lay dead on the threshold; the fire in the hearth had gone out. They did not notice Elsa, who had still not revived beneath the brushwood pile.

– Evidently the unwounded Swede has been here, – said the commander of the detachment, – where has he got to? Probably, he's got across the river; there'll be trouble if we don't catch him.

The Russians ran quickly out on to the river bank and enounterd poor Yakko.

– Where's the Swedish messenger? – asked the Russians.

Yakko did not actually understand them but, guessing what they meant, pointed downstream as the Vuoksi flowed.

– He must be quite near, – said the comander, – to horse, quickly!

With these words the commander leapt on his horse, seated poor Yakko across the saddle, and the whole detachment galloped off down the river bank. They galloped like that for a good kilometer. At the point where the foaming rapids come to an end, Yakko waved his hand; the Russians jumped down from their horses and could see how the waves had smashed the boat to pieces, along with the mangled bodies of the old fisherman and the Swede with the Finnish coat.

– The dear chap didn't make it across, – exclaimed the commander – it serves him right. Now let's get back, otherwise the Swedes will get us.

You, my fine fellow, can be our guide, – and the troop raced off, as fast as their horses could carry them.

Thus they galloped along for about ten kilometers. Yakko no longer knew what was happening: the swift movement of the horse had knocked all real consciousness out of him.

Suddenly musket shots could be heard in the forest; the Russian commander stopped his troop and listened carefully.

From the forest there appeared a crowd of Swedes. On seeing the Russians, they coldbloodedly disposed themselves in battle formation and discharged a volley at the troop. But they seemed not quite to get the distance: just a few of the Russian horses were wounded. Among these, however, was the troop commander's horse. He lowered Yakko on to the ground and, with a shout of 'After me, lads!' he charged at the Swedes brandishing his broadsword. The Swedes had no time to fire another volley. The Russian troop broke ranks, trampled them by horse and cut them down with their broadswords. The Swedes defended themselves bravely with bayonets; most of the Russian horses were wounded. Almost the whole troop hurried to reform swiftly into battle formation and like new, fresh troops marched on the wounded and confused Swedes. The fighting turned completely into hand-to- hand combat. Bayonets broke; the Swedes fought with rifle-butts and the Russians with broadswords. Pursued by two Swedish fusiliers, the commander of the Russian troop, his back to the cliff, courageously beat them off with a fractured broadsword. His comrades were some way off and his doom appeared sealed. The Russian was already composing a prayer for the moment of death, when suddenly one of his opponents, struck from behind, fell to the ground, and the other followed him. Only then did the Russian commander see in front of him little Yakko, with a broken musket in his hands. With flashing eyes, inflamed with vengeance, the little Finn was walking among the ranks, and when he came to a skirmish, he would strike the one in the Swedish uniform with his musket-butt. He spared no one, neither the wounded nor the dead, and maliciously struck at whatever heads came his way.

– Good boy, – shouted the Russians – that's nice, really nice, only there's no need to hit those on the ground.

After a while the badly beaten Swedes scattered again into the woods. The commander of the Russian troop, having placed several horsemen for observation purposes, hurried off to the main Russian force near Vyborg.

– You mustn't part from us, my brave lad, – he said to the young Finn.

Yakko understood nothing; his eyes were burning and there was but one feeling in them: hatred for the Swedes. All the rest was forgotten; he did not know what was happening to him and he submitted unwittingly to everything. Within a few kilometers, Lieutenant Zverev, the troop commander, had joined up with the main Russian force. He was getting ready to ride off with dispatches, when everything in the camp sprung to life. 'The Tsar's coming! The Tsar's coming!' – soldiers were saying to each other.

Yakko had no idea what was going on around him. He could see only that a lot of people were crowding round a tall black-haired man, before whom everyone took off their hats. Soon Yakko too was led into that same crowd. Lieutenant Zverev took Yakko by the hand and the tall black-haired man, before whom everyone removed their hats, patted him on the cheek and uttered something to those around in a language that was incomprehensible to the Finn.

Yakko kept on looking at the black-haired man and could not take his eyes off him; he wanted to put something into words to him, but could not....

In a little while, Yakko was seated in a cart and he raced off, he knew not where....

Thus three days went by: on the road a wounded soldier, who accompanied Yakko, looked after, tended and fed the poor Finn.

Unseen things, unknown people, unknown food: all this made a strong impression on the young Finn and brought him to a state of mind close to enchantment. Finally the Finnish mountains were left behind and they were on the level road, going between the marshes. Soon Yakko saw houses which seemed surprisingly huge. Travelling on a bit, he saw houses still bigger than the previous ones, a wide river and on the other side of the river another city of strange appearance: on the walls brass cannons glitter and sentries with guns march up and down. Huge boats, the like of which Yakko had never yet seen, are sailing along the wide river. Finally the cart stopped by a stone house; his companion got out, and pulled out Yakko, who was exhausted from the jolting on the road, leading him in to where a tiled stove, with images of people and various animals, restored the poor Finn to consciousness. After a minute a middle-aged man walked into the room. For some time he spoke to the companion and stroked Yakko's hair. Yakko, enlivened by these caresses, started to walk cheerfully around the room. Every object arrested his attention; he groped at the furniture, which was trimmed with green leather, and touched the window-panes, the purpose of which was lost on him. He was particularly struck by the small mirror between the windows. Yakko was delighted at first, catching sight of a Finn, but then grew frightened, ran off and hid in the corner.

Meanwhile a woman came into the room and behind her came her eight-year-old daughter. They reminded the Finn of his previous life, of

Gina and Elsa. Over the previous four days, Yakko had been so over-whelmed by everything that had happened to him that he had forgotten all the past, but now he threw up his hands, burst into tears and started to cry: 'Elsa, Elsa!'. But no one could understand the poor Finn; they caressed him and tried to console him, but he kept on crying and ate nothing the whole day. The next day Yakko was even on a ship, together with other young people of various ages, and in vain did he try to explain to himself where he was and whither he was being taken.

The indulgent reader will already, probably, have guessed that Yakko had been brought to Petersburg, to the new capital of the reformer of Russia, which had only just risen from the Finnish marshes. At that time, Russia's enlightener had given the order to send a number of young people to Holland. They were entrusted to the charge of Prince Kurakin. Rather unwillingly did Russian citizens set off overseas to learn the sciences of the infidel. The Finnish orphan, who had brought himself to Peter's attention, was a godsend in these circumstances. The ship was already loaded up, and the poor Finn was substituted for some adolescent from out of town whose mother had been bewailing him bitterly.

On the ship, Yakko met some old acquaintances and in particular the middle-aged man who had been so affectionate towards the young Finn. This middle-aged man was the father of Lieutenant Zverev, Prince Kurakin's secretary and personal assistant. With his entire household, he was setting sail for Holland, to join the Prince.

We shall not linger to describe how the half wild Finn was gradually transformed into an educated European, how he mastered foreign languages, how he became an excellent physicist and mechanical engineer.

Eleven years went by and Yakko, now having called himself Ivan Ivanovich Yakko, was living in Holland with old Zverev, who loved him like his own son. The servant girls even gossiped about Ivan Ivanovich taking an interest in the younger Zverev daughter, Maria Yegorovna, but the old man frequently affirmed that, before anything else, Ivan Ivanovich needed to establish himself in the Tsar's favour. There eventually came a time of separation: Ivan Ivanovich had to leave for Petersburg. At the same time a flattering testimonial on our Yakko was sent from Prince Kurakin to the monarch.

The adopted son of the poor fisherman scarcely recognised the young capital, so much had it grown in so short a time. The banks of the islands were lined with buildings and a forest of masts covered the azure surface of the Neva. The Finn felt fear and joy in his soul. Even now, as before, he knew about Russia only by hearsay. But its grandeur struck him all the more. He recalled the hut of his birth, recalled the fabulous tales of the Russian Tsardom, and only with difficulty could he believe that he was inside this fabulous world. He recalled how he had seen the monarch for the first time. Reality mingled with enchantment in the Finn's soul: Russia's great war-lord appeared to him in the first place as a giant, and secondly in the guise of a miraculous mage who had subjected the elements. This belief of Yakko's received a further boost when his educated mind formed the conviction, at every step, that Peter's miraculous exploits were not fiction, but reality. There then flared in Yakko's soul a rapturous love for the man who had transformed Russia and a feeling of certainty that he himself was unworthy to be the instrument of the monarch. The young Finn knew how he valued educated people who were equipped to comprehend his grandiloquent suppositions and the young Finn's heart dilated with pride and hope.

And these really were miraculous times then for the Russian realm. The Treaty of Nystad was concluded; Russia celebrated her power and treated her Tsar to the title of emperor and the Great. The fatherland was safe from enemies; the howl of war was not yet silenced, but it was a distant howl, not close to the young capital, but far away to the east. From Prince Kurakin's dealings, our young Finn knew that the monarch's attention was now directed to internal improvements. Russia was like a huge machine whose boundless strength knew no limits. Only the pendulum was lacking, which would have given this strength a measured momentum. The disorder of local affairs, the means of communication, the education of the people: all of this was entering Peter's mind and, from the heights of the throne, like powerful seed, was falling on to fertile Russian ground. The Finn told himself with delight that, for such matters, Peter needed people; he also knew that the monarch looked upon the up and coming generation as his best hope, and that he had been keeping an eye on the young man from his early years, attentively watching over his developing abilities. And suddenly he initiated him instantly into the highest mysteries of his works. At this point his old-time admirers grumbled their surprise at the Tsar's mistake. But they were even more surprised when the youth justified his splendid hopes, when the abilities of the Tsar's choice matched exactly the tasks allotted him. The veterans ascribed such fortune to chance, or attributed to the Tsar the art of guesswork, without realising that the great Tsar would long have been assiduous in keeping an eagle eye on the man he had picked out. Our Finn also noticed that, like all great people enriched by thoughts ahead of his time, Peter liked being anticipated and hated simple and literal fulfilment of his orders; that he sought in his assistants that love for the affair in hand which would overcome all hindrances, would exceed mere fulfilment, would transform new means for new goals and itself intuit the great intentions of the Great. Frequently, from the monarch's letters to Prince Kurakin, Yakko had seen that the Tsar cherished such people like the apple of his eye; he also saw how often the Great complained that he had no one to rely on.

In actual fact, the Tsar had long known in detail, from the reports of Prince Kurakin, of the abilities and the inclinations of the young Finn.

However, Yakko's imagination did not go beyond first lieutenant or similar rank, but something else unexpected was in preparation for him. In an audience with the sovereign he happened to mention Venice and the printing presses there. Just a few words from Yakko showed that he knew something of this matter, while it was a matter which had concerned Peter the Great for some time. Just at this moment, all his efforts were directed at this mighty instrument of enlightenment. The art of typography was still little known in Russia. Few people in Russia at that time were capable of dealing with it. Our Yakko was a find for Peter in this instance and he gave him several important assignments at the one time: he ordered him to get on with the translation of several foreign books and, while he was at it, to draw up a plan for the formation of a new typography and in particular to train printers in the typographical trade. Yakko's surprise and delight were inexpressible; he involuntarily fell on his knees before the great Tsar and from an overflow of feeling he was unable to utter a single word. And so the half wild Finn, under the mighty hand of Peter, was to become one of the instruments of Russian enlightenment.

At the end of the year 1722 a postal cart stopped close to the Vuoksi. A young man in a rich German kaftan jumped out of the vehicle, threw himself on to the ground and kissed it with the ardour of youth. With difficulty he pronounced a few Finnish words which the onlookers scarcely understood. However, they guessed that the traveller was asking for old Rusi's daughter.

Memory of the old man had not yet disappeared among the inhabitants of Imatra. Of a long winter's night they recalled the courageous fisherman and his amazing stories. They showed Yakko to the river bank and in an instant the young man had thrown himself into a boat.

When he got out on to the bank, tears gushed from his eyes; he recognised the hut of his childhood, his native rapids, and his heart began to beat strongly. 'Where's Elsa, then? Elsa?' – he asked.

Not far off, a few idle Finns were standing around a young girl of about twenty. She was running her fingers over the strings of the kantele, singing the old songs about the Finnish treasure, the Sampo, and dancing. In her apron there lay pieces of bread, which she had probably received from her listeners.

– That's Elsa, the grand-daughter of old Rusi, – said those who had accompanied the young man.

– Elsa! Elsa! – he cried and rushed to embrace her.

Elsa, greatly alarmed, cried out and wanted to run off.

– Elsa, little sister! do you really not recognise your Yakko?...

– You are trying to trick me, Yakko is dead, he was killed, – replied Elsa and wept bitterly.

– Your Yakko is alive, it is me, the adopted son of your grandfather, do you understand?

Elsa looked at him, but did not believe him and continued to cry.

Yakko could scarcely communicate his thoughts to her. Having learned almost every European language, he had forgotten his own and either could not think of the commonest of words, or else got the words muddled up. But the sight of his native surroundings aided his memory and the Finnish words, although with difficulty, sprouted through the layers of alien phrases and concepts, like birch roots through the Finnish granite.

– You don't believe that I am really Yakko? – he went on. – Look at me closely; have I really changed so much?

– Yakko was one of us, from Suomi, and you are not our's, you're a big lord.

– Elsa! Elsa! I am still the same, only the clothes on me are different. Look, there's the rock which we used to try to run up; there's the rowan tree from which I used to throw berries down to you; here's where I made you a little horn from a big ox-horn. Let's go into the hut and I'll tell you where everything was, where you and I used to sleep, where Rusi used to sit and where Gina sat, behind the stove....

They went into the hut. Everything in it was in its old position, except that the walls had somewhat warped: the same four-cornered stove, the same porthole, the same pine stumps, the same pile of brushwood that served as a bed. That horrific night, Rusi's saga, his death, the death of Gina – everything was renewed in the memory of the young Finn. He repeated it all in detail to Elsa.

Finally Elsa believed that Yakko really was standing before her and threw herself, sobbing, into his embraces.

They sat down.

– Tell me, Elsa, how do you live? Where do you live?

– I live here, in this hut.

– Alone?

– Alone. What's there to be afraid of? Everyone here's our own people.

The Salamander

In the day I go to the Pastor to learn writing – I can read already, Yakko. Then I go outside and play the kantele and I sing: the good people give me bread. Look how much I've got already, enough for the whole year. I've even got some *knakebre* here.* – Elsa pointed proudly at the pile of pieces she had collected. – In the evening I come here and think about my father, about grandfather and about you, Yakko; I cry a bit and then I go to sleep.

– Well, Elsa. I'll tell you, now it's not going to be like that. I am rich now and you are going to live well....

– What have you found, the Sampo is it?

– Almost.

– Where did you find it, Yakko?

– With the Russians....

– Ah, so the *Ruotsi* didn't kill you? – exclaimed Elsa, not quite understanding.

– Not *Ruotsi*, not the Swedes. The Russians: what you call *Veineleisi*.

– So you've been to their land?

– I live there and I'm going to take you back with me....

– Why? How can you? – Elsa cried in horror. – It's so far, so far from us.... Where would we sleep?...

– There, in my country....

– But this is your country, Yakko... it's my land, the Pastor said, and so it must be your's....

– You don't understand, my dear Elsa. In Russia I have a house, six times bigger than your hut. There you can go about in a coloured dress, eat clean bread every day....

– How is that possible? – asked Elsa.

– Listen! – she said to him finally – do you know what I've thought of? Instead of me going there with you, you bring your Sampo back here!...

– That's not possible, Elsa.

– Why isn't it possible? Do think I can't manage? I'm a good housekeeper, I can milk the cows, I can make sour milk, I can even bake *knakebre* on the stove for the whole year. And if you really have enough wealth, then we can buy salt and pickle the mushrooms – then we'll really be happy.

The young man shook his head, smiling:

– All that isn't possible, my dear Elsa. I serve the Tsar of the *Veineleisi*, I have to go to his land, and do you really want to forsake me?

---

*Flat cakes made of flour, current only among prosperous villagers. 'He eats clean bread the whole year round' is a Finnish expression of the greatest wealth (*Author's note*).

– How can I part from you, Yakko! Not for anything, not for anything. Many have already wanted to marry me, but I refused them all, I told them all that only Yakko will be my husband and now, I say, how can I part from you? But what you have to go for, I don't understand; at least, will we be able to make visits home?

– We will, perhaps, sometimes come here.

– Sometimes, but how often? Every day?...

– That's impossible.

– Well, once a week, on Sunday, to church.

– That's impossible, too. Maybe once a year.

Elsa did not reply, but wept bitterly.

However, Elsa's innocent suggestion of marriage to him gave the young man food for thought. Looking attentively at Elsa, he remarked that, despite her strange attire and her hair, which was swept up into a crown under an awful cap, Elsa could be considered a beautiful girl. Her face was not quite classical, but it did have an inexpressible charm, especially when she smiled. At times her blue eyes would ceaselessly flit from object to object; at times they would remain completely motionless, and then a feeling of sad mystery would be reflected in them which may be noted only among women of northern stock.

Strange thoughts entered the young man's head. He was already now looking at Elsa through different eyes. He imagined her dressed in the height of fashion, in his house, at a Petersburg court ball, and his heart beat strongly and violently. But, on the other hand, he felt loth to unite his fate for ever to an almost half wild woman whose language would not be understood by anyone and who comprehended only the most basic requirements in life. He imagined all the humiliations which she would undergo in a society which would be inaccessible to her, all the mockery which would follow in the wake of her unsophisticated simplicity and complete ignorance of the most usual subjects. He took fright at the thought of spending three days with her in the same carriage: the very innocence, the very straightforwardness of her feelings could be disastrous for them both.

– What are you thinking about, my dear Yakko? – Elsa said to him, gripping his face in her hands. – You've probably changed your mind and want to stay at home, isn't that it? – And with these words, before he knew what was happening, she kissed him passionately on the lips. An involuntary shudder ran over the young man's every limb.

– No, Elsa, that's not it, – replied the young man, trying to maintain an appearance of equanimity. – Do you know the way to the Pastor?

– What do you mean, I know the shortest way and every pathway....

– Take me to him.

– Let's go then, let's go, but you, I think, are hungry. Don't you want to eat? – And with these words she gave him a flat-cake made half and half of bark and flour....

Yakko looked at this strange comestible with a mixture of revulsion and pity. – No – he said, – I am not hungry; let's get going to the Pastor.

And Elsa ran off, grabbing Yakko by the hand and gnawing ravenously at her flat-cake.

Yakko found in the Pastor a kind and educated man. The young man explained to him the strangeness of his position and the Pastor understood him completely.

– I can help you, – said the good old man, – my wife is setting off today for Nienshants, that is to say, I mean, St Petersburg. She has room in the gig and your Elsa could travel with her in that carriage, as she's not yet used to better ones.

The young man, thanking the Pastor for this favour, added that he had nothing more than a *kibitka*, and that he must admit, he said, that *our* Russian carts are no good at all on your mountains.

When everything was ready for their departure, the Pastor took the young man aside: – 'I must warn you, – he said, – you are taking Elsa to foreign parts; you should know that she is prone to something like the falling sickness. In particular, keep her away from the fire and from the moonlight: both of these, it seems, produce a bad effect on her. From either of them she falls into a sort of trance and starts saying the strangest things. The simple folk consider her a sorceress.'

This story made Yakko shudder. He recalled what up until then he had forgotten: the old man's divinations; and, despite his own learning, in the spirit of the times, he could not get it out of his head that Elsa had indeed been bewitched. He did not, however, communicate his thoughts to the Pastor, but promised himself not to allow this state of affairs to slip his mind.

It cost much effort to persuade poor Elsa to take a seat in the gig. She did not want to leave her country, did not want not to be together with Yakko and did not want not to go. She sobbed violently; they put her almost unconscious into the cart.

Yakko noticed with surprise during the journey that nothing seemed to make any impression on Elsa; neither curiosity nor amazement had access to her soul. Only one thing was noticeable in her – fear at the sight of foreigners and the recollection of her native hut.

Finally the cart stopped at the Petersburg gates. The guards looked over the gig, which had been splendidly painted in red, and had a good look at our ladies.

– Here, – they were saying, – there's a Finnish girl arrived here in a red box. The younger one's not bad all right – do you see how cute she is...? – Elsa took fright at these moustachioed faces, enlivened by a whiff of gunpowder, looking out from under their spiked helmets. The Pastor's wife straightened up and wanted to say something to the soldiers, but the few Russian words which she knew got mixed up with Finnish and German ones.

– What are you prattling about, you Finnish witch? Or are you scared of having the eye put on you? – said one of the soldiers and the whole crowd laughed a raucous Russian laugh.

At that moment Yakko caught up with our lady travellers and went over to the gig. At the sight of a man in a German kaftan, and speaking Russian to boot, the crowd dispersed.

– Where have you brought me to? – said Elsa. – What horrible people there are here! And they can't even speak, but just keep shouting something awful!

Yakko laughed at poor Elsa's remarks and tried to console her. Meanwhile, the Pastor's wife had understood only one word in the Russians' conversation: the word 'witch', because she had happened to hear it several times before; she lost no time in telling Elsa that they were being sworn at and Elsa ingenuously enquired by what right were they being sworn at, when they hadn't done anything wrong.

Yakko whispered a couple of words to the guards officer who had arrived at that point; he shouted something and Elsa saw the horrible men in spiked helmets stand to attention as though turned to stone.

All this seemed both miraculous and frightening to Elsa.

To start off with, the Pastor's wife took Elsa to her relatives. Yakko, having entrusted them with the care of her costume, went off to see Zverev, telling him the story of his orphanhood, and how he had been cared for by Elsa's father, his sad end, and the miraculous preservation of his daughter. He asked him, in the name of gratitude and humanity to accept the poor girl into his home. Good old Zverev, after consultation with his wife, agreed.

And so our Elsa – the timid, capricious child of nature – found herself in farthingales and a gown; she was taught to hold herself straight, to walk quietly and not to throw her arms around Yakko's neck. She was constrained in all her movements, did not dare to raise her head, did not dare to budge and hardy dared to warble her sad Finnish songs.

Yegor Petrovich Zverev was Russian, but half German, or rather half Dutch. He had not had very much education, but a long stay in Holland had strongly affected him. He had become the personification of regularity: he got up every day at the appointed time, put on a white calico smock, plaited his hair, smoked a pipe of Dutch canaster and got down to work, which he unfailingly finished at the appointed time and every day he uttered his cherished phrase: 'It's already twelve, gone mid-day – isn't it time to dine, Fedosia Kuzminishna?'. He did not comprehend anything that was happening in Russia, but he did and said one thing and not another in accordance with *what was seemly*. His house would have been like an institutionalised machine if his wife, Fedosia Kuzminishna, had not interfered with it slightly. Although she also had lived in Holland and often, with a certain pride, told her neighbours all about it, the Dutch spirit had had little effect on her. She could not for the life of her understand why she should put on clean underwear every day; why at eight o'clock, and not later and not earlier, one should water the bulbs; why it is necessary every Saturday to wash all the floors, windows and walls and to polish the furniture with wax when guests were not expected. Because of this there would occur between the couple a certain amount of bickering. Spotting an armchair out of place, or a floor unpolished, Yegor Petrovich would say to his wife in a whisper, so that the servants wouldn't hear: 'It's beyond you, is all this, Fedosia Kuzminishna'.

And she would reply in a similar whisper: 'There's nothing else for it, you old fool of a chap: that's the way I've always lived and that's the way I'll die'. Never did these quarrels surface; it was just that the servants knew that, whenever the old couple started to address each other by the formal 'you', then they must have fallen out.

Maria Yegorovna was caught in the middle between her father and mother: plump, fresh, ruddy, but a little swarthy. Instead of being off to her beauty sleep on her stove-couch, she would chatter away of an evening to the baker of holy wafers about what was going on in the neighbourhood; but, come morning, and Maria Yegorovna would be laced into her corset, would put on her farthingales and become the complete Dutch girl; she would not speak, would not budge and would only adjust her starched cuffs.

Zverev's son was always away on the march.

Also attached to the family were Yevdokim, Zverev's old servant, and several maids, the main one of whom was Anisia the house-keeper, whose distinguishing quality was a terrible meanness – not on her own behalf, but that of her masters. When issuing the oil and other domestic stuffs, she would always measure out a little bit less than the proper amount and, for such observance of her masters' property, would hear out the fierce reproaches of the other menials.

So thus was the family in which our Elsa chanced to find herself. At first, confused by the novelty of her surroundings and the sight of strange people, she was blindly obedient, but, returning to her allotted room, she would take delight in throwing off her day-time attire, would start to quietly weep, to sing her Finnish songs and then to dance.

A day later Yakko visited Elsa. He could not do so more often. He was busy with important business, translating some book on the science of cyphers. He had a lot of work and very little time: our translator was being rushed.

– Yakko, Yakko, – Elsa said to him, – it's bad here, you can't go to the bath-house here....

– Why not, Elsa?

– Why not? I wanted to heat it on the quiet, so they don't bewitch me, but these *Veineleisi* are big sorcerers and they realised straight away and stopped me. They all want to go to the bath-house with me and they all laugh at me: they will bewitch me, it's the truth.... – And Elsa started to cry. In vain did Yakko try to reason with her.

– No, – she said, – whatever you say, it's a horrible country here and your *Veineleisi* are horrible people. The other day they took me along the streets, and what did I see? They were ganging up and punishing the earth....

– What? Punishing the earth?...

– Yes! You will say this is not true as well, but I saw it myself, they hewed a tree into a stake and with a great hammer on ropes they hit it into the ground, so that the earth moaned, and they were just shouting, shouting away... that horrible cry still sounds in my ears.

– You silly girl! They were driving in piles, to build houses!...

– But what for, at home on the Vuoksi they build houses without doing that!...

– Yes, on the Vuoksi there's plenty of stone, but here the soil won't support it....

– But here the soil won't support it! Nothing here is like it should be! It's horrible, horrible, Yakko! And listen, what does this mean? When we were travelling here, I saw on the road the *Veineleisi* putting fire under a big rock, the rock went bang and flew off into little pieces: were they trying to get the Sampo, or something?

– No, they wanted to loosen the soil....

– What? The soil is either too soft for them or it's too hard – you see how even you contradict yourself, Yakko. I find it sad, just sad! When I think of our mountains and our roads, I just dissolve in tears. There I was free, like a fish in water, the livelong day in the fresh air, the sky above my head, the mist around me, with our own songs nearby and our wonderful speech in my soul. But here there's neither sky, nor mist, nor songs, there's absolutely nothing, and your heart dies of fright. Believe me, Yakko, I haven't heard a Finnish song here once. What do you see out of the window, but moustachioed *Veineleisi* going to dig up the earth, looking for the Sampo. Listen to me, dear Yakko, let's run away, run away from here quickly, before the *Veineleisi* hammer us into the ground or blow us up....

– Where would we run to, Elsa?

– Where? Why, home, home, to the Vuoksi, to the Vuoksi – and not live here for ever! We can get married there, Yakko, and forget about the *Veineleisi*....

The approach of Fedosia Kuzminishna interrupted their conversation.

– Tell her, master Ivan Ivanovich, you see she doesn't know our language, or German, not to keep snivelling. Oh, to tell you the truth, just forget her, she's so strange. She won't eat soft bread, but collects the crusts; she doesn't put a thing in her mouth over dinner, and just gnaws her crusts all day....

– Eh! Fedosia Kuzminishna, – said Yegor Petrovich, – that's the sort of people they are, I know them. It's all right! She's young, she'll get used to things... it's seemly enough.

– Just as you please, – replied Fedosia Kuzminishna with visible displeasure, – but you're the one who wants the house kept just so and complains when there are crumbs or anything on the floor.

Maria Yegorovna remained silent, but the astute Yakko soon noticed that she was quietly jealous of Elsa.

Ivan Ivanovich indeed had both of them on his mind. He liked Maria Yegorovna, who was an attractive girl, meek and not badly educated for those days; her family were kind; Maria Yegorovna would not shame him at the Tsar's ball. But how did she compare with Elsa: now capricious, now pensive, now joyful Elsa? When, sitting under the window with her head in her hands, she would let down her blonde locks, her eyes darting uninhibitedly from one object to another as she sang her favourite song of the birch tree lamenting its loneliness, Yakko would forget his worldly interests and hopes. His native feelings would reverberate in his breast and he too, like Elsa, would be ready to throw up everything and escape with her to the meagre hut by the Finnish rapids.

A few hours later, Yakko would remember his new life, his part in the works of Peter the Great, and then the scales would fall from his eyes. He would see himself as the future head of the admiralty printing-house and a provincial governor, a man close to the sovereign. And then, by an inescapable train of thought, he would take fright at the idea of marriage to a half wild Finnish girl and Maria Yegorovna would present herself in all her splendour, in a rich costume at court, surrounded by foreign guests who could not but wonder at her skilful and courteous demeanour.

With such thoughts, Yakko, not knowing what decision to make, would go home and get down to his book on the science of printing.

Yegor Petrovich looked after poor Elsa with a fatherly kindness. As she was not literate, he engaged the local deacon to teach her Russian. But, whether it was the ineptitude of the teacher or the incapacity of the pupil, little learning was imparted. Elsa studied, tortured herself and cried like a child. A dancing master was also appointed for her. While the good German, Shtolzermann, had quite a battle with her, she acquired this skill rather more quickly: Elsa soon danced the minuet, bowed and curtseyed quite satisfactorily. Yegor Petrovich could not admire her enough. But after her lesson Elsa, as before, would run off to her room and, head in her hands, would again start singing of her birch tree.

Soon the opportunity presented itself to Elsa to display her dancing abilities in full glare.

Yegor Petrovich declared that everyone had to appear at the court ball which had been announced in their vicinity. Fedosia Kuzminishna started to protest, but Yegor Petrovich told her: 'Don't contradict me, Fedosia Kuzminishna, it's perfectly seemly: at court balls you get Dutch sea-captains and their wives, and the nobility, and the sovereign himself, and you just have to dress yourself up to the nines and get the girls dressed – in a seemly fashion, I tell you.'

– What? – objected Fedosia Kuzminishna, throwing up her hands, – are we taking that Finnish girl with us?

– Absolutely, Fedosia Kuzminishna, the Finnish girl too. Let people have a look at her, let her show herself, she needs to get to know the world.... That's seemly enough, I'm telling you, Fedosia Kuzminishna.

Fedosia Kuzminishna had no rejoinder to such speeches; she shook her head and went off to look out the dresses.

The day of the court ball arrived. Yegor Petrovich was in a blue silk kaftan with fancy paste buttons and striped hose with red arrows and a ship under the arm. Fedosia Kuzminishna was in a yellow ball gown and Maria Yegorovna a pink one. Elsa, now called Lizaveta Ivanovna, was in bright red, which she liked very much.

And so they arrived at the court ball. Yegor Petrovich, having exchanged bows with the host, soon met a Dutch sea-captain who invited him to a tankard of beer and a pipe of tobacco. Fedosia Kuzminishna installed herself with the girls amid the ladies, who clung tightly to the wall, awaiting the commencement of the dancing: the older ones with trepidation, the young ones with impatience.

Elsa saw and heard nothing of what was around her. She was so frightened from her very arrival, that she found herself continuously either in a state of alarm or of complete dumbness. She sat down in the same way and, as was her habit, unconsciously moved her eyes from side to side. The crowd appeared in front of her in all its colours and the faces, each one yielding its place to the next, almost disappeared as far as she was concerned. The noise of the conversation, the light, the movement – all deafened her, both physically and morally. Suddenly her eyes stopped on the opposite wall. She looked: there was something familiar there... yes, it was the banks of the Vuoksi, it was the rapids – the sun was shining above them, a rainbow was playing in the whimsical spray: here was her own hut and the cliff against which she had leaned.... Was this not a miracle? Had some sorcerer not brought Elsa back to her native land?... Elsa's heart beat strongly, her eyes darkened...she heard the noise of the rapids...a damp wind was blowing in her face...she seemed to hear the sounds of her mother tongue – were they not singing her favourite song? And Elsa started to sing it quietly...then...louder, louder – and then suddenly, what horror! Some sort of a crash rang out and Elsa was surrounded by the awful faces of the *Veineleisi*, and from among them Yakko was saying, with an angry face: 'Pull yourself together, come to your senses, Elsa...'.

And it all disappeared – Elsa saw herself once again at the ball, around her a crowd of people, all laughing; Yakko was looking at her with a discontented face.

– What's wrong with you, Elsa? – Yakko asked her.

Elsa could not reply, and could only point to the wall opposite.

That explained everything to Yakko. On the wall hung a large painting representing an Imatra waterfall. People crowded around Yakko and several times had to explain why the pretty Finnish girl had been singing away. They say that even the sovereign, from the other room, had wanted to find out the reason for the sudden alarm and had smiled upon hearing the story of this involuntary bursting of the soul of poor Elsa.

Yegor Petrovich was very embarrassed by this incident and did not know what to reply to the reproaches of Fedosia Kuzminishna, who was claiming that Lizaveta Ivanovna had shamed them for ever before the assembled company. But there was nothing to be done; it was impossible to go home from the ball as the Tsar had yet to leave and, like it or not, it was necessary to remain. Soon, in order to deflect attention from Elsa, Yakko invited Maria Yegorovna to dance a minuet. He was an excellent dancer and everyone got up from their place when he led out his lady and a small circle momentarily formed around the dancers. Among the spectators was

Elsa. She looked at her Yakko with astonishment and tried to arrive at some explanation as to why he had not come over to dance with her. She remained sorrowful and sullen all evening and did not answer any of Yakko's questions.

Meanwhile Fedosia Kuzminishna was trying everything she could to disencumber herself of this accursed Finnish girl, who shamed her in public and at home got up to all sorts of wonders. Let us pass on a private conversation between Fedosia Kuzminishna and Yegor Petrovich in their bedroom. Fedosia Kuzminishna, being a subtle woman, broached the subject obliquely.

– Do you know, Yegor Petrovich, – she said, – that life in Petersburg is getting quite costly....

– Yes, I notice that as well, Fedosia Kuzminishna, but what can we do? That's quite seemly, more and more people come into the city....

– And, there you are, Anisia has been reporting to me how our expenses are increasing: oil and bread and salt beef, all keep running out like nobody's business....

– But what are you on about that for, Fedosia Kuzminishna?

– Well, judge for yourself, Yegor Petrovich, an extra person in the house is no joke...today, tomorrow and every day at the table, a candle in her room...and extra soap....

– What a story you've started on! Is Liza eating you out of house and home, or something? – Well, old girl, you really can't complain about her on that score; she eats about as much as a young chick.... That's not the way our forbears ruined themselves, Fedosia Kuzminishna.

– It's at your discretion, Yegor Petrovich, as you yourself will judge, but it's my business to tell you that it's not good....

– What's not good?

– Well, in that court ball of yours, then? She shamed us....

– That's right, it wasn't good, but that's in the past now, Fedosia Kuzminishna. The Tsar himself knows about it and just allowed himself a smile....

– Well, but that's just one thing, but there's a lot more that's bad.

– Oh, yes, and what else is there?...

– Yes, well, it's not good, she's – oh, let's forget her – she's so odd: you know, Swedish girls....

– But Liza isn't Swedish....

– It's the same thing, she's from a Swedish land....

– So, what is she, then?... Come on, tell me.

– What is she? You see, you're only getting angry; I'll tell you quite simply – she's a witch, she bedevils....

Yegor Petrovich burst out laughing: – You don't know what you're talking about, Fedosia Kuzminishna, saying things like that... well, then, what is a witch?

– What am I to do, old chap, I'm a stupid thing, completely stupid. I've always lived like that and that's the way I'll die. I don't understand all your wisdom, I just judge everything simply: a witch is a witch. You just have to listen to what the whole house is saying.

– Well, what else are they gossiping on about?...

– I'll tell you what. The other day the maids were watching and Lizaveta Ivanovna was creeping into the bath-house and wanted to get the fire going. So the girls said to her: 'Eh, young mistress, you should have told us before, we could have heated up the bath-house for you'. They heated up the bath-house, they came for her and she was just going in when she saw...something going into the bathroom, all arms and legs – eh? What do you call that? We say it's because a witch has....

– There are no witches, Fedosia Kuzminishna, it's only old maids' chatter... she's just a bit wild yet, she hasn't got much polish yet among foreign people.

– Well, and what's she doing, I ask you, Yegor Petrovich, all day long singing to herself down her nose? – that's not for nothing....

– Yes, and what does she sing? Songs: that's their custom, that's what they all do, caterwaul away....

– Well, all right, but what about this? The girls heard a noise in her room one night...they looked through a chink and she was singing, and jumping about the floor and casting spells....

– It's just a young girl playing the fool....

– Oh, you can explain everything, Yegor Petrovich, and this? Recently some Finn came to our yard bringing provisions...she spotted him, jumped out, rushed straight over to him with her arms round his neck and started gabbling away in that language of hers....

– No wonder, she saw a fellow-countryman. However, let's talk about it later, Fedosia Kuzminishna, it'll soon be six o'clock already; I've got better things to do than ganging up on a poor girl. Give me my cloak – it's time for me to be about my business.

Fedosia Kuzminishna carried out her husband's command, but when she was alone she shook her head, threw her hands up and muttered:

– That's the way it always is...oh, you, better things to do...the poor girl...oh, you old sinner! Lord above, it seems she must have bewitched him!

Meanwhile another scene was taking place in the dining room. Yakko, who was passing the Zverev's house early in the morning, could not fail to call in to see the family which was a second home to him.

Maria Yegorovna was tidying up from breakfast. Her black locks, brushed back behind her ears, were covered in a white Dutch bonnet. A striped print blouse clasped her supple waist. Her cuffed sleeve, reaching only to the elbow, revealed a plump, malleable arm. Black shoes with red heels, fastened with a tin buckle, fitted tightly over a well-formed foot. Maria Yegorovna's sleepy eyes were rather languid; at times they blazed with brilliant sparks, or they could be covered with transparent moisture. Girlish dreams, nocturnal fancies perhaps, gave Maria Yegorovna's face a thoughtfulness which usually disappeared during the course of the day.

– How nicely dressed you are today! – said Ivan Ivanovich, kissing her hand.

– You are joking, – said Maria Yegorovna with a smile, – I've got my homespun dress on, which you've seen lots of times before.

Ivan Ivanovich became confused and did not know at all what to say. His inner voice would have said: 'How pretty you are today, Maria Yegorovna, there's something particularly attractive about you today.' But such phrases were not then said to young girls and would have been considered indecent.

In order to change the subject, Ivan Ivanovich asked:

– And where is everyone?

– Father is at business, mother is seeing about the housework....

Yakko went silent and started to examine the tablecloth with great curiosity. But when Maria Yegorovna left the table, Yakko looked at her fine figure and fell into a severe state of hesitation. He could not help admiring both Maria Yegorovna's beauty, her dexterity and her love of order – 'a good wife! a good housekeeper!' – these words resounded involuntarily in his ear. Maria Yegorovna moved a chair to the cupboard, to put some dishes back on the upper shelf. She jumped nimbly on to the chair, her one foot resting on the cushion and the other raised in the air, and this well-shaped leg in a grey stocking with arrows was displayed to full advantage. The young man's heart started to beat faster, his eyes sparkled...he wanted to say something, but the door opened and in came Elsa. Her blouse was barely fastened and her fair flaxen locks spread over her fair half-revealed breast; she was sorrowful and her eyes expressed something half wild. Instinctively she had understood the feeling with which Yakko was looking at Maria Yegorovna and she turned away angrily.

– Hello, Elsa! – said Ivan Ivanovich in Russian, giving her his hand.

– *Än mujsta!* – replied Elsa, puffing out her cheeks and drawing back her hand.

162

– Yes, and will it be long before you manage to learn Russian?

– *Än mujsta!* – repeated Elsa.

– What's wrong with you, Elsa? – said Ivan Ivanovich in Finnish. – Who are you angry with? Have you really been insulted?

– What do you want with me? Go and dance with her, that's all you're good for.

– Oh, so you're angry because I danced with Maria Yegorovna? What's wrong with that? It's time you got used to the customs here....

– Our custom says you only dance with your betrothed....

– Explain to Lizaveta Ivanovna, – interrupted Maria Yegorovna, looking daggers at Elsa – that she shouldn't forget to lace herself up. Mama will be angry and we just can't make her understand that it isn't decent.

Yakko conveyed these words to Elsa. Elsa threw up her hands.

– Oh, Yakko, how the *Veineleisi* have bewitched you. Everything that they think up seems good to you, and all our ways are bad. Now what do they want to tie me up with braids for? What for? Tell me! They just want me not to be able to walk, or talk, or breathe – and you just say the same thing. Now you tell me, why should I be laced up? Will I be better if I am, or something?

Yakko paused to think how to reply to this strange question and meanwhile involuntarily looked at his beautiful compatriot.

It is true that her breast was half exposed, but this breast was as white as snow; her locks hung in disorder over her shoulders, but he found her all the more appealing for that. Her slippers were scarcely on her feet, so all the more could be seen of her slender and beautiful leg. Peculiar thoughts struggled for supremacy within the young man.

Elsa continued:

– There's Yusso, he's cleverer than you, the *Veineleisi* can't deceive him. You should listen to what he says.

– Who's Yusso?

– Don't you know Yusso, Yuxano's son? You've forgotten all your own people, Yakko, the *Veineleisi* have knocked your memory out of you.

– Where have you met him?

– The *Veineleisi* made him bring various stores here – I recognised him right away from the window....

– So what was he saying to you, then?

– Oh, lots of things, lots! Annie's cow has calved, Mary's got married to Mattie....

– What else did he tell you?...

– You want to know everything? – said Elsa, clapping her hands with a mocking expression, – well, perhaps I'll tell you: he said he and I should go home.

– Home, with him?

– Yes! He's a bit cleverer than you. He says that, however cunning the *Veineleisi* may be, they are going to catch it, and the *Ruotsi* want to let the sea in on them again....

– What nonsense, Elsa... the Swedes? That's just a fairy tale....

– Yes! fairy tale! – Yusso doesn't say that. He explains that poor people like us are not fit to live with the *Veineleisi*; and he said that he's got a lot of money here for oil – God doesn't give the *Veineleisi* any oil.... – Come with me, he says, I'll marry you, I've plenty of money, and we can eat clean bread the whole year round.

– And did you agree?

– Not yet, – replied Elsa craftily, – I said I would have to ask my chap about it.

– Maria Yegorovna, seeing that they were paying no attention to her, left the room.

Yakko thought for a while. What decision should he make? Whether to wait on for the long, long drawn out education of the half wild Elsa, subjecting her to all the unpleasantnesses of an unaccustomed lifestyle, or whether to give her up as a bad job and return her to her homeland. At the thought of their homeland, his heart automatically beat faster: the charms of Elsa, his childhood playmate, seemed to him all the greater and to part from her, to part for evermore, seemed to him unthinkable.

Elsa realised the effect her story had. She clapped her hands, jumped over to Yakko and, on her knees, seized him by the head and pressed him to her, and her fresh, silky breast slid over the young man's face; he shuddered and almost pushed her from him.

Elsa burst into tears. Yakko ran from the room.

– He doesn't even want to kiss me, – muttered Elsa through her tears, – oh, there's a reason for it, that Maria has cast a spell on him; he dances with her, and the way he looks at her – all right, we shall see...it wasn't for nothing that the old people taught me....

With these words Elsa ran off to her room and put the door on its hook. An hour later she came out and quietly tip-toed into Maria Yegorovna's room. She looked round and, seeing no one was there, hurriedly approached the bed and shoved something under the feather mattress.

Elsa turned and behind her flapped the starched wings of a maid's cap and a pair of eyes flashed at her through copper spectactles. From under the cap could be heard the menacing voice of Anisia the housekeeper:

– What are you doing creeping about in here, my young lady? With these words the old woman put her hand under the feather bed and pulled out a small packet. Straight away she went to Fedosia Kuzminishna and then the fun started.

After general consultation with Anisia and the other maids it was proposed to open the packet. They undid it – not without fear and not without a few superstitious sayings – and found: two rags, a piece of paper, a small piece of coal and some clay, all tied up crosswise with black thread. Witchcraft – there was not the slightest doubt.

They send for Elsa, they show it to her and they ask her about it: she just laughs slyly.

There was already talk of tying up the witch and presenting her to the police but, fortunately, Yegor Petrovich returned. Having found out the reason for the commotion, he smiled outwardly, but inwardly he was a bit scared himself: 'Who knows what she's up to?' – he thought. After a short silence he said: what's the use of us questioning her? She doesn't even understand us and can't explain to us. That sort of thinking must be stupid. Ivan Ivanovich will be coming in the evening; let him ask her all about it: what she was doing and why.

– All right, all right, – replied Fedosia Kuzminishna – you see it and you still don't believe it. Have it your own way, only allow me to keep her locked up until then. It's no joke, you know, father; Maria Yegorovna is not exactly a stranger to us. – Yegor Petrovich said nothing.

By the evening they had released the unfortunate captive.

It was already about seven in the evening; outside it was frosty. In the Zverevs' livng room they had stoked up the huge Swedish stove. The oven doors had been left open. Light from its opening permeated the room with· a purple mist. The shadow of the windows, illuminated by a full moon, was sharply outlined on the wooden floor. Two lit candles stood on the table and flickered from the current of air. All these modes of illumination intermingled; the whimsical shadows which they cast fluttered on the ceiling, on the wide wooden fretted cornice and on the walls, which were upholstered with black leather, complete with shining insignia.

At the table were seated Zverev, his wife and Yakko. They seemed to have just finished a long and unpleasant conversation, which was followed by complete silence. Eventually the doors were opened and in came a pale, quivering Elsa, rather like a criminal. With an imposing expression, Yakko showed her to the chair opposite the fire. Elsa did not want to sit down, but Yakko underlined his instruction in a menacing voice and Elsa obeyed. She sat on the chair, folded her arms and fixed her immobile gaze into the hearth's orifice.

– Don't be afraid, Elsa, – said Yakko in Finnish, in a quiet voice, – no one's going to do you any harm; but tell me quite frankly what that packet means, which you see on the table. What was your intention? – Elsa made no reply and concentrated all the more on fixing her gaze into the opening of the fire. Her face grew redder. Her locks hung down over her eyes. The moonlight lay on her white dress in a wide stripe. Her whole body shuddered, like a Pythian priestess on a charmed tripod. – Well, then, tell us, – said Yakko, directing his angry eyes at Elsa.

– What are you asking me about, Yakko, – said Elsa finally, in a halting voice, – that packet is a mere trifle...a childish joke.... I thought by this means to wean you away from that Maria, who wants to take you away from me.... But now that's not it...that's not it at all...now...I know everything, I can see everything; now I am strong and you are all...nothing...before me....

– What are you saying, Elsa? – said Yakko, visibly perturbed, – you have taken leave of yourself.

Elsa began to laugh with a strange guffaw.

– Or don't you see? – she continued, – there... far away... in the middle of the flame... the scarlet halls of my little sister... there she is... in the corona of the shining coals; she is smiling... she is nodding to me... she says that I must talk to you....

At this point, Yakko remembered the Pastor's words and wanted to throw himself upon Elsa and put an end to her bewitchment; but curiosity and some sort of invisible power held him back on his chair.

Elsa went on:

– I was still a child when old Rusi used to take me on his knee and sit me opposite the fire. He would cover my head with his hands and, pointing to the opening of the stove, would say: 'Elsa, Elsa, look for your little sister'. I was silly then and afraid and I wanted to fight my way out of the old man's hands, but my eyes unwittingly fixed on the fire and soon I couldn't tear them away. Before long, in the depths, amongst the white-hot coals, I saw, as I see now, magnificent halls. That's where columns of living flame entwine, stretch up to the sky and don't go out. Crimson sparks fly off and shine on the white flaming wall. In the middle of those halls a child's face appeared to me, one exactly like mine; it would smile, beckon me in, disappear in streams of flame and appear again with the same smile. 'Little sister, little sister, – it would say to me, – when shall you and I be united?' And my heart would long for this beautiful child, and it would keep on smiling and beckoning to me. And I just had to think about something, or old Rusi would ask me something, and from the distant wall a veil would be removed and I would see everything on the earth and under the earth, and the mountains and the forests and the watery chasms, and the people, and hear what they were saying, and see what they were doing. 'Run away from here', – my little sister says to me now, – 'here they will distract you, they will keep you away from me, they'll stifle you, you'll forget our language! On the banks of the Vuoksi people will not lead you astray, there the pines and the cliffs are silent, the moon shines with its life-giving power and animates the coarse body. There in the moon's rays, in the streams of flame, we shall mingle in a merry round-dance, fly round the whole earth and the whole earth for us will be bright and transparent'. Do you hear, Yakko, what little sister says; you are the only thing we lack; the mighty power of old Rusi vitalised you too, you silly; you are ours, Yakko! You are mine and nothing can part us: if you forget about me, you'll rue the day. Leave these people, Yakko; in our fiery chambers it is bright and joyful; there we shall meet and we shall merge with you into a single flaming thread. It's true, my time has not yet come, but will it be soon? I am asking my miraculous sister: 'Not soon', – she replies, – 'everything grows by degrees, like the tree from the seed. First on the earth, then under the earth, and then... above the earth, Elsa, and there are no limits to our strength and our bliss!'

Yakko did not let her continue.

– There's something strange happening here, – he said to Yegor Petrovich, – she is out of her mind: I advise you to send for the doctor.

– But what did she tell you? – asked Yegor Petrovich.

– Nothing, – replied Yakko, – you mustn't be afraid of her; she is ill, she's got a fit of.... Send for the doctor, I tell you, let him see her in this state.

– All right, then, – replied Yegor Petrovich. – Ivan Khristianovich lives quite near us and he's at home in the evenings. – They sent for the doctor and Elsa still sat opposite the fire, now laughing, now uttering incomprehensible speeches, now putting her hands together, as though imploring someone about something. Yakko watched her with curiosity, proposing, come what may, to await the resolution of this riddle.

A quarter of an hour later Ivan Khristianovich arrived, a prim German in a brown kaftan with steel buttons; he carried a cane with an ivory knob. He knocked with it, assuming an important air, spitting on one side then the other, for he had the habit of ceaselessly chewing tobacco, which was then thought to be a universal medicine against all diseases.

– Where's the patient? – he asked in German.

– I am considered the patient, – replied Elsa in German. Yakko's amazement was inexpressible. He knew that, in normal circumstances, Elsa could not speak a word of German.

– How do you feel, my dear child? – said Ivan Khristianovich.

– Good physician, silly physician, you want to treat me. Do you know whom you want to treat? Do you know how to treat with fire and flame? Look, my little sister is laughing at you, good physician, silly physician.

Ivan Khristanovich listened, listened to her with astonishment: he sniffed some tobacco and did not understand a thing.

Meanwhile the fire was going out slowly in the hearth and the moon had gone behind a nearby house; and at the same time there was a lessening in Elsa's loquacity. Finally, it was as if she had woken up.

– Where am I? What's wrong with me? – she said in Finnish.

The doctor felt her pulse; Zverev and Yakko were looking at her with concern. Meanwhile Yakko told the physician all that had happened.

Furrowing his brows and eagerly sniffing his tobacco, Ivan Khristiano-vich pronounced:

– It's a strange case, but there have been examples of this sort of thing when nervous spirits rise from the effects of the heat and act upon the brain. And from that you can get a nervous condition, as Celsius writes. However, pyromania, or fortune-telling by fire, was known among the ancients and produced similar symptoms with them. Strange that it should have been preserved until now. but there's nothing to fear! Put the patient to bed and I shall bring you from the house a fine medicine which, as our famous Dutch physician Van Ander has proved, helps against all illnesses: namely opium. Give her four drops every day and plenty of coffee to drink and you will see, it will remove these whims from her like magic.

The next day and the day after poor Elsa was indeed ill from the effects of the unversal medicine; the day after that she could hardly get up: from agitation of the blood and sleepiness.

The poor child of nature understood nothing that was being done to her: why she was being kept locked in; or why they kept pouring some drug into her, the effects of which, however, seemed to her to be quite pleasant. But she ofen forgot all that was going on around her and turned all her attention to the hero of Finnish legend, the famous Väinämöinen. She recalled how he made himself a kantele from the pike's ribs, as he didn't know where to get wood-chips and hair on his strings, and in a state of oblivion she sang:

> An oak grew in a barnyard
> a tall tree at a yard's end;
> on the oak were shapely boughs
> on each bough was an acorn
> on the acorn was a golden whorl
> on the golden whorl was a cuckoo.

The Salamander

When the cuckoo calls
and utters five words
gold wells from its mouth
and silver pours forth
on a golden knoll
on a silver hill:
from there the kantele's pegs
the screws for the curly birch!
The old Väinämöinen said
he uttered, spoke thus:
'I've got the kantele's pegs
the screws for the curly birch
but still something is missing:
five strings the kantele lacks.
Where should I get the strings from
for it, put on the voices?'

He went in search of a string.
    He steps through a glade:
a lassie sat in the glade
a young maiden on the marsh.
The lass was not weeping, nor
indeed was she rejoicing
but just singing to herself:
she sang to pass her evening
hoping a bridegroom would come
thinking about her lover.
Steady old Väinämöinen
yonder crept with no shoes on
without toe-rags he tiptoed;
    then when he got there
he began to beg tresses
and he put this into words:
'Lass, give some of your tresses
    damsel, of your hair
    for kantele strings
voices of eternal joy!'

The lass gave of her tresses
    some of her fine hair;
    gave tresses five, six
    even seven hairs:
from there the kantele strings
sounders of eternal joy.

But suddenly Elsa's voice was raised; her eyes shone and with great pride she sang out:

> Then, when old Väinämöinen
>   played the kantele
> with small hands, slender fingers
>   thumbs curving upward
> the curly birch tree uttered
> the leafy sapling lilted
>   the cuckoo's gold called
> and the lassie's hair rejoiced.
> With his fingers Väinämöinen played
> with its strings the kantele rang out:
> mountains thundered, boulders boomed
>   all the cliffs trembled
>   rocks lapped upon waves
> gravels on waters floated
>   the pines made merry
>   stumps leapt on the heaths.
>
> It is heard, the fine music
> was heard in six villages
> and there was no animal
> that did not come to listen
>   to that sweet music
> the sound of the kantele;
> what beasts were in the forest
>   crouched on their claws to
> listen to the kantele
> marvel at the merriment;
> the flying birds of the air
> gathered upon twigs
> and all manner of fishes
>   crowded on the shore;
>   the very earthworms
> moved to the top of the mould –
>   they turned, they listened
> to that sweet music, to the
> kantele's eternal joy
>   Väinämöinen's tune.
> There the old Väinämöinen
>   played finely indeed
> and rang out beautifully.

The Salamander

When he played at home
in his room of fir
the rafters echoed
and floorboards thudded
the loft beams sang, the doors creaked
all the windows made merry
the hearth of stone moved
the curly-birch post chanted;
when he walked among spruces
and roamed among pines
the spruces bowed down
the pines on the hill turned round
the cones rolled upon the lea
the sprigs showered down on the root;
when he wandered in a grove
or tripped in a glade
the groves played a game
the glades were glad all the time
the flowers had a fling
the young saplings bobbed about.

But often the words of the song approached her own situation and with a pitiful lament she would reply to Väinämöinen, as he asked the weeping, spreading birch tree why it was crying:

'Well, some people say
certain people think
that I live in joy
in delight revel;
but lean in my cares
in my longings I ring out
set forth in my suffering-days
in sorrows murmur. Empty
for my silliness I weep
for my shortcomings complain
that I am hapless, wretched
utterly woeful, helpless
in these evil spots
on these vast pastures.
Often in my gloom
and often, a gloomy wretch
I am felled for slash-and-burn
for firewood chopped up:
men have stood under me, have

whetted their axes
to dispatch my luckless head
to end my weak life.
So I with small means
a poor wretched birch
am left quite naked
utterly undressed
to quake in the chill
to howl in the frost.'

And towards the end of the song, Elsa began to weep and to weep bitterly. Thus would Yakko find her and all his attempts to console her and reason with her would be fruitless. This strange obsession with her homeland grew even stronger in Elsa through her seclusion. Yakko did not know what to do: over a three-month period Elsa's education had not really progressed at all. Her ideas had not developed; all her folkloric prejudices were still in full cry. It was no longer possible to leave her in the Zverevs' home. To marry her? The very thought turned Yakko cold. He could not help comparing his situation with a fine machine, in which just one wheel had been wrongly installed, which had the effect of spoiling the motion of all the other wheels. He could not but admit that Elsa was for him a drawback in life. His inward displeasure was reflected in his words and, from this, Elsa grieved all the more.

And at the same time Elsa was beautiful; at the same time his native sky shone at him in her eyes, the fabulous world of his childhood, and Yakko would go home as before with despair in his heart.

The month of November came. For several days on end it poured with rain and the sea wind drove the Neva over its banks. One morning Yakko was sitting in his secluded room which had been allotted to him in the Admiralty and, deep in his work, he did not notice what was happening around him. In the meantime, the whole city was in a state of alarm, the water was rising excessively, inhabitants of the embankment areas of the city were moving their possessions up to the garrets, and in a few places they had already moved up to the roof. The high granite embankment wall did not yet exist. What would now be an insignificant water rise was, in 1722, a real disaster for the city. Yakko glanced out of the window: Admiralty Square had become a sea, awash with boats, logs, roofs and coffins. The Zverevs' house was situated in the part of the town most liable to flooding. The thought of the fate awaiting the family immediately struck Yakko: but how was he to help, how could he get there?

172

The Salamander

The waves were already breaking against the upper section of the lower storeys! Wringing his hands in desperation, Yakko watched the overflow of the Neva, seeking some means of leaving the building through the window. At that minute he noticed a smallish launch with a broken mast sailing over the Neva. Two sailors were vainly attempting to retrieve a chunk of the mast which was submerged in the water, or to cut the ropes in two. Already the launch was leaning to one side. At the stern stood a tall man; his black hair spread over his shoulders. With one hand he clenched the helm, with the other he was encouraging the flustered mariners, but – in another minute the launch was bound to capsize. Yakko looked, and couldn't believe his eyes – it was the Tsar himself!

At this sight, the young Finn forgot all danger. With a strong fist he knocked through the window frame and threw himself out of the window. At this moment a strongly fastened raft was thrown against the wall of the building. From the movement of the raft, Yakko hit his head hard against the wall and in an almost unconscious state grasped at some slippery logs. In that condition he was picked up by people on one of the admiralty boats.

Hardly had Yakko come to – and his first question was about the Tsar. 'He changed launch', was the reply. Then Yakko remembered again about the family and the boat swiftly turned in the direction of the Zverevs' house. As they approached, Yakko could see water already pouring from the windows; in the whole house there was no sign of a living person. Sorrow gripped the young Finn's heart; the last people whom me might call his own had perished. But soon his attention turned to a large launch which was trying to get near to the house with its oars. Looking again, he could see in the launch Zverev, his wife and all the domestics; as the launch came nearer and nearer, Yakko could distinguish all the faces and everyone was there – excepting only Elsa.

– And Elsa? – he shouted in despair.

– We don't know! – Zverev answered sadly.

The young man fell senseless to the floor of the boat.

By evening the water had subsided. The inhabitants gradually returned to their houses, trying to efface the traces of the flooding, and soon everything in the young, courageous capital returned to its usual order.

Our Yakko lay in Zverev's bedroom with a swollen head and in the grip of a strong fever. He tossed about on the bed, pronouncing now incomprehensible words and now calling for family members, and for Elsa. This went on for entire days. Finally Yakko returned to his senses and the first person whom his weakened memory recognised was Maria Yegorovna. She was sitting beside the bed and looking with concern at the sick man.

– Where am I? What's wrong with me? – asked Yakko.

– With the people who love you, – replied a quiet voice.

Everything returned again to the young man's memory. He took Maria Yegorovna's hand and pressed it tightly to his lips. Maria Yegorovna lowered her eyes and reddened.

Fedosia Kuzminishna came into the room.

– What happened to Elsa? – asked Yakko.

– Ah, thanks be to God! He's come to! Why, young man, you've been unconscious for three weeks, that's no laughing matter. Now, as for your sister, she's alive and well, young man – she's gone home with some Finn or other. Yegor Petrovich went to quite a bit of trouble; they had a job to find out where she had vanished to, to some Vox place, was it?

Indeed, at the time of the flood, when the yard had already filled with water and Yegor Petrovich, together with the household, was preparing to embark in an admiralty launch which had reached them from the street, in all the confusion they had forgotten about Elsa. At that time she was in her room, her windows looking out on to the yard, and locked in, in accordance with the wise instructions of Fedosia Kuzminishna. The unfortunate recluse watched with horror as the water rose higher by the minute: – 'it's all over, – she told herself, – the *Ruotsi* have let the sea in on to the *Veineleisi*: everything must perish, there's no salvation' – and with these words she folded her arms, sat down opposite the window and coolly watched the water lift the roof off a low barn. Suddenly she saw a boat appearing in the yard and in the boat was a familiar face. 'Yusso, Yusso! – yelled Elsa, opening the wide top window, – I'm here, I'm here! Save me!'

And the agile Finn approached the window, grasped the shutters, helped Elsa scramble on to his bark, sat her down, took up the oars and soon the bark had disappeared from view.

Meanwhile, seating himself in the launch, old Zverev remembered Elsa. He rushed back to her room, but she wasn't there; they ran round the whole house and went into the attics – Elsa had disappeared. Time was precious; the commander of the launch said that he still had to give assistance to many more houses; and Yegor Petrovich was dragged almost forcibly into the launch.

Yakko improved with every day. One day, when Maria Yegorovna came into the room to see him, he said:

– You seem to have forgotten about me, Maria Yegorovna, you visit me so rarely.

– When you were in danger, – the girl replied, – I didn't leave you, as

God's my witness. But now that you're starting to get better, thanks be to God, it's not seemly for me to remain alone with you.

– Are there no means by which to cure that ill? – said Ivan Ivanovich, with a smile.

– What means? I don't know.

– It's very simple. Be my wife! What would you say to that, Maria Yegorovna?

Maria Yegorovna muttered the usual thing for the circumstances: 'The answer does not depend on me', and the young man tenderly kissed her hand.

The matter was negotiated with the old people; they gave their blessing. 'But before the wedding, there is one thing I have to do', – said Yakko to Yegor Petrovich, – 'I want to see Elsa right'.

– That's very noble, – said the old man, – most seemly.

A few days later a sledge was propelling the young Finn towards his native river banks. About forty kilometers before Imatra he was already asking around the settlements about Elsa, the grand-daughter of old Rusi. But the inhabitants told him that Imatra was far away and that they knew no one there.

Another twenty kilometers and it was a different story: 'how could we not know Elsa? – said the Finns, – we haven't had a sorceress like her for ages. She knows everything, whatever you ask her; if someone is sick, or one of the animals, you go to her, bow low, and it's gone like magic. And in return she'll soon be happy; Yusso says he'll marry her, for sure.'

Swiftly the wide sleigh raced over the deep snow; the mist lay on the plains, the green firs quietly swayed over the snowdrifts, the moon shimmered from the clouds and with its pale rays cut through the layers of mist; the mist cleared, allowing through a strip of brightness, and then it again obscured the wayside rocks. A sad feeling weighed on Yakko's soul: he was travelling over his native earth, which was at the same time foreign to him. From time to time Petersburg presented itself to his imagination, with its active and enlightened life, and then again the Finn's gaze turned involuntarily to the sorrowful panorama of his original homeland.

Not far from Imatra, Yakko noticed an unusual illumination in a hut which stood alone amid the rocks. In part it was curiosity and in part some involuntary feeling or other that caused him to stop. Yakko got out of his sledge, went over to the hut, looked through the porthole and saw that there was some sort of a celebration going on: a wedding or some such event.

Looking more closely, Yakko soon saw Elsa there in the hut. She was wearing a rather rich Finnish dress and was seated in the place of honour; everyone was treating her with the greatest respect, as they regaled her and bowed. Elsa was joyful and content, laughingly telling the tale of how the *Ruotsi* let the sea loose on the *Veineleisi* and wanted to drown her and how she and Yusso had tricked them.

Yakko thought to himself: 'Here she is joyful, respected by all, speaking her own language; she is free and happy. Back there she is sorrowful, tied in her every movement, the subject of mockery and hatred. Why should I take this happiness from her, in the hope of finding another sort which is incomprehensible to her and perhaps even unobtainable?'

At this point Elsa stood up and bid farewell to her hosts, who most respectfully escorted her out. The crowd of people walked past Yakko; he saw Elsa at a distance of two paces, but kept quiet amd just sadly watched her go, until she had disappeared in the mist.

Then Yakko waked into the hut and, handing a purse of money over to the host, he said: 'Tell Elsa, the grand-daughter of old Rusi, that Yakko sends her this for her wedding'. Yakko knew the honesty of his fellow-countrymen and was certain that the purse would be passed on as instructed.

While the the good people were still reeling at the sight of such incalculable wealth, Yakko left the hut and glanced once more at his native rocks.

– The last thread is broken, – he said to himself, – my land is foreign to me. Farewell, Suomi – farewell for ever! And greetings to Russia, my real motherland!

The young Finn buried his face in his hands, jumped into the sledge and the bells began to jingle!

Until this day on the banks of the Vuoksi a legend is preserved of the girl whom a rich lord wanted to take away to Petersburg, but who ran away from riches out of love for her native hut. They also tell how, long ago, strangers, or spirits, wealthily dressed, suddenly appeared in the local huts and left money on the table, asking for it to be passed on to Elsa, the aged sorceress.

II

Elsa

Dedicated to Count V.A. Sollogub

Errant, erraverunt ac errabunt, eo quod
proprium agens non posuerunt Philosophi.

Ioannes Pontanus, Theatro Alchemico

We were sitting in front of the fire; suddenly
father hit me so hard that I cried. 'Don't cry',
said father, 'you've done nothing wrong'; at
that moment the Salamander appeared in the
fire; 'I hit you so you don't forget it and so
you'll pass this event on to your children'.

Autobiography of Benvenuto Cellini

There lived in Moscow an uncle of mine, a man no longer at all young, but
with a mind, a heart and an education – and in these three qualities, they
say, there lies concealed the secret of never growing old. Uncle did not lose
his mind, because he did not lose his interest in people. Three generations
passed him by, but he understood the language of each of them. Novelty
held no terrors for him because nothing was new to him. Constantly following the wondrous path of knowledge, he had grown accustomed to
watching the natural development of this huge tree, in which discovery
ceaselessly followed discovery, observation followed observation, and
from one theory there grew another, which, in its turn, brought forth once
again the original. Therefore his conversation was always interesting, although strange. You would not find in it those opinions which had long
been steeped and squeezed dry, like old sugar-beet in a sugar factory. Nor
did it contain those phrases which in other people lie in wait for you in one
situation or another, like the inscription on a pot in the Kunstkamera or like
the refrain of a vaudeville couplet. But he had many ideas with which it
was not possible to agree: he maintained, for instance, that to know a lot, to

know a very great deal, was not at all advisable; that in olden days people were worse than us but knew much more than us; and that, for example, human knowledge has never again reached the same magnitude as before the flood!... It should be added that Uncle had travelled a lot in his younger days and – in the fashion of the times – had been a member of every possible mystical society: he had made gold, called up spirits, jumped and made others jump on wax nails or across rugs, played the role of the fathomless pit, and so on, and so on. Much that was wondrous on these subjects had been preserved in his memory; but, when speaking, he would employ such a strange mode of expression, at one and the same time both portentous and whimsical, that it was usually impossible to divine whether in actual fact Uncle believed what he was saying or was poking fun at it. When we pressed him by demanding insistently that he should say whether he was joking or serious, and that he should drop this ambiguous tone, Uncle would smile and with simple-hearted archness he would remark that it was impossible to get by without such a tone when speaking of many of the things of this world, and especially of the things not entirely of this world.

One morning I caught the old man in over a cup of coffee.

– What's the meaning of this, Uncle? I seem to remember that you never drank coffee in the mornings before.

– Yes, what am I going to do with all your scientists and doctors? First they affirmed that two cups of coffee a day, in the morning and after dinner, are too much for me: so I gave up my morning cup and used to wait calmly for my after-dinner one. And now recently the devil has possessed a certain German to write a whole book (with these words Uncle struck a quarto volume with his fist) in proof of there being nothing more harmful than coffee after dinner, and so persuaded me, sinner that I am, that from then on I replaced my after-dinner cup by a morning one.

– And meanwhile the vacancy left by the after-dinner cup is filled by something else, Uncle, isn't that the case?

Uncle gave up on the subject.

– You, young people, you never believe us old codgers. You, I'm sure, would not believe, for example, that you can have noise and shouting in a house without any visible reason?

– I would half believe....

– Half measures are never any use for anything; everything in nature is a whole – isn't that right? What are you, a Schellingist or a Hegelian?

– A bit of each, and perhaps neither the one nor the other....

– What's that? Whats's that? Scepticism?... How strange! But in this case, have the decency not to be a sceptic, for what I am saying is true. Just now the owner of the house came to me and told me, though, what I have long known. Yes, indeed! I've known that house for forty years. In my day it used to belong to Prince A., with whom I was friendly in my youth. In those days the nobility lived more like boyars: at every step in the house you could see that its owner had a father, a grandad a great grandad and their ancestors, which is not a thing you notice in the rented apartments of today, in which our top historical names languish so tediously and lavish their wealth....

– Well aimed, Uncle! You've hit the bull's eye with me there....

– I know, I know, the new generation!... Our fathers lived cautiously. They didn't take care either of your name or your health. And I'm not blaming you: you are cleansing your fathers' sins. But in my day it was not like that: the grandfather of the present inheritor lived thirty years in his Moscow boyar house without leaving the place. The whole neighbourhood thrived on it. A whole street was called after it, for he precisely fulfilled his boyar's position: doing good, not just counting and forgetting; and from his light and generous hand several merchants were raised, whose children now are millionaires. A father would profit from this bottomless purse to send his son to college, the industrialist who acquired the weaving mill; the generosity of this purse has educated several good painters at the academy and a whole orchestra of musicians.... However, many did that in those days and you can believe me that the beginning of the present wealth of the Muscovite middle class and its flourishing industry was marked by the boyar talent of those times, which lay in knowing how not to lavish one's wealth.

– I often used to visit the Prince. Even then, and that's forty years back, he would show me a room in which, sometimes at night, a strange noise could be heard, like a sort of howling. I even deliberately stayed the night for several days running in the Prince's house and myself twice heard this noise. We would barely open the door, and everything would be quiet; the room was empty and everything in its place. Scientists, sorcerers and various conspirators were invited to this room, but nothing helped and nothing was ever explained. Since then I have had plenty of time to forget about this house; but the other day the last inheritor, in his absence, sold the house of his fathers to a local merchant of my acquaintance, who wants to establish some sort of spinning works in the boyar chambers. The day before yesterday he came to me and, telling me all about the advantages of his purchase (for I had him well trained not to give me any nonsense), he remarked that there was just one snag. – What's that? – I asked. – It's just, – he replied, scratching himself and smiling, – as we would say simply, I've bought a house with brownies in it. – What do you mean, brownies? –

179

Exactly that, old chap; we had hardly moved in when at night we heard someone howling in the main room. We thought one of the workers must have stayed behind and went in there, but it was all quiet and as calm as you like. The next night – the same thing, and the night after that: howling away and suddenly it goes quiet, and then it's there again. You get it two or three times a night, so it's given everyone the willies. Don't you know any remedy, old chap?... – So I went off with the merchant to his new house and with no difficulty recognised the same room in which I had conducted my observations back in the late prince's time; nothing had changed in it.

– So what did you advise the poor merchant to do? – I asked my uncle.

– I advised him to place a steam-engine in this huge room, assuring him that that had the particular capability of chasing out goblins. But before the room is completely altered, Mister Physicist, wouldn't you like to have a look at it and explain this strange phenomenon by the latest theories? Seeing that you nowadays take it upon yourselves to explain everything!

– No, nowadays we don't take it upon ourselves to explain anything.... We maintain that each thing is, because it is....

– That's very useful for the march of science, it makes sense and it saves all the trouble of researching and pushing back the frontiers....

– However, it would be interesting to have a look at the room....

– Right, – said Uncle, – carriage! Only, be assured that all this is no imaginary daydream; and that I, a coldblooded fellow, have heard these howls with my own ears. Neither is there any need to doubt the merchant.

When we entered the old boyar dwelling, I sadly examined the princely coats of arms which were generously dispersed over the walls; the rows of family portraits whose origins were lost back in the legendary periods of our history; the old crystal candelabra which illuminated the boyars' feasts, that were open to all passers by; the princes' study, with its huge armchairs, where he perhaps would think about which new good deed to throw his gold at next – and my heart shrunk at the thought that coarse mechanical work was to take the place of lofty moral acts. Uncle was quiet, but he too seemed to be thinking the same thing, while our garrulous host was still plaguing us with his plans: 'Here will be the drying room, here the combing room, here the bleachery, the study will be the lumber room, and so on'. Calico and printed cloth! Are you worth this? Under your mills will vanish the memory of our ancestors' ancient virtue; our history will vanish! Amid these ruminations, we quite forgot the object of our visit. Eventually our host opened the door into a huge reception hall, lit from above: 'So here's where I shall place the steam engine, according to your advice, old chap; that's just the ticket. Right here...'; our host made a particular kind of a face and crossed himself.

I examined this strange room attentively and finally said to Uncle:

– This is not a room, but a wind instrunment.

– Ah, so that's it! – said Uncle with a derisive smile, – have the goodness to explain yourself a little more clearly. Of course nowadays you pursue clarity; you think that there is something in this world that is actually clear to mankind! Explain then, explain.

– It would be difficult to explain, but guesses can be made. I am not joking. This room does indeed resemble a wind instrument. Just look at that long gallery which, like a funnel, adjoins this chamber: this chamber acts like the bell-mouth of a French horn, and in the room itself look at the arch built into the ceiling: this arch is a segment of the cone: on this arch the window frames sink in the form of a segment of an octahedron....

– Spare us, spare us! – shouted Uncle, – or if not me, then at least this model of innocence! (With these words he indicated the owner of the house who, goggleyed, was listening to me with all possible attention.) Don't be astonished, Pantelei Artamonovich old chap: my nephew is a past master at casting charms; and you know that in 'charms' you get goodness knows what words, like cones and octahedrons....

– We understand, old chap, – replied our host.

– So what's your conclusion? – Uncle asked me.

– The following: that every sound in that gallery, which is built in an arc, passing through to this hall, must be magnified ten times. Now imagine that this sound hits the tone of this arc – then the sound would probably be a hundred times stronger. Add to that the echo produced by the inclined frames, and then you can convince yourself that the cheep of some rat in an acoustic microscope like this would seem like the howl of a human....

– That's all true enough, – remarked Uncle, – except that you, as a man of the nineteenth century, must prove your words by experiment....

I went off to the gallery and shuffled, sang and whistled: all these sounds resounded loudly in the gallery but nothing like a howl materialised in the room. Uncle smiled; the owner of the house looked upon all this with some surprise, not knowing what was going on in front of him, a joke or serious business. I exhausted myself, pacing up and down the gallery.

– Now, what do you say, Mister Scientist? – said Uncle to me in French.

– I say that I believe you, and I believe our host, but....

– But you want to test out for yourself whether we are deceiving you?

– More or less, Uncle; an experiment would be purer, as the chemists say.

– If then it happens, then you'll deign to admit it! So, Panteleimon Artamonovich, – Uncle continued, turning to the owner of the house, – our expert says he deserves to spend a night in your house, so he can get rid of the goblins straight away...he has this potion.

The owner bowed and expressed his gratitude.

– And so that it won't be too awful for you, – added Uncle, – I shall be with you for company, Mister Philosopher.

In the evening we appeared at the lodge. We were allotted a small room beside the door of the enchanted hall. I took all possible precautions, examined all the adjacent rooms, locked all the doors, lit plenty of candles everywhere and pulled out of my pocket a few issues of the French political press. Uncle was more gloomy than usual.

– What's that? – he asked, pointing to the newspapers.

– That's my potion, – I replied, – the potion which you told the owner of the house I had.

– A genuine potion, – retorted Uncle, – and a very effective one even. Nothing so removes a man from his inner, mysterious, real life, nothing makes him so deaf and dumb as the picture of these petty passions and petty crimes which calls itself the world of politics....

– What is to be done? A person is forced to live in this world....

– That is to say wants to live in it. The beast in him really enjoys beating the air and assuring himself that he is engaged in something important and worthwhile. All these flights of cunning, all these little tricks to little purpose suit him fine. Do these gentlemen not know how they foul the air which we breathe!

– Foul the air?

– I should say so!

I laughed.

– It would be interesting, – I said, – to research what chemical changes in the air are wrought by newspapers....

– You'd do better, Mister Scientist, to research why a speck of musk fills a whole room with its smell. You may have heard that the empress Josephine was very partial to musk. Recently a room was entered which she had occupied thirty years ago; in the course of that time this room had been washed and ventilated and the furniture changed – and what do you think? The smell of musk still remained in it to this day.

– That was in all the journals; but it doesn't prove anything: the divisibility of musk is well known....

– Well known? – retorted Uncle, with a laugh. – Congratulations if it's well known to you. And is it well known to you why you don't go into the room of a patient with an infectious disease?

– Of course! Because of the exhalation; a diseased, infectious atmosphere is formed from the breathing of the patient....

– Diseased atmosphere! And you think, child, that a power which is a thousand times stronger than bodily breathing and material divisibility, the power of criminal thought, criminal feeling, the criminal word or deed does not produce a diseased, noxious atmosphere around itself? Tell me, have you never noticed yourself that you breathe easier in the presence of a good man, your nerves calm down, as though a fragrant balm had been applied to them, your head is clearer, your heart beats evenly and merrily – while, on the contrary, a spectre unwittingly takes over in the presence of a scoundrel, something oppresses you, crushes you; your thoughts are constrained, your heart beats drearily, you are afraid to fix your eyes on such a man, as though you are ashamed of him or afraid that he might burn your innards with his gaze?... Your instinct does not deceive you! Believe me, young man, that around every thought, every feeling, every word and action a magic circle forms, to which are involuntarily subordinated the less powerful thoughts, feelings and actions which fall into it. This truth is contemporary with the world; its crude emblem is preserved in those magic circles which the fairy-tale mages draw around themselves.

– All that could very well be true, if it could only be proved.

– Proved, proved! – Uncle retorted testily. – Do you have the capacity to prove things? What do you have that's proven?...

– Very little, but at least at this moment it is proven, for example, that this candle is standing on the table, because I can see it....

Uncle began to guffaw. – See it, you can see it? But by what right do you see? By what right do you think you see? Who told you what you see? Who told you that there's a candle in front of you? I, on the contrary, assure you that there isn't a candle now in front of you; prove to me the opposite.

– I began to laugh in my turn.

– And I assure you that there's a big concert going on now on the moon, at which all the lunary inhabitants are gathered; prove to me the opposite.

– That's just it! – shouted my uncle. – That's where your nineteenth-century logic gets you! You see nothing beyond it. You, of course, are right in relation to it, but it is not right in relation to me. You may laugh, Mister Philosopher, but it's quite certain that there are places to which the whole past is as though attached, on which are traced in secret letters for people who are centuries removed from us their thoughts, their will.... Don't laugh. I also the other day had occasion to laugh at your scientists, who tempered and soaked magnetised things and then were surprised when, despite all their tricks, these things brought on mesmeric sleep to somnambulists with a single touch.... Materialists! They wanted to temper and steep away the magnetiser's will! You want facts? Very well! Do you know, Mister Scientist, that there are people who carry with them all their possessions? In my young days, I knew a man who seduced a girl and the unfortunate threw herself in the river. And what do you think? As soon as he began telling the story of this, his hair stood on end, his face went pale and he trembled all over: at that moment he saw in front of him, as clearly as I see you now, the river, the unfortunate girl and her death agonies....

– Oh, yes, I know about that! One of my friends acts out that comedy very well....

– Yes, I know that that event has been turned into a joke, but it has its basis in truth: I knew the man it happened to very well, and I can assure you that for him it was no joke, but a proof – he died tormented by this vision....

– Permit me to remark though, Uncle, that you are not conducting such a conversation to no purpose. You want to infect my imagination, to prepare me for the unusual, and then to frighten me, so that afterwards, as is your wont, you can have a good laugh at me, and at our century, and at our accomplishments.

– Just read your potion, – he said and with these words he pulled a book out of his pocket.

– What's that I see? – I exclaimed, – why that's *Brius' Calendar*! So that's where you draw your wisdom from, esteemed Uncle? You must admit that it's my turn to laugh.

– There is a lot of nonsense in this book, – replied my uncle with a semi-important and semi-mocking expression, – but that is not the compiler's fault.... But however that may be, I need this book: today I want to check a certain cypher, which seems to me to be doubtful.

It was already eleven o'clock in the evening. Everyone in the house had gone to bed. It was quiet on the streets. Only from the watch-towers there resounded the drawn-out cries of the sentries which were soon lost in the distance. The candles were burning and the flickering shadows lay on the cornices, which were adorned by the princely coats of arms. Everything was quiet.

The newspapers were interesting just at that minute; I was completely absorbed in them; all my attention was fixed on this positive European world with its activity, its industry, its passions and its steam engines. In particular, an article on the railways occupied me greatly and unwittingly there arose in me a certain pride at the thought of the gigantic enterprises of the industry of our time. In a word, I was completely engrossed in my reading when, suddenly... could I believe it?... No, there was no mistake... exactly within the bewitched room there resounded, and very clearly, a groaning. I shall never forget that moment; those sounds are ringing in my ears to this day. This groan sounded neither like a human voice nor the cry of an animal, but there was in it something unutterably sad. It penetrated to the innards of the soul and it was impossible to hear it without feeling a particular alarm: it seemed as though this sound was repeated in the very depths of my heart.... At this moment, twelve o'clock struck. The striking of the clock brought me to my senses: I rushed to the doors of the room – everything in there was quiet. The candles which had been placed by me on the tables burned calmly. All the doors were locked and there was no one in the room. I again went round all the walls and looked into the neighbouring rooms – everything was silent and peaceful. Somewhat perturbed, I returned to Uncle's room: he was sitting calmly, attentively looking through his book and making a few notes in it.

– Did you hear it? – he said.

– I heard it, – I replied.

– Do you understand what it is?

– Not at all.

– Well, perhaps it was a squeaking door, – Uncle went on, in his mocking tone.

I said nothing. Uncle continued: – Do you still want to stay?

– Until morning, at least. But why don't we go into our hall?

– I don't know for sure whether that would interfere with our experiment. We'll wait for the second time. If you like, this is what we'll do: I shall go into that room which has a door into it from the opposite side of our hall; you will remain here; we'll both start off by the doors and the moment the howling starts we'll enter the room simultaneously.

I agreed although, I must admit, an infantile fear had come over me and I felt terrified alone in the room. My heart beat fiercely and the groaning resounded constantly in my ears.

I tried to pull myself together by enumerating all the acoustic possibilities for the generation of such a sound. Meanwhile with one hand I took a candle and the other I placed on the door handle, so as to be ready at any moment. I don't know whether I was in that position for long. Everything around me was quiet. I seemed to hear the quivering of my pulse. Suddenly, just when I was feeling like moving away from the door, from right beside it, almost under my ear, the howl rang out again: but this was a howl of a different character. It also did not resemble any sounds known to me and seemed more an expression of rage than of sorrow.

A coldness ran along my veins. However, I quickly opened the door and very nearly stepped straight back again when, at the other end of the hall, I saw a human figure.... Only a minute later did I recognise it as my uncle, who, as arranged, had opened his door at the same time as I.

– Did you hear it? – said my uncle in his usual tone.

– It's strange, very strange! – I replied. – Now listen, Uncle; we have to try one last thing: let's stay in this room and see for sure whether these dreadful phenomena are being produced in it.

– Agreed, – replied Uncle, – although, I don't mind telling you, I have particular reasons for not wanting to remain here, and I wouldn't guarantee success. Nevertheless, – my uncle added, after some thought, – we'll give it a try.

Once again I examined all the neighbouring rooms and all the doors, checked the candles and, so as to give my thoughts another direction, I got down to my paper again. We were seated in the middle of the hall, beside the card table. Uncle drew upon it, with great attention, some sort of figures and signs that to me were unintelligible.

– What's all that? – I asked.

– Never mind, – Uncle replied in a tone more portentous than usual. – This is my pigeon; you are outside this sphere.

– Uncle, – I yelled, – for God's sake, cut out the mystery! I could do now with preserving all my presence of mind.

We stopped talking. More than half an hour went by of complete silence, when suddenly... how can I express my amazement! From the depths of the hall, the groaning was heard again, at first quietly, but then louder, louder.... Finally it resounded right above my ear. This time I clearly distinguished two sounds in which was expressed an inconsolable sort of despair, rage and sorrow – in a word, everything doleful which the human soul could devise. I leaped from my chair and looked at my uncle; he too seemed alarmed and, leaning heavily on the table, was following with some disquiet the movement of the sound.... But how can I describe my horror when, looking up at the opposite wall, I caught sight, between the shadows cast by me and by my interlocutor, of yet a third shadow which was quite distinct, but whose shape it was impossible to catch, for it was constantly changing. It was something beyond expression, resembling a human figure which, seemingly, was straining and struggling, constantly changing its form. Here there was the likeness of a head, and hands which extended themselves and then clenched, like figures on the optical scenes known as 'amorphous pictures'. All this went on for not more than a minute.... I glanced behind: there was no one but us in the room. I looked up again at the wall and the incomprehensible shade was paling, together with the howl, which was getting lost at the other end of the hall. It seemed to have flown past us.

– Well, thank God for that, it's disappeared! – said my uncle, taking his hands from the table. – The poor wretches! – he added, taking a long breath – when are you going to pay off your debt for this?

186

After a few minutes, my uncle calmed down and resumed his derisive expression, saying:

– Well, did you hear it?

– I heard it, – I replied.

– And you saw it?

– I saw it, – I replied.

– Was the experiment on the level?

I remained silent.

– Now we can calmly go off home, – went on Uncle, – it won't happen any more.

– How do you know that?

– Three epochs of life and three groans.

– For God's sake, that's enough of this mysterious tone. Let's try and combine our efforts to make some sense of this strange phenomenon.

– It's very clear to me.

– Then, tell me.

– What's the use? You will still understand nothing and you'll just say that I'm playing a joke on you, that none of this can be proved and so on, the way you usually do in response to my candid explanations – yes, candid – he repeated with an expression of mockery.

– No, tell me, Uncle, tell me what you know and what you make of it. In a phenomenon as strange as this, anything is possible.

– Anything? – asked Uncle, looking at me intently.

– Well, what I mean is that we must make use of every means in order to explain it....

Uncle smiled. I remained silent.

We remained until morning in the bewitched hall and, as my uncle had predicted, really did hear nothing more.

The following is what my uncle called the explanation of this strange phenomenon. I shall try, as far as my memory permits, to reproduce here his story in full.

– In order to explain to you this phenomenon, – my uncle said, – I must begin from afar. Chronologically it relates to the third decade of the eighteenth century. You will not find my story in history, because what is described in your history is only the external events, only the deceptive images of real inner events. Over and above your philologists, archeologists, antiquarians and so on there exist in this world other historians; they open up their annals to those phenomena which usually remain unmentioned by others or are misinterpreted. I have chanced in my life to have dealings with these unknown chroniclers and what I am about to tell you has been wrested by me from that mysterious tradition of theirs. You may believe me or not, as you wish. If my story seems insufficiently clear to you, then you are welcome to provide your own explanation. As far as I am concerned, I don't need other explanations.

Around the year 1726, in a secluded room not far from Sukhareva Tower, at about midnight, two men – the one quite an old man, the other of more middling years – were bustling around by a strangely shaped stove. The younger man was sitting right opposite the hearth and adjusting the burning coals with his tongs. Having fruitlessly examined the opening, he set about reading the huge book lying in front of him on the lectern. The old man, in a wide velvet kaftan, sat down, after the examination, in the armchair and listened with great attention to the reading: the young man read lingeringly.

'...Having got the stone by means of successful control of the white of the fire, as already instructed above, if you wish to see it red, then increase the heat of the stove, for our Salamander lives only in a strong fire and amidst the fire and feeds on fire and does not fear the fire. From light heat, tincture and sulphur are not to be separated from the stone. For this work forty-one days and nights are required.'

– And what day are we today? – asked the old man.

– The thirty-second day from the start of the fixation, – replied the young man.

– And still we don't see the red dragon, and we don't even see the rust that Basilius Valentinus talks about. We must have made a mistake somewhere in the procedure.

– We'll wait until the forty-first day, and then we shall see.

– It's all very well for a young man like you to wait, but what about me – an old man? This is already the fourth time we have started this procedure: we seem to be getting near, we seem to have forgotten nothing – and still we don't get anywhere! And meanwhile my strength is weakening: so many nights without sleep.... If it wasn't for you, Ivan Ivanovich, then I wouldn't have the strength for our great business. Oh, if we could only get to the red dragon! At least from that we could get some nourishing gold, which affords a man life almost eternal and perfect health. While I'm securing the elixir of life, I'm afraid of losing my health altogether. Even now I'm inclined to drowsiness; suppose I fall asleep, maybe you won't sleep, dear chap. Stand me in good stead; after all, I am letting you in on a great secret – please, don't go to sleep. Every minute now is important. Don't stint on the coal, don't leave the athanor:* if the fire goes down just

*An alchemist's stove (*Author's note*)

188

for a minute, everything's lost and we'd have to start all over again. So, don't go to sleep; oh, I'm feeling sleepy, beware...the Salamander...because...dragon's blood...the athanor...quint...essence...elixir....

Gradually the old man's words mingled; he dozed and dozed and finally fell asleep completely, rehearsing in his sleep the secret words of the alchemists.

The young man continued to watch over the fire assiduously, not removing his eyes from it, and ajusted the burning coals.

Sad thoughts were whirling in the head of the man sitting in front of the hearth. – So that's how all my hopes have finished, – he was thinking; – so that's why fate tore me away from my poor Finnish shack. Much that was fine glittered before me; I saw *the Great,* I talked to him, I thought with his thoughts, I felt with his feelings – and when the Great was no more all my hopes were buried with him. There was no support for the poor parvenu. I was slandered and banished.... Is anything being done now in my fine room in the admiralty? Is anyone working there with the same fervour with which I used to work? And my translations on the science of cyphers and my plan for the printing works?... All that was in vain! Just booty for the worms. And what now? The governor to be, the boyar – is now the assistant, almost the slave of a peevish, half mad old man; I spend sleepless nights in front of burning coals on work which is scarcely marketable and very nearly criminal!... And then there's my wife with her demands and reproaches; she says that I can't support her and recalls her previous lifestyle, her previous prosperity. What am I supposed to do? Is it my fault that they took my post from me, that others wanted it? Is it my fault that they all spurn me and scorn me, a poor Finn? It's sad, sad!... Ah, my golden hopes, where are you? Where are you? If the Great were alive, it would not be like this.... And now, is everything really finished? Am I really not to live in lordly mansions? Really not to see any more admirers? Really to die not a governor? Oh, why, why did I ever leave my shack? What did fate drag me away to see other countries for? Why did I receive the enlightenment of science and why was my mind educated? If all that hadn't been the case, my heart would not have languished; I would not have known, would not have suffered from this unquenchable thirst; I would have spent my life peacefully within the sound of our native rapids, in that poor shack.... And Elsa, Elsa! My little sister! Where are you, what's happening to you? Where are your light brown locks, your languid eyes? Where is your white breast? You would have loved me, you would not have cribbed at a fate which would have entailed you living with your poor Finn; on your simple-hearted breast I would have slept calmly, listening to our native songs....

– The young man covered his face with his hands; tears spattered from his eyes....

– Hearth of mystery! – he went on – what have you fixed your fiery orifice on me for? What is hidden in you? Ashes and coal...but who knows... perhaps... in another few days gold will be pouring out of you, and the poor Finn will look people proudly in the eye. Oh, then it's not you I will be loading with riches, wicked wife, not you! – only snakes hiss on your tongue! – no, I shall throw you over then, leave you.... All is permitted to a rich man; I shall fly off to my native banks, embrace my Elsa and together with her I shall laugh at the whole world. Oh, Elsa, Elsa! Where are you?

At that moment someone knocked at the door. The young man looked up: – 'So! It's my wife, the snake in the grass. What do you want?' – said Yakko (for that was the young man's name). Into the room came a woman of about thirty, pale, her face distorted from rage; her dress was in some disorder.

– What? – she said in an angry voice, – is the old fool asleep? Dowse the fire down, less coals will fall out.

– How can I! – replied Yakko.

– You can do the same as you did before. What's going on here anyway – a demon's tea party! I can't get rid of the two of you. Day and night your fire is smouldering. Passers by see your smoke and that smoke of yours is no Orthodox smoke – the whole street stinks of sulphur and bogeymen. Everyone says you're making poisons or raising devils.

– Let them prattle away as much as they like, but this time I don't want to trick the old man any more, I'm not going to move the fire until I've finished the job.

– Just listen to you! Don't be afraid! You've got the old man on the brain. He doesn't want to do the devil knows what in his own house, so he comes here to you. Never mind him, but it's you they'll burn in the end and me together with you. Oh, what a poor, miserable orphan I am! I have neither father nor mother, neither family nor tribe, there's no one to stand up for me; God treated me to married life with an accursed Finn, a sorcerer, a heretic....

– Away from here, – shouted the angered husband – or it will be the worse for you. If the old man wakes up and sees you here, there'll be trouble, that's for sure. Get out, I'm telling you.

– And thanks to you, my lord and master, Ivan Ivanovich, I have nothing to walk out in! Give me the money for some shoes.

– And where am I supposed to get it? You won't get it from the old man; and when he wakes up and catches you here, there won't be another crust of bread.... Look, he's beginning to stretch – get out of here, you've been told!

The woman looked at Yakko with inexpressible spite and went out, muttering to herself: – Finn, sorcerer, heretic, beggar....

– And that's the woman, – thought Yakko, – who once seemed an angel of goodness to me! What happened to her maidenly gentleness, her feminine modesty? Is that the Masha who, before, in her Dutch bonnet, laced into her smock, sweet and simple-hearted, was afraid to utter an unnecessary word? Everything has changed now! While we were living in comfort, she seemed an angel; but that angel could not bear the most usual of calamities – penury! Oh, Elsa, Elsa! You won't have changed! Where are you? Am I really fated never to see you again?...

Meanwhile the light was starting to break through; the crimson northern sun began to peek through the clouds and silently make its way over the roofs. The old man woke up.

– What! Is it morning already? – he said, rubbing his eyes. - How's our affair doing? Hasn't the fire gone down a bit? – He stood up, went over to the athanor, examined it from all sides and, seemingly, was satisfied.

– And you didn't fall asleep, even for a minute?

– Not for a minute, – replied Yakko.

– Thank you, my son. Work at it, work at it; help an old man and, I assure you, you won't be the loser.... I am entrusting an important secret to you, young man. You should know, all the sages of the world, from the dawn of the ages, have been seeking what comprises our marvellous work...marvellous, I tell you. It is all-powerful; it saves the body from rotting, it, I repeat, can endlessly prolong human existence.... The one thing they didn't know was where to start; but I, I know. Since the highest heavens form around the earth not of their own accord, but from the influence of the sun and the other planets, so our quintessence awaits animation from the sun – the brilliant, omnipotent and equable: against this sun all earthly fires can do nothing. I am telling you, with all the emotion of my heart, that this sun, unconquered by fire, this root of our life, this seed of metals, created for the adornment of our sky, has been – in this hand!

Yakko listened to the old man and did not know whether to believe him or not: the old man spoke with such power, with such vehement conviction.... It was true that they had set about their wonderful task three times already and three times they had found – just ash. But Yakko knew that more than one learned mage in Holland, France and Germany had believed in alchemy and had laboured over the philosopher's stone. Many laughed at these efforts, but no one had yet made so bold as to prove manifestly the impossibility of the philosopher's stone. In Paris Yakko had seen the living witness of this truth: he saw the building, erected in gold, created by Nicolas Flamel; he had seen the wonderful symbols which Nicolas Flamel had left on the buildings which he had built in memory of his feat and as a clue to the wise men of all ages. He had seen with his own eyes in Vienna the iron nail, half of which had been turned to gold by a celebrated alchemist to the glory of that mysterious science. Why, even that very man who was working with him now belonged to a select band of the most erudite men of their time: a military man, high official, respected for his high title – how could he not be believed?... But at the same time, the old man seemed to him suspicious; at times it could be doubted whether he had any common sense left: sometimes he would cry, sometimes laugh, like a child, or jump around the floor snatching at his hair, or launch into some barely comprehensible but majestic speech, riddled with contradictions, and then his eyes would burn, he would be in a frenzy and his whole body would shake.

Trusting neither the old man nor his own doubts, Yakko endeavoured to find explanations to the enigma in books. Paracelsus, Arnold of Villanova, Geber, Basilius Valentinus scarcely left the young alchemist's hands. Their arguments were seductive and they seemed to have opened up their souls; all of them to a man promised wealth, happiness, health and long life to that person who had the patience to follow the pursuit to its conclusion. Yakko found in their descriptions all the details of the wonderful task; nothing was left out; it seemed as though you only had to get down to doing it: they themselves said that a woman could do it without leaving her spindle. There was just one thing that they did not reveal: the substance from which the tree of life was supposed to spring up – and in front of Yakko was a man who boasted that he knew this mysterious substance, the name of which had never been entrusted to paper. This substance was in front of him, concealed in a crude clay flask.... Yakko became lost in thought.

Over the final few days, the alchemists had not left their hearth for a minute. When Yakko went to sleep, for two or three hours, not more, the old man supervised the athanor.

Finally there dawned the fatal forty-first day. The alchemists did not sleep the whole night and exactly at the prescribed hour, on the minute, they put out the fire. Oh, how their hearts were beating when the decisive moment came! Yakko's hand shook, as he carefully began to clean off the grease which had stuck together all the parts of the secret apparatus. Another minute – and before them would shine the wondrous purple stone, the seed of metals, the elixir against all illnesses, the marvellous tincture which raised crude lead up to gold....

And so the lid of the mysterious vessel was removed – and what do you think?... On the bottom of it lay a black, formless, baking mass, and that was all.

– The black crow swallowed our red dragon, – exclaimed the old man, – we did something wrong.... We'll have to start all over again. Rest for a few days, about three, not more; then get the athanor ready again. Meanwhile I'll go through the whole process in my mind; I'll try to spot where we could have gone wrong. Farewell. Don't come and see me. We don't want the profane to know of our links. Don't neglect the books: read Paracelsus again – my memory is weak, I might overlook something.

With these words the old man pulled a silver rouble out of his pocket, put it on the table in front of poor Yakko and went.

Yakko – pale, exhausted and tormented from lack of sleep – went out from the laboratory into the next room and threw himself in despair on to the bed. He slept a light and troubled sleep, but, little by little his visions became more fascinating. He saw the bank of the Vuoksi and heard the sound of the Imatra rapids. Elsa was before him in all her beauty. She bent her head against Yakko's breast and kissed him. His face was bestrewn with her locks which were surrounded by gold pieces and precious stones. A radiant sun shone on them and was reflected in their irridescent tints.

A coarse voice brought Yakko out of his sweet oblivion.

– Are you going to stop sleeping, you lazy devil? – said Maria Yegorovna, – all you do is sleep. Now, where's this gold? Hand it over. Did you make a lot?

Yakko could barely come to; however, he dipped his hand into his pocket and pulled out the silver rouble, throwing it scornfully on to the floor....

– Is that all? – said his wife, picking up the coin. – We give humble thanks, I'm sure, Mister Ivan Ivanovich! And that's all there is for food and drink?... How far do you think that will go? You just consider: they want to throw us out of the apartment; the baker says he won't give us bread on tick any more, and the butcher and the grocer.... Oh, how poor and miserable I am!... Down to my last dress!... I've nothing even to go to God's church in, to pray to God not to punish me for your sins, you damned sorcerer!... Oh, mother, that poor mother of mine! Did you ever think or guess that I would come to such a fate?...

– What can I do? – Yakko asked in despair.

– Do what you know, you are the man of the house...mine is woman's business.

– I swear to you by God, Maria Yegorovna, – Yakko replied weakly, – that I'd be pleased to give you my blood, if only you wouldn't reproach me.

– That's enough of taking the name of God, you heretic! You don't take me in; we've heard all these tales before.

– So, what am I supposed to do, then? – Yakko replied, starting to get angry.

– What you should have done was to stay in Petersburg. That was the place to be, with a salary and everything my father did for you....

– But don't you know that I was driven out?

– Driven out? And what for...? Because your back was far too stiff. You should have gone along to them and bowed a bit lower...but oh, no... how can one!... Proud at the wrong times. And now it's you who can whistle for it.... Well, give me some money, then! You're supposed to support me, by law.

Yakko jumped up from his bed.

– Be quiet! – he shouted.

– No, I won't keep quiet, I shall go and denounce you for your sorcery, for making poisons. When they take you to the torture chamber and start wrenching your shoulder-blades, then you'll sing a different tune, you accursed heretic! Beggar!...

We shall not here describe the scene which followed this conversation. It would, in our epoch, seem too strange....

Three days passed. Yakko did not manage to rest at all. His wife gave him not a minute's peace and he was able to subdue her only by methods totally unphilosophical. All this tormented and abased his soul. Often he was almost ready to lay hands on himself; more often still he felt like fleeing Moscow and making his way to his own land. Yet hope still beckoned; seemingly it even increased with each misfortune. 'Just another forty days, – he finally said to himself, – and one of two things will happen: either I shall be the possessor of treasure, or I shall be no more'.

On the fourth day someone knocked at he door. It was the old man.

– I've found it! – he said, – and how could we have forgotten it!... We should have started on a Thursday, on the day dedicated to Jupiter; and we started on a Monday, on the day of the moon! It's quite understandable that her cold moisture penetrated our athanor and prevented the dragon from maturing. Today is Thursday, so at exactly mid-day we shall get down to our task. Is everything ready?

– Everything, – replied Yakko dolefully, – but before we get down to work, allow me to ask a favour, your excellency.... I haven't got a kopeck in the house...with the rouble you gave me I paid the most essential debts.... – Tears of shame and humiliation rolled down Yakko's cheeks.

– So! I was expecting that! – shouted the old man angrily. – Money, always money! A genuine son of Adam! I really don't know why I ordained you into our task. You work only out of self-interest. You don't have in you the spiritual feeling for a great task because your soul is unclean. You do not understand the aspirations of my soul, you do not understand the whole importance of our sacrament. You think that this is just a job, like any other. I am training you in the greatest wonder in the world, the only one which a man should worry about – and you come to me with worldly thoughts, with your money...you're despicable!... Go and look for money wherever you like.

– I assure you, most excellent Count, that if it hadn't been a matter of utmost need, – replied the affronted Yakko, – then...then I should have left you long ago. Look for another assistant, another as diligent as I am.

The irate old man paced around the room. His meanness tormented him but, on the other hand, he counted up all the advantages which Yakko brought him. The old man realised full well how difficult it would be to find another secluded place in Moscow for his secret experiments. It would be difficult to conceal the actions of a titled boyar, a rich man. But he hoped that no one would pay attention to this poor hovel. He pulled out of his pocket a silver rouble, looked at it with regret and, giving it to Yakko, muttered with a feigned smile: 'All right, don't get angry; here's some money for you; just a bit more work and then you'll look upon coins with the same scorn as I do. Now, to business'.

Exactly at mid-day the old man took a small golden box out of his pocket, opened it in a mysterious manner, poured out the contents into the athanor and hurriedly closed the lid, so that Yakko could not see what the box contained. The flask was smeared over; beneath it the fire was kindled and once again for Yakko there began the long sleepless nights, once again the anguished waiting – now fearful, now confident, again the reading of the seductive pages, again this monotonous, agonising actuality.

Twenty days passed. Once again neither the old man nor Yakko noticed those alchemical signals which would herald a successful conclusion to the task. One night the old man fell asleep; Yakko remained alone before the hearth. He felt sad, inexpressibly sad, that day. Again he had been forced to ask the old man for money; again the old man responded in his usual skinflint tone and again his wife tormented him with her reproaches. Yakko, fixing his eyes on the fire, tried to sweeten the bitter present with recollections from the past. Unexpectedly there came to mind the words which Elsa had once said to him: 'you are our's', – said Elsa to him, – 'and ours you must be'. What was the meaning of those words, pronounced by that strange woman at a moment of enchanted visions?...

– Elsa, Elsa! – said Yakko, – where are you? Has your mysterious power really been extinguished?... Do you really not feel your Yakko suffering, your Yakko calling you? Oh, if only you were with me, perhaps you would instruct me what to do!

Yakko's thoughts becamme gloomier and gloomier by the hour.

– What, – he said in the depths of his soul, – what are all these fairy tales about virtue and about punishments in the future world? Is man really condemned to suffer on earth?.. Is he really not permitted all means, in order to escape from his sufferings?... All means, – he repeated, unwittingly shuddering, – yes, all, – he said with bitterness, – oh, what wouldn't I sacrifice at this moment, so as to achieve my purpose! There is still one way which I have not encountered in the books; perhaps the sages hide it from the senseless crowd; perhaps what we need is a sacrifice on the mysterious flask – perhaps we need a human life.... Why not?... Why not try it?... – Yakko's eyes, inflamed and immobile, transfixed upon the sleeping old man.

This feeling, which had been born only that very minute, frightened Yakko himself. He jumped up from his bench, but had hardly turned the other way when he looked and...on the circle illuminated by the hearth was the outline of some shadow of indeterminate shape. Yakko shuddered, a cold feeling ran along his veins and he rushed over to the hearth and there, exerting all his inner strength, he muttered: 'Elsa, Elsa! Is it you?'

And in the middle of the flames a vague image appeared to him... getting nearer, nearer...he was no longer in any doubt...it was the face of Elsa, smiling...she was beckoning him...and she said to him: 'Yes, Yakko, it is I, your Elsa; I heard you; it's high time you remembered me...and there you are, working away in vain. Foolish people! You want to discover the greatest secret without calling on the Salamander! Your fire is quite dead without her. You expect it to vitalise the dragon? Even for us it's a difficult thing; even we undertake it with fear. But for you I am ready for anything. Go to sleep, go to sleep, dear Yakko; get your strength back; instead of you, I shall look after your work'.

– Elsa, Elsa! – exclaimed Yakko, stretching out his arms to her.

– No, Yakko, you cannot embrace me now; in the daytime I shall appear before you in my earthly mode and you will not leave me, Yakko, will you?... Will you be true to me?

Yakko shuddered: – And my wife?

– Wife? – replied Elsa in a derisive tone, – your wife won't interfere....

– How do you mean, she won't interfere?... – shouted Yakko.

– Don't be afraid; I am not going to lead you into sin, foolish boy. It's enough just to desire, Yakko. Or have you even still not grasped what human will means? All you have to do is to love me; nothing mortal can stand against our mysterious flame. But there is one condition: be mine, be mine, Yakko, swear it....

– I swear it, – Yakko murmured darkly....

He watched while Elsa turned into a stream of white flame, but in this stream he could still recognise his Elsa. He saw her wind herself around the mysterious vessel and cascade over it in the form of golden rain. Was this not a marvel? The vessel became transparent; within it a fiery lion was struggling with a fiery dragon, and there was the lion almost at its last breath...the dragon was swallowing it...in an instant a brilliant corona appeared on it and the vessel filled with a ruby coloured light...the dragon wagged its fiery wings and, at every flap, irridescent rays surged around the vessel.

Yakko saw nothing more for, as it seemed to him, he fell into a heavy sleep. A knock at the door awakened him. It was already morning. The old man was still asleep. The young man thought it was his wife and was not keen to open the door; but the knock was repeated. Yakko heard someone saying in Finnish: 'Open, open up, dear Yakko'. Yakko shuddered, unlocked the door – and before him stood Elsa in her usual coarse Finnish dress; her hair was taken up under a shapeless cap. She threw her arms around Yakko. Yakko was beside himself with joy.

– I bet you forgot about me, Yakko, – she said, – but I certainly remembered. As soon as I knew that you had been chased out, ruined and were poor I left everything and came to you. It didn't half cost me something! If it hadn't been for Yusso....

– Your husband? – asked Yakko.

– No, Yakko, I didn't get married. Yusso very much wanted to marry me, but I kept telling him: wait, my brother-chap will come. He waited and waited, the poor thing, and then stopped waiting. But he still loves me; when he knew that I was grieving for you he said straight away: 'Go on, I'll take you, Elsa; perhaps you can help your brother'. And Yusso is such a clever fellow, he does a bit of business in Petersburg and even knows people here; oh, we looked and looked for you here...and we'd still be at it, but a kind man came along, the one who brings you coal. They say you are a blacksmith or a locksmith...he brought me here, right to the door, such a kind....

– Elsa, Elsa!... – said Yakko, – so you really can help me?... Do you know what our task is?...

– No, I don't know a smith's business, but I can help you. Just look how much I saved without you.

And with these words she pulled out from her bosom a piece of linen, from which there poured silver and gold money. There were a hundred roubles and more here.

– Elsa! – said Yakko, – but this past night, here in the hearth,...

– What was that? – asked Elsa.

– Do you remember what you said to me?...

– When? – asked Elsa in surprise.

At that moment Maria Yegorovna was returning from the market. – And what is the meaning of this? – she shrieked, – have you brought another sorceress here again?...

But no sooner had she caught sight of the money than her face brightened up; she threw her arms around Elsa: – Oh, my dearest Yelisaveta Ivanovna!... And I didn't recognise you.... And you haven't changed at all: the same beauty as you always were. How did you manage to find us?... And didn't we miss you, miss you.... But perhaps, don't refuse, stay a while with us.... And whatever's all this money you've scatterd here?... Let me put it away.

– Our kind sister, – said Yakko to his wife, – is giving us this money: it's ours.

Maria Yegorovna again rushed to embrace Elsa, gathered the coins into her pocket and ran off to the kitchen, muttering in a whisper: 'Now I'll have some fun!'.

As from this miraculous appearance, Yakko applied himself even more diligently to his work. Frequently he recognised Elsa in the twisting currents of flame. He understood very clearly that this was she, and no other, for her face often flashed before him amid the blaze. He spoke to her and she replied. Frequently the vessel became transparent for a moment, and inside it strange visions were enacted. Yakko saw in it first an unearthed grave and in the grave a horrifying skeleton; through the skull and the bones of the skeleton a fiery jet was passing; the eye holes, jaws and ribs lit up, and with a sickly groan the dead man rose from the grave. Then he saw a field, strewn with dead bones and fiery birds swooped down to peck at them. Then there appeared in the vessel two lions which devoured one another; then he saw Elsa in the form of a Salamander, with a crown on her head. The Salamander splashed voluptuously in the fiery sea and two flaming jets were issuing forcefully from her virginal breasts.

Closely observing these wonderful phenomena, Yakko recalled that he had seen something of the sort in the books of Basilius Valentinus and other hermetic philosophers, but previously he had considered these depictions to be simple symbols, under which the sages concealed their secrets, but now everything was comprehensible and clear to our young alchemist.

– Tell me, – said Yakko, fixing his eyes on the white-hot orifice, – tell me, Elsa, by what miracle I see you *here*, completely different from *there*.

There you don't even understand your existence here.

– Dear Yakko, – replied Elsa, stretching out to him from the opening her fiery arms, from which radiant sparks were cascading like rain, – sweet Yakko, you are too inquisitive. Can I embrace you here? Your mortal membrane would perish from my touch. I can approach you only in the form of cooled ashes; be content with that for the time being. Forget your curiosity, carry on assisting me in our task, which neither we alone, nor humans without us, are in a position to carry through. It's a difficult business, Yakko, a very difficult business, not all the mysteries of which are accessible even to us. We only undertake it out of love for humans; do you know that we have to penetrate to the root of the metals with all our being; from our own breasts we must secrete the life-giving moisture which alone can awaken its dead power. It's not easy for us to do, Yakko: in order to do that we have to wrestle with all the elemental spirits which in the form of beasts and various animals wage a war of attrition on us; they don't want, in fact they are terrified of, the awakening of the supreme ruler over all elements. But sooner or later we must conquer them.

– Will it be soon? How soon? – exclaimed the impatient Yakko.

– I don't know; many mistakes were made by you. But I will tell you this in consolation: this time, with my help, you will attain one of the lower powers of the mysterious stone. And it will stand you humans in good stead.

The old man continued to come every day to Yakko as before and to fuss zealously around the stove. 'Now', – he would say, – 'I am sure that we shall achieve our goal. I don't think we have forgotten anything and the fire is burning evenly. Another few nights and the phoenix will be spreading her wings for us'.

– Most excellent Count, – said Yakko with a significant smile, – do you think that our task can be crowned with success if, by means of mysterious invocation, we do not summon a Salamander?

– You're barking up the wrong tree there, dear boy, – replied the old man, – you read the books, but you don't understand them. Now what is a Salamander? It's just a symbolic term, by which our sages sometimes understand the action of the fire in our business, and sometimes the stone itself, because it burns in the fire without burning. Study, study away, dear boy....

Yakko again smiled and remained silent.

Meanwhile, from the time of Elsa's appearance, everything in Yakko's house went on other than as before. She completely took over the running of the household. Cleanliness, tidiness and order came into the house. Elsa acquired a cow, and then a second and a third, and little by little from the boyars' houses people started to come to buy milk and butter which, in distinction from the usual, they called 'Finnish'. Efficiency was once again a feature of poor Yakko's house. Maria Yegorovna was delighted to see in her house once again copper, silver and sometimes even gold coins. She began to sport classy dresses, Dutch bonnets, chintz smocks and red-heeled boots. All this was fine enough; but there was something not so fine: during her time of penury Maria Yegorovna succumbed to drinking vodka. When she drank it, her spirits were lifted. The second time she tried it – the same thing, she liked it. Gradually she provided herself with a modest carafe which, however, she concealed from her husband in a hiding place. Gradually she more and more often started to make for the consolatory beverage; a habit became a passion and we have to admit that the greater part of her reproaches to her husband came about due to Maria Yegorovna's lack of money for the filling of her cherished carafe. Now Maria Yegorovna was in a state of bliss. From the morning she would be quite merry and, while Elsa saw to the running of the house, Maria Yegorovna would sit at the table, her sides propped up by her arms, rocking her head and singing:

'Glasses of vodka are on the move round the table!'

Elsa often found her in that condition and, probably not understanding what was going on, looked at Maria Yegorovna with such strange eyes that Maria Yegorovna became fearful and sad – and she would again take refuge in her consolation. After dinner Maria Yegorovna would already be in an unwakable sleep and sometimes she would not even dine at all. At night, having woken up, she would again make her way on tiptoe to her hiding place… and then fall asleep again. The next day she would start all over again.

Yakko paid no attention to his wife's behaviour. Absorbed in his mysterious enterprise, Yakko forgot everything worldly. Spending every day by the hearth, he rarely approached the members of his family and when he did approach them he had time only for Elsa, rejoicing that his wife left him in peace, and he impatiently awaited the fateful forty-first day.

Finally it dawned…. The mysterious lid was raised and on the bottom of the vessel was a blue coloured alloy…. Both the old man and Yakko palpitated with excitement.

– This is something wondrous, – said the old man, – our stone must be of a purple colour…this is not it…but isn't it at least of the sapphire family?... We'll experiment….

With these words the old man melted some lead, broke a few filings off the newly obtained alloy and threw them on to the lead… the filings flew off and the lead remained lead, as before. Our alchemists laboured the whole day. What they didn't try to do with the newly obtained alloy! They united it with copper, with iron and with all the metals, but in vain: the base crackled and scattered but nothing turned either into silver or gold.

– This is just a kind of glass, – said the old man finally with some annoyance, – we made a mistake somewhere. We'll have to start all over again. Rest for three days and then prepare the athanor again.

Meanwhile Yakko clearly heard Elsa laughing loudly amid the coals.

– Don't listen to that foolish old man, – she said, – take this stone; it's not gold, but it's worth gold: but don't tell the old man that. Immerse this stone in water and you will see what happens. The fool! He thinks he understands the writings of the sages; he read that you need forty days' work over the phoenix, but he read only a dead letter. He doesn't realise that a cabbalistic number is concealed in these words, that the circle here depicts the world and the number is the four seasons of the year, the essential timespan for the full maturity of the wonderful stone.

– What are you thinking about? – said the old man.

– Don't you hear anything? – replied Yakko.

– What's there to hear? Only the crackling of the coals in the hearth.

Yakko realised that the Salamander's words were audible to him alone and kept quiet.

– So, what did you mean, then? – the old man continued.

– I think, wasn't it perhaps that we opened the athanor too early? Doesn't the number forty signify the four seasons of the year?...

– Not a bad idea, – remarked the old man, – oh! I can see we'll make something of you yet! We'll try it. So then, prepare two athanors: one we'll open every forty days and the other we'll open after a whole year has elapsed....

With these words the old man placed a silver rouble on the table as usual and departed, muttering to himself: 'Four seasons of the year... forty... four... why didn't that occur to me?... that's strange!...

With the departure of the old man, Yakko immediately again heated up the stone which they had obtained and threw it into water. After this operation had been conducted a few times, there remained in the vessel a liquid of a beautiful blue colour. Yakko dipped a piece of cloth into it and the cloth coloured.

Yakko's knowledge of chemistry quickly told him what advantage could be derived from this discovery. He decomposed the substance in accordance with scientific rules, found its composition, again repeated the experiment on a bigger scale and soon there appeared in Yakko's house vats and boilers. He declared to guests from the textile sphere that he was taking up the dyeing of cloth not inferior to the overseas product – and in the city they were amazed, talking of an indigo dye.

And these new arrangements fell to the good Elsa: the whole day she bustled about, hired workers, kept the accounts, checked the vats, collected the dye, sold it, did the dyeing and the hanging out. Yakko served at times as translator, but otherwise just took in the money.

But could this type of success satisfy the proud expectations of an alchemist? Was the dye trade enough for he who intended to grasp in his hand the root of all the world's treasures!...

Once again the athanor was lit and once again the old man appeared with his mysterious box. But at the moment when he was preparing to pour its contents into the flask, Yakko again heard a scoff from the Salamander: 'Your old man knows a lot; even we could do worse than consult him, but he falls down on the details: all his compounds will get him nowhere if he doesn't extract some oil from flint'.

– Oil of flint? – asked Yakko.

– Yes; you know, there is a wonderful and mighty liquid concealed inside flint....

– But I also know that this liquid annihilates all earthly bodies; there is not a vessel that could hold it: one drop of it on a human body and a person would dissolve in the most horrible torment....

– Yakko, Yakko! the embryo of life – is death... – pronounced the Salamander in a strong voice, and disappeared.

When Yakko started talking to the old man about oil of flint, the old man began shaking. 'I know, – he replied, – I have heard of this horrific fluid, I've come across references to it in the books, but until now I always thought that the alchemists mentioned it just to scare off the profane, or to punish them when they undertake our great task with impure or ignorant hands'.

The work went on as previously and, as previously, without success. Every night an irresistible sleep came over the old man. Yakko looked after the athanor and when his strength waned the Salamander appeared in the middle of the fire, consoled her favourite, comforted him, stretched out her fiery fingers to him and in a golden jet entwined herself around the athanor.

One evening the old man was dozing and Yakko, lost in thought, sat in front of the fire. The alchemist felt a deep sadness in his soul. He was not gratified by trifling domestic advantages; even hope was no longer enough to console him. He looked gloomily around him and his gaze was involuntarily drawn to the old man, who was dozing, leaning on his elbows in the armchair.

– Why is he not me? – the thought drifted into Yakko's mind, - why am I not him? – he added, losing himself in this train of thought, – he is of noble birth, he's rich, he keeps coming here, exploiting a pauper's hospitality for his dangerous business, and at the same time despising me...why should he not be me?... me – him? He – I?...

His thoughts became gloomier and gloomier and sometimes they even frightened the alchemist himself.

Someone crept up on the young man from behind; a quivering, feverish kiss made him shudder; he turned and before him was Elsa.

– It's you, Elsa: how did you get in here?

– Oh, how pleased I am, you forgot to lock the doors! I hardly ever get in here to see you. Do you know how boring it is for me without you, Yakko? All day and night you're here and I'm alone, completely alone. There's so much work about the house and sometimes I so want to kiss you, it's like a tormenting thirst....

So Elsa sat on Yakko's knees and embraced him. Yakko pressed her to him. – Elsa, Elsa! – murmured Yakko unwittingly, – if you only knew how I love you! I love you so much that it's awful to say....

– Yes! you love...! and Mari, Mari....

– I can't even look at Mari without revulsion; Mari is wicked, Mari nags me, Mari is bloated, she's ill or something, isn't she?

– Perhaps, I don't know, – replied Elsa, smiling mockingly, – or perhaps she's not ill, but like that from being too merry.... She sleeps a lot, Yakko, ever such a lot. – Meanwhile, Elsa's face had flushed and she continued: – In sleep a person, you know, is unarmed...much can affect them....

– I've noticed too that all too often she seems not to be herself....

– Yes! That's right...as though not herself....

– But what's the point of talking about her! You are my only consolation, you take the place of everything for me – both wife and family... Your father brought me up when I was a poor, helpless orphan. When again penury visited me, you took on your father's role: you run my whole household, you have made me rich, you calm me...you love me....

Again Yakko squeezed Elsa to his chest and Elsa wound herself around the young man, as ivy winds itself around the stately oak. She nestled against his face as though wanting to hide on his breast, as though wanting to bite into it. Her cheeks became more and more inflamed, both from the effect of the fire and from her inner excitement....

– What's that? – said Elsa, pointing to the alchemical apparatus.

– I'm searching for the Sampo, – replied Yakko, with a smile, wishing to approximate as far as possible to Elsa's notions.

Elsa's face was burning more and more strongly; her eyes were radiant.

– Sampo...Sampo...yes, exactly, the Sampo...nothing else but what the wise Finns understood by this word...the one thing that must be sought, the one thing that people have sought since the dawn of the ages; the wonderful legends are about it alone; their labours and hopes are devoted to it alone.... To the few has it been revealed...to the few...and only by uniting body and soul with us...and now to you, a mortal, this path has been revealed...and to you...if you...you...love me....

Elsa again entwined her arms around the young man.... Yakko was in an ecstatic frenzy: pale and quivering, he clasped Elsa and, having cooled a little from his wild agitation, he sought with his lips the burning hot lips of the girl.

But suddenly he recoiled from her and covered his face in his hands.

– What am I doing!... – he said in desperation, – Elsa, Elsa, spare me!

Elsa stared at him with enraged eyes.

– Elsa! – he went on, – why can't I belong to you completely... why do I have to have that Mari...as my wife?...

– Mari! Mari!... – repeated Elsa in a strange voice.

At that moment Yakko saw that fiery sparks spattered from Elsa's eyes; she stretched out her arms... and fiery jets spurted from her fingers... flame extended from her lips, it crackled around Elsa and around Yakko... at this point everything became confused...the walls of the room were screened by columns of fire...the athanor broadened to fill an immense space.... Elsa and Yakko floated and sank amid the fiery waves...lions, dragons, the dead skeleton and monstrous birds were flying round them... everything entwined and untwined and went round....

When Yakko returned to his senses, everything was quiet: the old man was dozing; the hearth was smouldering calmly; there was no Elsa.

A loud knock at the door made Yakko shudder. – Who's there? – he asked as he opened it.

– Master, master! – came the voice of a workman, – the mistress is in a bad way.

Yakko hurriedly opened up.

– What's wrong with her? – he asked.

– It's not good, boss, in fact it's beyond saying... you'll see for yourself.

Yakko ran in to his wife's room. On entering, a powerful and strange smell stunned him. He hurriedly approached the bed; in Maria Yegorovna's place there lay an indescribable black mass. A working girl was crying beside the bed; in the corner sat Elsa, her head bent and also bitterly crying.

– What's happened here? – shouted Yakko in horror.

– We can't rightly say, – replied the working lass, sobbing – not that many minutes past, Maria Yegorovna sort of took sick, started moaning and groaning, she did, with her heart like – so me and Yelisaveta Ivanovna both went to her, saying: oh, what's wrong with you?... We were looking and she had little blue flames running down her body, and her body was going blacker and blacker... and smoke was pouring out and this stink; and we tried to do this and that, and splashed water on her and put it out with our hands, but nothing helped. You could hardly blink your eyes before she'd burnt away – look, like you see; we couldn't even send for the priest....

Yakko stood dumbstruck before the ashes of his wife; a doleful feeling, resembling despair, constrained his heart. He looked up at Elsa and asked:
– 'Were you with me?'

– I did go in to you for a minute, – relied Elsa, sobbing, – you said a few words to me and then dozed off, so that I didn't feel like waking you; so I went away on tiptoe and shut the door on the latch; I came in here, had a look, and Mari was bad; I sent the workman for you, but he couldn't knock you awake.... Poor Mari! Poor Mari! How she suffered, – affirmed Elsa, – it's good though that it didn't last long.

Yakko threw himself into the armchair: – Was all that really only a dream? – he was thinking.

It was soon known in the locality that the dyer's wife had burned to death: people gathered around, discussed it and expressed their amazement. The German physician asserted that she had burned as though from excessive usage of strong spirits, but the Russian populace just laughed at him: – 'Did you hear that', – they said, – 'she's supposed to have burned up from drinking wine! These Germans! No, there's more to it than that.'

They discussed it, speculated and dispersed.

His wife's funeral did not distract Yakko for long from his secret business. The athanor blazed as before and, as before, Elsa, in the image of the Salamander, entwined herself around the vessel. As before, the old man, who grew weaker by the day, fixed his dimmed eyes on the subject of their expectations and little by little he sunk into oblivion. He had already lost count of the days, relying for that on Yakko.

– Soon the four hundred and first day will come, – said the Salamander – and the business will be completed; our mysterious fruit is ripening and growing strong....

Yakko's heart beat strongly in his breast. And so, that which was impossible for others was to be possible for him. A few more days – and he would have in his hands the mysterious talisman which gives health, long life and incalculable wealth. But at that moment another thought pressed involuntarily into Yakko's soul.

'Why, – he thought, – why should I share my secret with this feeble old man? He did not discover it, so it is not for him to profit from it. The treasure in my hands would be fully mine, but shared – who knows? It would fall into unclean hands; this imbecilic old man would entrust it to someone else and, when everyone makes themselves rich, what would my wealth mean?'

– Well, there's no great difficulty here, – interjected the Salamander, having read his thoughts, – why remind the old man of the vital day? Let him spend it in oblivion and place all his hopes upon a completely fruitless vessel.

And so on mid-night of the four hundred and first day the athanor again became transparent. A purple flame spread in it, like a light cloud. In the middle of it there grew a luxuriant flower; light and airy, it floated in space. Around it there crowded a long row of men in Tsarish robes with crowns on their heads. They stood in reverential silence, waiting for the spine of the wondrous flower to unfold.

Then everything disappeared and the lid flew off the athanor, as though the strings had been torn from sonorous harps, and a fragrance spread through the air.... At the bottom of the vessel lay a purple stone and it illuminated the whole room with a pink glow. Yakko fell to his knees... and looked; the coarse clay vessel gradually turned to gold. Yakko approached, carefully lifted up the vessel and carefully placed it in a prepared hiding place, replacing it with another clay vessel of the same form.

A few minutes later the old man awoke.

– Well, what's happened? – he said, rubbing his eyes, – hasn't the fire gone down a bit?

– It's wrecked! – Yakko replied, – the lid has flown off the athanor.

– Oh! – exclaimed the old man, – evil spirits are against us. Though that's a misfortune suffered not only by me: Paracelsus himself had his athanor torn apart ten times by the motions of elemental spirits. What can be done! We'll have to start all over again. It's a pity that we didn't use oil of flint. An explosion of it is dangerous, as it can destroy a man, but then it preserves the vessel from explosion itself. Tomorrow we'll see about the preparation of this wondrous liquid.

With these words the old man, as usual, put his hand in his pocket and placed a silver rouble on the table. Yakko bowed, smiling.

– Yakko, Yakko! – said the Salamander, – beware, do not scorn the old man's money; hide your wealth, exploit it and revel in it on the quiet. People will find out and pester you; you will never satisfy them even with ingots of gold: they won't stop short of the tortures of the rack to get the cherished secret from you. Most of all, watch out for the old man: he is powerful and important in the human world and will soon fathom your secret; let him go on thinking that you haven't discovered it yet.

Over the first days, Yakko's rapture knew no bounds. At night, when the old man was asleep, the euphoric alchemist would bring out his wonderful stone. A few grains of it would fall on the melted lead – and the lead would turn into a gold ingot. During the daytime, Yakko was beside himself with joy, jumping around and kissing Elsa, who could not, for the life of her, account for, as she put it, Yakko being so pleased with himself. The domestics reckoned that there would soon be an opportunity to make merry at a wedding and laid bets on how soon the period of mourning would be lifted.

Meanwhile the ingots were accumulating. Yakko hid them under the floor; but soon another feeling entered the alchemist's soul, in place of joy. As the treasure multiplied, a fear began to overcome him that someone would fathom his secret, would steal his wealth. He doubled the iron locks on the doors and windows, instituted watchmen, himself never closed his eyes – but nothing could calm his agitation. Soon there remained to him only one happy minute in the course of the day: that minute in which the lead in his hands was transformed into gold and, following that, he would look at the gold ingot almost in horror. Where was he to put it? How was he to hide it? How was he to profit from it? And his life turned into an endless torment: he had become the guard of his own treasure! With regret he recalled that time when, inspired with hope, he had spent sleepless nights in front of the athanor; he didn't sleep now, either, but now it was because he was listening for the slightest noise, for a thief scraping away under the earth, for the old man to wake up, for his secret to be fathomed.

During the day he wandered about sad and half demented; nothing was any comfort to him: neither a rich table, nor Elsa's smile. In vain did she ask him what he was grieving for.

– Don't you understand my depression? – said Yakko to Elsa, replying sadly to her caresses.

– Perhaps you are missing Mari?

– Oh, don't remind me about Mari.... I'm certainly not depressed over her... you'd do better to tell me, teach me, what I am supposed to do about what you have given me, which has only multiplied my sufferings.

– I'll tell you what to do, – said Elsa, – sell everything you have and we'll go home to Imatra, settle down in our hut and forget about the whole world.

– You don't understand, Elsa! – said Yakko impatiently.

Such conversations recommenced over and again. Elsa remained Elsa; the Salamander no longer manifested itself in the mouth of the now barren athanor.

Now Yakko sat over the athanor still more diligently. The old man's appearance became more and more dubious by the hour. Yakko noticed doubt on his face; it seemed as though the old man had begun to guess and his every word was, for Yakko, laced with a double meaning. Alarmed and quivering, he would follow the old man's every movement: now he lowered his gaze to the ground – perhaps he could sense the gold ingots in the cellar; now he gazes vaguely around – is the radiance from the wondrous stone not translucent? Then he approaches the hearth and looks up at Yakko – has he not fathomed the secret?

What did Yakko not devise, in order to keep doubt away from the Count! Meanwhile, whether as a consequence of time or of failure, the old man was becoming more querulous and more exacting by the hour; but the fortunate alchemist had lost his feeling of haughty poverty. He carried out all of the old man's whims, not daring to contradict him; put up with his derisive comments with the humility of a slave; and grovelled in utter degradation, completely oblivious to any human dignity. In vain did he call on the assistance of the Salamander: the Salamander did not reply.

One day, his patience exasperated, Yakko could hardly restrain himself.... Fortunately, the old man dozed off. Like a madman, Yakko ran out of the laboratory and rushed over to Elsa. She was quite frightened, but Yakko dragged her with him, come what may, in to the hearth, sat her on a chair, squeezed her shoulders in an iron grip and, in a threatening whisper, said:

– In the name of your old grandfather, Elsa, tell me, how can I be rid of this old man?

Elsa at first started to quiver...then gradually calmed down...and finally replied in a halting voice:

– To be rid...of the old man...is easy...you just have to...just... desire....

– Desire? – shouted Yakko, – like with Mari....

– I don't know...but what's so terrible in that?...man...has to... desire...and the old man...will be no more....

– Be no more? But he's a titled nobleman: if he vanishes, they'll look for him, they'll guess where he is and come to me.

– Why does...the old man...need to vanish?... Couldn't you just take his place...be like him...titled...live in rich chambers...not be afraid of your gold ingots?...

– What are you saying, Elsa? Is this possible?

– There's nothing...that's impossible...for a man's will...you just have to desire....

– How can I not desire that? – exclaimed Yakko so loudly that the old man woke up, fixed his frozen eyes on Yakko and wanted to say something....

At that moment it seemed to the alchemist that before him stood not the Count but old grandfather Rusi, who had died thirty years before.

The frightened Yakko wanted to rush over to him; but a terrifying and deafening crash resounded...a flame rose up from the athanor and a fiery lava issued forth. A thick crimson smoke filled the room and within the smoke whirled the faces of the old man, Elsa, Mari, the old grandfather....

When Yakko came to, there was no sign of the old man; the athanor lay in smithereens. Yakko could feel he was wearing a velvet costume and recognised it as that same kaftan that the old Count always used to wear and, in some confusion, went over to the small round mirror which hung in the laboratory. In the mirror, instead of himself, he caught sight of a wrinkled face and grey hair – in a word, the old Count.

Late in the evening the Count returned to his boyar's chambers and the crowd of servants which met him on the staircase accompanied him respectfully to his study. Remaining alone, the Count found a key in his pocket, opened a secret lock in his sideboard and placed in it some sort of a package, through which a pink radiance could be seen and which he had pulled out from his bosom. Then the Count went over to a table with papers on it, read through a few letters and a memorandum and rang the bell; his estate manager came in.

– Old chap, send a cart tomorrow to Yakko the dyer and ask for the Finnish girl there – his wife, or whatever she is – and take from her some boxes, which are not to be opened, and bring them carefully here to me in the study. After that I'll tell you what to do with them.

In the circles which he frequented, the old Count noticed that people could not get over the change in him; they could not understand where his familiarity, his sprightliness, his cordiality and his gallantry had come from.... The ladies, amongst themselves, whispered that, probably, he had swallowed some elixir of life and claimed that, soon, he would look quite young again.

The old Count gave himself over to his dissipated Moscow life with all the ardour of youth. Balls and masquerades had replaced the old court assemblies and the Count didn't miss a single one. He himself held open house and squandered gold with never a caution. The populace crowded around the Count's chambers from morning until night. For all those passing down the street a place was set in the Count's dining room and wine by the full goblet was drunk to the health of the benificent boyar.

Thus long years went past. The old man grew no older, his gold did not run out; but whether he was happy, that no one knew. It was remarked that frequently, amid the noisy feasting, a dismal sadness would appear on the Count's face. The indistinct murmurings of the mob would reach the lucky man.

— Surely, there's a demon tormenting him, – said some.

— He's busy with affairs of state, – opined others.

— The old fart's just in love, – replied a third.

— Who with? Who with? – whispered several voices amongst themselves.

— I know who with, – muttered one voice, – with that young Princess Vorotynskaia; just watch how he pays court to her, his eyes never leave her....

— Oh, but he's old! And she can't be more than sixteen....

— What does that matter! Grey hair in his beard and the very devil in his appendage!

— Well, how far has it got, then?

— I know that the parents are quite keen on it, though the girl isn't half jibbing a bit: she says he's too bloody old.

— I'm not going to argue with you any more, – the old princess said to the Count, sitting with him on the divan in one of the further-flung rooms of the Count's house, – I can tell you quite candidly that this match suits us very well, but I must also tell you that the girl can't stand you: we shall be giving her away forcibly. You should know that and, in actual fact and to be quite truthful, you are no longer young, old chap.

The impassioned old man kissed the princess's hands.

— Rest assured, dear madam; don't look upon me as old: your young beauty will soon get used to me and will fall in love. The exterior can be deceptive. Believe me, no young blade could love the young princess as I would. I shall bestrew her with diamonds, and you too, and all your family.

— Oh, dear me, old chap, your kindness overwhelms me; I don't know where to put myself.

Down the marble steps went the bridegroom in his rich and brilliant costume. By the doorway stood a gilded coach with the Count's coat of arms, harnessed in tandem with black and skewbald horses. Magnificently dressed lackeys and footmen crowded around.

– Where do you think you're going? – they said, shoving away a woman in a Finnish dress, – now's not the time for you! Don't you see? Now the boyar's off to get married.

The Count, hearing a commotion, stopped on the staircase. They even say that he turned pale, but that is improbable because his face had been heavily rouged.

– Let her in, let her in! – he said in a weak voice, – let her in! You know that everyone has free access to me.

They let the Finnish woman through. The Count went back into the reception room and, as was his custom, leaned on the marble table, trying to assume a calm and self-important expression.

– Now, what can I do for you, my dear? – he said to the Finnish girl, as she walked in, – out with it quickly because, as you see, I have no time.

– So, then, Yakko, – Elsa replied, – are we soon going home to Imatra? We don't want to live here for ever....

– Listen, my dear, – said the Count portentously, – you realise that I have no possibility now of going with you to Imatra, and there's no need to. As far as you are concerned, I advise you to go there and put your mind at rest. If not, I shall have to...you understand.... I don't mind telling you, my beauty, that you are getting above yourself; here's some money to see you off, don't worry; and henceforth I shall not abandon you....

With these words the Count gave her a purse filled with gold.

Elsa roared with laughter; and again and again...her voice got louder and louder... it was no longer a guffaw, but a crash, then thunder...the walls began swaying, loosening, falling.... Yakko saw himself in his former room; in front of him was the mysterious stove, from the orifice of the stove shot a flame which was winding itself around him; he wanted to run...but there was no salvation! The walls were breathing fire, the ceiling was collapsing, one more minute...and the alchemist, his stove and Elsa were no more!

– That's a pity! – said the parishioners, as they passed the smouldering ruins on the following day, – the dyer's house has burned down. He was just starting to do well, too; and he himself, they say, didn't manage to jump out... bad heart.

– Where did you get that from? He was boiling oil and the oil went up in flames, poured all over the place. He ran this way and that, trying to snuff it out, but you can't do anything with oil, and so the lot went up.

– Pity! He was a good chap; good to do business with.

– Except he was sometimes at his wit's end.

— That's right. But isn't it time for a drop, matey?...

With this, Uncle's story came to an end.

— Tell me then, Uncle, — I remarked, — what is there to link this story with our adventures in your friend the merchant's house?

— It seems clear enough, — Uncle replied with a smile, — the smouldering ruin was bought by the late prince. He built a house on it, which now belongs to the merchant.

— Well, and so?

— You still don't understand! The bewitched hall, in which we passed the night, occupies the very spot where the alchemist's laboratory used to be.

— So you are assuming, Uncle, that these cries....

— I am not assuming anything... but I understand very clearly what I wish for you.

— But listen, Uncle: do you really believe that, in actual fact, the Salamander burned up your Finn?

— Others, very likely, would say that Mister Yakko was just making false money and then, so as to cover everything up, he burned down the house and ran away, together with his assistant, the Finnish girl: or so many supposed in Moscow. Others claimed he was a madman. A third view was that he feigned madness.... From all these opinions you may choose whichever you like....

I must confess that, to this day, I am convinced that all this was invention, that my uncle wanted to play a joke at my expense, and that all those cries and shadows were nothing but phantasmagoria. I am hopeful that every reasonable reader will agree with me on this.

1841

NOTES

NEW YEAR

Lucullus: Roman general (c. 117-56 BC), famed for luxurious lifestyle

THE TALE OF A DEAD BODY, BELONGING TO NO ONE KNOWS WHOM

Bova Korolevich: hero of a popular old Russian tale
Vanka Kain: celebrated Moscow thief and police spy
Korobeynikov: journey of a Moscow merchant to the Middle East of 1583
(All these were represented in popular reading matter in the early nineteenth century)
interment of the cat: popular print of a procession of mice burying a cat

THE STORY OF A COCK, A CAT AND A FROG

one of our latest writers: probably refers to Gogol's 'Old-World Landowners', read by Odoevsky in manuscript
mice burying the cat: see above
Lorenz Heister (1683-1758): famous German surgeon
Herman Boerhaave (1668-1738): Dutch physician and scientist

THE SYLPH

Charles X...Don Carlos: confusion between Charles [Karl] X of France and the pretender to the Spanish throne who launched the Carlist Wars.
Paracelsus (1493-1541): celebrated alchemical thinker and physician

The Count of Gabalis: book on elemental spirits, written by the Abbé Monfaucon de Villars (Paris, 1670)

Arnold of Villanova (1235-1313): an alchemical Hermetic writer

Raimondo Lulli (1235-1316): [Ramón Lull/Raymond Lully] Platonic and occult thinker

Undine…her uncle: refers to de la Motte Fouqué's tale *Undine* (1811)

Platon Mikhailovich: characteristic (deliberate ?) mistake over name

LETTER IV

Count Saint-Germain (c. 1707-84): see Introduction

Robertson, E.: presumed to be the Belgian physicist who made a balloon flight from St. Petersburg in 1804

THE LIVE CORPSE

Karolina Ivanovna [cf. earlier and later 'Karolina Karlovna']: confusion over name, going back to first edition, which may be deliberate (although   standardised by the editors of the most recent edition)

THE COSMORAMA

la Valière: a particular hairstyle (mod. French *lavallière:* a large floppy bow-tie)

Khreraskov, Mikhail Matveyevich (1733-1807): Russian neo-classical writer

'The Dragon-Fly and the Ant': fable by La Fontaine (1621-95)

Krummacher, Friedrich Adolph (1767-1845): German author of *Parables* (1805)

Vladimir Andreyevich [otherwise 'Vladimir Petrovich']: here presumed to be a mistake

Marschner, Heinrich (1795-1861): composer of German romantic operas

Puységur, Marquis Chastenet de; Deleuze, Joseph P.F.; Wolfart, Karl C.; and Kieser [?]: exponents of the pseudo-sciences of animal magnetism and Mesmerism, which were much in vogue during the late eighteenth and early nineteenth centuries.

THE SALAMANDER

Grot, Yakov Karlovich (1812-93): Russian philologist and specialist in Scandinavian affairs; translator of Finnish sagas etc. into Russian.

Lönnrot, Elias (1802-84): Finnish folklorist who collected and published the Finnish epic, *The Kalevala*.

Wolf, Friedrich August (1759-1824): German philologist

Imatra: rapids on the River Vuoksi, and surrounding region

Veineleisi [Venäläiset]: popular Finnish name for the Russians

'A Finnish Legend': stylised allegorical-folkloric account of the Great Northern War, between Charles [Karl] XII and Peter the Great

Suomi: Finnish name for Finland

Sampo: legendary Finnish treasure (see *The Kalevala*)

Iumala and Pergola: god of the sky and devil respectively in Finnish myth

Kukari: further Finnish mythological entity

Kurakin, Prince Boris Ivanovich (1676-1727): Russian diplomat

Treaty of Nystad: peace agreement between Russia and Sweden (1721)

Nienshants [Nyenshans]: Finnish name for Petrozavod and subsequently for St Petersburg itself.

Kunstkamera: (German) collection of valuables established by Peter I in St Petersburg (1714)

'An oak grew in a barnyard': this and subsequent quotations are taken from The World's Classics edition of *The Kalevala*, translated by Keith Bosley (Oxford University Press, 1989), pp. 577-84.

Brius's Calendar: astrological prophesies appearing first in Moscow in 1709; ascribed to Yakov Vilimovich Brius (1670-1735), a Petrine soldier and scholar of Scottish (Bruce) origin, but compiled by librarian Vasilii Kiprianov. The figure of the old Count may be based partly on Brius, who had a reputation as a black magician.

Basilius Valentinus: a supposed fifteenth-century alchemist, whose writings are a seventeenth-century forgery.

Nicolas Flamel (1330-1418): French alchemist

Paracelsus and Arnold of Villanova: see under *The Sylph* above

Geber: thirteenth-century author of 'classic' alchemical texts